Robert Williams Buchanan

A Poet's Sketch-book

Selections From the Prose Writings of Robert Buchanan

Robert Williams Buchanan

A Poet's Sketch-book
Selections From the Prose Writings of Robert Buchanan

ISBN/EAN: 9783337010898

Printed in Europe, USA, Canada, Australia, Japan

Cover: Foto ©Andreas Hilbeck / pixelio.de

More available books at **www.hansebooks.com**

A

POET'S SKETCH-BOOK

Selections from the Prose Writings

OF

ROBERT BUCHANAN

London
CHATTO AND WINDUS, PICCADILLY
1883

CONTENTS.

PREFATORY NOTE.

THIS volume of Prose Selections is intended as a companion to the lately-published volume of selections from the author's Poems. Special prominence has been given in it, therefore, to personal and descriptive matter, to the exclusion of mere criticism. It is, in fact, what it is called, a Poet's Sketch-Book, and will be chiefly interesting to those who take an interest in the author as a writer of poems.

The prose tale with which the selection concludes requires, perhaps, a word of special explanation. It is a study in the manner of the Celtic genius, and is, to the author's own thinking, far more completely a poem than anything he has published in verse.

THE POET, OR SEER:
A DEFINITION

# THE POET, OR SEER.

I.—VISION.

WHAT is the Poet, or Seer, as distinguished from the philosopher, the man of science, the politician, the tale-teller, and others with whom he has many points in common? He is, indeed, a student as other students are, but he is emphatically the student who sees, who feels, who sings. The Poet, briefly described, is he whose existence constitutes a new experience—who sees life *newly*, assimilates it *emotionally*, and contrives to utter it *musically*. His qualities, therefore, are triune. His sight must be individual, his reception of impressions must be emotional, and his utterance must be musical. Deficiency in any one of the three qualities is fatal to his claims for office.

I. And first, as to the Glamour, the rarest and most important of all gifts; so rare, indeed, and so powerful, that it occasionally creates, in very despite of nature, the othei poetic qualities. Yet that individual sight may exist in a character essentially unpoetic, in a temperament purely intellectual, might be proven by reference to more than one writer—notably, to a leading novelist. That proof, however, is immaterial. The point is, how to detect this individual sight, this Glamour, how to describe it,—how, in fact, to find a criterion which will prove this or that person to be or not to be a Seer.

The criterion is easily found and readily applied. We find it in the special intensity, the daring reiteration, the unwearisome tautology, of the utterance. The Seer is so occupied with his vision, so devoted in the contemplation of the new things which nature reserved for his special seeing, that he can only describe over and over again—in numberless ways—in infinite moods of grief, ecstasy, awe—the character of his sight. He has discovered a new link, and his business is to trace it to its uttermost consequences. He beholds the world as it has been, but under a new colouring. While small men are wandering up and down the world, proclaiming a thousand discoveries, turning up countless moss-grown truths, the Seer is standing still and wrapt, gazing at the apparition, invisible to all eyes save his, holding his hand upon his heart in the exquisite trouble of perfect perception. And behold ! in due time, his inspiration becomes godlike, insomuch as the invisible relation is incorporated in actual types, takes shape and being, and breathes and moves, and mingles in tangible glory into the approven culture of the world.

For, let it be noted, Nature is greedy of her truths, and generally ordains that the perception of one link in the chain of her relations is enough to make man great and sacerdotal; only twice, in supreme moments, she creates a Plato and a Shakespeare, proving the possibility, twice in time, of a sight imperfect but demi-godlike. "Life is a stream of awful passions, yet grandeur of character is attainable if we dare the fatal fury of the torrent." Thus said the Greek tragedians, but how variously! The hopelessness of the struggle, yet the grandeur of struggling at all, is uttered by all three— each in his own fashion. In despite of madness, adultery, murder, incest,—in connection with all that is horrible,—in defiance of the very gods, Œdipus, Ajax, Medea, Orestes, Antigone, agonize divinely, and, perishing, attain the repose of antique sculpture. The same undertone pervades all this antique music, but is never so obtruded as to be wearisome. Never was the tyranny of circumstance, the inexorable penalties enforced even on the innocent when laws are broken, represented in such wondrous forms. Under such penalties the innocent may perish, but their reward is their very innocence. Even when they lament aloud, when they exclaim against the direness of their doom, these figures lose none of their nobility. In the *Philoctetes*, the very cries of physical pain are dignified; in the *Œdipus*, the bitterness of the blind sufferer is noble; in the *Prometheus*, the shriek of triumphant agony is sublime.

These three dramatists uttered the truth as they beheld it; nor do they interfere in any wise with higher interpretations of the same conditions. They used the light of their generation; and the value of their revelation lies in the sincerity and splendour of the contemporary utterance. The same thing is not to be said again. It was a cry heard early in time; it is an echo haunting the temple of extinct gods. But its truth to humanity is eternal. We have the same agonies to this day, but we regard them differently. All that can be said on the heathen side has been said supremely.

While the dramatist depicts the fortunes and questionings of small groups and individuals, the epic poet chronicles the history of the world. It is not every day we can have an epic; for only twice or thrice in time are there materials for an epic. Homer is the historian of the gods, and of the social life under Jove and his peers; through his page blows the fresh breeze of morning, the white tents glimmer on Troy plain, horses neigh and heroes buckle on armour,—while aloft the heavens open, showing the glittering gods on the snowy shoulder of Olympus, Iris darting on the rainbow, whose lower end reddens the grim features of Poseidon, driving his chariot through the foam of the Trojan sea. The passion of the *Iliad* is anger, the action, war; in the *Odyssey*, we have the domestic side of the same life, the softer touches of superstition, the milder influences of gods and goddesses, heroes and their queens. But the life is the same in both—large, primitive, colossal—absorbing all the social and religious significance of a period.

What Homer is to the polytheism of the early Greeks, the Old Testament is to the monotheism of the Hebrews. It is the epic of that life—the wilder, weirder, more spiritual poem of a wilder, weirder, more spiritual period. It is the utterance of many mouths, the poem of many episodes, but the theme is unique, pre-eminent—the spirit of the one God, breathing on His chosen peoples, and steadily moving on to fixed consummations foreshadowed in the Prophets. We have had no such wondrous epic as this since, and can have none such again. It is the poem of the one God, when yet He was merely a voice in the thundercloud, a breath between the coming and going of the winds.

Where else, in Virgil's time, subsisted the matter for an epic? To sing of Æneas and his fortunes was certainly patriotic, but the subject, at the best, was merely local—a contemporary, not an eternal, theme. The two great forms of early European life had been phrased in the two great early epics; and till Christ taught, the time for the third great poem of masses had not come. In point of fact, the third great poem has not yet been written. The *New Testament*, of course, is didactic, not poetic; and the *Paradise Regained* of Milton is purely modern and academic.

The fourth European epic is the *Divine Comedy* of Dante; the fifth and last is the *Paradise Lost* of Milton. It is scarcely necessary to describe in detail the character of the vision in each of these cases. Dante saw Roman Catholicism as no eye ever saw it before, watched it to

its uttermost results, made of it an image enduring by
the very intensity of its outlines,—framed of it the epic
of the early church.   Milton's perfect sight pictured,
under latter lights, the wonders of the primeval world.
The theme was old, but, the light was new; and no man
had *seen* angels till Milton saw them, having been first
blinded, that his spiritual sight might be unimpeded.

Thus, all these men,—Homer, the framers of the
biblical epos, Æschylus, Sophocles, Euripides, Dante,
Milton,—were.poets by virtue of having seen some side
of truth as no others saw it.   If some were greater than
others, their materials were perhaps greater.   Not every
one is so situated in time as to see the subject of a new
epos, waiting to· be sung.   But the Seer "shines in his
place, and is content."   Even Goethe had his truth to
utter, and was so far a Seer.   He was great in literature,
by virtue of his spiritual littleness.   It needed such a
man to see Nature in the cold light of self-worship, to
betoken the futility of pure artistic striving.   Yet
this, at the best, was negative teaching, and so far, inferior.

But, it may be objected, these men surely expressed
more than one truth in their generation.   In no wise, for
each had but one point of view; there was no hovering,
no doubting; their gaze was fixed as the gaze of stars.
The object is eternal, it is the point of view which
changes.   Take Milton, for example; the peculiarity of
Milton as a Seer is the angelic spirituality of his sight,
its rejection of all but perfectly noble types for poetic

contemplation. It would seem that, from having once walked with angels, he sees even common things in a divine white light. He breathes the thin serene air of the mountain-top. He seems calm and passionless; his heart beats in great glorified throbs, with no tremor; his speech is stately and crystal clear; he is for ever referring man to his Maker; for ever comparing our stature with that of angels. Mark, further, that his spiritual creatures are profoundly intellectual creatures, strangely subtle and lofty reasoners. He holds pure intellect so divine a thing that, in spite of himself, he makes the Devil his hero. "The end of man," he says in effect, "is to contemplate God, and enjoy Him for ever." But he says this in a way which is not final; there may be truth beyond Milton's truth, but one does not belie the other; this blind man saw as with the eye, and spake as with the tongue, of angels.

Utterances such as these once attained, perceptions so peculiar once welded into the culture of the world, it behoves no man to re-utter them in the reiterative spirit of their first discoverers. He who looks at life exactly as Milton, or Chaucer, or Dante did, may be an excellent being, but he is certainly too late to be a Seer. Yet each new Seer is, of necessity, familiar with the discoveries of his predecessors; the white light of Milton's purity chastens and solemnises Wordsworth's diction; while the glow of Elizabethan colour tinges the pale cheek of Keats the lover. The Seer is not the person of Goethe's epigram,—

> Ein Quidam sagt : " Ich bin von keiner Schule ;
> Kein Meister lebt mit dem ich buhle ;
> Auch bin ich weit davon entfernt,
> Dass ich von Todten was gelernt."
> Das heisst, wenn ich ihn recht verstand—
> "Ich bin ein Narr auf eigne Hand ! "

Nay, as each great Poet sings, we again and again catch tones struck by his predecessors—Homer, Æschylus, Dante, Job, Solomon, Milton, Goethe, and the rest,—but deeper, stronger, more permanent than all, we catch the broken voice of the man himself, saying a mystic thing that we have never heard before. The later we come down in time, the frequenter are the echoes; they are the penalty the modern pays for his privileges. Æschylus and the rest echo Homer and the minstrels. The Hebrew prophets, the heathen poets, the Italian minstrels,—Homer, Moses, Tasso, Dante,—reverberate in every page of Milton; yet they only add volume to the English voice. Shakespeare catches cries from all the poetic voices of Europe,[1] daringly translating into his own phraseology the visions of other and smaller singers, and mellowing his blank verse by the study even of contemporaries. In Chaucer's breezy song come odours from the Greek Ægean, and whispers from Tuscany and Provence. Aristophanes, again and again, inspires the poetically humorous twinkle in the eyes of

---

[1] Note how he spiritualises still further what is already spiritual in the poetic prose of Plutarch ; as an example, compare with the original passage in the Life of Antony the Speech of Enobarbus, descriptive of Cleopatra in her barge.

Molière. But the plagiarism of such writers is kingly plagiarism; the poets ennoble the captives they take in conquest; refusing instruction from no voice, however humble; accepting the matter as divinely sent by nature, but seldom imitating the tones of the medium which transmits the matter.

There is no better sign of unfitness for the high poetic ministry than a too tricksy delight in imitating other *voices*, however admirable. Racine caught the Greek stateliness so well that he has scarcely an accent of his own, save, of course, the mere general accentuation of his people. In reading him, therefore, we have constantly before our mind's eye the picture of a Frenchman on the stage of the great amphitheatre; we see the masks, the fixed lineaments expressive of single passions; and we hear the high-pitched soliloquies of Greece translated into a modern tongue. Racine, indeed, is better reading than any translator of the tragedians, but he is no Seer. On the other hand, Molière was nearly as much under influence as Racine, but the splendour of his individual vision lifted him high into the ranks of poetic teachers. He was an arrant thief, robbing the playwrights of all countries without mercy, but the roguish gleam of the thief's eyes is never lost under the load of stolen raiment. We think of *him*, not of what he is stealing; the dress makes plainer, instead of hiding, the natural peculiarities of the wearer.

There is, then, no danger in echoes, where they do not drown the voice; when they are too audible, that is

the case. The greatest artists utter old truths with all
the force of novelty; not in philosophy only, but in
poetry also, are the worn cries repeated over and over
again.   These cries are common to all the race of Seers,
and may be described as the poetic "terminology."

According to the dignity of the revelation will be the
rank of the Seer in the Temple.   The epic poet is great,
because his matter is great in the first place, and because
he has not fallen below the level of his matter.   The
dramatist is great by his truth to individual character
not his own, and his power of presenting that truth
while spiritualising into definite form and meaning some
vague situation in the sphere of actual or ideal life.   The
lyric poet owes his might to the personal character of
the emotion aroused by his vision.   Then, there are
ranks within ranks.   Not an eye in the throng, however,
but has some object of its own, and some peculiar
sensitiveness to light, form, colour.   To Milton, a prospect of heavenly vistas, where stately figures walk and
cast no shade; but to Pope (a seer, though low down
in the ranks) the pattern of tea-cups, and the peeping of
clocked stockings under farthingales.   While the rouge
on the cheek of modern love betrays itself to the languid
yet keen eyes of Alfred de Musset, Robert Browning is
proclaiming the depths of tender beauty underlying
modern love and its rouge; each is a Seer, and each is
true, only one sees a truth beyond the other's truth.
After Wordsworth has penetrated with solemn-sounding
footfall into the aisle of the Temple, David Gray follows,

and utters a faint cry of beautiful yearning as he dies upon the threshold.

II.—EMOTION.

The second essential peculiarity of the Poet is that of emotional assimilation of impressions. Where intellect coerces emotion, by however faint an effort, the result is criticism of life, however exquisite. Where emotion coerces intellect, the result is poetry.

It is not enough, observe, to *see* vividly. Sir Walter Scott could see as vividly as Keats,—but he was incapable of such emotion. Scott, indeed, is the greatest modern writer who may unhesitatingly be described as unpoetic. He was true both to human types and to society. He was able to clothe the bare outline of history with vivid form and colour. Writing at a time when individualism was at its height in England, ere Whig and Tory had merged into one vacuous nonentity, he could not fail to shadow forth those higher aspirations which are the exclusive property of individual men of genius. Yet no man ever laboured to depict trifles with a more lofty devotion to general truth. There was no finicism in the author of "Waverley." He depicted in faithful æsthetic photography the manners and qualities of ordinary or extraordinary men and women. He was not always profound, nor always noble. But over all his works lies the brilliant radiance of the artistic sympathies, giving, to what might otherwise have been simply

a colourless likeness, the marvellous beauty of an exquisite literary painting.   Scott, however, was no poet.
His very success in prose fiction, as well as the failure of
his metrical productions, betokens his unpoetic nature.
He *saw*, but was not *moved* enough to *sing*.   For there
is this marked difference between poetic and all other
utterance: it owes everything to concentration.   Deep
emotion is invariably rapid in its manifestation, as we
may mark in the case of the ordinary cries of grief; and
the temperament of the poet is so intense, so keen, that
nought but concentrated utterance suffices him.   On the
other hand, the true secret of novel-writing is the power
of expanding.

The *apparence* of pure coercive intellect varies, of
course, according to the nature of the singer.   In Sappho
and Catullus, and all purely lyrical Seers, the intellectual
note is hardly heard at all; in Ovid and Chaucer, it is
heard faintly; in the subjective school of writers, such
as Shelley, it is painfully audible.   But even in Shelley,
where he writes poetry, emotion prevails.   "Queen Mab"
has justly been styled a pamphlet in verse, and the "Re-
volt of Islam" is only occasionally poetic.

It follows that we are, on the whole, more powerfully
moved by purely lyrical utterance than by utterances of
higher portent.   Sappho *troubles* us more than Sophocles,
Keats more than Wordsworth.   The personal cry, so
sharp, so rapid, so genuine, can never fail to find an echo
in our hearts.   The manly exclamation of Burns,—

> For pity's sake, sweet bird, nae mair,
> Or my puir heart is broken !

the fetid breath of Sappho, screaming,—

> Cold shiverings o'er me pass,
> Chill sweats across me fly !
> I am greener than grass,
> And breathless seem to die !

the passionate voice of Catullus,—

> Cœli, Lesbia nostra, Lesbia illa,
> Illa Lesbia, quam Catullus unam
> Plus quam se, atque suos anavit omnes !

the tender lament of Spenser over Sidney, the scream of Shelley, the warm sigh of Keats, all move deeply in the region of melancholy and tears. But the happy calls move us deliciously, although truly "our sweetest songs are those that tell of saddest thought." The lighter strains of Burns, the songs of Tannahill, some verses of Horace, others of Ovid, the lyrics of Drayton and George Wither, and many other glad poems which will occur rapidly to every student, possess the lyrical light in great intensity and sweetness.

But not only in poems professedly lyrical is this lyrical light to be found; it is noticeable in poetry of any form, wherever there is extreme emotion, and may invariably be looked for as the characteristic of the true singer. Œdipus piteously exclaiming in his blindness,—

> τί γὰρ ἔδει μ' ὁρᾶν,
> ὅτω γ' ὁρῶντι μηδὲν ἦν ἰδεῖν γλυκύ ;

Dante, in the great joy of his divinely beloved one, feeling his pale studious lips and cheeks turn into rose-leaves.[1]   Samson Agonistes groaning,—

> O dark, dark, dark, amid the blaze of noon,
> Irrevocably dark, total eclipse,
> Without all hope of day.

Macbeth's last twilight murmur,—

> I have lived long enough; my way of life
> Is fallen into the sear, the yellow leaf;
> And that which should accompany old age,
> As honour, love, obedience, troops of friends,
> I must not look to have!

Cleopatra in the heyday of her bliss; the Sad Shepherd, chasing the footsteps of his love, and warbling in tune-ful ecstasy,—

> Here she was wont to go! and here! and here!
> Just where those daisies, pinks, and violets grow:
> The world may find the spring by following her,
> For other print her airy steps ne'er left;
> Her treading would not bend a blade of grass,
> Or shake the downy blow-ball from his stalk;
> But like the soft west wind she shot along,
> And where she went the flowers took thickest root,
> As she had sow'd them with her odorous foot.

And Bernardo Cenci, in the horror and anguish of that last parting, screaming,—

> O life! O world!
> Cover me! let me be no more!   To see

[1] Purgatory, xxx.

That perfect mirror of pure innocence
Wherein I gazed and grew happy and good,
Shiver'd to dust! To see thee, Beatrice,
Who made all lovely thou didst look upon—
Thee, light of life, dead, dark! While I say "sister"
To hear I have no sister ; and thou, mother,
Whose love was a bond to all our loves,—
Dead ! the sweet bond broken !

These utterances, one and all, sad or glad, are essentially lyrical, only differing from the first class of lyric utterances in belonging to fictitious personages, not to the writer. Romeo and Juliet swarms with lyrics ; every great play of Shakespeare is more or less full of them. They betoken the true dramatic force, and are less distinct in the lesser dramatist. They are plentiful in Beaumont and Fletcher, in Ford, in Webster ; less plentiful in Massinger ; scarcely audible at all in Shirley and Ben Jonson. Where they should appear in the bombastic tragedies of Dryden, rhetoric and rhodomontade appear instead ; and to come down to modern times, where shall we look for the lyrical light in the pretentious tentatives of Sheridan Knowles and Johanna Baillie ? If these tentatives sometimes rise to dignity of movement, that is the most which can be said of them. We have powerful emotional situations, and no emotion.

It is here that all professed imitations of the classics fail. They reproduce the *repose* so admirably, as in many cases to send the reader to sleep. But we search in vain in them for the representation of the great fires, the burning passions of the originals. Insensibly, as has been shrewdly remarked, we derive our notions of Greek art from Greek sculpture, and forget that although calm evolution was rendered necessary by the requirements of the great amphitheatre, it was no calm life, no dainty passion, no subdued woe that was thus evolved. The lineaments of the actor's mask were fixed, but what sort of expression did each mask wear?—the glazed hopeless stare of Œdipus, the white horror-stricken look of Agamemnon, the stony glitter of the eyes of Clytemnestra, the horridly distorted glare of the Promethean Furies, the sick, suffering, and ghastly pale features of Philoctetes. Where was the calm here? The movement of the drama was simple and slow, yet there was no calm in the heart of .the actors, each of whom must fit to his mask a monotone—the sneer of Ulysses, the blunted groan of Cassandra, the fierce shriek of Orestes. The passion and power have made these plays immortal; not the slow evolution, the necessity of the early stage. They are full of the lyrical light.

But though lyrical emotion is the intensest of all written forms of emotion, and must invariably be attained wherever poetry interprets the keenest human feeling and passion, there are forms of emotion wherein intellect is not coerced so strongly. Two forms may be mentioned, and briefly illustrated here—emotional meditation and emotional ratiocination. Either of these forms is of subtler and more mixed quality than the purely lyrical form.

We have numberless examples of emotional meditation in Wordsworth; the thought is strong, solemn, unmistakably intellectual, but it is spiritualised withal by profound feeling.   Observe, as an example of this, the following portion of the " Lines composed a few miles above Tintern Abbey :"—

O sylvan Wye ! thou wanderer through the woods,
How often has my spirit turned to thee,
And now, with gleams of half-extinguished thought,
With many recognitions dim and faint,
And somewhat of a sad perplexity,
The picture of the mind revives again ;
While here I stand, not only with the sense
Of present pleasure, but with pleasing thoughts,
That in this moment there is life and food
 For future years.   And so I dare to hope,
Though changed, no doubt, from what I was when first
I came among these hills ; when like a roe
I bounded o'er the mountains, by the sides
Of the deep rivers, and the lonely streams,
Wherever nature led ; more like a man
Flying from something that he dreads, than one
Who sought the thing he loved.   For Nature then
(The coarser pleasures of my boyish days,
And their glad animal movements all gone by),
To me was all in all.   I cannot paint
What then I was.   The sounding cataract
Haunted me like a passion : the tall rock,
The mountain, and the deep and gloomy wood,
Their colours and their forms were then to me
An appetite ; a feeling and a love
That had no need of a remoter charm,
By thought supplied, or any interest
Unborrowed from the eye.   That time is past,
And all its aching joys are now no more,
And all its dizzy raptures.   Not for this
Faint I, nor mourn, nor murmur ; other gifts

> Have followed, for such loss, I would believe,
> Abundant recompense.　For I have learned
> To look on Nature, not as in the hour
> Of thoughtless youth ; but hearing oftentimes
> The still, sad music of humanity,
> Not harsh nor grating, though of ample power
> To chasten and subdue.　And I have felt.
> A presence that disturbs me with the joy
> Of elevated thoughts: a sense sublime
> Of something far more deeply interfused,
> Whose dwelling is the light of setting suns,
> And the round ocean, and the living air,
> And the blue sky, and in the mind of man,
> A motion and a spirit, that impels
> All thinking things, all objects of all thought,
> And rolls through all things.

By the side of this exquisite passage, let me place another by the same great reflective writer,—

> When, as becomes a man who would prepare
> For such an arduous work, I through myself
> Make rigorous inquisition, the report
> Is often cheering ; for I neither seem
> To lack that first great gift, the vital soul,
> Nor general truths, which are themselves a sort
> Of elements and agents, under-powers,
> Subordinate helpers of the living mind.
> Nor am I naked of external things,
> Forms, images, nor numerous other aids
> Of less regard, though won perhaps with toil,
> And needful to build up a poet's praise.
> Time, place, and manners do I seek, and these
> Are found in plenteous store, but nowhere such
> As may be singled out with steady choice ;
> No little band of yet remembered names
> Whom I, in perfect confidence, might hope

To summon back from lonesome banishment,
And make them dwellers in the hearts of men
Now living, or to live in future years.
Sometimes the ambitious power of choice, mistaking
Proud spring-tide swellings for a regular sea,
Will settle on some British theme, some old
Romantic tale by Milton left unsung;
More often turning to some gentle place
Within the groves of chivalry, I pipe
To shepherd swains, or seated, harp in hand,
Amid reposing knights, by a river side
Or fountain, listen to the grave reports
Of dire enchantments faced and overcome
By the strong mind, and tales of warlike feats,
Where spear encountered spear, and sword with sword
Fought, as if conscious of the blazonry
That the shield bore, so glorious was the strife,
Whence inspiration for a song that winds
Through ever-changing scenes of voting quest;
Wrongs to redress, harmonious tribute paid
To patient courage and unblemished truth,
To firm devotion, zeal unquenchable,
And Christian meekness hallowing faithful loves.

There can be no mistaking the qualities of these two passages. The first is poetry, the second is the merest prose; the emotion in the first extract so breathes on the thought as to fill it with exquisite music and subtle pleasure not to be coerced by meditation. Yet the mood of both is a meditative mood. In the "Prelude," from which the above extract is taken, and in the "Excursion," prose and poetry alternate most significantly. Where the feeling is vivid and intense, the lines lose all that cumbrousness and pamphletude which have blinded so many readers to the real merits of these two compositions.

All these moods, indeed, are but the consequence of that first mood, wherein the Seer receives his impression. If that first mood be too purely intellectual, if the Seer be not stirred extremely in the process of assimilation, there is a certainty that, in spite of clear vision, he will produce prose,—as Milton did occasionally, as Wordsworth did very often ; as Shakespeare seldom or never does, and as Keats never did.

It is certain, then, that clear vision can exist independently of emotion ; that, however, emotion is generally dependent on clear vision ; and that, in short, he who sees vividly will in most cases feel deeply, but not in all cases.

Let me mention one more notable case in point. I mean Crabbe,—the writer to whom modern writers are fondest of alluding, and whom, to judge from their blunders concerning him, they appear to have been least fond of reading. A careful study of his works has revealed to me abundant knowledge of life, considerable sympathy, little or no insight, and no emotion. The poems are photographs, not pictures. There is no spiritualisation, none of that fine selective instinct which invariably accompanies deep artistic feeling. There is too constant a consciousness of the "reader," too painful an attempt to gain force by means of vivid details. Now, these are not the poetic characteristique. The poet derives his force from the vividness of the feeling awakened by his subject or by his meditation ; he does not betray himself by clumsy efforts to gain attention. A thought— a touch—a gleam of colour—often suffice for him. Whereas Crabbe betrays his purely intellectual attitude at every step. He describes every cranny of a cottage, every gable, every crack in the wall, every kitchen utensil, —when his story concerns the soul of the inmate. He pieces out a churchyard like so much grocery, into so many lives and graves. There is no glamour in his eyes when he looks on death ;—he is noting the bedroom furniture and the dirty sheets. There is no weird music in his ears when he stands in a churchyard ;—he is re- cording the quality of the coffin-wood, sliding off into an account of the history of the parish beadle, and observing whose sheep they are that browse inside the stone wall of the holy place.

III.—MUSIC.

I am now led directly to the discussion of the third poetic gift,—that of music; for metrical speech is the most concentrated of all speech, and proportions itself to the quality of the poetic emotion. The most powerful form of emotion is lyrical emotion, and the sweetest music is lyrical music.

Poetic vision culminates in sweet sound,—always in- adequate, perhaps, to represent the whole of sight, but interpenetrating through the medium of emotion with the entire mystery of life. Nothing, indeed, so distinguishes

the variety of Seers as their melody.   It is the soul's perfect speech.   A break in the harmony not seldom betrays
a dizziness of the eyes, an inactivity of the heart.   A false
note betrays the false maestro.   A cold or forced expression indicates insincerity.

This music, this last wondrous gift, carries with it its
own significance and wisdom ; it has a wondrous glamour
of its own, like the dim light that is in falling snow.
What exquisite sound is this,—where the thought and
the emotion die away into a murmur like the wash of a
summer sea ?—

> Thou wast not born for death, immortal bird !
>   No hungry generations tread thee down ;
> The voice I hear this passing night was heard
>   In ancient days by emperor and clown.
> Perhaps the self-same song that found a path
>   Through the sad heart of Ruth, when, sick for home,
>   She stood in tears among the alien corn ;
>   The same that oft-times hath
>   Charmed magic casements, opening on the foam
>   Of perilous seas, in faery lands forlorn.

Or this,—so perfect in its fleeting rapture :

>   Sound of vernal showers,
>   On the twinkling grass,
>   Rain-awakened flowers,
>   All that ever was
>   Joyous, and clear, and sweet, thy music doth surpass.
>   Teach us, sprite or bird,
>   What sweet thoughts are thine :
>   I have never heard
>   Praise of love or wine
>   That panted forth a rapture so divine !

> Teach me half the gladness
> That thy brain must know,
> Such harmonious madness
> From my lips would flow,—
> The world should listen then, as I am listening now.

Or these lines from the "Willow, Willow," of Alfred de Musset :—

> Mes chers amis, quand je mourrai,
> Plantez un saule au cimetière.
> J'aime son feuillage éploré,
> La pâleur m'en est douce et chère,
> Et son ombre sera légère
> A la terre où je dormirai.

I might fill pages with such quotations.

The examples just given are examples of purely lyrical music,—from its personal nature, the most concentrated of all music. For the sake of contrast, now, let me turn to the least concentrated form of all, as it is represented in particular writers.

At a first view, it would seem that epic poetry is most apt to be unmelodious, on account of the diffuse character of its materials as generally conceived. But this is an error *à priori*. The materials are not diffuse—they are only large and various ; and the music is emotional and concentrated, though not to the extent noticeable in less dignified forms of writing. Like dramatic poetry, it is all-embracing, and includes in its compass all elements, from lyrical feeling to emotional meditation. The stateliness and constancy of its movement do not preclude the sharp lyrical cry or the deep meditative pause,

Homer is the most various of singers. His successors are less various, precisely because they are less great. Again and again in the sharp solemn progress of Dante through Hell are we startled by bursts of wilder melody. Even in " Paradise Lost " there are some occasions when the deep organ bass changes into a scream.

This is but saying what has been already said of lyrical emotion. In brief, lyrical emotion and lyrical music as its expression intersect all great poetry, whatever its nature ; and the reason need not be further explained. Lyric music is the *ideal* speech of intense personal feeling ; and that is why the exquisite music of Greek tragedy is not confined to the choruses.

But just as all emotion is not markedly personal, all music is not lyrical. No music is so exquisite, so profoundly interesting to men ; but there are more complex kinds of expression, sounds more variegated and diffuse. Take the following passage from the " Paradise Lost " of Milton :—

> For now, and since first break of dawn, the Fiend,
> Mere serpent in appearance, forth was come,
> And on his quest, where likeliest he might find
> The only two of mankind, but in them
> The whole included race, his purpos'd prey.
> In bower and field he sought where any kind
> Of grove or garden plot more pleasant lay,
> Their tendence or plantation for delight ;
> By fountain or by shady rivulet
> He sought them both, but wish'd his hap might fin l
> Eve separate ; he wish'd but not with hope
> Of what so seldom chanc'd, when to his wish,

Beyond his hope, *Eve separate he spies,*
Veil'd in a cloud of fragrance, where she stood,
Half spy'd, so thick the roses blushing round
About her glow'd, oft stooping to support
Each flower of slender stalk, whose head, though gay
Carnation, purple, azure, or speck'd with gold,
Hung drooping, unsustained; them she upstays
Gently with myrtle band, mindless the while
Herself, tho' fairest unsupported flower,
From her best prop so far, and storm so nigh.
Nearer he drew, and many a walk travers'd
Of stateliest covert, cedar, pine or palm,
Then voluble and bold, now hid, now seen
Among thick-woven arborets and flowers
Imborder'd on each bank, the hand of Eve :
Spot more delicious than those gardens feign'd,
Or of reviv'd Adonis, or renown'd
Alcinous, host of old Laertes' son,
Or that, not mystic, where the sapient king
Held dalliance with his fair Egyptian spouse.

  * * * * *

So spake the enemy of mankind, enclos'd
In serpent, inmate bad, and toward Eve
Address'd his way, not with indented wave,
Prone on the ground, as since, but on his rear.
Circular base of rising folds, that tower'd
Fold above fold, a surging maize, his head
Crested aloft, and curbuncle his eyes ;
With burnish'd neck of verdant gold, erect
Amidst his circling spires, that on the grass
Floated redundant; pleasing was his shape
And lovely ; never since of serpent kind
Lovelier, not those that in Illyria chang'd
Hermione and Cadmus, or the God
In Epidaurus ; nor to which transform'd
Ammonian Jove, or Capitoline was seen
He with Olympias, this with her who bore

> Scipio the height of Rome.   With tract oblique
> At first, as one who sought access, but fear'd
> To interrupt, side-long he works his way :
> As when a ship, by skilful steersman wrought
> Nigh river's mouth, or foreland, where the wind
> Veers oft, as oft so steers and shifts her sail :
> So varied he, and of his tortuous train
> Curl'd many a wanton wreath in sight of Eve,
> To lure her eye ; she, busied, heard the sound
> Of rustling leaves, but minded not, as us'd
> To such disport before her through the field,
> From every beast, more duteous at her call
> Than at Circean call the herd disguis'd.
> He bolder now, uncall'd before her stood,
> But as in gaze admiring : oft he bow'd
> His turret crest, and sleek enamel'd neck,
> Fawning, and lick'd the ground whereon she trod.

In these exquisite passages of pure description, the music
perfectly represents the subdued emotion of the artist ;
there is no excitement, but vivid presentment ;—and we
hear the very movement of the snake in the involution
and picturesqueness of the lines.   I cannot do better
than place by the side of the above a passage from the
same great poet, which seems to me especially false and
inharmonious.   It is very brief :—

> The Most High
> Eternal Father, from his secret cloud,
> Amidst in thunder utter'd thus his voice :
> Assembled angels, and ye powers return'd
> From unsuccessful charge, be not dismay'd,
> Nor troubled at these tidings from the earth,
> Which your sincerest care could not prevent,
> Foretold so lately what would come to pass,

> When first this Tempter cross'd the gulf from Hell.
> I told ye then he should prevail and speed
> On his bad errand, man should be seduc'd
> And flatter'd out of all, believing lies
> Against his Maker ; no decree of mine
> Concurring to necessitate his fall,
> Or touch with lightest moment of impulse
> His free will, to her own inclining left
> In even scale.   But fall'n he is, and now
> What rests but that the mortal sentence pass
> On his transgression, death denounc'd that day?
> Which he presumes already vain and void,
> Because not yet inflicted, as he fear'd,
> By some immediate stroke ; but soon shall find
> Forbearance no acquittance ere day end,
> Justice shall not return as bounty scorn'd.
> But whom send I to judge them? whom but thee
> Vicegerent Son? to thee I have transferr'd .
> All judgment, whether in Heaven, or Earth, or Hell.
> Easy it may be seen that I intend
> Mercy colleague with justice, sending thee
> Man's friend, his mediator, his design'd
> Both ransome and redeemer voluntary,
> And destin'd man himself to judge men fall'n.

Where is the thunder here ?   Where is the solemn music? Instead of awe-inspiring sound, we have bald and turgid prose, pieced out clumsily into ten-syllable lines, every one of which limps like Vulcan.   And why ?   Precisely because Milton had no spiritual glamour of the Highest, such as he had of Satan, for example,—felt no real emotion in recording His utterances, not even the cold meditative emotion which just redeems many other parts of " Paradise Lost " from sheer prose.   He was forcing his mind to hear a voice, attempting to represent the utterance of a personality ungrasped by his imagination.

Mere rhetorical music is the least poetic of all, although sometimes it has an exceeding charm, as in Virgil's famous lines on Marcellus, and much of the poetry of rhetorical periods in England.

Akin to such rhetorical music is the melody of the French school of writers, singers who mar expression by too elaborate effort, by habitual verbosity, and by fatal fluency of sound. Melody, indeed, as represented in our true singers, may be divided into three kinds, just as the singers themselves may be divided into three classes,—the simple, the ornate, and the grotesque. The first kind is the sweetest and best ; we find it in the great lyrists, from Sappho to Burns. Wherever Shelley sings perfectly, as in the " Ode to the Skylark," his music loses all its insincerities and affectations. Ornate and grotesque music have common faults,—the first sacrifices the emotion and meaning by thinning and straining them too carefully; the second loses in portent what it gains in mannerism ; and both, therefore, betray that dangerous intellectual self-consciousness which is a barrier to the production of true poetry. A thing cannot be uttered too briefly and simply if it is to reach the soul. Music that conceals, instead of expressing, thought, music that is nothing but sweet sounds and luscious alliterations, is not poetry. We have the sweet sounds everywhere, in fact : in the wash of the sea, in the rustle of leaves, in the song of birds, in the murmur of happy living things. The world is full of them, its heart aches with them; they are mystical and they are homeless. It is the offices of poetry not barely to imitate them, but to link them with the Soul, and by so doing to use them as symbols of definite form and meaning. They issue from the soul's voice with a new wonder in their tones, and are then ready to be used as man's perfect language and speech to God.

I need delay little more on this branch of poetic power, which, indeed, contains matter for a whole volume. It is clear that there is no poetry without music, but that music varies extremely, according to the quality and intensity of the emotion. It may safely be affirmed that no subject is unfit for poetic treatment which can be spiritualised to this uttermost form of harmonious and natural numbers. So closely is melody woven in with and representative of emotion and of sight, that it has been called the characteristique of the true Seer. But let us never lose sight of the fact that music *is* representative, and valuable, not for the sole sake of its own sweetness, not for the sole sake of the emotion it represents, but mainly and clearly valuable for the sake of the poetic thought and vision which it brings to completion. There may be melodious sound without meaning, fine versification without thought; but the most exquisite melody and versification are those which convey the most exquisite forms of poetic vision.

DAVID GRAY:

A MEMOIR

DAVID GRAY:

SITUATED in a by-road, about a mile from the small town of Kirkintilloch, and eight miles from the city of Glasgow, stands a cottage one storey high, roofed with slate, and surrounded by a little kitchen-garden. A white-washed lobby, leading from the front to the back-door, divides this cottage into two sections; to the right, is an office fitted up as a hand-loom weaver's workshop; to the left is a kitchen paved with stone, and opening into a tiny carpeted bedroom.

In the workshop, a father, daughter, and sons worked all day at the loom. In the kitchen, a handsome cheery Scottish matron busied herself like a thrifty housewife, and brought the rest of the family about her at meals. All day long the soft hum of the loom was heard in the workshop; but when night came, mysterious doors were thrown open, and the family retired to sleep in extraordinary mural recesses.

In this humble home, David Gray, a hand-loom weaver, resided for upwards of twenty years, and managed to rear a family of eight children—five boys and three girls. His eldest son, David, author of " The Luggie and other Poems," is the hero of the present true history.

David was born on the 29th of January, 1838. He alone, of all the little household, was destined to receive a decent education. From early childhood, the dark-eyed little fellow was noted for his wit and cleverness; and it was the dream of his father's life that he should become a scholar. At the parish-school of Kirkintilloch he learned to read, write, and cast up accounts, and was, moreover, instructed in the Latin rudiments. Partly through the hard struggles of his parents, and partly through his own severe labours as a pupil-teacher and private tutor, he was afterwards enabled to attend the classes at the Glasgow University. In common with other rough country lads, who live up dark alleys, subsist chiefly on oatmeal and butter forwarded from home, and eventually distinguish themselves in the class-room, he had to fight his way onward amid poverty and privation ; but in his brave pursuit of knowledge nothing daunted him. It had been settled at home that he should become a minister of the Free Church of Scotland. Unfortunately, however, he had no love for the pulpit. Early in life he had begun to hanker after the delights of poetical composition. He had devoured the poets from Chaucer to Wordsworth. The yearnings thus awakened in him had begun to express themselves in many wild fragments—contributions, for the most part, to the poet's corner of a local newspaper—"The Glasgow Citizen."

Up to this point there was nothing extraordinary in the career or character of David Gray. Taken at his best, he was an average specimen of the persevering young Scottish student. But his soul contained wells of emotion which had not yet been stirred to their depths. When, at fourteen years of age, he began to study in Glasgow, it was his custom to go home every Saturday night in order to pass the Sunday with his parents. These Sundays at home were chiefly occupied with rambles in the neighbourhood of Kirkintilloch; wanderings on the sylvan banks of the Luggie, the beloved little river which flowed close to his father's door. On Luggieside awakened one day the dream which developed all the hidden beauty of his character, and eventually kindled all the faculties of his intellect. Had he been asked to explain the nature of this dream, David would have answered vaguely enough, but he would have said something to the following effect: "I'm thinking none of us are quite contented; there's a climbing impulse to heaven in us all that won't let us rest for a moment. Just now I would be happy if I *knew* a little more. I'd give ten years of life to see Rome, and Florence, and Venice, and the grand places of old; and to feel that I wasn't a burden on the old folks. I'll be a great man yet ! and the old home, the Luggie and Gartshore wood, shall be *famous* for my sake." He could only measure his ambition by the love he bore his home. "I was born,

bred, and cared for here, and my folk are buried here. I
know every nook and dell for miles around, and they are all
dear to me.   My own mother and father dwell here, and
in my own *wee* room " (the tiny carpeted bedroom above
alluded to) " I first learned to read poetry. I love my
home, and it is for my home's sake that I love fame."

Nor is that home and its surroundings unworthy of
such love.   Tiny and unpretending as is Luggie stream,
upon its banks lie many nooks of beauty, bowery glimpses
of woodland, shady solitudes, places of nestling green
here and there.   Not far off stretch the Campsie fells,
with dusky nooks between, where the waterfall and the
cascade make a silver pleasure in the heart of shadow;
and beyond, there are dreamy glimpses of the misty blue
mountains themselves.   Away to the south-west, lies Glasgow in a smoke, most hideous of cities, wherein the very
clangour of church-bells is associated with abominations.
Into the heart of that city David was to be slowly drawn,
a subject of fascination only death could dispel,—the
desire to make deathless music, and the dream of moving
therewith the mysterious heart of man.

At twenty-one years of age, when this dream was strong
within him, David was a tall young man, slightly but
firmly built, and with a stoop at the shoulders.   His head
was small, fringed with black curly hair. Want of can-
dour was not his fault, though he seldom looked one in
the face; his eyes, however, were large and dark, full of
intelligence and humour, harmonising well with the long
thin nose and nervous lips. The great black eyes and

woman's mouth betrayed the creature of impulse; one whose reasoning faculties were small, but whose temperament was like red-hot coal. He sympathised with much that was lofty, noble, and true in poetry, and with much that was absurd and suicidal in the poet. He carried sympathy to the highest pitch of enthusiasm; he shed tears over the memories of Keats and Burns, and he was corybantic in his execution of a Scotch "reel." A fine phrase filled him with the rapture of a lover. He admired extremes—from Rabelais to Tom Sayers. Thirsting for human sympathy, which lured him in the semblance of notoriety, he perpetrated all sorts of extravagancies, innocent enough in themselves, but calculated to blind him to the very first principles of art. Yet this enthusiasm, as I have suggested, was his safeguard in at least one respect. Though he believed himself to be a genius, he loved the parental roof of the hand-loom weaver.

And what thought the weaver and his wife of this wonderful son of theirs? They were proud of him, proud in a silent undemonstrative fashion; for among the Scottish poor concealment of the emotions is held a virtue. During his weekly visits home, David was not overwhelmed with caresses; but he was the subject of conversation night after night, when the old couple talked in bed. Between him and his father there had arisen a strange barrier of reserve. They seldom exchanged with each other more than a passing word; but to one friend's bosom David would often confide the love and tenderness he bore for his over-worked, upright parent. When the boy first began to write verses the old man affected perfect contempt and indifference, but his eyes gloated in secret over the poet's-corners of the Glasgow newspapers. The poor weaver, though an uneducated man, had a profound respect for education and cultivation in others. He felt his heart bound with hope and joy when strangers praised the boy, but he hid the tenderness of his pride under a cold indifference. Although proud of David's talent for writing verses, he was afraid to encourage a pursuit which practical common sense assured him was mere trifling. At a later date he might have spoken out, had not his tongue been frozen by the belief that advice from him would be held in no esteem by his better educated and more gifted son. Thus, the more David's indications of cleverness and scholarship increased, the more afraid was the old man to express his gratification and give his advice. Equally touching was the point of view taken by David's mother, whose cry was, "The kirk, the free kirk, and nothing but the kirk!" She neither appreciated nor underrated the abilities of her boy, but her proudest wish was that he should become a real live minister, with home and "haudin'" of his own. To see David,—"our David,"—in a pulpit, preaching the Gospel out of a big book, and dwelling in a good house to the end of his days!

But meantime the boy was swiftly undermining all such cherished plans. He had saturated his heart and mind with the intoxicating wines of poesy,—drunken deep of such syrups as only very strong heads indeed can carry calmly. He differed from older and harder poets in this only,—that he had not the trick of disguising his vanity, knew not how to ape humanity. The poor lad was moved, maddened by the strange divine light in his eyes, and he cried aloud: "The beauty of the cloudland I have visited! the ideal love of my soul!" Thus he expressed himself, much to the amusement of his hearers. "Solitude," he exclaimed on another occasion, "and an utter want of all physical exercise, are working deplorable ravages in my nervous system; the crows'-feet are blackening about my eyes, and I cannot think to face the sunlight. When I ponder over my own inability to move the world, to move one heart in it, no wonder that my face gathers blackness. Tennyson beautifully and (so far) truly says, that the face is 'the form and colour of the mind and life.' If you saw *me!*" His verses written at that period, although abounding with echoes of his two pet poets, show great intensity and the sweetness of perfect feeling. Some of the lyrics in his volume, printed among the Poems Named and without Names, belong to this period. His productions, however, were for the most part close reproductions of the manner of Keats; and so conscious was he of this fact, that in one of these pieces he expressly styled himself, "a foster son of Keats, the dreamily divine." Wordsworth he did not not reproduce so much until a later and a purer period. One of these unpublished pieces I shall quote here, to show that David, even at the crude assimilate period, showed 'brains" and vision noticeable in a youth of twenty.

EMPEDOCLES.

> " He who to be deem'd
> A god, leap'd fondly into Ætna flames, —
> Empedocles."—MILTON.

How, in the crystal smooth and azure sky,
Droop the clear, living sapphires, tremulous
And inextinguishably beautiful !
How the calm irridescence of their soft
Ethereal fire contrasts with the wild flame
Rising from this doomed mountain like the noise
Of ocean whirlwinds through the murky air !
Alone, alone ! yearning, ambitious ever !
Hope's agony !   O, ye immortal gods !
Regally sphered in your keen-silvered orbs,
Eternal,.where fled that authentic fire,
Stolen by Prometheus ere the pregnant clouds
Rose from the sea, full of the deluge !   Where
Art thou, white lady of the morning ; white
Aurora, charioted by the fair Hours
Through amethystine mists weeping soft dews
Upon the meadow, as Apollo heaves
His constellation through the liquid dawn ?
Give me Tithonus' gift, thou orient
Undying Beauty ! and my love shall be
Cherubic worship, and my star shall walk
The plains of heaven, thy punctual harbinger !
O with thy ancient power prolong my days
For ever ; tear this flesh-thick cursed life
Enlinking me to this foul earth, the home
Of cold mortality, this nether hell !
  Rise, mighty conflagrations ! and scarce wild
These crowding shadows !   *Far on the dim sea*
Pale mariners behold thee, and the sails
Shine purpled by thy glare, and the slow oars
Drop ruby, and the trembling human souls

Wonder affrighted as their pitchy barks,
Guided by Syrian pilots, ripple by
Hailing for craggy Calpe; O, ye frail
Weak human souls, I, lone Empedocles,
Stand here unshivered as a steadfast god,
Scorning thy puny destinies.

                         I float
To cloud-enrobed Olympus on the wings
Of a rich dream, swift as the light of stars,
Swifter than Zophiel or Mercury
Upon his throne of adamantine gold.—
Jove sits superior, while the deities
Tread delicate the smooth cerulean floors.
Hebe (with twin breasts, like twin roes that feed
Among the lilies), in her taper hand
Bears the bright goblet, rough with gems and gold,
Filled with ambrosia to the lipping brim.
O, love and beauty and immortal life !
O, light divine, ethereal effluence
Of purity ! O, fragrancy of air,
Spikenard and calamus, cassia and balm,
With all the frankincense that ever fumed
From temple censers swung from pictured roofs,
Float warmly through the corridors of heaven.

Hiss ! moan ! shriek ! wreath thy livid serpentine
Volutions, O ye earth-born flames ! and flout
The silent skies with strange fire, like a dawn
Rubific, terrible, a lurid glare !
Olympus shrinks beside thee ! I, alone,
Like deity ignipotent, behold
Thy playful whirls and thy weird melody
Here undismayed. O gods ! shall I go near
And in the molten horror headlong plunge
Deathward, and that serene immortal life
Discover? Shriek your hellish discord out
Into the smoky firmament ! Down roll

Your fat bituminous torrents to the sea,
Hot hissing !   Far away in element
Untroubled rise the crystal battlements
Of the celestial mansion, where to be
Is my ambition ; and O far away
From this dull earth in azure atmospheres
My star shall pant its silvery lustre, bright
With sempiternal radiance, voyaging
On blissful errands the pure marble air.

O, dominations and life-yielding powers,
Listen my yearning prayer : To be of ye—
Of thy grand hierarchy and old race
Plenipotent, I do a deed that dares
The draff of men to equal.   You have given
Immortal life to common human men
Who common deeds achieved ; nay, even for love
Some goddesses voluptuous have raised
Weak whiners from this curst sublunar world,
Pillowed them on snow bosoms in the bowers
Of Paradise !   And shall Empedocles,
Who from the perilous grim edge of life
Leaps sheer into the liquid fire and meets
Death like a lover, not be sphered and made
A virtue ministrant ?   All you soft orbs
By pure intelligences piloted,
Incomprehensibly their glories show
Approving.   *O ye sparkle-moving fires*
Of heaven, now silently above the flare
Of this red mountain shining, which of you
Shall be my home ?   Into whose stellar glow
Shall I arrive, bringing delight and life
And spiritual motion and dim fame ?
Hiss, fiery serpents !   Your sweet breathings warm
My face as I approach ye.   Flap wild wings,
Ye dragons ! flaming round this mouth of hell,
To me the mouth of heaven.

The influence of Keats soon decayed, and calmer influences supervened. He began a play on the Shakesperian model. This ambitious effort, however, was soon relinquished for a dearer, sweeter task,—the composition of a pastoral poem descriptive of the scenery surrounding his home. This subject, first suggested to him by a friend who guessed his real power, grew upon him with wondrous force, till the lines welled into perfect speech through very deepness of passion. His whole soul was occupied. The pictures that had troubled his childhood, the running river, the thymy Campsie fells, were now to be again before his spirit; and all the human sweetness and trouble, the beloved faces, the familiar human figures, added to the soft music of a flowing river and the distant hum of looms from cottage doors. The result was the poem entitled "The Luggie," which gives its name to the posthumous volume, and which, though it lacked the last humanising touches of the poet, remains unique in contemporary literature.

But even while his heart was full of this exquisite utterance, this babble of green fields and silver waters, the influence of cities was growing more and more upon him, and poesy was no more the quite perfect joy that had made his boyhood happy. It was not enough to *sing* now; the thirst for applause was deepening; and it is not therefore extraordinary that even his fresh and truthful pastoral shows here and there the hectic flush of self-consciousness,—the dissatisfied glance in the direction of the public. The natural result of this was occasional merry-making, and grog-drinking, and beating the big city during the dark hours. There was high poetic pleasure in singing songs among artizans in familiar public-houses, flirting with an occasional milliner, and singing her charms in broad Scotch,—even occasionally coming to fisticuffs in obscure places, possibly owing to a hot discussion on the character of that demon of religious Scotch artizans,—the poet Shelley. I do not hesitate the least in mentioning these matters, because Gray has been too frequently represented as a morbid, unwholesome young gentleman, without natural weaknesses—a kind of aqueous Henry Kirke White, branded faintly with ambition. He was nothing of the kind. He was a young man, as other young men are—foolish and wild in his season, though never gross or disreputable. The very excess of his sensitiveness led him into outbreaks against convention. While pouring out the sweetness of his nature in " The Luggie," he could turn aside again and again, and relieve his excitement by such doggerel as this, addressed to a companion,—

> Let olden Homer, hoary,
> Sing of wondrous deeds of glory,
> In that ever-burning story,
>   Bold and bright, friend Bob !
> *Our* theme be Pleasure, careless,
> In all stirring frolics fearless,
> In the vineyard, reckless, peerless,
>   Heroes dight, friend Bob !

Be it noted, however, that there was in Gray's nature a

strange and exquisite femininity,—a perfect feminine purity and sweetness. Indeed, till the mystery of sex be medically explained, I shall ever believe that nature originally meant David Gray for a female; for besides the strangely sensitive lips and eyes, he had a woman's shape, —narrow shoulders, lissome limbs, and extraordinary breadth across the hips.

Early in his teens David had made the acquaintance of a young man of Glasgow, with whom his fortunes were destined to be intimately woven. That young man was myself. We spent year after year in intimate communion, varying the monotony of our existence by reading books together, plotting great works, writing extravagant letters to men of eminence, and wandering about the country on vagrant freaks. Whole nights and days were often passed in seclusion, in reading the great thinkers, and pondering on their lives. Full of thoughts too deep for utterance, dreaming, David would walk at a swift pace through the crowded streets, with face bent down, and eyes fixed on the ground, taking no heed of the human beings passing to and fro. Then he would come to me crying, " I have had a dream," and would forthwith tell of visionary pictures which had haunted him in his solitary walk. This " dreaming," as he called it, consumed the greater portion of his hours of leisure.

Towards the end of the year 1859, David became convinced that he could no longer idle away the hours of his youth. His work as student and as pupil teacher was ended, and he must seek some means of subsistence. He imagined, too, that his poor parents threw dull looks on the beggar of their ¸ bounty. Having abandoned all thoughts of entering into the Church, for which neither his taste nor his opinions fitted him, what should he do in order to earn his daily bread? His first thought was to turn schoolmaster; but no! the notion was an odious one. He next endeavoured, without success, to procure himself a situation on one of the Glasgow newspapers. Meantime, while drifting from project to project he maintained a voluminous correspondence, in the hope of persuading some eminent man to read his poem of "The Luggie."

Unfortunately, the persons to whom he wrote were too busy to pay much attention to the solicitations of an entire stranger. Repeated disappointments only increased his self-assertion; the less chance there seemed of an improvement in his position, and the less strangers seemed to recognise his genius, the more dogged grew his conviction that he was destined to be a great poet. His letters were full of this conviction. To one entire stranger he wrote: "I am a poet; let that be understood distinctly." Again: "I tell you that, if I live, my name and fame shall be second to few of any age, and to none of my own. I speak this because I *feel* power." Again: "I am so accustomed to compare my own mental progress with that of such men as Shakespeare, Goethe, and Wordsworth, that the dream of my life will not be fulfilled, if my fame equal not, at least, that of the latter of these three!" This was extraordinary language, and it is not surprising that little heed was paid to it. Let some explanation be given here. No man could be more humble, reverent-minded, self-doubting, than David was in reality. Indeed, he was constitutionally timid of his own abilities, and he was personally diffident. In his letters only he absolutely endeavoured to wrest from his correspondents some recognition of his claim to help and sympathy. The moment sympathy came, no matter how coldly it might be expressed, he was all humility and gratitude. In this spirit, after one of his wildest flights of self-assertion, he wrote: "When I read Thomson, I despair." Again: " Being bare of all recommendations, I lied with my own conscience, deeming that if I called myself a great man you were bound to believe me." Again: " If you saw me you would wonder if the quiet, bashful, boyish-looking fellow before you was the author of all yon blood and thunder." In a lengthy correspondence with Mr. Sydney Dobell, who is also known as a writer of verse, David wrote wildly and boldly enough ; but he was quite ready to plead guilty to silliness when the fits were over. But the grip of cities was on him, and he was far too conscious of outsiders. How sad and pitiable sounds the following ! " Mark !" he cried, "it is not what I have done, or can now do, but what I feel myself able and born to do, that makes me so selfishly stupid. Your sentence, thrown back to me for reconsideration, would certainly seem strange to any one but myself; but the thought that I had so written to you only made me the more resolute in my actions, and the

wilder in my visions.   What if I sent the same sentence
back to you again, with the quiet stern answer, that it is
my intention to be the 'first poet of my own age,' and
second only to a very few of any age.   Would you think
me 'mad,' 'drunk,' or an 'idiot,' or my 'self-confidence'
one of the '*saddest* paroxysms?'   When my biography
falls to be written, will not this same self-confidence be
one of the most striking features of my intellectual development?   Might not a poet of twenty *feel* great
things?   In all the stories of mental warfare that I have
ever read, that mind which became of celestial clearness
and godlike power did nothing for twenty years but *feel*."
The hand-loom weaver's son raving about his "biography!"   The youth that could babble so deliciously
of green fields, looking forward to the day when he would
be anatomised by the small critic and chronicled by the
chroniclers of small beer!   It was not in this mood that
he wrote his sweetest lines.   The world was already too
much with him.

Here, if anywhere in his career, I see signs which con-
sole me for his bitter suffering and too early death; signs
that, had he lived, his fate might have been an even
sadder one.   Saint Beuve says, as quoted by Alfred de
Musset :—

> Il existe, en un mot, chez les trois quarts des hommes,
> Un poëte mort jeune à qui l'homme survit !

A dead young poet whom the man survives !—and
dead through that very poison which David was beginning

to taste.   I dare not aver that such would have been the
result ; I dare not say that David's poetic instinct was
too weak to survive the danger.   But the danger existed
—clear, sparkling, deathly.   Had David been hurried
away to teach schools among the hills, buried among
associations pure and green as those that surrounded his
youth and childhood, the poetic instinct might have sur-
vived and achieved wondrous results.   But he went
southward,—he imbibed an atmosphere entirely unfitted
for his soul at that period ; and—perhaps, after all, the
gods loved him and knew best.

For all at once there flashed upon David and myself
the notion of going to London, and taking the literary
fortress by storm.   Again and again we talked the
project over, and again and again we hesitated.   In the
spring of 1860, we both found ourselves without an
anchorage ; each found it necessary to do something for
daily bread.   For some little time the London scheme
had been in abeyance ; but, on the 3rd of May,
1860, David came to me, his lips firmly compressed, his
eyes full of fire, saying, " Bob, I'm off to London."
" Have you funds ? " I asked.   " Enough for one, not
enough for two," was the reply.   " If you can get the
money anyhow, we'll go together."   On parting, we
arranged to meet on the evening of the 5th of May, in
time to catch the five o'clock train.   Unfortunately,
however, we neglected to specify which of the two
Glasgow stations was intended.   At the hour appointed,
David left Glasgow, by one line of railway, in the belief

that I had been unable to join him, but determined to try the venture alone.　With the same belief and determination, I left at the same hour by the other line of railway.　We arrived in different parts of London at about the same time.　Had we left Glasgow in company, or had we met immediately after our arrival in London, the story of David's life might not have been so brief and sorrowful.

Though the month was May, the weather was dark, damp, cloudy.　On arriving in the metropolis, David wandered about for hours, carpet-bag in hand.　The magnitude of the place overwhelmed him; he was lost in that great ocean of life.　He thought about Johnson and Savage, and how they wandered through London with pockets more empty than his own; but already he longed to be back in the little carpeted bedroom in the weaver's cottage.　How lonely it seemed!　Among all that mist of human faces there was not one to smile in welcome; and how was he to make his trembling voice heard above the roar and tumult of those streets　The very policemen seemed to look suspiciously at the stranger. To his sensitively Scottish ear the language spoken seemed quite strange and foreign; it had a painful, homeless sound about it that sank nervously on the heart-strings.　As he wandered about the streets he glanced into coffee-shop after coffee-shop, seeing "beds" ticketed in each fly-blown window.　His pocket contained a sovereign and a few shillings, but he would need every penny.　Would not a bed be useless extravagance? he asked himself. Certainly. Where, then, should he pass the night? In Hyde Park! He had heard so much about this part of London that the name was quite familiar to him. Yes, he would pass the night in the park. Such a proceeding would save money, and be exceedingly romantic; it would be just the right sort of beginning for a poet's struggle in London ! So he strolled into the great park, and wandered about its purlieus till morning. In remarking upon this foolish conduct, one must reflect that David was strong, heartsome, full of healthy youth. It was a frequent boast of his that he scarcely ever had a day's illness. Whether or not his fatal complaint was caught during this his first night in London is uncertain, but some few days afterwards David wrote thus to his father : " By-the-bye, I have had the worst *cold* I ever had in my life. I cannot get it away properly, but I feel a great deal better to-day." Alas ! violent cold had settled down upon his lungs, and insidious death was already slowly approaching him. So little conscious was he of his danger, however, that I find him writing to a friend : " What brought me here? God knows, for I don't. *Alone* in such a place is a horrible thing. . . . People don't seem to understand me . . . Westminster Abbey; I was there all day yesterday. If I live I shall be buried there—so help me God ! A completely defined consciousness of *great* poetical genius is my only antidote against utter despair and despicable failure."

I suppose his purposes in coming to Babylon were about as definite as my own had been, although he had the advantage of being qualified as a pupil teacher. We tossed ourselves on the great waters as two youths who wished to learn to swim, and trusted that by diligent kicking we might escape drowning. There was the prospect of getting into a newspaper office. Again, there was the prospect of selling a few verses. Thirdly, if everything failed, there was the prospect of getting into one of the theatres as supernumeraries.* Beyond all this, there was of course the dim prospect that London would at once, and with acclamations, welcome the advent of true genius, albeit with seedy garments and a Scotch accent. It doubtless never occurred to either that besides mere "consciousness" of power, some other things were necessary for a literary struggle in London—special knowledge, capability of interesting oneself in trifles, and the pen of a ready writer. What were David's qualifications for a fight in which hundreds miserably fail year after year? Considerable knowledge of Greek, Latin, and French, great miscellaneous reading, a clerkly handwriting, and a bold purpose. Slender qualifications, doubtless, but while life lasted there was hope.

We did not meet until upwards of a week after our arrival in London, though each had soon been apprised of the other's presence in the city. Finally we came together. David's first impulse was to describe his lodgings, situated in a by-street in the Borough. "A cold, cheerless bed-room, Bob ; nothing but a blanket to

* Each of the friends, indeed, unknown to each other, actually applied for such a situation ; and one succeeded.

cover me. For God's sake get me out of it!" We were walking side by side in the neighbourhood of the New Cut, looking about us with curious puzzled eyes, and now and then drawing each other's attention to sundry objects of interest. "Have you been well?" I inquired. "First-rate," answered David, looking as merry as possible. Nor did he show any indications whatever of illness; he seemed hopeful, energetic, full of health and spirits; his sole desire was to change his lodging. It was not without qualms that he surveyed the dingy, smoky neighbourhood where I resided. The sun was shedding dismal crimson light on the chimney-pots, and the twilight was slowly thickening. We climbed up three flights of stairs to my bedroom; dingy as it was, this apartment seemed, in David's eyes, quite a palatial sanctum; and it was arranged that we should take up our residence together. As speedily as possible I procured David's little stock of luggage; then, settled face to face as in old times, we made very merry.

My first idea, on questioning David about his prospects, was that my friend had had the best of luck. You see, the picture drawn on either side was a golden one; but the brightness soon melted away. It turned out that David, on arriving in London, had sought out certain gentlemen whom he had formerly favoured with his correspondence, among others Mr. Richard Monckton Milnes, now Lord Houghton. Though not a little astonished at the appearance of the boy-poet, Mr. Milnes had received him kindly, assisted him to the best of his power, and made some work for him in the shape of manuscript-copying. The same gentleman had also used his influence with literary people,—to very little purpose, however. The real truth turned out to be that David was disappointed and low-spirited. "It's weary work, Bob; they don't understand me; I wish I was back in Glasgow." It was now that David told me all about that first day and night in London, and now he had already begun a poem about "Hyde Park;" how Mr. Milnes had been good to him, had said that he was "a poet," but had insisted on his going back to Scotland and becoming a minister. David did not at all like the notion of returning home. He thought he had every chance of making his way in London. About this time he was bitterly disappointed by the rejection of "The Luggie" by Mr. Thackeray, to whom Mr. Milnes had sent it, with a recommendation that it should be inserted in the "Cornhill Magazine."

Lord Houghton briefly and vividly describes his intercourse with the young poet in London. He had written to Gray strongly urging him not to make the hazardous experiment of a literary life, but to aim after a professional independence. "A few weeks afterwards," he writes, "I was told that a young man wished to see me, and when he came into the room I at once saw that it could be no other than the young Scotch Poet. It was a light, well-built, but somewhat stooping figure, with a countenance that at once brought strongly to my recollection a cast of the face of Shelley in his youth, which I

had seen at Mr. Leigh Hunt's.   There was the same
full brow, out-looking eyes, and sensitive melancholy
mouth.   He told me at once that he had come to London in consequence of my letter, as from the tone of it
he was sure I should befriend him.   I was dismayed at
this unexpected result of my advice, and could do no
more than press him to return home as soon as possible.
I painted as darkly as I could the chances and difficulties
of a literary struggle in the crowded competition of this
great city, and how strong a swimmer it required to be
not to sink in such a sea of tumultuous life.   ' No, he
would not return.'   I determined in my own mind that
he should do so before I myself left town for the country,
but at the same time I believed that he might derive
advantage from a short personal experience of hard
realities.   He had confidence in his own powers, a simple
certainty of his own worth, which I saw would keep him
in good heart and preserve him from base temptations.
He refused to take money, saying he had enough to go
on with ; but I gave him some light literary work, for
which he was very grateful.   When he came to me again,
I went over some of his verse with him, and I shall not
forget the passionate gratification he showed when I told
him that, in my judgment, he was an undeniable poet.
After this admission he was ready to submit to my criticism or correction, though he was sadly depressed at the
rejection of one of his poems, over which he had evidently spent much labour and care, by the editor of a
distinguished popular periodical, to whom I had sent it

with a hearty recommendation. His, indeed, was not a spirit to be seriously injured by a temporary disappointment ; but when he fell ill so soon afterwards, one had something of the feeling of regret that the notorious review of Keats inspires in connection with the premature loss of the author of 'Endymion.' It was only a few weeks after his arrival in London, that the poor boy came to my house apparently under the influence of violent fever. He said he had caught cold in the wet weather, having been insufficiently protected by clothing ; but had delayed coming to me for fear of giving me unnecessary trouble. I at once sent him back to his lodgings, which were sufficiently comfortable, and put him under good medical superintendence. It soon became apparent that pulmonary disease had set in, but there were good hopes of arresting its progress. I visited him often, and every time with increasing interest. He had somehow found out that his lungs were affected, and the image of the destiny of Keats was ever before him."

It has been seen that Mr. Milnes was the first to perceive that the young adventurer was seriously ill. After a hurried call on his patron one day in May, David rejoined me in the near neighbourhood. "Milnes says I'm to go home and keep warm, and he'll send his own doctor to me." This was done. The doctor came, examined David's chest, said very little, and went away, leaving strict orders that the invalid should keep within doors and take great care of himself. Neither David nor I liked the expression of the doctor's face at all.

It soon became evident that David's illness was of a most serious character. Pulmonary disease had set in, medicine, blistering, all the remedies employed in the early stages of his complaint, seemed of little avail. Just then David read the "Life of John Keats," a book which impressed him with a nervous fear of impending dissolution. He began to be filled with conceits droller than any he had imagined in health. "If I were to meet Keats in heaven," he said one day, "I wonder if I should know his face from his pictures?" Most frequently his talk was of labour uncompleted, hope deferred; and he began to pant for free country air. "If I die," he said on a certain occasion, "I shall have one consolation,—Milnes will write an introduction to the poems." At another time, with tears in his eyes, he repeated Burns's epitaph. Now and then, too, he had his fits of frolic and humour, and would laugh and joke over his unfortunate position. It cannot be said that Mr. Milnes and his friends were at all lukewarm about the case of their young friend; on the contrary, they gave him every practical assistance. Mr. Milnes himself, full of the most delicate sympathy, trudged to and fro between his own house and the invalid's lodging; his pockets laden with jelly and beef-tea, and his tongue tipped with kindly comfort. Had circumstances permitted, he would have taken the invalid into his own house. Unfortunately, however, David was compelled to remain, in company with me, in a chamber which seemed to have been constructed peculiarly for the purpose of making the occupants as uncomfortable as possible. There were draughts everywhere : through the chinks of the door, through the windows, down the chimney, and up through the flooring. When the wind blew, the whole tenement seemed on the point of crumbling to atoms; when the rain fell, the walls exuded moisture ; when the sun shone, the sunshine only served to increase the characteristic dinginess of the furniture. Occasional visitors, however, could not be fully aware of these inconveniences. It was in the night-time, and in bad weather, that they were chiefly felt ; and it required a few days' experience to test the superlative discomfort of what David (in a letter written afterwards) styled "the dear old ghastly bankrupt garret." His stay in these quarters was destined to be brief. Gradually, the invalid grew homesick. Nothing would content him but a speedy return to Scotland. He was carefully sent off by train, and arrived safely in his little cottage-home far north. Here all was unchanged as ever. The beloved river was flowing through the same fields, and the same familiar faces were coming and going on its banks ; but the whole meaning of the pastoral pageant had changed, and the colour of all was deepening towards the final sadness.

Great, meanwhile, had been the commotion in the handloom weaver's cottage, after the receipt of this bulletin : "I start off to-night at five o'clock by the Edinburgh and Glasgow Railway, right on to London, in good health and spirits." A great cry arose in the household. He was fairly "daft ;" he was throwing away all his chances in the world; the verse-writing had turned his head.

Father and mother mourned together. The former, though incompetent to judge literary merit of any kind, perceived that David was hot-headed, only half-educated, and was going to a place where thousands of people were starving daily. But the suspense was not to last long, The darling son, the secret hope and pride, came back to the old people, sick to death. All rebuke died away before the pale sad face and the feeble tottering body ; and David was welcomed to the cottage hearth with silent prayers.

It was now placed beyond a doubt that the disease was one of mortal danger ; yet David, surrounded again by his old cares, busied himself with many bright and delusive dreams of ultimate recovery. Pictures of a pleasant dreamy convalescence in a foreign clime floated before him morn and night, and the fairest and dearest of the dreams was Italy. Previous to his departure for London he had conceived a wild scheme for visiting Florence, and throwing himself on the poetical sympathy of Robert Browning. He had even thought of enlisting in the English Garibaldian corps, and by that means gaining his cherished wish. " How about Italy ? " he wrote to me, after returning home. " Do you still entertain its delusive notions ? Pour out your soul before me ; I am as a child." All at once a new dream burst upon him. A local doctor insisted that the invalid should be removed to a milder climate, and recommended Natal. In a letter full of coaxing tenderness, David besought me, for the sake of old days, to accompany him thither. I answered indecisively, but immediately made all endeavours to grant my friend's wish.   Meantime I received the following :—

"Merkland, Kirkintilloch,
" 10th November, 1860.

"EVER DEAR BOB,

" Your letter causes me some uneasiness; not but that your numerous objections are numerous and vital enough, but they convey the sad and firm intelligence that you cannot come with me.   It is absolutely impossible for you to raise a sum sufficient !   Now you know it is not necessary that I should go to Natal ; nay, I have, in very fear, given up the thoughts of it; but we—or I—could go to Italy or Jamaica—this latter, as I learn, being the more preferable.   Nor has there been any 'crisis' come, as you say.   I would cause you much trouble (forgive me for hinting this), but I believe we could be happy as in the dear old times.   Dr. —— (whose address I don't know) supposes that I shall be able to work (?) when I reach a more genial climate; and if that should prove the result, why, it is a consummation devoutly to be wished.   But the matter of money bothers me.   What I wrote to you was all hypothetical, *i.e.* things have been carried so far, but I have not heard whether or no the subscription had been gone on with.   And, supposing for one instant the utterly preposterous supposition that I had money to carry us both, then comes the second objection—your dear mother !   I am not so far gone, though I fear far enough, to ignore that blessed feeling.   But if it were for your good? Before God, if I thought it would in any way harm your health (that cannot be) or your hopes, I would never have mooted the proposal. On the contrary, I feel from my heart it would benefit you ; and how much would it not benefit *me?* But I am baking without flour. The cash is not in my hand, and I fear never will be; the amount I would require is not so easily gathered.

"Dobell[1] is again laid up. He is at the Isle of Wight, at some establishment called the Victoria Baths. I am told that his friends deem his life in constant danger. He asks for your address. I shall send it only to-day; wait until you hear what he has got to say. He would prefer me to go to Brompton Hospital. *I would go anywhere for a change.* If I don't get money *somehow* or *somewhere* I shall die of *ennui.* A weary desire for change, life, excitement of every, *any* kind, possesses me, and without *you* what am I? There is no other person in the world whom I could spend a week with, and thoroughly enjoy it. Oh, how I desire to smoke a cigar, and have a pint and a chat with you.

"By the way, how are you getting on ? Have you lots to do? and well paid for it ? Or is life a lottery with

---

[1] Sydney Dobell, author of "Balder," "The Roman," &c. This gentleman's kindness to David, whom he never saw, is beyond all praise. Nor was the invalid ungrateful. "Poor, kind, half-immortal spirit here below," wrote David, alluding to Dobell, "shall I know thee when we meet new-born into eternal existence ? . . . Dear friend Bob, did you ever know a nobler? I cannot get him out of my mind. I would write to him daily. would it not pest him. '

you? and the tea-caddy a vacuum? and—a snare? and —a nightmare? Do you *dream* yet, on your old rickety sofa in the dear old ghastly bankrupt garret at No. 66? Write to yours eternally,

" DAVID GRAY."

The proposal to go abroad was soon abandoned, partly because the invalid began to evince a nervous home-sickness, and chiefly because it was impossible to raise a sufficient sum of money. Yet be it never said that this youth was denied the extremest loving sympathy and care. As I look back on those days it is to me a glad wonder that so many tender faces, many of them quite strange, clustered round his sick bed. When it is reflected that he was known only as a poor Scotch lad, that even his extraordinary lyric faculty was as yet only half-guessed, if guessed at all, the kindness of the world through his trouble is extraordinary. Milnes, Dobell, Dobell's lady-friends at Hampstead, never tired in devising plans for the salvation of the poor consumptive invalid,—goodness which sprang from the instincts of the heart itself, and not from that intellectual benevolence which invests in kind deeds with a view to a bonus from the Almighty.

The best and tenderest of people, however, cannot always agree; and in this case there was too much discussion and delay. Some recommended a long sea-voyage; one doctor recommended Brompton Hospital; Milnes suggested Torquay in Devonshire. Meantime, Gray, for the most part ignorant of the discussions that were taking place, besought his friends on all hands to come to his assistance. Late in November he addressed the editor of a local newspaper with whom he was personally acquainted and who had taken interest in his affairs :—

" I write you in a certain commotion of mind, and may speak wrongly. But I write to *you* because I know that it will take much to offend you when no offence is meant ; and when the probable offence will proceed from youthful heat and frantic foolishness. It may be impertinent to address you, of whom I know so little, and yet so much ; but the severe circumstances *seem* to justify it.

" The medical verdict pronounced upon me is *certain and rapid death if I remain at Merkland.* This is awful enough, even to a brave man. But there is a chance of escape ; as a drowning man grasps at a straw I strive for it. Good, kind, true Dobell writes me this morning the plans for my welfare which he has put in progress, and which most certainly meet my wishes. They are as follows : Go *immediately*, and *as a guest* to the house of Dr. Lane, in the salubrious town of Richmond ; thence, when the difficult matter of admission is overcome, to the celebrated Brompton Hospital for chest diseases ; and in the Spring to Italy. Of course, all this presupposes the conjectural problem that I will slowly recover. 'Consummation devoutly to be wished !' Now, you think, or say, what prevents you from taking advantage of all these plans ? At once, and without any squeamishness, *money for an outfit.* I did not like to ask Dobell, nor do I ask you ; but hearing a 'subscription' had been *spoken of*, I urge it with all my weak force. I am not in want of an immense sum, but say £12 or £15. This would conduce to my safety, as far as human means could do so. If you can aid me in getting this sum, the obligation to a sinking fellow-creature will be as indelible in his heart as the moral law.

"I hope you will not misunderstand me. My barefaced request may be summed thus : If your influence set the affair a-going quietly and *quickly*, the thing is done, and I am off. Surely I am worth £15 ; and for God's sake overlook the strangeness and the freedom and the utter impertinence of this communication. I would be off for Richmond in two days, had I the money, and sitting here thinking of the fearful probabilities makes me half-mad."

It was soon found necessary to act with decision. A residence in Kirkintilloch throughout the winter was, on all accounts, to be avoided. A lady, therefore, subscribed to the Brompton Hospital for chest complaints for the express purpose of procuring David admission.

One bleak wintry day, not long after the receipt of the above letter, I was gazing out of my lofty lodging-window when a startling vision presented itself in the shape of David himself, seated with quite a gay look in an open Hansom cab. In a minute we were side by side, and one of my first impulses was to rebuke David for the folly of exposing himself during such weather in such a vehicle. This folly, however, was on a parallel with David's general habits of thought. Sometimes, indeed, the poor boy became unusually thoughtful, as when, during his illness, he wrote thus to me: "Are you remembering that you will need clothes? These are things you take no concern about, and so you may be seedy without knowing it. By all means hoard a few pounds if you can (I require none) for *any* emergency like this. Brush your excellent top-coat; it is the best and warmest I ever had on my back. Mind, you have to pay ready money for a new coat. A seedy man will not get on if he requires, like you, to call personally on his employers."

David had come to London in order to go either to Brompton or to Torquay,—the hospital at which last-named place was thrown open to him by Mr. Milnes. Perceiving his dislike for the Temperance Hotel, to which he had been conducted, I consented that he should stay in the "ghastly bankrupt garret," until he should depart to one or other of the hospitals. It was finally arranged that he should accept a temporary in-vitation to a hydropathic establishment at Sudbrook Park, Richmond. Thither I at once conveyed him. Meanwhile, his prospects were diligently canvassed by his numerous friends. His own feelings at this time were well expressed in a letter home: "I am dreadfully afraid of Brompton; living among sallow, dolorous, dying consumptives is enough to kill me. Here I am as com-fortable as can be: a fire in my room all day, plenty of meat, and good society,—nobody so ill as myself; but there, perhaps, hundreds far worse (the hospital holds

218 in all stages of the disease; ninety of them died last report) dying beside me, perhaps,—it frightens me."

About the same time he sent me the following, containing more particulars :—

"Sudbrook Park, Richmond,
Surrey.

"MY DEAR BOB,

"Your anxiety will be allayed by learning that I am little worse. The severe hours of this establishment have *not* killed me. At 8 o'clock in the morning a man comes into my bedroom with a pail of cold water, and I must rise and get myself *soused*. This *sousing* takes place three times a day, and I'm not dead *yet*. To-day I told the bathman that I was utterly unable to bear it, and refused to undress. The doctor will hear of it; that's the very thing I want. The society here is most pleasant. No patient so bad as myself. No wonder your father wished to go to the water cure for a month or two; it is the most pleasant, refreshing thing in the world. But *I* am really too weak to bear it. Robert Chambers is here; Mrs. Crowe, the authoress; Lord Brougham's son-in-law; and at dinner and tea the literary tittle-tattle is the most wonderful you ever heard. They seem to know everything about everybody but Tennyson. Major ———— (who has a *beautiful* daughter here) was crowned with a laurel-wreath for some burlesque verses he had made and read, last night. Of course you know what I am among them—a pale cadaverous young person, who sits in dark corners, and is for the most part silent; with a horrible fear of being pounced upon by a cultivated unmarried lady, and talked to.

"Seriously, I am not better. When the novelty of my situation is gone, won't the old days at Oakfield Terrace seem pleasant? Why didn't they last for ever?

"Yours ever,

"DAVID GRAY."

All at once David began, with a delicacy peculiar to him, to consider himself an unwarrantable intruder at Sudbrook Park. In the face of all persuasion, therefore, he joined me in London, whence he shortly afterwards departed for Torquay.

He left me in good spirits, full of pleasant anticipations of Devonshire scenery. But the second day after his departure, he addressed to me a wild epistle, dated from one of the Torquay hotels. He had arrived safe and sound, he said, and had been kindly received by a friend of Mr. Milnes. He had at first been delighted with the town, and everything in it. He had gone to the hospital, had been received by "a nurse of death" (as he phrased it), and had been inducted into the privileges of the place; but on seeing his fellow-patients, some in the last stages of disease, he had fainted away. On coming to himself he obtained an interview with the matron. To his request for a private apartment, she had answered that to favour him in that way would be to break written rules, and that he must content himself with the common privileges of the establishment. On leaving the matron, he had furtively stolen from the place, and made his way through the night to the hotel. From the hotel he addressed the following terrible letter to his parents :—

" Torquay, January 6, 1861.

"DEAR PARENTS,

"I am coming home—home-sick. I cannot stay from home any longer. What's the good of me being so far from home, and sick and ill? I don't know whether I'll be *able* to come back—sleeping none at night—crying out for my mother, and her so far away. Oh God, I wish I were home never to leave it more ! Tell everybody that I'm coming back—no better—worse, worse. What's about climate—about frost or snow or cold weather when one is at home ? I wish I had never left it.

" But how am I to get back without money, and my expenses for the journey newly paid yesterday? I came here yesterday scarcely able to walk. O how I wish I saw my father's face—shall I ever see it? I have no money, and I want to get home, home, home ! What shall I do, O God? Father, I shall *steal* to see you again, because I did not use you rightly—my conduct to you all the time I was at home makes me miserable, miserable, miserable ! Will you forgive me ? —do I ask that ? forgiven, forgiven, forgiven ! If I can't get money to pay for my box, I shall leave box and everything behind. I shall try and be at home by Saturday, January 12th. Mind the day—if I am not home—God knows where I shall be. I have come through things that would make your heart ache for me —things which I shall never tell to anybody but you, and you shall keep them secret as the grave. Get my own little room ready, quick, quick; have it all tidy and clean and cosy against my home-coming. I wish to die there, and nobody shall nurse me, except my own dear mother, ever, ever again. O home, home, home!

"I will try and write again, but mind the day. Perhaps my father will come into Glasgow, if I *can* tell him beforehand *how*, *when*, and *where* I shall be. I shall try all I can to let him know.

"Mind and tell everybody that I am coming back, because I wish to be back, and cannot stay away. Tell everybody; but I shall come back in the dark, because I am so utterly unhappy. No more, no more. Mind the day.

"Yours,

"D. G.

" Don't answer—not even *think* of answering."[1]

---

[1] While lingering at Torquay, however, his mood became calmer, and he was able to relieve his overladen mind in the composition of these lines—deeply interesting, apart from their poetic merit.

HOME SICK.

Lines written at Torquay, January, 1861.

Come to me, O my Mother! come to me,
Thine own son slowly dying far away!
Thro' the moist ways of the wide ocean, blown

Before I had time to comprehend the state of affairs,
there came a second letter, stating that David was on the
point of starting for London. "Every ring at the hotel
bell makes me tremble, fancying they are coming to take
me away by force. *Had you seen the nurse!* Oh! that
I were back again at home—mother! mother! mother!"
A few hours after I had read these lines in miserable
fear, arrived Gray himself, pale, anxious, and trembling.
He flung himself into my arms with a smile of sad relief.
"Thank God!" he cried; "*that's* over, and I am here!"
Then his cry was for home; he would die if he remained
longer adrift; he must depart at once. I persuaded him

> By great invisible winds, come stately ships
> To this calm bay for quiet anchorage;
> They come, they rest awhile, they go away,
> But, O my Mother, never comest thou!
> The snow is round thy dwelling, the white snow,
> That cold soft revelation pure as light,
> And the pine-spire is mystically fringed,
> Laced with encrusted silver. Here—ah me!—
> The winter is decrepit, underborn,
> A leper with no power but his disease.
> Why am I from thee, Mother, far from thee?
> Far from the frost enchantment, and the woods
> Jewelled from bough to bough? Oh home, my home!
> O river in the valley of my home,
> With mazy-winding motion intricate,
> Twisting thy deathless music underneath
> The polished ice-work—must I nevermore
> Behold thee with familiar eyes, and watch
> Thy beauty changing with the changeful day,
> Thy beauty constant to the constant change?

M. S.

to wait for a few days, and in the meantime saw some of
his influential friends.   The skill and regimen of a
medical establishment being necessary to him at this
stage, it was naturally concluded that he should go to
Brompton ; but David, in a high state of nervous excitement, scouted the idea.   Disease had sapped the founda-
tions of the once strong spirit.   He was now bent on
returning to the north, and wrote more calmly to his
parents from my lodgings :—

"London, Thursday.

"My very Dear Parents,

" Having arrived in London last night, my friends have
seized on me again, and wish me to go to Brompton.
But what I saw at Torquay was enough, and I will come
home, though it should freeze me to death.   You must
not take literally what I wrote you in my last.   I had
just *ran away* from Torquay hospital, and didn't know
what to do or where to go.   But you see I have got to
London, and surely by some means or other I shall get
home.   I am really home-sick.   *They all tell me my life
is not worth a farthing candle if I go to Scotland in this
weather, but what about that ?*   I wish I could tell my
father when to come to Glasgow, but I can't.   *If* I start
to-morrow I shall be in Glasgow very late, and what am
I to do if I have no cash ?   If he comes into Glasgow by
the twelve train on Saturday, I may, if possible, see him
at the train, but I would not like to say positively.   Surely
I'll get home somehow.   I don't sleep any at night now

for coughing and sweating—I am afraid to go to bed.
Strongly hoping to be with you soon.

"Yours ever,

"DAVID GRAY."

"Home—home—home!" was his hourly cry. To
resist these frantic appeals would have been to hasten
the end of all. In the midst of winter, I saw him into
the train at Euston Square. A day afterwards, David
was in the bosom of his father's household, never more
to pass thence alive. Not long after his arrival at home,
he repented his rash flight. "I am not at all contented
with my position. I acted like a fool; but if the hospital
were the *sine qua non* again, my conduct would be the
same." Further, "I lament my own foolish conduct, but
what was that quotation about *impellunt in Acheron?* It
was all nervous impulsion. However, I despair not, and,
least of all, my dear fellow, to those whom I have de-
serted wrongfully."

Ere long, poor David made up his mind that he must
die; and this feeling urged him to write something which
would keep his memory green for ever. "I am working
away at my old poem, Bob; leavening it throughout with
the pure beautiful theology of Kingsley." A little later:
"By-the-bye, I have about 600 lines of my poem written,
but the manual labour is so weakening that I do not go
on." Nor was this all. In the very shadow of the
grave, he began and finished a series of sonnets on the
subject of his own disease and impending death. This

increased literary energy was not, as many people imagined, a sign of increased physical strength; it was
merely the last flash upon the blackening brand. Gradually, but surely, life was ebbing away from the young
poet.

In March, 1861, I formed the plan of visiting Scotland
in the spring, and wrote to David accordingly. His
delight at the prospect of a fresh meeting—perhaps a
farewell one—was as great as mine. He wrote me the
following, and burst out into song:[1]—

"Merkland, March 12, 1861.

"My Dear Bob,

"I am very glad to be able to write you to-day. Rest
assured to find a change in your old friend when you

---

[1] I subjoin the poem, not only as lovely in itself, but as the last
sad poetic memorial of our love and union. I find it in his printed
volume, among the sonnets entitled, "In the Shadows:"—

> Now, while the long-delaying ash assumes
> Its delicate April green, and loud and clear
> Thro' the cool, yellow, mellow twilight glooms,
> The thrush's song enchants the captive ear;
> Now, while a shower is pleasant in the falling,
> Stirring the still perfume that shakes around;
> Now that doves mourn, and, from the distance calling,
> The cuckoo answers, with a sovereign sound—
> Come, with thy native heart, O true and tried!
> But leave all books; for what with converse high,
> Flavoured with Attic wit, the time shall glide
> On smoothly, as a river floweth by,
> Or as on stately pinion, through the gray
> Evening, the culver cuts his liquid way!

come down in April. And do, old fellow, let it be the end of April, when the evenings are cool and fresh, and these east-winds have howled themselves to rest. When I think of what a fair worshipful season is before you, I advise you to remove to a little room at Hampstead, where I only wish too, too much to be with you. Don't forget to come north since you have spoken about it ; it has made me very happy. My health is no better,—not having been out of my room since I wrote, and for some time before. The weather here is so bitterly cold and unfavourable, that I have not walked 100 yards for three weeks. I trust your revivifying presence will electrify my weary relaxed limbs and enervated system. The mind, you know, has a′ great effect on the body. Accept the wholesome common place. . . . By-the-way, how about Dobell ? Did your mind of itself, or even against itself, recognise through the clothes *a man—a poet?* Young speaks well :—

> *I never bowed but to superior worth,*
> *Nor ever failed in my allegiance there.*

Has he the modesty and make-himself-at-home manner of Milnes ? " The remainder of this letter is unfortunately lost.

In April, I saw him for the last time, and heard him speak words which showed the abandonment of hope. " I am dying," said David, leaning back in his arm-chair in the little carpeted bedroom ; " I am dying, and I've only two things to regret : that my poem is not published,

and that I have not seen Italy." In the endeavour to in-
spire hope I spoke of the happy past, and of the happy
days yet to be. David only shook his head with a sad
smile. "It is the old *dream*—only a dream, Bob—but I
am content." He spoke of all his friends with tenderness,
and of his parents with intense and touching love. Then
it was "farewell!" "After all our dreams of the future,"
he said, "I must leave you to fight alone; but shall there
be no more 'cakes and ale' because I die?" I returned
to London; and ere long heard that David was eagerly
attempting to get "The Luggie" published. Delay after
delay occurred. "If my book be not immediately gone
on with, I fear I may never see it. Disease presses closely
on me. . . . The merit of my MSS. is very little—mere
hints of better things—crude notions harshly languaged;
but that must be overlooked. They are left not to the
world (wild thought!), but as the simple, possible, sad,
only legacy I can leave to those who have loved and love
me." To a dear friend and fellow poet, William Freeland,
then sub-editor of the *Glasgow Citizen*, he wrote at this time:
"I feel more acutely the approach of that mystic dissolution of existence. The body is unable to perform its
functions, and like rusty machinery creaks painfully to the
final crash. . . . About my poem,—it troubles me like
an ever present demon. Some day I'll burn all that I
have ever written,—yet no! They are all that remain of
me as a living soul. Milnes offers £5 towards its publica-
tion. I shall have it ready by Saturday first." And to
Freeland, who visited him every week, and cheered his

latter moments with a true poet's converse, he wrote out a wild dedication, ending in these words; " Before I enter that nebulous uncertain land of shadowy notions and tremulous wonderings—standing on the threshold of the sun and looking back, I cry thee, O beloved ! a last farewell, lingeringly, passionately, without tears." At this period I received the following :—

"Merkland, N. S., Sunday Evening.

" Dear, dear Bob,

" By all means and instantly, 'move in this matter' of my book. Do you really and without any dream-work, think it could be gone about *immediately ?* If not soon I fear I shall never behold it. *The doctors give me no hope*, and with the yellowing of the leaf 'changes' likewise 'the countenance' of your friend. Freeland is in possession of the MSS., but before I send them (I love them in so great temerity) I would like to see, and, *if at all possible*, revise them. Meanwhile, act and write. Above all, Bob, give me (and my father) no hope unless on sound foundation. Better that the rekindled desire should die than languish, bringing misery. I cannot sufficiently impress on you how important this 'book,' is to me : with what ignoble trembling I anticipate its appearance : how I shall bless you should you succeed.

" Do not tempt me with your kindness. The family have almost got over the strait, only my father being out of work. It is indeed, a 'golden treasury' you have sent me. Many thanks. My only want is new interesting books. I shall return it soon when I get *Smith.* Do not, like a good fellow, disappoint an old friend by forgetting to send *that* work. With what interest (thinking on my own probable volume) shall I examine the print, &c. *I am sure, sure to return it.*

"When *you* complain of physical discomfort I believe. What is the matter? Your letters now are a mere provoking adumbration of your condition. I know positively nothing of you, but that you are mentally and bodily depressed, and that you will never forget Gray. In God's name let us keep together the short time remaining.

"You tell me nothing; write sooner too. Recollect I have no other pleasure. How is your mother? and all? Are your editorial duties oppressive? Is life full of hope and bright faith, *yet, yet?* Tell me, Bob, and tell me quickly.

"What a fair, sad, beautiful dream is *Italy!* Do you still entertain its delusive motions? Pour your soul before me; I am as a child.

"Yours for ever,

"DAVID GRAY."

Still later, in an even sweeter spirit, he wrote to an old schoolmate, Arthur Sutherland, with whom he had dreamed many a boyish dream, when they were pupil teachers together at the Normal School:—

"As my time narrows to a completion, you grow dearer. I think of you daily with quiet tears. I think of the happy, happy days we might have spent together at Maryburgh; but the vision darkens. My crown is laid in the dust for ever. Nameless too! God, how that troubles me! Had I but written one immortal poem, what a glorious consolation! But this shall be my epitaph if I have a gravestone at all,—

> 'Twas not a life,
> 'Twas but a piece of childhood thrown away.

O dear, dear Sutherland! I wish I could spend two *healthy* months with you; we would make an effort, and do something great. But slowly, insidiously, and I fear fatally, consumption is doing its work, until I shall be only a fair odorous memory (for I have great faith in your affection for me) to you—a sad tale for your old age.

> Whom the gods love die young.

Bless the ancient Greeks for that comfort. If I was not ripe, do you think I would be gathered?

"Work for fame for my sake, dear Sutherland. Who knows but in spiritual being I may send sweet dreams to you—to advise, comfort, and command! who knows? At all events, when I am *mooly*, may you be fresh as the dawn.

"Yours till death, and I trust *hereafter too*,

"DAVID GRAY."

At last, chiefly through the agency of the unwearying Dobell, the poem was placed in the hands of the printer. On the 2nd of December, 1861, a specimen-page was sent to the author. David, with the shadow of death even then dark upon him, gazed long and lingeringly at the printed page. All the mysterious past—the boyish yearnings, the flash of anticipated fame, the black surroundings of the great city—flitted across his vision like a dream. It was "good news," he said. The next day the complete silence passed over the weaver's household, for David Gray was no more. Thus, on the 3rd of December, 1861, in the twenty-fourth year of his age, he passed tranquilly away, almost his last words being, "God has love, and I have faith." The following epitaph, written out carefully a few months before his decease, was found among his papers :—

MY EPITAPH.

Below lies one whose name was traced in sand—
He died, not knowing what it was to live ;
Died while the first sweet consciousness of manhood
And maiden thought electrified his soul :
Faint beatings in the calyx of the rose.
Bewildered reader, pass without a sigh
In a proud sorrow !   There is life with God,
In other kingdom of a sweeter air ;
In Eden every flower is blown.   Amen.

DAVID GRAY.

Sept. 27, 1861.

Draw a veil over the woe that day in the weaver's cottage, the wild broodings over the beloved face, white in the sweetness of rest after pain. A few days later, the beloved dust was shut for ever from the light, and carried a short journey in ancient Scottish fashion, on hand-

G

spokes, to the Auld Aisle Burial-Ground, a dull and lonely square upon an eminence, bounden by a stone wall, and deep with the "uncut hair of graves." Here, in happier seasons, had David often mused; for here slept dust of kindred, and hither in his sight the thin black line of rude mourners often wended with new burdens. Very early, too, he blended the place with his poetic dreams, and spoke of it in a sonnet not to be found in his little printed volume :—

OLD AISLE.

Aisle of the dead ! your lonely bell-less tower
　Seems like a soul-less body, whence rebounds
No tones ear-sweetening, as if 'twere to embower
　The Sabbath tresses with its soothing sounds.
In pity, crumbling aisle, thou lookest o'er
　Your former sainted worshippers, whose bones
　Lie mouldering 'neath these nettle-girded stones,
Or 'neath yon rank grave weeds ! Now from afar
Is seen the sacred heavenward spire, which seems
　An intercessor for the mounds below :
And doth it not speak eloquent in dreams ?
　In dreams of aged pastors who did go
Up to the hallowed mount with homely tread :
　While there, old men and simple maids and youths
　Throng lovingly to hear the sacred truths
In gentle stream poured forth. But he is dead ;
　And in this hill of sighs he rests unknown,
　As that wild flower that by his grave hath blown.

Standing on this eminence, one can gaze round upon the scenes which it is no exaggeration to say David has immortalized in song,—the Luggie flowing, the green woods of Gartshore, the smoke curling from the little hamlet of Merkland, and the faint blue misty distance of the Campsie Fells. The place though a lonely is a gentle and happy one, fit for a poet's rest; and there, while he was sleeping sound, a quiet company gathered ere long to uncover a monument inscribed with his name. The dying voice had been heard. Over the grave now stands a plain obelisk, publicly subscribed for, and inscribed with this epitaph, written by Lord Houghton :—

THIS MONUMENT OF

AFFECTION, ADMIRATION, AND REGRET,

IS ERECTED TO

DAVID GRAY,

THE POET OF MERKLAND,

BY FRIENDS FAR AND NEAR,

DESIROUS THAT HIS GRAVE SHOULD BE REMEMBERED

AMID THE SCENES OF HIS RARE GENIUS

AND EARLY DEATH,

AND BY THE LUGGIE NOW NUMBERED WITH THE STREAMS

ILLUSTRIOUS IN SCOTTISH SONG,

BORN, 29TH JANUARY, 1838; DIED, 3RD DECEMBER, 1861.

Here all is said that should be said; yet perhaps the poet's own sweet epitaph, evidently prepared with a view to such a use, would have been more graceful and appropriate.

"Whom the gods love die young," is no mere pagan consolation; it has a tenderness for all forms of faith, and even when philosophically translated, as by Wordsworth, who said sweetly that "the good die first," it still possesses balm for hearts that ache over the departed.

That the young soul passes away in its strength, in its prismatic dawn, with many powers undeveloped, yet no power wasted, is the beauty and the pity of the thought, the inference of the apotheosis.   The impulse has been upward, and the gods have consecrated the endeavour. The thought hovers over the death-beds of Keats and Robert Nicoll; it is repeated even by weary old men over those poets' graves.   No hope has been disappointed, no eye has seen the strong wing grow feeble and falter earthward, and the possibility of a future beyond our seeing is boundless as the aspiration of the spirit which escaped us.   "Whom the gods love die young," said the Athenians; and "bless the ancient Greeks for *that* comfort," wrote David, with the thin, tremulous, consumption-wasted hand.   Beautiful, pathetically beautiful, is the halo surrounding the head of a young poet as he dies.   We scarcely mourn him,—our souls are so stirred towards the eternal.   But what comfort may abide when, from the frame that still breathes, poesy arises like an exhalation, and the man lives on.   In life as well as in death there is a Plutonian house of exiles, and they abandon all hope who enter therein; and that man inhabits the same.   How often does this horror encounter us in our daily paths?   The change is rapid and imperceptible.   Without hope, without peace, without one glimpse of the glory the young find in their own aspirations, the doomed one buffets and groans in the dark. Which of the gods may he call to his aid?   None; for he believes in none.   Better for him, a thousand times better, that he slept unknown in the shadow of the village where he was born. The strong hard scholar, the energetic literary man of business has a shield against the demons of disappointment, but men like David have no such shield. Picture the dark weary struggle for bread which must have been his lot had he lived. He had not the power to write to order, to sell his wits for money. He sleeps in peace. He has taken his unchanged belief in things beautiful to the very fountain-head of all beauty, and will never know the weary strife, the poignant heart-ache of the unsuccessful endeavourers.

The book of poems written, and the writer laid quietly down in the auld aisle burying ground, had David Gray wholly done with earth? No; for he worked from the grave on one who loved him with a love transcending that of women. In the weaver's cottage at Merkland sub-sisted tender sorrow and affectionate remembrance; but something more. The shadow lay in the cottage; a light had departed which would never again be seen on sea or land; and David Gray, the handloom-weaver, the father of the poet, felt that the meaning had departed out of his simple life. There was a great mystery. The world called his darling son a poet,—and he hardly knew what a poet was; all he *did* know was that the coming of this prodigy had given a new complexion to all the facts of existence. There was a dream-life, it appeared, beyond the work in the fields and the loom. His son, whom he had thought mad at first, was crowned and honoured for the very things which his parents had thought useless.

Around him, vague, incomprehensible, floated a new atmosphere, which clever people called *poetry;* and he began to feel that it was beautiful—the more so, that is was so new and wondrous.   The fountains of his nature were stirred.   He sat and smoked before the fire o' nights, and found himself dreaming too ! He was conscious, now, that the glory of his days was beyond that grave in the kirkyard.   He was like one that walks in a mist, his eyes full of tears.   But he said little of his griefs,—little, that is to say, in the way of direct complaint.   "We feel very weary now David has gone !" was all the plaint I knew him to utter ; he grieved so silently, wondered so speechlessly.   The new life, brief and fatal, made him wise.   With the eager sensitiveness of the poet himself he read the various criticisms on David's book; and so subtle was the change in him, that, though he was utterly unlearned and had hitherto had no insight whatever into the nature of poetry, he knew by instinct whether the critics were right or wrong, and felt their suggestions to the very roots of his being.

With this old man, in whom I recognised a greatness and sweetness of soul that has broadened my view of God's humblest creatures ever since, I kept up a correspondence—at first for David's sake, but latterly for my correspondent's own sake.   His letters, brief and simple as they were, grew fraught with delicate and delicious meaning ; I could see how he marvelled at the mysterious light he understood not, yet how fearlessly he kept his soul stirred towards the eternal silence where his son was lying. "We feel very weary now David has gone!" Ah, how weary! The long years of toil told their tale now; the thread was snapt, and labour was no longer a perfect end to the soul and satisfaction to the body. The little carpeted bedroom was a prayer-place now. The Luggie flowing, the green woods, the thymy hills, had become haunted; a voice unheard by other dwellers in the valley was calling, calling, and a hand was beckoning; and tired, more tired, dazzled, more dazzled, grew the old weaver. The very *names* of familiar scenes were now a strange trouble; for were not these names echoing in David's songs? Merkland, "the summer woods of dear Gartshire," the "fairy glen of Wooilee," Criftin, "with his host of gloomy pine-trees," all had their ghostly voices. Strange rhymes mingled with the humming of the loom. Mysterious "poetry," which he had once scorned as an idle thing, deepened and deepened in its fascination for him. All he saw and heard meant something strange in rhyme. He was drawn along by music, and he could not rest.

Beside him dwelt the mother. Her face was quite calm. She had wept bitterly, but her heart now was with other sons and daughters. David was with God, and the minister said that God was good—that was quite enough. None of the new light had troubled her eyes. She knew that her beloved had made a "heap o' rhyme,"—that was all. A good loving lad had gone to rest, but there were still bairns left, bless God!

But the old man lingered on, with hunger in his heart,

wonder in his soul.   This could not last for ever.   In the winter of 1864, he warned me that he was growing ill ; and although he attributed his illness to cold, his letters showed me the truth.   There was some physical malady, but the aggravating cause was mental.   It was my duty, however, to do all that could be done humanly to save him ; and the first thing to do was to see that he had those comforts which sick men need.   I placed his case before Lord Houghton ; but generous as that man is, all men are not so generous.   "It is exceedingly difficult to get people to assist a man of genius himself," wrote Lord Houghton, gloomily; "they won't assist his relations."   Lord Houghton, however, personally assisted him, and was joined by a kind colleague, Mr. Baillie Cochrane.

I felt then, and I feel now, that the condition of the old man was even more deeply affecting than the condition of David in his last moments, as deserving of sympathy, as universal in its appeal to human generosity ; and I felt a yearning, moreover, to provide for the comfort of David's mother, and for the education of David's brothers.   Who knew but that, among the latter, might be another bright intellect, which a little schooling might save for the world ?   After puzzling myself for a plan, I at last thought that I could attain all my wishes by publishing a book to be entitled "Memorials of David Gray," and to contain contributions from all the writers of eminence whom I could enlist in the good cause.   Such a thing would *sell*, and might, moreover, be worth buying.   The fine natures were not slow in responding to the appeal, and I mention some names, that they may gain honour. Tennyson promised a poem ; Browning another ; George Eliot agreed to contribute ; Dickens, because he was too busy to write anything more, offered me an equivalent in money. All seemed well, when one or two objections were raised on the score of propriety ; and it was even suggested, that, " It looked like begging for the father on the strength of Gray's reputation." Confused and perplexed, I determined to refer the matter to one whose good sense is as great as his heart, but (luckily for his friends) a great deal harder. "Should I or should I not, under the circumstances, go on with my scheme ? " His answer being in the negative, the book was not gone on with, and the matter dropped.

Meantime, the old man was getting worse. On the 27th April I received this letter :—

" Merkland.

" DEAR MR. BUCHANAN,

" We hope this will find you and Mrs Buchanan in good health. I am not getting any better. The cough still continues. However, I rise every day a while, but it is only to sit by the fire. Weather is so cold I cannot go out, except sometimes I get out and walks round yard. *I am not looking for betterness.* I have nothing particular to say, only we thought you would be thinking us ungrateful in not writing soon.

" I remain, yours ever,

" DAVID GRAY.

"I understand there is some movement with David's stone* again."

On the 9th of May he wrote, "I have Dr. Stewart to attend me.   He called on Sunday and sounded me ;—he says I am a dying man, and dying fast. You cannot imagine what a weak person I am ; I am nearly bedfast." On the 16th May came the last lines I ever received from him.   They are almost illegible, and their purport prevents me from printing them here.   A few days more, and the old man was dead. His green grave lies in the shadow of the obelisk which stands over his beloved son. Father and child are side by side. A little cloud, a pathetic mystery, came between them in life, but that is all over.   The old handloom-weaver, who never wrote a verse, unconsciously reached his son's stature some time ere he passed away. The mysterious thing called "poetry," which operated such changes in his simple life, became all clear at last—in that final moment when the world's meanings became transparent, and nothing is left but to swoon back with closed eyes into the darkness, confiding in God's mercy, content either to waken at His footstool, or to rest painlessly for evermore.

* The monument, not then erected.

LITERARY SKETCHES.

THOMAS LOVE PEACOCK.

A PERSONAL REMINISCENCE.

IN the neighbourhood of the picturesque village of Chertsey, close to which the Thames winds broad and clear between deep green meadow-flats and quiet woods still stand the ruins of Newark Abbey. Situated in a lonely field, eight miles from the village, and near to the Weybridge canal, they lie comparatively unknown and little visited ; a mill murmurs close at hand, turned by a small fall ; and all around stretch the level fields and meadows of green Surrey. Here, at the beginning of the present century, when these ruins stood as now, a young man and maiden, betrothed to each other, were accustomed to meet and exchange their quiet vows ; and here, half a century afterwards, a grey-haired old man of seventy, beautiful in his age as the old Goethe, would wander musing summer day after summer day. The lovers had been parted ; the maiden had married and died young, while the man had also married and become the father of a household; but that first Dream had never been forgotten by one at least of the pair, and that surviving one was Thomas Love Peacock, known to general English readers as the author of "Headlong Hall." With a constancy and a tenderness which many more famous men would have done well to emulate, he clung to the scene of his first and perhaps his only love: a love innocent, like all true love; and far preferable, to quote his own words, to—

"The waveless calm, the slumber of the dead,

which weighs on the minds of those who have never loved, or never earnestly." Looking on the face of Peacock in his old age, and knowing his secret, well might one remember in emotion the beautiful words of Scribe : "Il faut avoir aimé une fois en sa vie, non pour le moment où l'on aime, car on n'éprouve alors que de tourmens, des regrets, de la jalousie; mais peu à peu ces tourmens-la deviennent des souvenirs, qui charment notre arrière-saison. Et quand vous verrez la vieillesse douce, facile, et tolérante, vous puissez dire comme Fontenelle— *L'amour a passé par-la !*"

Yes, Love had passed that way, and set on the old man his gracious seal, which no other deity can counterfeit; so that, looking upon the old man's face, one read of gentleness, high-mindedness, toleration, and perfect chivalry. These may seem odd words to apply to one whom the world knew rather as a retrograde philosopher and satirical pessimist than a lover of human nature, as a scholar rather than a poet, as a country gentleman of the old school rather than a humanitarian of the new: but they can be justified; and it' may be questioned, moreover, whether he had not learned of the eighteenth century certain modest virtues which the nineteenth century has incontinently forgotten. To children he was gentleness itself, and all children loved him; and there could be no prettier sight in the world than the picture of him, as I saw him first, and as in my mind's eye I see him now, sitting one summer day, seated on his garden lawn by the river, while a little maiden of sixteen rested on his knees the great quarto *Orlando Innamorato* of Bojardo, and, following with her finger the sun-lit lines, read soft and low, corrected ever and anon by his kind voice, the delicate Italian he loved so well. Who that looked at him, then, could fail to perceive, to quote Lord Houghton's words, " that he had gone through the world with happiness and honour?" But the secret of his beautiful benignity lay deeper. " L'amour a passé par-la !"

While a student in Scotland, I had known him as the friend of Shelley, and had read his delightful works with pleasure and profit; until at last I was prompted to write to him, expecting (I remember) to receive but a cold response from one who, to judge him by his works, was too much of a Timon to care for boys' homage. I was agreeably disappointed. The answer came, not savage like a rap on the knuckles, but cordial as a hand-shake. Afterwards, when I was weary "climbing up the breaking wave" of London, I thought of my old friend, and determined to seek him out. Mainly with the wish to be near him, I retreated to quiet Chertsey; and thence past Chertsey Bridge, through miles of green fields basking in the summer sun, and through delightful lanes to Lower Halliford, I went on pilgrimage, youth in my limbs, reverence in my heart, a pipe in my mouth, and the tiny Pickering edition of Catullus (a veritable "lepidum libellum," but alas, far from "novum!") in my waistcoat pocket. And there, at Lower Halliford, I found him as I have described him, seated on his garden lawn in the sun, with the door of his library open behind him, showing such delicious vistas of shady shelves as would have gladdened his own Dr. Opimian, and the little maiden, reading from the book upon his knee. Gray-haired and smiling sat the man of many memories, guiding the utterances of one who was herself a pretty two-fold link between the present and the past, being the granddaughter (on the paternal side) of Leigh Hunt, and also the granddaughter (on the maternal side) of the Williams who was drowned with Shelley. Could a youthful student's eyes see any sight fairer?

> "And did you once see Shelley plain,
>> And did he stop and speak to you? . . .
>> . . . How strange it seems, and new!"[1]

And this old man had spoken with Shelley, not once, but a thousand times; and had known well both Harriet

[1] Robert Browning.

Westbrook and Mary Godwin; and had cracked jokes
with Hobhouse, and chaffed Proctor's latinity; and had
seen, and actually criticised, Malibran; and had bought
"the vasty version of a new system to perplex the sages,"[1]
when it first came out, in a bright, new, uncut quarto;
and had dined with Jeremy Bentham; and had smiled at
Disraeli, when, resplendently attired, he stood chatting in
Hookham's with the Countess of Blessington; and had
been face to face with that bland Rhadamanthus, Chief-
Justice Eldon; and was, in short, such a living chronicle
of things past and men dead as filled one's soul with delight and ever-varying wonder. "How strange it seemed,
and new!"

The portrait prefixed to the new edition of his works[2]
conveys a very good idea of the man as I first saw him—
a stately old gentleman with hair as white as snow, a keen
merry eye, and a characteristic chin. His dress was plain
black, with white neckcloth, and low shoes, and on his
head he wore a plaited straw hat. One glance at him was
enough to reveal his delightful character, that of his own
Dr. Opimian. "His tastes, in fact, were four: a good
library, a good dinner, a pleasant garden, and rural walks."
This was the man who, as a beautiful boy, had been
caught up and kissed by Queen Caroline; who, when he
grew up to manhood, had been christened "Greeky
Peeky," on account of his acquirement in Greek; and
who had been thus described, in a passage I have not

---

[1] Byron's description of Wordsworth's Excursion.
[2] Peacock's Works, 3 vols. (Bentley, 1875).

seen quoted before, by Shelley, in the "Letter to Maria Gisborne."

> "You will see P—, with his mountain Fair [1]
> Turned into a Flamingo . . . .
> When a man marries, dies, or turns Hindoo,
> His best friends hear no more of him ; but you
> Will see him and will like him, too, I hope,
> And that snow-white Snowdonian antelope,
> Matched with the cameo-leopard.   His fine wit
> Makes such a wound, the knife is lost in it ! "

Age had mellowed and subdued the "cameo-leopard," but the "fine wit," as I very speedily discovered, was as keen as ever.   His life had been passed in comparative peace and retirement.   He spoke French with the good old-fashioned English accent, and he had never been to Paris or up the Rhine ; Italy he knew not, nor cared to know ; and much as he loved the sea, he had sailed it little.   His four tastes had kept him well anchored all his life.   In his youth he had had a fifth, the Italian Opera, but the long modern performances, and the decadence of the ballet, had alienated him.   He had his "good library," and it *was* a good one—full of books it was a luxury to handle, editions to make a scholar's mouth water, bound completely in the old style in suits as tough as George Fox's suit of leather.   The "good dinner" came daily.   "He liked to dine well, and withal to dine quickly, and to have quiet friends at his table, with whom he could discuss questions which might afford ample room for pleasant conversation, and none for acri-

[1] Peacock's wife.

monious dispute."[1] In the "pleasant garden" he was sitting with the clear winding Thames below him and his rowing-boat swinging at the garden steps. And the "rural walks" lay all around him, on the quiet river side, through the green woods of Esher, down the scented lanes to Chertsey, by winding turns to Walton and Weybridge—scenes familiar to him since boyhood and hallowed with the footprints of dead relatives and departed friends. For the old man was, so to speak, alone in the world—his wife and best-loved daughters lay asleep in Shepperton churchyard, his son was somewhere abroad, and the cries of the children around him were not those of his own family. His gifted daughter Rosa, who died in her prime, was gone before, but another daughter, not of the flesh, had risen in her place. Many years before, when she was grieving sorely for the loss of a little child, Margaret, his wife had noticed, on Halliford Green, a little girl in its mother's arms, and seeing in it a strange likeness to her own dead child, had coaxed it into her own house, and dressed it in the dead babe's clothes. Peacock returning from the India House, looked in through the dining-room window, and seeing the child within was almost stunned by its resemblance to Margaret. This little girl, Mary Rosewell, had been adopted by the Peacocks ; and now, when all the rest were dead, she remained—a bright loving foster-daughter, whose baptismal name of "Mary" had long ago been sweetened into "May." I cannot describe her better

[1] Gryll Grange.

than in Peacock's own words when describing Miss Gryll: " The atmosphere of quiet enjoyment in which she had grown up seemed to have steeped her feelings in its own tranquillity ; and still more, the affection which she felt for her foster-father, and the conviction that her departure from his house would be the severest blow that fate could inflict on him, led her to postpone what she knew must be an evil day for him, and might peradventure not be a good one to her."   She has never married, but she has fulfilled her woman's mission perfectly, and the final years of Peacock owed much of their tranquil sunshine to her tender and pathetic care.

Knowing Peacock only from his books, I was not prepared to find in him that delightful *bonhomie* which was in reality his most personal characteristic, in old age at least ; and when we became acquainted, and read and talked together, I was as much astonished at the sweetness of his disposition as amused and captivated by his quaint erudition.   In that green garden, in the lanes of Halliford, on the bright river, in walks and talks such as " brightened the sunshine," I learned to know him, and although he was so much my senior he took pleasure (I am glad to say) in my society, partly because I never worried him with " acrimonious dispute," which he hated above all things.

There was for the moment one dark cloud of misunderstanding between us—a cloud of smoke; for, like Hans Andersen's parson,[1] I " smoked a good deal of

[1] *At være eller ikke at være.*

tobacco, and bad tobacco," and to Peacock tobacco was poison. He forgave me, however, on one condition, that I never smoked within five hundred yards of his house—an arrangement which, I am ashamed to say, I violated, for well I remember, one night stealthily opening the bed-room window in the house at Halliford, and "blowing a cloud" out into the summer night. I am not sure that much of his hate of tobacco did not arise from his morbid dread of fire. He would never have any lucifer matches in his house, save one or two which were jealously kept in a tin box in the kitchen. Morning after morning he arose with the sun, lit his own fire in the library, and read till breakfast, laying in material for talk which flowed like Hippocrene—as crystal, and as learned! His chief, almost his only, correspondent was Lord Broughton, who had been his friend through life. The two old gentlemen interchanged letters and verses, and capped quotations, and doubtless felt like two antediluvian mammoths left stranded, and yet living, after the Deluge—that Deluge being typified to them by the submersion of Whig and Tory in one wild wave of Progress, and the long career of Lord Brougham as a sort of political Noah. The old landmarks of society were obliterated. Lord Byron was a dim memory, and the stage-coach was a dream. The poetry of Nature had triumphed, and the poetry of Art had died. Germany had a literature, and it was part of polite education to know German. Beards were worn. Rotten boroughs were no more. The *Times*, like a colossal Podsnap, dominated journalism, but the *Daily*

Telegraph was stirring the souls of tradesmen to the sub-
blime knowledge of Lempriere's Dictionary and Bohn's
" Index of Quotations." Special correspondents were
invented, competitive examination was consecrating medio-
crity, and a considerable number of Englishmen drank
bad champagne.   What was left for an old scholar, but,
like the Hudibrastic Mirror of Knighthood,

> " To cheer himself with ends of verse,
>   And saying of philosophers ! "

For the rest, the world was in a bad way; best keep
apart, and let it wag.   ψῦξον τὸν οἶνον, Δωρι !   Quaff a
cool cup in the green shade, and drink confusion to
Lord Michin Mallecho and the last Reform Bill !
It must be conceded at once that Peacock was no
friend to modern progress—the cant of it, hoarsely roared
from the throats of journalistic Jews and political Merry
Andrews, had sickened him ; and he was not for one
moment prepared to admit that the world was one whit
wiser and happier than before the advent of the steam en-
gine.   The pessimism which appears everywhere in his
books was the daily theme of his talk ; but to understand
it rightly we must remember it was purely *satiric*—
that, in truth, Peacock abused human nature because he
loved it.   Genial at heart as Thackeray, he delighted
to condemn man and society in the abstract.   Hence
much of his writing must be read between the lines.   In
the clever little sketch of Peacock, prefixed to the new
edition of the works, Lord Houghton errs to some ex-

tent in trying to construct Peacock out of his books.[1] The "unreasoning animosity" Lord Houghton speaks of was purely ironic. For example, so far from having "an indiscriminate repugnance to Scotland and to everything Scotch," he was very fond of Scotchmen, having many correspondents among them ; but he could not spare them for all that, any more than Thackeray could spare the Irish, whom he loved with all his heart. When, in "Gryll Grange," he makes Dr. Opimian say of the Americans : " I have no wish to expedite communication with them. If we could apply the power of electric repulsion to preserve us from ever hearing any more of them, I should think we had *for once* derived a benefit from science ! "—he is merely, in a mood of what Lord Houghton felicitously called "intellectual gaiety," in an after-dinner mood, expressing a comic prejudice with no deep root in reason. The animosity is Aristophanic. No one reverenced Socrates more than his unmerciful "chaffer," and no man knew the benefit of science better than Peacock. He tried to shut out humanity, but he felt for it very intensely. He could fain have resembled the gods of Epicurus—thinking, feeling nothing, as Cicero

---

[1] "In the same spirit he clung to the old religious ideas that haunted all early Roman history, and indeed went far into the Empire, and thus *he liked to read Livy, and did not like to read Niebuhr.*"—LORD HOUGHTON'S PREFACE. The words in italics are put by Peacock into the mouth of a young lady in "Gryll Grange," and by no means express his own sentiments ; indeed, Niebuhr was regarded by him with the highest admiration, as having almost unique intuition.

expresses it, but "Mihi pulchre est," and "Ego beatus sum"—but in reality, he felt for human suffering very acutely. He would fain have had the world one vast Maypole, with all humanity dancing round it, or one mighty Christmas tree, with all humanity waiting to get a prize from it. Every year, on May-day, he crowned a little May-queen—generally one of his grandchildren—as queen of the May, and all the little children of the village flocked in to her with garlands, to be rewarded, as the case might be, with a bright new penny or a silver coin. He loved the old times for their old customs, and he loved the old customs because they made men gentle and children glad. "He had no fancy," he said, "for living in an express train; he liked to go quietly through life, and to see all that lay in his way." His life, indeed, might be described as one long rural walk, in company with Dr. Opimian, occasionally diversified by a visit to London, and a night at the Italian Opera. He belonged, as Lord Houghton says, "to the eighteenth century," and I may add that he had every one of its virtues without one of its vices.

His literary tastes were very interesting; although they, too, belonged to the eighteenth century. His favourite classical authors were Aristophanes and Cicero. His knowledge of the latter was extraordinary; there was scarcely a passage of any force which he had not by heart. As to Aristophanes, he simply revelled in that quaint satire so akin to the keen writings of his own modern Muse. At a time when he was reading Pickwick, and delighting in its extravagances, he cried characteristically, with a delicious twinkle of his eye, at dinner—"Dickens is very comic, but—not *so* comic as Aristophanes!" His mind was not so much attracted by the Greek tragedians, though of course he knew them well, as by the comic writers and the satirists; and, on the whole, I fancy he preferred Euripides to Sophocles, for the very reasons which make critics like him less. His sympathies, indeed, were less with the grand, the terrible, and the sublimely pathetic, than with the brilliant, the exquisite, and the delicately artistic. Comedy fascinated him more than Tragedy awed him. Although he was a profound student of the mystical hymns of Orpheus, he read them more as a scholar than as a mystic. It must be admitted, moreover, that his mind was in itself a terrible "thesaurus eroticus," and there was to be found in it many a Petronian quibble and Catullian *double entendre* not to be discovered in Rambach. To the last he loved Petronius—a writer who has never yet received justice for his marvellous picture-painting and delicate graces of diction, and who can be vindicated to the moralist far more easily than Rabelais. Rabelais he loved too, of course; who does not? Like Swift, he preferred Plautus to Terence :—

> Despite what schoolmasters have taught us,
> I have a great respect for Plautus,
> And think our boys may gather *there* hence
> More wit and wisdom than from Terence!

From these tastes of his in the classical direction, the

reader may readily guess what authors and what books he selected from more modern fields. It will readily be understood that he was partial to Molière, to Voltaire's satirical works, and to the dramatists of the Restoration; that he admired "Sir Roger de Coverley" and the *Spectator*, and had by heart "Clever Tom Clinch" and the other sardonic verses of Dean Swift; and that he did *not* care much for the poetic transcendentalism of Coleridge. He esteemed the poetry of Milton, but far preferred Milton's prose. At the time I knew him, he could repeat by heart nearly the whole of Redi's "Bacchus in Tuscany"—a bibulous masterpiece which had been admirably translated by Leigh Hunt. Of modern non-poetical works, I should say his three favourites were Monboddo's "Ancient Metaphysics," Drummond's "Academical Questions," and Horne Tooke's "Diversions of Purley;" to which may be added, with a reservation, Harris's "Hermes." He was always very fond of philosophic philology, and one of the last works of his life was to issue to his private friends a new interpretation of the *Aelia Lælia Crispis*.

But the above brief catalogue of his favourites affords no glimpse of his true attainment. In reality he had not read so many books as many less masterly men; but his peculiarity was that he had so read and re-read his favourite ones that he had completely attained the interior of them. Thoreau used to say that the Bible and Hafiz were books enough for any one man's lifetime; and certainly, a lifetime might be spent on the study of the

Bible alone. Peacock had some dozen authors virtually by heart,—and thus, the polyglott of his delightful talk was really surprising. He never forgave a false quantity; Browning's Avat*ar*, in "Waring," would have driven him into a fever, and, in speaking of America, he never forgot the fact that its most popular poet, at that time, had committed the false Latin of "Excelsior."[1] His tastes in poetry may be presumed; but I ought to mention to his honour that he was one of the few early lovers of Wordsworth, despite his personal dislike to the Lake School. He was never, till the day of his death, quite *en rapport* with Shelley's moonshine-genius; he far preferred such a solid, flesh and blood poet as Burns, and of Burns' poems his favourite was "Tam o' Shanter;" and he had little or no appreciation for John Keats. Indeed, he never passed the portico of the green little Temple erected by Keats to Diana, remembering with indignation the barbarous fancies consecrated therein; for he could prove by a hundred quotations that the sleep of Endymion was eternal, whereas in the modern poem the Latmian shepherd is for ever capering up and down the earth and ocean like the German chaser of shadows.[2] The ancient

[1] Is it possible that Peacock himself is responsible for the translation in the verses to "Gryll Grange" of a passage from the Metamorphoses of Apuleius; wherein "fluctibus educata" is rendered by "the educated in the waves," etc. There are several errors in the new edition, not to speak of the many unaccentuated Greek quotations.

[2] For similar reasons, he was perpetually wroth with Byron. He gives one frightful instance of incongruity in the notes to "Night-

conception, as briefly incorporated by Cicero in the passion where Diana is described as watching for ever the sleep of "her beloved Endymion," is certainly very lovely. And here I may remark incidentally that the influence of Peacock on the lurid genius of Shelley, though doubtless chilling on occasion, was certainly beneficial and in the interests of Art. He checked a thousand extravagances, and helped to form Shelley's later and more massive style as exemplified in such pieces as "Alastor, or the Spirit of Solitude." Peacock suggested the title for this poem, and was amused to the day of his death by the fact that the public, and even the critics, persisted in assuming Alastor to be the name of the hero of the poem, whereas the Greek work Ἀλάστωρ signifies an evil genius, and the evil genius depicted in the poem is the Spirit of Solitude.

Nothing can be more gentle, more guarded, than Peacock's printed account of Shelley. His private conversation on the subject was, of course, very different. Two subjects he did not refer to in his articles may safely be mentioned now—Shelley's violent fits of passion, and the difficulty Peacock found in keeping on friendly terms

mare Abbey."—"In Manfred, the great Alastor, or Κακος Δαιμων, of Greece is hailed king of the world by the Nemesis of Greece, in concert with three of the Scandinavian Valkyriœ, under the name of the Destinies; the astrological spirits of the alchemysts of the middle ages; an elemental witch, transplanted from Denmark to the Alps; and a chorus of Dr. Faustus's devils, who came in at the last act for a soul. It is difficult to conceive where this heterogeneous mythological company could have met originally, except at a *table d'hote*, like the six kings in "Candide."—"Nightmare Abbey," p. 332, vol. i. of collected edition.

with Mary Godwin. Many were the anecdotes he told with a twinkling eye, of Shelley's comic outbursts. One I particularly remember. When the two friends were rowing one day on the Thames, as it was their constant custom to do, they came into collision with a flat-bottomed boat moored in the centre of the stream, in which an old tradesman and his wife were contentedly seated, bottom-fishing. Remonstrances and strong expressions from the "lady" ensued; and, as the friends pulled away from the scene of the encounter, Shelley shrieked out, in his peculiarly unmusical voice, "There's an old woman angling for unfortunate fishes, as the Devil will angle for her soul in H—!" As to Mary Godwin, I fancy Peacock never really liked her; and this fact, of course, must be weighed in estimating his opinions relative to her and her predecessors. On one occasion, at least, he refused to enter Shelley's house while "she was in it," and was only constrained to do so by an entreaty from Mary herself. On the whole he is just, even generous, to her memory; but he certainly preferred Harriett, if only on the ground of her surpassing beauty.

It is well known that Peacock pourtrayed Shelley in the "Scythrop" of "Nightmare Abbey," and it is pleasant to remember that Shelley admitted the truth of the portrait, and was amused by it. Specially pointed was the passage wherein Scythrop, who loves two young ladies at once, tells his distracted father that he will commit suicide :—There is no doubt that if Shelley could have kept *both* Harriett and Mary he would have been happy; for he, more than most men, needed the triple wifehood so amusingly described in "Realmah." Seriously speaking, the picture of the man Shelley, as depicted by Peacock, directly in his "Memorials," and indirectly in the novel, is far more loveable and fascinating than the "divine" characterless humanitarian whom hero-worshippers love to paint.

I do not propose to attempt, on the present occasion, any estimate of Peacock's novels, although I believe they are entitled to a far higher place in literature than Lord Houghton seems inclined to give them; but they are full of opinions which he expressed even more admirably in conversation. His detestation of the literary class lasted until the end. "The understanding of literary people," he affirmed, "is exalted, not so much by the love of truth and virtue, as by arrogance and self-sufficiency; and there is, perhaps, less disinterestedness, less liberality, less general benevolence, and more envy, hatred, and uncharitableness among them, than among any other description of men." In his young days he had cut and slashed at his brethren, especially at the Lake Poets, whom he appreciated very much notwithstanding. Latterly he was wont to affirm, as in "Gryll Grange," that "Shakespeare never makes a flower blossom out of season, and Wordsworth, Coleridge, and Southey are true to nature in this *and in all other respects.*" He hated Moore as much as he loved Burns. "Moore's imagery," he makes Mr. MacBorrowdale say, "is all false. Here is a highly applauded stanza :—

> " 'The night dew of heaven, though in silence it weeps,
> Shall brighten with verdure the sod where he sleeps ;
> And the tear that we shed, though in secret it rolls,
> Shall long keep his memory green in our souls.'

But it will not bear analysis. The dew is the cause of the verdure, but the tear is not the cause of the memory —the memory is the cause of the tear." I am sorry to say he could never be persuaded to appreciate Tennyson. Specially offensive to him was the laureate's picture of Cleopatra as "a queen with swarthy cheeks and bold black eyes, brow-bound with burning gold." "Thus," he writes, "one of our most popular poets describes Cleopatra ; and one of our most popular artists has illustrated the description by a portrait of a hideous grinning Ethiop. . . . . Cleopatra was a Greek, the daughter of Ptolemy Auletes and a lady of Pontus. The Ptolemies were Greeks, and whoever will look at their genealogy, their medals, and their coins, will see how carefully they kept their pure Greek blood uncontaminated by African inter-mixture. Think of this description and this picture applied to one who, Dio says—and all antiquity confirms him—was 'the most superlatively beautiful of women, splendid to see, and delightful to hear.'[1] For she was eminently accomplished : she spoke many languages with grace and facility. Her mind was as wonderful as her personal beauty. There is not a shadow of intellectual expression in that horrible portrait." For the rest,

---

[1] Περικαλλεστάτη γυναικῶν. . . λαμπρά τε ἰδεῖν καὶ ἀκουσθῆναι οὖσα.—DIO. xlii. 34.

the Cleopatra of Shakespeare delighted him, as having not
one feature in common with that other abominable
"Queen of Bembo."

He was a great believer in Greek painting, with its
total absence of perspective; nevertheless, he abhorred
pre-Raphaelism, though it loves perspective as little as
the Greeks!   But in fact, he was generally inclined to
cry, with his own Gryllus, in "Aristophanes in London,"

> "—All the novelties I yet have seen,
> Seem changes for the worse."

New schools of painting and poetry attracted him as little
as new science.   One of his prejudices was amusing in
the extreme, and it is foreshadowed, like so many of his
latter peculiarities, in "Gryll Grange."   Great as was his
knowledge of Greek, Latin, Italian, and French,—which
Horne Tooke calls "the usual bounds of a scholar's
acquisition,"—and considerable as was his interest in
Goethe and the Weimer circle, he disliked everything
German, and never attempted to learn that wonderful
language, which may be said to be the key to the
golden chamber of modern poetry and philosophy.   Mr.
Falconer observes in "Gryll Grange," quoting a dictum
of Porson's, that "Life is too short to learn German;
meaning, I apprehend, not that it is too difficult to be
acquired within the ordinary space of life, but that there
is nothing in it to compensate for the portion of life
bestowed in its acquirement, however little that may be!"
He used to quote with a chuckle Porson's doggrel—

> " The German's in Greek
> Are sadly to seek ;
> Save only Hermann,
> And Hermann's a German ! "

It is strange that he was not curious in this direction, for his literary appetite was unbounded. When we first met, and when he was approaching his eightieth year, he was studying Spanish, in order to read the *Autos* and other masterpieces of Calderon. Conceive the literary vitality, in an old man of that age, which would urge him on to the study of a tongue almost new to him ! The task was a comparatively easy one, of course, from his consummate knowledge of other kindred tongues, but it still possessed difficulties enough to daunt a less earnest lover of learning. His cry for more light, like that of the old Goethe, was heard till the very last.

As I write of him, and look again upon the photograph of his genial features, I am reminded, by a certain general resemblance to the portraits of Thackeray, that the author of " Vanity Fair " was one of his greatest admirers, and wrote to him several pleasant letters, in one of which, which I saw, he promised to pay a long visit to Lower Halliford. I do not think the visit was ever paid; but it is pleasant to think of those two men in company, for they possessed many characteristics in common. What evenings there would have been in the old house at Halliford if Thackeray had come ! What capping of quotations, what mellow music of eighteenth century voices, while these two kindred spirits drank their after-dinner wine! For Thackeray's heart was with the eighteenth century too; and either one or the other of these two white-headed "old boys" would have been quite at home, if suddenly translated back in time, and set down by Temple Bar with the Dean of St. Patrick's, or with Pope in his villa at Twickenham, or in a Whitefriars hostelry with Dick Steele. On such an evening, when the old heart was warm with wine, and after Thackeray, perhaps, had trolled out to his host's delight, the ballad of "Little Billee," or "Peg of Linavaddy," I can conceive the author of "Gryll Grange" reciting, in that rich mellow voice of his, his own lovely verses called, "Love and Age;"—

> I played with you 'mid cowslips blowing,
> When I was six and you were four;
> When garlands weaving, flower-balls throwing,
> Were pleasures soon to please no more.
> Through groves and meads, o'er grass and heather,
> With little playmates, to and fro,
> We wandered hand in hand together;
> But that was sixty years ago.
>
> You grew a lovely roseate maiden,
> And still our early love was strong;
> Still with no care our days were laden,
> They glided joyously along;
> And I did love you very dearly,
> How dearly words want power to show;
> I thought your heart was touched as nearly;
> But that was fifty years ago.
>
> Then other lovers came around you,
> Your beauty grew from year to year;

And many a splendid circle found you
The centre of its glittering sphere.
I saw you then, first vows forsaking,
On rank and wealth your hand bestow;
Oh then I thought my heart was breaking,—
But that was forty years ago.

And I lived on, to wed another:
No cause she gave me to repine;
And when I heard you were a mother,
I did not wish the children mine.
My own young flock, in fair progression,
Made up a pleasant Christmas row:
My joy in them was past expression,—
But that was thirty, years ago.

You grew a matron plump and comely,
You dwelt in fashion's brightest blaze;
My earthly lot was far more homely;
But I too had my festal days.
No merrier eyes have ever glistened
Around the hearthstone's wintry glow,
Than when my youngest child was christened,—
But that was twenty years ago.

Time passed.   My eldest girl was married,
And I am now a grandsire grey;
One pet of four years old I've carried
Among the wild-flowered meads to play.
In our old fields of childish pleasure,
Where now, as then, the cowslips blow,
She fills her baskets ample measure,—
And that is not ten years ago.

But though first love's impassioned blindness
Has passed away in colder light,

> I still have thought of you with kindness
> And shall do, till our last good-night.
> The ever-rolling silent hours
> Will bring a time we shall not know,
> When our young days of gathering flowers
> Will be a hundred years ago.

And we know that this was the very sort of music to fill the great guest's eyes with tears, though it spoke only, like his more sad prose muse, of "Vanity, Vanity!" Thackeray touched the same note repeatedly—it was a habitual one with him—but he never touched it more delicately, or with a truer pathos. A little longer, and both were at rest, the veteran worn out with years, and the great good. man struck down in the prime of his powers.

Ignorant of the world as it is, circumscribed in his vision like all students of books, narrowed to the knowledge of a good library and a few green walks, thus Thomas Peacock passed away. He lived to see the curious theories which he developed so wonderfully in "Melincourt," and to many of which he was indebted to Lord Monboddo, assuming an importance in the history of science which fairly startled him. The generalisations made by quidnuncs from Darwin's facts, and which, rather than Darwin's own teaching, constitute "Darwinism," were sufficiently portentous to fill an eighteenth century satirist with comic wonder. What Peacock's own views were as to the origin and destiny of Man, I cannot tell: on such subjects he was reticent; but his sympathies were with the antique world, and I daresay

he would not have discountenanced a proposal once
entertained by Mr. Ruskin, to revive the worship of
Diana. At any rate, he was quite pagan enough to
astonish conventional people. Miss Nichols, in her
excellent and thoroughly sympathetic little sketch of her
grandfather, prefixed to the collected works, tells a
striking anecdote illustrative of his pleasant paganism.
Shortly before his death, a fire broke out in the roof of
his bed-room, and he was taken to the library, which lay
at the other end of the house. "At one time it was
feared the fire was gaining ground, and that it would be
needful to move him into one of the houses of the
neighbourhood, but he refused to move. The curate,
who came kindly to beg my grandfather to take shelter
in his house, received rather a rough and startling reception, for in answer to the invitation, my grandfather
exclaimed with great warmth and energy, 'By the immortal gods, I will not move!'"

Smile as we may at the formality and pedantry of the
eighteenth century, there were giants in those days; and
Peacock resembled them in intellectual stature. His
books will live, if only for their touches of quaint erudition; but they abound in delicious little pictures, such
as that of Mr. Falconer and his seven Vestal attendants
in "Gryll Grange," or those of Coleridge and Shelley in
"Nightmare Abbey." Sir Oran Haut-ton is perfect, a
masterpiece of characterisation, and as for Dr. Opimian,
he is as sure of immortality as "my Uncle Toby" himself.
But the true glory of Peacock was his delicious personal-

ity.   To have known and spoken with such a man, is in itself part of a liberal education.   I shall not soon forget that we sipped "Falernian" together, though the "Falernian" was no stronger than May Rosewell's cowslip-wine.   Circumstances called me back to Scotland, and during the short period preceding his decease we did not meet.   Only a few days before his death he dreamed of his "dear Fanny," the maiden who had been his first love, and for weeks together she came to him in his sleep, gently smiling.   Thus the Immortal Ones, call them by what names we may, were good to him until the very end; and while that first and last dream was bright within him, he sank to rest.   Let us fancy that, though life parted him from his first love, in death they were not divided; nor shall be, even when—

> The ever-rolling silent hours
>   Have brought a time they do not know,
> When their young days of gathering flowers
>   Will be a hundred years ago !   .

THE GOOD GENIE OF FICTION.

CHARLES DICKENS.

THERE was once a good Genie, with a bright eye and a magic hand, who, being born out of his due time and place, and falling not upon fairy ways, but into the very heart of this great city of London wherein we write, walked on the solid earth in the nineteenth century in a most spirit-like and delightful dream. He was such a quaint fellow, with so delicious a twist in his vision, that where you and I (and the wise critics) see straight as an arrow, he saw everything queer and crooked ; but this, you must know, was a terrible defect in the good Génie, a tremendous weakness, for how *can* you expect a person to behold things as they are whose eyes are so wrong in his head that they won't even make out a straight mathematical line.

To the good Genie's gaze everything in this rush of life grew queer and confused. The streets were droll, and the twisted windows winked at each other. The Water had a voice, crying, "Come down! come down!" and the Wind and Rain became absolute human entities, with ways of conducting themselves strange beyond expression. Where you see a clock, *he* saw a face and heard the beating of a heart. The very pump at Aldgate became humanised, and held out its handle like a hand for the good Genie to shake. Amphion was nothing to him. To make the gouty oaks dance hornpipes, and the whole forest go country-dancing, was indeed something, but how much greater was the feat of animating stone houses, great dirty rivers, toppling chimneys, staring shop windows, and the laundress's wheezy mangle! Pronounce as we may on the wisdom of the Genie's conduct, no one doubts that the world was different before he came: the same world, doubtless, but a duller, more expressionless world; and perhaps, on the whole, the people in it—especially the poor, struggling people—wanted one great happiness which a wise and tender Providence meant to send.

The Genie came and looked, and after looking for a long time, began to speak and print; and so magical was his voice, that a crowd gathered round him, and listened breathlessly to every word; and so potent was the charm, that gradually all the crowd began to see everything as the charmer did (in other words, as the wise critics say, to *squint* in the same manner), and to smile in the same odd, delighted, bewildered fashion. Never did pale faces brighten more wonderfully! never did eyes that had seen straight so very long, and so very, very sadly, brighten up so amazingly at discovering that, absolutely, everything was crooked! It was a quaint world, after all, quaint in both laughter and tears, odd over the cradle, comic over the grave, rainbowed by laughter and sorrow in one glorious Iris, melting into a thousand beautiful hues. " My name," said the good Genie, " is Charles Dickens, and I have come to make you all—but especially the poor and lowly—brighter and happier." Then, smiling merrily, he waved his hands, and one by one, along the twisted streets, among the grinning windows and the human pumps, quaint figures began to walk, while a low voice told stories of Human Fairyland, with its ghosts, its ogres, its elves, its good and bad spirits, its fun and frolic, oft culminating in veritable harlequinade, and its dim, dew-like glimmerings of pathos. There was no need any longer for grown-up children to sigh and wish for the dear old stories of the nursery. What was Puss in Boots to Mr. Pickwick in his gaiters ? What was Tom Thumb, with all its oddities, to poor Tom Pinch playing on his organ all alone up in the loft? A new and sweeter Cinderella arose in Little Nell ; a brighter and dearer little Jack Horner eating his Christmas pie was found when Oliver Twist appeared and " asked for more."

It was certainly enchanting the earth with a vengeance, when all life became thus marvellously transformed. In the first place, the world was divided ; just as old Fairyland had been divided, into good and bad fairies, into beautiful Elves and awful Ogres, and everybody was either very loving or very spiteful.   There were no composite creatures, such as many of our human tale-tellers like to describe.   Then there was generally a sort of Good Little Boy who played the part of hero, and who ultimately got married to a Good Little Girl, who played the part of heroine.

In the course of their wanderings through human fairyland, the hero and heroine met all sorts of strange characters—queer-looking Fairies, like the Brothers Cheeryble, or Mr. Toots, or David Copperfield's aunt, or Mr. Dick, or the convict Magwitch; out-and-out Ogres, ready to devour the innocent, and without a grain of goodness in them, like Mr. Quilp, Jonas Chuzzlewit, Fagin the Jew, Carker with his white teeth, Rogue Riderhood, and Lawyer Tulkinghorn; comical Will-o'-the-wisps, or moral Impostors, flabby of limb and sleek of visage, called by such names as Stiggins, Chadband, Snawley, Pecksniff, Bounderby, and Uriah Heep.   Strange people, forsooth, in a strange country.   Wise critics said that the country was not the world at all, but simply Topsy-turvyland; and indeed there might have seemed some little doubt about the matter, if every now and again, in the world we are speaking of, there had not appeared a group of poor people with such real laughter and tears that their humanity was indisputable.   Scarcely had we lost sight for a moment of the Demon Quilp, when whom should we meet but Codlin and Short sitting mending their wooden figures in the churchyard? and not many miles off was Mrs. Jarley, every scrap on whose bones was real human flesh ; the Peggotty group living in their upturned boat on the sea-shore, while little Em'ly watches the incoming tide erasing her tiny footprint on the sand ; the Dorrit family, surrounding the sadly comic figure of the Father of the Marshalsea ; good Mrs. Richards and her husband the Stoker, struggling through thorny paths of adversity with never a grumble ; Trotty Veck sniffing the delicious fumes of the tripe a good fairy is bringing to him ; and Tiny Tim waving his spoon, and crying, " God bless us all ! " in the midst of the smiling Cratchit family on Christmas Day.

This was more puzzling still—to find " real life " and " fairy life " blended together most fantastically. It was like that delightful tale of George M'Donald's, where you never can tell truth from fancy, and where you see the country in fairyland is just like the real country, with cottages [and cooking going on inside], and roads, and flower-gardens, and finger-posts, yet everything haunted most mysteriously by supernatural creatures. But let the country described by the good Genie be ever so like the earth, and the poor folk moving in it ever so like life, there was never any end to the enchantment. On the slightest provocation trees and shrubs would talk and dance, intoxicated public-houses hiccup, clocks talk in measured tones, tombstones chatter their teeth, lamp-posts reel idiotically, all inanimate nature assume animate qualities. The better the real people were, and the poorer, the more they were haunted by delightful Fays. The Cricket talked on the hearth, and the Kettle sang in human words. The plates on the dresser grinned and gleamed, when the Pudding rolled out of its smoking cloth, saying perspiringly, " Here we are again ! " Talk about Furniture and Food being soulless things ! The good Genie knew better. Whenever he went into a mean and niggardly house, he saw the poor devils of chairs and tables attenuated and wretched, the lean time-piece with its heart thumping through its wretched ribs, the fireplace shivering with a red nose, and the chimney-glass grim and gaunt. Whenever he entered the house of a good person, with a loving, generous heart, he saw the difference—jolly fat chairs, if only of common wood, tables as warm as a toast, and mirrors that gave him a wink of good-humoured greeting. It was all enchant-ment, due perhaps in a great measure to the strange twist in the vision with which the good Genie was born.

Thus far, perhaps, in a sort of semi-transparent allegory, have we indicated the truth as regards the wonderful genius who has so lately left us. Mighty as was the charm of Dickens, there have been from the beginning a certain select few who have never felt it. Again and again has the great Genie been approached by some dapper *dilettante* of the superfine sort, and been informed that his manner was wrong altogether, not being by any means the manner of Aristophanes, or Swift, or Sterne, or Fielding, or Smollett, or Scott. This man has called him, with some contempt, a " caricaturist." That man has described his method of portrayal as " sentimental." M'Stingo prefers the humour of Galt. The gelid, heart-searching critic prefers Miss Austen.   Even young ladies have been known to take refuge in Thackeray.   All this time, perhaps, the real truth as regards Charles Dickens has been missed or perverted.   He was not a satirist, in the sense that Aristophanes was a satirist.   He was not a comic analyst, like Sterne ; nor an intellectual force, like Swift ; nor a sharp, police-magistrate sort of humourist, like Fielding ; nor a practical-joke-playing tomboy, like Smollett.   He was none of these things.   Quite as little was he a dashing romancist or fanciful historian, like Walter Scott.   Scott found the Past ready made to his hand, fascinating and fair.   Dickens simply enchanted the Present.   He was the creator of Human Fairyland. He was a magician, to be bound by none of your commonplace laws and regular notions : as well try to put Incubus in a glass case, and make Robin Good-fellow the monkey of a street hurdy-gurdy.   He came to put Jane Austen and M. Balzac to rout, and to turn London into Queer Country.

One never forgets how Aladdin, when he got possession of the ring, and rubbing the tears out of his eyes, accidentally rubbed the ring too, discovered all in a moment his power over spirits and things unseen.   Much in the same way did Dickens discover his gift.   It was an accidental rub, as it were, when he was crying sadly, that brought the brilliant help.   But in his case, unlike that of Aladdin, the power grew with using.   The first few figures summoned up in the "Sketches" were clever enough, but vague and absurdly thin, mere shadows of what was coming. But suddenly, one morning, descended like Mercury the angel Pickwick beaming through his spectacles ; and the man-child revelled in laughter, utterly abandoning himself to the madest mood. He was not as yet quite spell-bound by his own magic, and was merely full of the fun. The tricksy Spirit of Metaphor, which he compelled to such untiring service afterwards, scarcely got beyond such an image as this, in the vulgarising style of "Tom Jones:"—"That punctual servant-of-all-work, the sun, had just risen and begun to strike a light." But the book was full of quiddity, rich in secret unction. It was in a sadder mood, with the recollections of his hard boyish sufferings still too fresh upon him, that he wrote "Oliver Twist." This book, with all its faults, shows what its writer might have been, if he had not chosen rather to be a great magician. Putting aside altogether the artificial love story with which it is interblended, and which is the merest padding, there is scarcely a character in this fiction which is not rigidly drawn from the life, and that without the faintest attempt to secure quiddity at the expense of verisimilitude. The character of Nancy, the figures of Fagin and his pupils, the conduct of Sykes after the murder, are all studies in the hardest realistic manner, with not one flash of glamour. Even the Dodger is more life-like than delightful. There are touches in it of mar-vellous cunning, strokes of superb insight, bits of descrip-tion unmatched out of the writer's own works ; but the lyric identity (if we may apply the phrase to one who, although he wrote in prose, was specifically a poet) had yet to be achieved. The charm was not all spoken. The child-like mood was not yet quite fixed.

Not at the "Oliver Twist" stage of genius could he have written thus of a foggy November day : "Smoke lowering down from chimney-pots, making a soft black drizzle, with flakes of soot in it as big as full-grown snow-flakes—gone into mourning, one might imagine, for the death of the sun ;" or thus about shop-windows on the same occasion : "Shops lighted two hours before their time—as the gas seems to know, for it has a haggard and unwilling look ;" or thus of a sleeping country town, where "nothing seemed to be going on but the clocks, and they had such drowsy faces, such heavy lazy hands, and such cracked voices, and they surely must have been too slow." Still less could he have pictured the wonderful figure of little Nell surrounded by oddities animate and inanimate, and moving through them to a sweet sleep and an early grave. Still less could he have written such an entire description as that of the Court of Chancery in "Bleak House," where the fog of the weather penetrates the whole intellectual and moral atmosphere, and renders all phantasmic and ludicrously strange. Yet all these things are seen and felt as a child might have seen and felt them—are just like the world little Dombey or little Nell might have described, if they had wandered as far, and been able to put their impressions upon paper.

It is not to be lost sight of, as being a most significant and striking fact, that Dickens is greatest when most personal and lyrical, and that he is most lyrical when he puts himself in a child's place, and sees with a child's eyes. In the centre of his best stories sits a little human figure, dreaming, watching life as it might watch the faces in the fire. Little Oliver Twist, little David Copperfield, little Dombey, little Pip (in "Great Expectations"), wander in their turn through Queer Land, wander and wonder; and life to them is quaint as a toy-shop and as endless as a show. And where Dickens does *not* place a veritable child as the centre of his story, as in "Little Dorrit" or "Bleak House," he employs instead a soft, wax-like, feminine, *child-like* nature, like Amy Dorrit or Esther Summerson, which may be supposed to bear the same sort of relation to the world as children of smaller growth, and to feel the world with the same intensity. In any case, in any of his best passages, whether humorous or pathetic, emotion precedes reflection, as it does in the case of a child or of a great lyric poet. The first flash is seized; the picture, whether human or inanimate, is taken instantaneously and steeped in the feeling of the instant. Thus, when Carker first appears upon the scene in "Dombey and Son," the author, with a quick infantine perception, first notices "two unbroken lines of glistening teeth, whose regularity and whiteness were quite distressing," and in another moment perceives that in the same person's smile there is "something like the snarl of the cat." With any other author but the present this first impression would possibly fade : but with him, as with a child, it grows and enlarges, till the white teeth of Carker absolutely haunt the reader, and in Carker's very look and gesture is seen a feline resemblance. The feeling never disappears for a moment. " Mr. Carker reclined against the mantelpiece. In whose sly look and watchful manner; in whose false mouth, stretched but not laughing; in whose spotless cravat and very whiskers; *even in whose silent passing of his left hand over his white linen and his smooth face:* there was something desparately cat-like."

And the further the book proceeds the more is the feline metaphor pursued, so that when Carker is planning the downfall of Edith Dombey we all feel to be watching, with intense interest, a cat in the act to spring. " He seemed to purr, he was so glad. And in some sort Mr Carker, in his fancy, basked upon a hearth too. Coiled up snugly at certain feet, he was ready for a spring, or for a tear or for a scratch, or for a velvet touch, as the humour seized him. Was there any bird in a cage that came in for a share of his regards ? " Nay, so unmistakable is his nature that it even provokes Diogenes the dog; for " as he picks his way so softly past the house, glancing up at the windows, and trying to make out the pensive face behind the curtain looking at the children opposite, the rough head of Diogenes came clambering up close by it, and the dog, regardless of all soothing, barks and howls, as if he would tear him limb from limb. Well spoken Di !" adds the author; "so near your mistress ! Another and another, with your head up, your eyes flashing, and your vexed mouth ringing for want of him. Another, as he picks his way along. You have a good scent, Di,—cats, boys, cats !"

K

Note here the positive *enchantment* which this lyrical feeling casts over every subject with which it deals. There can be no mistake about it—we are in Fairyland ; and every object we perceive, animate or inanimate, is quickened into strange life. Wherever the good person goes all good things are in league with him, help him, and struggle for him ; trees, flowers, houses, bottles of wine, dishes of meat, rejoice with him, and enter into him, and mingle identities with him. He, literally "brightening the sunshine," fills the place where he moves with Fairies and attendant spirits. Read, as an illustration of this, the account of Tom Pinch's drive in " Martin Chuzzlewit." But wherever the bad person goes, on the other hand, only ugly things sympathise. He darkens the day ; his baleful look transforms every fair thing into an ogre. The door-knockers grin grimly, the door hinges creak with diabolical laughter. There is not a grain of good in him, not a gleam of hope for him. He is, in fact, scarcely a human being, but an abstraction, representing Selfishness, Malice, Envy, Sham-piety, Hate ; moral ugliness of some sort represented invariably by physical ugliness of another sort. He, of course, invariably gets beaten in the long run. This is all as it ought to be—in a fairy tale.

The pleasantest creatures in this pleasant dream of life, seen by our good Genie with the heart of a child, are (undoubtedly) the Fools. Dickens loved these forms of helplessness, and he has created the brightest that ever were imagined—Micawber, Toots, Twemlow, Mrs. Nickleby, Traddles, Kit Nubbles, Dora Spenlow, the gushing

Flora,[1] and many others whose names will occur to every reader. They are perhaps truer to nature than is generally conceded. The critical criterion finds them silly, and the pathos wasted over them somewhat maudlin. The public loves them, and feels the better for them ; for, however wrong in the head, they are all right at heart—indeed, with our good Genie, a strong head and a tender heart seldom go together, which is a pity. There can be no doubt that the creator of these creatures was violently irrational, had an intense distaste for hard facts, and an equally intense love for sentimental chuckle-heads.

> The heart, the heart, if that beats right,
> Be sure the brain thinks true.

It may be observed, in deprecation, that Dickens' good people, and especially his Fools, too often wear their hearts "upon their sleeves," and give vent to the disagreeable "gush" so characteristic of his falsetto pathetic passages, such as the well-known scene between Dr. and Mrs. Strong in "David Copperfield :" —

"Annie, my pure heart !" said the doctor, "my dear girl !"

"A little more ! a very few words more ! I used to think there were so many whom you might have married, who would not have brought such charge and trouble on you, and who would have made your home a worthier home. I used to be afraid that I had better have remained your pupil, and almost your child. I used to fear

---

[1] Not the least interesting portion of Mr. Forster's life is the part showing us that Dora and Flora are photographs from the life, taken at different periods from the same person, and that this person was regarded by Dickens himself at one time just as Copperfield regarded Dora, and at a later period just as Clennam regarded Mrs F. !

that I was so unsuited to your learning and wisdom. If all this made me shrink within myself (as indeed it did), when I had that to tell, it was still because I honoured you so much, and hoped that you might one day honour me."

"That day has shone this long time, Annie," said the doctor, "and can have but one long night, my dear."

"Another word! I afterwards meant—steadfastly meant, and purposed to myself—to bear the whole weight of knowing the unworthiness of one to whom you had been so good. And now a last word, dearest and best of friends! The cause of the late change in you, which I have seen with so much pain and sorrow, and have sometimes referred to my old apprehension—at other times to lingering suppositions nearer to the truth—has been made clear to-night; and by an accident. I have also come to know, to-night, the full measure of your noble trust in me, even under that mistake. I do not hope that any love and duty I may render in return will ever make me worthy of your priceless confidence; but with all this knowledge fresh upon me, I can lift my eyes to this dear face, revered as a father's, loved as a husband's, sacred to me in my childhood as a friend's, and solemnly declare that in my lightest thought I had never wronged you; never wavered in the love and the fidelity I owe you!"

She had her arms round the doctor's neck, and he leant his head down over her, mingling his gray hair with her dark brown tresses.

"Oh, hold me to your heart, my husband! Never cast me out! Do not think or speak of disparity between us, for there is none, except in all my many imperfections. Every succeeding year I have known this better, as I have esteemed you more and more. Oh, take me to your heart, my husband, for my love was founded on a rock, and it endures!"—(*David Copperfield,* chap. xlv., pp. 402, 403, Charles Dickens' Edition.)

There is, of course, far too much of this sort of thing in Dickens' pictures, but it does not go beyond bad *drawing.* His conception of the pathetic circumstances is always psychologically right, only he has too little experience not to make it theatrical. A child might think such a scene, on or off the stage, very affecting. And why does it only repel grown-up people? For the very reason that it is childishly and absurdly candid, that the speakers in it lack the loving reticence of full-grown natures, that it is full of " words, words, words," from which proud and affectionate men and women shrink. Our good Genie's pets were far too fond, children-like, of pouring out their own emotions; they lacked the adult reserve. This is a fault they share with many contemporary creations, such as Browning's " Balaustion," whose

> O *so glad*
> To tell you the adventure!

and general guttural liquidity of expression, is quite as bad in itself (and far worse in its place) as anything in Dickens.

Even more precious than the Fools are, in our eyes, the Impostors. What a gallery; alike, yet how different! Pecksniff, Pumblechook, Turveydrop, Casby, Bounderby, Stiggins, Chadband, Snawley, the Father of the Marshalsea! Although a brief inspection of these gentlemen shows them all to belong to the same family, each in turn comes upon us with pristine freshness. They are infinitely ridiculous and quite Elf-like in their moral flabbiness.

And this brings us to one point upon which we would willingly dwell for some time, did space permit us. A great humorist like our good Genie, is the very sweetener and preserver of the earth, is the most beneficent Angel that walks abroad ; for it is a most cunning and delightful law of mental perception, that as soon as any figure presents itself to us in a funny light, hate for that figure is impossible. If you have any enemy, and if any peculiarity of his makes you smile or laugh, be sure that you and he are closer united than you know. Humour and love are twin brothers, one beautiful as Eros, the other queer as Incubus, but both made of the very same materials ; and therefore, to call a man a great humorist is simply to call him the most loving and lovable type of humanity that we are permitted to study and enjoy. And this, all the world feels, was Charles Dickens. It would be hard indeed to over-estimate what this good Genie has done for human nature, simply by pointing out what is odd in it. Here come Hypocrisy, Guile, Envy, Self-conceit ; you are ready to spring upon and rend them ; yet when the charm is spoken, you burst out laughing. What comical figures ! You couldn't think of hurting them ! Your heart begins to swell with sneaking kindness. Poor devils, they were made thus ; and they are so absurd ! Fortunately for humanity, this comical perception has grown with the growth of the world. Mystic touches of it in Aristophanes sweetened the Athenian mind when philosophy and the dramatic muse were souring and curdling, and at the mad laughter of Rabelais the cloud-pavilion of monasticism parted to let the merry sky peep through. But the deep human mirth of the popular heart was as yet scarcely heard.

Shakespeare's humour, even more than Chaucer's, is of the very essence of divine quiddity.

Between Shakespeare and Dickens, only one humorist of the truly divine sort rose, fluted magically for a moment, and passed away, leaving the Primrose family as his legacy to posterity. Swift's humour was of the earth, earthy; Gay's was shrill and wicked; Fielding's was judicial, with flashes of heavenlike promise; Smollett's was cumbrous and not spiritualising; Sterne's was a mockery and a lie (shades of Uncle Toby and Widow Wadman, forgive us, but it is true!); and—not to catalogue till the reader is breathless—Scott's was feudal, with all the feudal limitations, in spite of his magnificent scope and depth. Entirely without hesitation we affirm that there is more true humour, and consequently more helpful love, in the pages of Dickens than in all the writers we have mentioned put together; and that, in *quality*, the humour of Dickens is richer, if less harmonious, than that of Aristophanes; truer and more human than that of Rabelais, Swift, or Sterne; more distinctively unctuous than even that of Chaucer, in some respects the finest humorist of all; a head and shoulders over Thackeray's, because Thackeray's satire was radically unpoetic; certainly inferior to that of Shakespeare only, and inferior to *his* in only one respect—that of humorous pathos. It is needless to say that in the last-named quality Shakespeare towers supreme, almost solitary. Falstaff's death-bed scene[1] is, taken relatively to the preceding life,

[1] See *King Henry V.*, act ii. scene 3.

and history, and rich unction of Sir John, the most wonderful blending of comic humour and divine tenderness to be found in any book—infinite in its suggestion, tremendous in its quaint truth, penetrating to the very depths of life, while never disturbing the first strange smile on the spectator's face. Yes; and therefore overflowing with unutterable love.

The humour of our good Genie seems, when we begin to analyse it, a very simple matter—merely the knack, as we have before said, of seeing crooked—of posing every figure into oddity. A tone, a gesture, a look, the merest trait, is sufficient; nay, so all-sufficient does the trait become that it absorbs the entire individuality; so that Mr. Toots becomes a Chuckle, Mr. Turveydrop incarnate Deportment, Uriah Heep a Cringe; so that Newman Noggs cracks his finger-knuckles, and Carker shows his teeth, whenever they appear; so that Traddles is to our memory a Forelock for ever sticking bolt upright, and Rigaud (in " Little Dorrit ") an incarnate Hook-Nose and Moustache eternally meeting each other. Enter Dr. Blumber: "The Doctor's walk was stately, and calculated to impress the juvenile mind with solemn feelings. It was a sort of march; but when the Doctor put out his right foot, he gravely turned upon his axis, with a semicircular sweep towards the left; and when he put out his left foot, he turned in the same manner towards the right. So that he seemed, at every stride he took, to look about him as though he were saying, 'Can anybody have the goodness to indicate any subject, in any direction, on which I am uninformed?'" Enter Mr. Flintwinch: "His neck was so twisted, that the knotted ends of his white cravat actually dangled under one ear; his natural acerbity and energy always contending with a second nature of habitual repression, gave his features a swollen and suffused look; and altogether he had a weird appearance of having hanged himself at one time or other, and of having gone about ever since, halter and all, exactly as some timely hand had cut him down." This first impression never fades or changes as long as we see the figure in question.

Akin to this perception of Oddity, and allied with it, is the perception of the Incongruous. Never did the brain of human creature see stranger resemblances, funnier coincidences, more side-splitting discrepancies. This man was for all the world like (what should he say?) a Pump, the more so as his feelings generally ran to water. That man was a Spider, such a comical Spider—" horny-skinned, two-legged, money-getting, who spun webs to catch unwary flies, and retired into holes until they were entrapped." Yonder trips the immaculate Pecksniff, "carolling as he goes, so sweetly and with so much inno-cence, that he only wanted feathers and wings to be a Bird."

The summer weather in his bosom was reflected in the breast of nature. Through deep green vistas, where the boughs arched over-head, and showed the sunlight flashing in the beautiful perspective; through dewy fern, from which the startled hares leaped up, and fled at his approach; by mantled pools, and fallen trees, and down in hollow places, rustling among last year's leaves, whose scent woke memory of the past, the placid Pecksniff strolled. By meadow gates and hedges fragrant with wild roses; and by thatch-roofed cottages, whose inmates humbly bowed before him as a man both good and wise ; the worthy Pecksniff walked in tranquil meditation. The bee passed onward, humming of the work he had to do ; the idle gnats, for ever going round and round in one contracting and expanding ring, yet always going on as fast as he, danced merrily before him ; the colour of the long grass came and went, as if the light clouds made it timid as they floated through the distant air. The birds, so many Pecksniff consciences, sang gaily upon every branch ; and Mr. Pecksniff paid *his* homage to the day by enumerating all his projects as he walked along.—*Martin Chuzzlewit*, p. 302.

Here, as elsewhere, the whole power lies in the incongruity of the whole comparison, in the reader's perfect knowledge that Pecksniff is a Humbug and an Impostor, and that there is nothing bird-like or innocent in his nature. The vein once struck, there was nothing to hinder our good Genie from working it for ever. His path swarmed with oddities and incongruities ; Wagner-like he mixed these elements together, and produced the Homunculus, Laughter. And just as the perception of oddity and incongruity varies in men, varies the enjoyment of Dickens. Quiddity for quiddity—the reader must give as well as receive ; and if the faculty is not *in* him, he will turn away contemptuously. A weasel looking out of a hole is enough to convulse some people with laughter ; they see a dozen odd resemblances. Other people, again, walk through all this Topsyturvyland with scarcely a smile. Life in all its phases, great and small, seems perfectly congruous and ship-shape ; much too serious a matter for any levity.

But it is time we were drawing these stray remarks to a close, or we may be betrayed into actual criticism—a barbarity we should wish to avoid. Truly has it been said, that the only true critic of a work is he who enjoys it ; and for our part, our enjoyment shall suffice for criticism. The Fairy Tale of Human Life, as seen first and last by the good Genie of Fiction, seems to us far too delightful to find fault with—just yet. A hundred years hence, perhaps, we shall have it assorted on its proper shelf in the temple of Fame. We know well enough (as, indeed, who does not know?) that it contains much sham pathos, atrocious bits of psychological bungling, a little fine writing and a thimbleful of twaddle ; we know (quite as well as the critical know) that it is peopled, not quite by human beings, but by Ogres, Monsters, Giants, Elves, Phantoms, Fairies, Demons, and Will-o'-the-Wisps ; we know, in a word, that it has all the attractions as well as all the limitations of a Story told by a Child. For that diviner oddity, which revels in the Incongruity of the very Universe itself, which penetrates to the spheres and makes the very Angel of Death share in the wonderful laughter, we must go elsewhere—say to Jean Paul. Of the Satire, which illuminates the inside of Life and reveals the secret beating of the heart, which unmasks the Beautiful and anatomises the Ugly, Thackeray is a greater master ; and his tears, when they do flow, are truer tears. But for mere magic, for simple delightfulness commend us to our good Genie. He came, when most needed, to tell the whole story of life anew, and more funnily than ever; and it seems to us that his childlike method has brightened all life, and transformed this awful London of ours—with its startling facts and awful daily phenomena—into a gigantic Castle of Dreams. And now, alas! the magician's hand is cold in death. What a liberal hand that was, what a great heart guided it, few knew better than the writer of this paper.

> But he is fled
> Like some frail exhalation, which the dawn
> Robes in its golden beams,—ah! he is fled!
> The brave, the gentle, and the beautiful,
> The child of grace and genius.   Heartless things
> Are done and said in the world, and many worms
> And beasts and men live on, and mighty earth,
> From sea and mountain, city and wilderness,
> In vesper low of joyous orison,
> Lifts still its solemn voice; but he is fled—
> He can no longer know or love the shapes
> Of this phantasmal scene, who have to him
> Been purest ministers, who are, alas!
> Now he is not![1]

Now, all in good time, we get the story of his life; and let us hesitate a little, and know the truth better, ere we sit in judgment.   Against all that can be said in slander, let our gratitude be the shield.   Against all that may have been erring in the Man (few, nevertheless, to our thinking, have erred so little), let us set the mighty services of the Writer.   He was the greatest work-a-day Humorist that ever lived.   He was the most beneficent Good Genie that ever wielded a pen.

[1]Shelley's "Alastor."

OSSIAN.

LAVEN stands alone, separated from the chain of Cuchullins proper, and with the arms of the Red Hills encircling him and offering tribute. It is seldom he deigns to put aside his crown of mist, but on this golden day he is nnkinged. "The sunbeam pours its light stream before him ; his hair meets the wind of his hills, his face is settled from war, the calm dew of the morning lies on the hill of roses, for the sun is faint on his side, and the lake is settled and blue in the vale."

It is thus, as we gaze, that the thin sound of the voice of Cona breaks in upon our meditations ; "O bard ! I hear thy voice : it is pleasant as the gale of the spring that sighs on the hunter's ear, when he wakens from dreams of joy, and has heard the music of the spirits of the hill." In the dreamy wanderings of our mind we had almost forgotten Ossian, the true spirit of the mystic scene.   Oh ! ye ghosts of the lonely Cromla !   Ye souls of chiefs that are no more ! ye are " like a beam that has shone, like a mist that has fled away."   "The sons of song are gone to rest."   But one voice remains, strange and sad, " like a blast that roars loudly on a sea-surrounded rock, after the winds are laid."

What the Cuchullins are to all other British mountains Ossian is to all other British bards.   He abides in his place, neither greater nor less, challenging comparison with no one, solitary, sad, wrapt in eternal twilight.   Just in the same way as Glen Sligachan repelled Alexander Smith, the song of Ossian tires and wearies Brown and Robinson : fashionable once, it is now in disrepute ; by Byron, Goethe, and Napoleon cherished as a solemn inspiration, and lately pooh-poohed as conventional and artificial by the Saturday Reviewer, it abides forgotten, like Blaven, till such time as humorous critics may care to patronise it again.   It keeps its place, though, as surely as Scuir-na-Gillean and Blaven keep theirs.   It is based on the rock, and will endure.   Meantime, let us for once exclaim with Mr. Arnold, "Woody Morven, and echoing Lora, and Selma with its silent halls—we all owe them a debt of gratitude ; and when we are unjust enough to forget it, may the Muse forget us ! " [1]

As to the question of authenticity, that need not be introduced at this time of day.   Gibbon's sneer and Johnson's abuse prove nothing.   In this, as in all matters, Gibbon was a sceptic, as worthy to be heard on Ossian as

[1] " On the Study of Celtic Literature."   By Matthew Arnold.

Voltire on Shakespeare, or Gigadibs on Walt Whitman.
In this, as in everything else, Johnson was a bully, a dear,
lovable, shortsighted bully, as fit to listen to Fingal as to
paint the scenery of the Cuchullins. The philological
battle still rages ; but few of those competent to judge now
doubt that Macpherson did receive Gaelic MSS., that
the originals of his translations were really found in the
Highlands—that, in a word, Macpherson's Ossian is a
bona-fide attempt to render into English a traditionary
poetic literature similar in origin and history to the Ho-
meric poems. Truly has it been said that "Ossian drew
into himself every lyrical runnel, augmented himself in
every way, drained centuries of their songs : and living
an oral and gipsy life, handed down from generation to
generation without being committed to writing, and having their outlines determinately fixed, these songs become
vested in a multitude, every reciter having more or less to
do to them. For centuries the floating legendary material
was reshaped, added to, and altered by the changing
spirit and emotion of the Celt." What remains to us is a
set of titanic fragments, which, like the scattered boulders
and *blocs perchés* of Glen Sligachan, show where a mighty
antique landscape once existed. The translation of
Macpherson, made as it was by a scholar familiar with
modern literature, has numberless touches showing that
the chisel has been used to polish the original granite,
but it is on the whole a marvellous bit of workmanship,
strong, free, subtle, full of genius—better than any English translation of the Iliad, nearer to the true antique

than Chapman's, or Pope's, or Derby's, or Blackie's ver-
sions of the Greek.   In this translation, retranslated,
Goethe read it; and Napoleon; and each stole something from it, if only a phrase.   Veritably, at first sight,
it has a barbarous look.   The prose breathes heavily, in
a series of gasps, each gasp a sentence.   The sound is to
a degree monotonous, like the voice of the wind; it rises
and falls, that is all, breaks occasionally into a shriek,
dies sometimes into a sob; but it is always a wind-like
voice.   Yet just as hour after hour we have sat by the
fireside, hearkening to the wind itself, feeling the sadness
of Nature creep into the soul and subdue it, so have we
sat listening to the sad "sound of the voice of Cona."
It is a wind, a wind passing among mountains.   Only a
sound, yet the soul follows it out into the darkness—where
it blows the beard from the thistle on the ruin, where it
mists the pictures in the moonlight mere, where it meets
the shadows shivering in the desolate corry, where it dies
away with a divine whisper on the fringe of the mystic
sea.   A wind only, but a voice crying, " I have seen the
walls of Balclutha, but they were desolate.   The fire had
resounded in the halls, and the voice of the people is
heard no more.   The stream of Clutha was removed
from its place by the fall of the walls.   The thistle shook
there its lonely head; the moss whistled to the wind.
The fox looked out from the windows; the rank grass of
the wall waved round his head."   It is an eerie wail out
of the solitude.   We are blown hither and thither on it,
through the mists of Morven, over the livid Cuchullins,

through the terror of tempest, the dewy dimness of dawn —where the heroes are fighting, where a thousand shields clang—where rises the smoke of the ruined home, the moan of the desolate children—where the dead bleed, and " the hawks of heaven come from all their winds to feed on the foes of Auner "—where the sea rolls far distant, and the white foam is like the sails of ships—where the narrow house looks pleasant in the waste, and " the gray stone öf the dead." But ever and anon we pause listening, and know that we are hearkening to a sound only, to the lonely cry of the wind.

After all, it is unfair to call this monotonousness a demerit. Ossian's poems have much more in common with the Theogony than the Iliad and Odyssey. Ulysses and Thersites were comparatively modern products of the Greek Epos. In the Ossianic period humanity dwelt in the twilight which precedes the dawn of culture. The heroes are not only colossal, but shadowy—dim in a dim light—figures vaguer than any in the Eddas ; you see the gleam of their eyes, the flash of their swords, you hear the solemn sound of their voices ; but they never laugh, and if they uplift a festal cup, it is with solemn armsweep and hushed speech. The landscape where they move is this landscape of Glen Sligachan, with a frequent glimpse of woodier Morven, and a far-off glimmer of the western sea ; all this shadowy, for the "morning is gray on Cromla," or the " pale light of the night is sad." " I sit by the mossy fountain ; on the top of the hill of wind. One tree is rustling above me. Dark waves roll over the heath.   The lake is troubled below.   The deer descend from the hill.   It is mid-day, but all is silent."   This is a day picture, but there is little sunlight.   It is in this atmosphere that some readers expect variety.   They weary of the wind, and the gray stone on the waste, and the shadows of heroes.   O for one gleam of humour, of the quick spirit of life! they cry.   As well might they look for Falstaff in the Iliad, or for Browning's Broad Church Pope in Shakespeare!   Blaven and his brethren are not mirth-breeding; nor is Ossian.   Here in the waste, and there in the book, humanity fades far off; though coming from both, we drink with fresher breath the strong salt air of the free waves of the world.

In these days of metre-mongers, in these days when poetry is a tinkling cymbal or a pretty picture, when Art has got hold of her sister Muse and bedaubed her with unnatural colour, we might well expect the public to be indifferent to Ossian.   Not the least objection to the Gael, in the eyes of library-readers, is the peculiar gasping prose in which the translation is written : and it is an objection ; yet it affords scope for passages of wonderful melody, just as does the prose of Plato, or of Shakespeare,[1] or the semi-Biblical line of Walt Whitman. "Before the left side of the car is seen the snorting horse!   The thin-maned, high-headed strong-hoofed, fleet-bounding son of the hill; his name is Dusronnal,

---

[1] Take Hamlet's speech about himself (commencing "I have of late, but wherefore I know not," &c.) as an example of what Coleridge calls "the wonderfulness of prose."

among the stormy sons of the sword." Such a passage is prose as fully acceptable as a more literal translation, broken up into lines like the original :   .

> " By the other side of the chariot
>   Is the arch-necked, snorting,
>   Narrow-maned, high-mettled, strong-hoofed,
>   Swift-footed, wide-nostril'd steed of the mountains;
>   Dusrongeal is the name of the horse."   ·

Music in our own day having run to tune, in poetry as in everything else, we eschew unrhymed metres and poetical prose; yet it is as legitimate to call Beethoven a barbarian as to abuse Ossian and Whitman for their want of melody.   And as to the charge that Ossian lacks *humour*, where in our other British poetry is humour so rife that we imperatively demand it from the Gael?   Where is Milton's humour? or Shelley's?   Where in contemporary poetry is there a grain of the divine salt of life, such as makes Chaucer prince of tale-tellers, and gladdens the academic period of rare Ben, and makes Falstaff loveable, and Bardolph's red nose delicious, and preserves the slovenly-scribbled " Beggar's Opera " for all time?   In sober truth, humour and worldly wisdom, and all we *blasés* moderns mean by variety, were scarcely created in the Ossianic period.   Why, they are rare enough in the lonely Hebrides even now.   Now, in the nineteenth century, the Celtic islander smiles as little as old Fingal or Cuthullin.   His laugh is grim and deep ; he is too far back in time to laugh lovingly.   His loving mood is earnest, tearful, almost painful, sometimes full of a dim brightness, but never exuberant and joyful.

Yet we moderns, who love hoary old Jack for his sins, and stand tearfully at his bed of death,[1] and like all fat men and sinners better for his sake, we to whom life is the quaintest and drollest of all plays as well as the deepest and divinest of all mysteries, may listen very profitably, ever and anon, to the monotonous wail of Cona, may pass a brooding hour in the twilight shadow of this eerie poetry. The influence of Ossian upon us is quite specific: not religious at all; not merely ghostly; but solemn and sad and beautiful; with just enough life to preserve a thread of human interest; with too little life to awaken us from the mood of brooding mystic feeling produced by the lonely landscape, and the dim dawn, and the changeful moon. Ossian dreams not of a Supreme Being, has no religious feelings, but he believes

[1] *Host.* "Nay, sure, he's not in hell: he's in Arthur's bosom, if ever man went to Arthur's bosom. 'A made a finer end, and went away, an it had been any christom child; 'a parted even just between twelve and one, e'en at turning o' the tide; for after I saw him fumble with the sheets, and play with flowers, and smile upon his fingers' ends, I knew there was but one way; for his nose was as sharp as a pen, and 'a babbled of green fields. 'How now, Sir John?' quoth I: 'what, man! be of good cheer. So 'a cried out 'God, God, God!' three or four times: now I, to comfort him, bid him, 'a should not think of God; I hoped there was no need to trouble himself with any such thoughts yet. So, 'a bade me lay more clothes on his feet: I put my hand into the bed, and felt them, and they were as cold as any stone; then I felt to his knees, and so upward and upward, and all was as cold as any stone."—*Henry V.*, ii. 3.

in gracious spirits "fair as the ghost of the hill, when it moves in a sunbeam at noon, over the silence of Morven." If there is no humour in his poems, there is a great deal of exquisitely human tenderness. Nothing can be more touching in its way than the death of Fellan: "Ossian, lay me in that hollow rock. Raise no stone above me, lest one should ask about my fame. I am fallen in the first of my fields, fallen without renown." Perfect in its way, too, is the imagery in the lament of Malvina over the death of Oscar: "I was a lovely tree in thy presence, Oscar! with all my branches round me. But thy breath came like a blast from the desert and laid my green head low. The spring returned with its showers, but no leaf of mine arose."

Sweetest and tenderest of all Ossian's songs, the song which fills the soul here in the gorges of Glen Sligachan, is "Berrathon," the "last sound of the voice of Cona." It is a wind indeed, strange and tender, deep and true. All the strife is hushed now, Malvina the beautiful is dead, and the old bard, knowing that his hour is drawing nigh, murmurs over a fair legend of the past. "Such were my deeds, son of Appin, when the arm of my youth was young. But I am alone at Lutha. My voice is like the last sound of the wind, when it forsakes the woods. But Ossian shall not be long alone; he sees the mist that shall receive his ghost; he beholds the mist that shall form his robe when he appears on his hills. The sons of feeble men shall behold me and admire the stature of the chiefs of old. They shall creep to their caves. . . . Lead, son of Appin, lead the aged to his woods. The winds begin to rise; the dark wave of the lake resounds. . . . Bring me the harp, son of Appin. Another song shall arise. My soul shall depart in the sound. . . . Bear the mournful sound away to Fingal's airy hall; bear it to Fingal's hall, that he may hear the voice of his son. . . . The blast of north opens thy gates. O king! I behold thee sitting on mist, dimly gleaming in all thine arms. Thy form now is not the terror of the valiant. It is like a watery cloud, when we see the stars behind it with their weeping eyes. Thy shield is the aged moon: thy sword a vapour half kindled with fire. Dim and feeble is the chief who travelled in brightness before. . . . I hear the voice of Fingal. Long has it been absent from mine ear! 'Come, Ossian, come away!' he says. . . . 'Come, Ossian, come away!' he says. 'Come, fly with thy fathers on clouds.' I come, I come, thou king of men. The life of Ossian fails. I begin to vanish on Cona. My steps are not seen in Selma. Beside the stone of Mora I shall fall asleep. The winds whistling in my gray hair shall not awaken me. . . . Another race shall arise." If this be not a veritable voice, then poesy is dumb indeed. The desolate cry of Lear is not more real.

Read these poems to-day on Glen Sligachan, or on the slopes of Blaven. Is not the solemn grayness everywhere? Is there a touch, a tint, of the quiet landscape lost? Not that Ossian described Nature; that was left for the modern. He contrives, however, while using the simplest imagery, while never pausing to transcribe, to conjure up before us the very spirit of such scenes as this. Mere description, however powerful, is of little avail; and painting is not much better. Ossian's verse resembles Loch Corruisk more closely than Turner's picture, powerful and suggestive as that picture is.

TWO POETS.

IN a quiet set of chambers in the Avenue Matignon, No. 3, Paris, there lingered for eight long years a quaint figure, paralysed to his chair and watching, with an eye where love and jealousy blended, the figure of his wife sewing at his side, while an old negress moved about in household duties. This man spent most of his time in composition, using alternatively the French and the German tongues. He had few friends and not many visitors. His life was lonely, his heart was sad, and he uttered shrill laughter. Though tender and affectionate beyond measure (witness his treatment of his mother, "the old woman at the Damenthor") he loved to gibe at all subjects, from the majesty of God to the littleness of man. His name was known through all the length of Germany as the greatest poet after Goethe. His wild, sweet poems were household words. He had sung the wonderful song of the

"Lorelei," and the delightful ballad of the daughters of King Duncan :

> Mein Knecht ! steh' auf und sattle schnell,
>   Und wirf dich auf dein Ross,
> Und jage rasch, durch Wald und Feld,
>   Nach König Duncan's Schloss !

He was the author of the most dreadfully realistic poem of modern times, the fragment entitled " Ratcliffe," where we have the terrible meeting of two who "loved once : "

> "Man sagte mir, Sie haben sich vermählt ? "
> " Ach ja ! " sprach sie gleichgültig laut und lachend,
> " Hab' einen Stock von Holz, der überzogen
> Mit Leder ist, Gemahl sich nennt ; doch Holz
> Ist Holz ! "—*Und klanglos widrig lachte sie, &c.*[1]

He had (not to speak of his other achievements) been the German lyrical poet of his generation.   On February 17, 1856, he died, and the only persons of note who attended his funeral were Mignet, Gautier, and Alexander Dumas. This man was Heinrich Heine, author of the " Buch der Lieder " and the " Romanzero."

At the same period there was moving in the heart of

[1] " They tell me thou art *married?* "
" Ah, yes ! " she said, indifferently, and laughing,
" A wooden stick I have, with leather cover'd,
And called a Husband !   Still, wood is but wood !"
And here she broke to hollow, empty laughter, &c.

We know few poems more powerfully affecting the imagination, by more terribly simple means, than this piece of bitter psychology.

Paris another poet, who was to France what Heine was to Germany, and perhaps something more. In verses of the most delicate fragrance he had chronicled the lives and aspirations, the ennui and despair, of the inhabitants of the most cultured and debased city under the sun. He had exhausted life too early, like most Frenchmen. His fellow-beings had listened with him, in the theatre, to Malibran, and sighingly exclaimed in his words that, in this world,

> Rien n'est bon que d'aimer, n'est vrai que de souffrir !

They had listened delightedly to the talk of his two seedy dilettantes, who exchange notes together inside the cabaret, and finally disappear in a fashion worthy of Montague Tigg in his adversity :

DUPONT.
Les liqueurs me font mal. Je n'aime que la bière.
Qu'as-tu sur toi ?

DURAND.
Trois sous.

DUPONT.
Entrons au cabaret.

DURAND.
Après vous !

DUPONT.
Après vous !

DURAND.
Après vous, s'il vous plaît ![1]

[1] *Poesies nouvelles*, p. 116.

They have beaten time to his delicious song of " Mimi
Pinson : "

Mimi Pinson est une blonde,
Une blonde que l'on connaît ;
Elle n'a qu'une robe au monde,
Landerirette !
Et qu'un bonnet !

They had seen him, as his own Rolla, enter the Rue des
Moulins, where his little mistress will greet him with a
kiss.   Poor little thing! her body is bought and sold ; and
yet, see! she is lying in sweet and innocent sleep :

Est-ce sur de la neige, ou sur une statue,
 Que cette lampe d'or, dans l'ombre suspendue,
Fait onduler l'azur de ce rideau tremblant ?
Non, la neige est plus pâle, et le marbre est moins blanc,
C'est un enfant qui dort.—Sur ses lèvres ouvertes
Voltige par instants un faible et doux soupir,
Un soupir plus léger que ceux des algues vertes
Quand, le soir, sur les mers voltige le zéphyr,
Et que, sentant fléchir ses ailes embaumées
Sous les baisers ardents de ses fleurs bien-aimées,
Il boit sur ses bras nus les perles des roseaux.
C'est un enfant qui dort sous ces épais rideaux,
Un enfant de quinze ans,—presque une jeune femme.
Rien n'est encor formé dans cet être charmant.
Le petit cherubim qui veille sur ton âme
Doute s'il est son frère ou s'il est son amant.
Ses longs cheveux épars la couvrent tout entière.
La croix de son collierre pose dans sa main,
Comme pour témoigner qu'elle a fait sa prière,
Et qu'elle va la faire en s'éveillant demain.
Elle dort, regardez :—quel front noble et candide !
Partout, comme un lait pur sur une onde limpide,
Le ciel sur la beauté répandit la pudeur.

Elle dort toute nue et la main sur son cœur.
N'est-ce pas que la nuit la rende encor plus belle ?
Que ces molles clartés palpitent autour d'elle,
Comme si, malgré lui, le sombre Esprit du soir
Sentait sur ce beau corps frémir son manteau noir?

This poet was Alfred de Musset, and those who loved his strange voice, issuing from the lupanar, soon found it fade away. He died in the height of life and power. Whenever we think of him, we think of his own story imitated from Boccaccio.[1] Like Pascal in that story, he was revelling in all the delights of sensual love when, from the flowery couch where he sat with his mistress, he unaware plucked a flower, and held it between his lips as he talked; and alas ! the poisonous belladonna crept into his veins, and he fell a corpse, with the words of love on his poor trembling lips.

[1] Simone.

HUGO IN 1872.

ANY a long year has now elapsed since the advent of the Romantic School filled the aged Goethe with horror, causing him to predict for modern Art a chaotic career and a miserable termination; and gray now are the beards of the students who flocked in cloaks and slouch hats to applaud the first performance of "Hernani" at the national theatre. Since those merry days a new generation has arisen, and more than one mighty land-mark has been swept away. Goethe is dead; so are dozens of minor kings—not to speak of Louis Philippe.

The sin of December has been committed and expiated; the man of Sedan has been arraigned before the bar of the world, and received as sentence the contempt and execration of all humanity; and meantime, the exile of Guernsey, after a period of fretful probation, has gone back to the bosom of his beloved France. Political changes have been fast and furious. Not less fast and furious have been the literary revolutions. The poor bewildered spectator, be his proclivities political or literary, has been hurried along so rapidly that he has scarcely had time to get breath.   There lies France, a mighty Ruin.   Beyond rises Deutschthumm, a portentous Shadow, at which the veteran of Weimar would have shivered.   Here comes Victor Hugo, with his new poem.[1] And Chaos, such as Goethe predicted, is every way fulfilled !

How great we hold Victor Hugo to be in reference to his own time we need not say ; veritably, perhaps, there is no nobler name on the whole roll of contemporary creators ; but we surely express a very natural and a very common sentiment when we say that every fresh approach of this prodigy is bewildering to the intellect.   We have had so frequently during the last generation the spectacle of reckless trading in high departments—in politics more particularly ; we have beheld so constantly the collapse of governmental windbags and social balloons of the Haus-mann sort ; we have stood by helpless so often while the mad Masters of the world played their wild and fantastic tricks before high heaven, and moved sardonically from one bloody baptism to another ; we have seen so much evil come of empty words and vain professions, and moral bunkum generally—that we may be pardoned, perhaps, for regarding with a certain alarm that sort of *literature* which, with all its wonderful genius, may fairly be described as reckless also—reckless and blind to all artistic consequences.

[1] " L'Année Terrible."

"Worts ! worts ! worts !" said Sir Hugh Evans ; and here, in all the latest efflorescence of what was once the Romantic, and may now fairly be called the Chaotic, School, we have Words innumerable—brilliant and musical, doubtless, but wild and aimless ; every sentence with a cracker in its tail, till we get utterly indifferent to crackers ; image piled on image, epithet on epithet, phrase choking phrase ; here a catherine-wheel of ecstasy, there a rocket of fierce appeal ; a blaze of colour everywhere, all the hues of the prism (except the perfect product of all, which is pure white light) ; the whole forming a dazzling, hissing, spluttering Firework of human speech. " How very fine !" we exclaim ; " there's a rocket for you ! look at these raining silver lights ! Ah, this is something like an exhibition !" But after it is all over, and the sceptical ones point out to us the wretched darkened canvas framework where the last sparks are lingering and the last smuts falling, we are angry at our own enthusiasm, and feel like men who have been befooled. After all, we reflect, the place is only Cremorne ; the object merely the amusement of a crowd of gaping pleasure-seekers who pay so much a head. It has been a vulgar entertainment at the best ; and we try to forget it, looking up, as the smoke clears, at the silent stars. This mood, however, is still more unfair than the other. Truly enough, we have been present at fireworks, but on a scale of tremendous genius. A great master has been condescending for our amusement, and has actually worked wonders with his materials.

Nor is this all.   When a poet like Victor Hugo, yield
ing to the daimonic influence of his own spirit, produces
for us in public all the wild resources of his fearless art,
he cannot fail to awaken in us forces which slumber at
the touch of any other living man.   We may resent the
emotion as a weakness, but the emotion exists : we are
lifted by it as on the wings of the wind, and driven
"darkly fearfully afar."   The scenery of the spectacle
may be tawdry, but it is outlined with a mighty hand ;
the lights may be only wretched rushlights, but what a
strange lurid gleam they shed over the rude and gigantic
towers and battlements of the scene !   It is magnificent,
although it is not nature ; it is full of infinite suggestion,
though it is not art.   The power is unbounded ; the only
question that remains being, "Is the power squandered ?
Much, doubtless, is squandered ; and it is this persistent
waste which, corresponding as it does to French waste
generally, fills one with suspicion and alarm.   Reckless
writing has its delights, like reckless trading, like reckless
fighting and swaggering ; but will it not lead to the same
end as these others ?   Concentrated and reserved for
specific efforts, instead of being frivolously spent in every
direction, the same genius who limned Jean Valjean and
Fantine might yet rise to his due place and glory as the
Æschylus of his generation.

After all, it is doubtful if Æschylus, doomed to live in
these latter days, would have kept his head.   Even as
it was, he "let go" tremendously, and was far, very far,
from being a steady-brained bard ; his vision repeatedly

overmastering him, and his utterance becoming thick and confused with portentous weight of matter. His lot was easy, however, compared with that of the modern who has aspired to perform Æschylean functions in the nineteenth century, by chronicling in tremendous poetic cipher the ravings and sufferings of *our* Titan ; and it is, therefore an open question whether Victor Hugo is not a greater than even Æschylus, in so far as he has grappled with, and to some extent triumphed over, difficulties to all intents and purposes insuperable.

We, for our part, find more to move our homage in Jean Valjean than in the Prometheus. We hold that one figure, rudely as it is drawn, to be in some respects the very noblest conception of this generation ; and we would look on at fireworks for ever, if once or twice such a face as Jean's shone out with its heaven-like promise. Gilliatt, too, is noble in the Promethean direction ;—and so is Quasimodo. Indeed, we know not where to look, out of Æschylus, for figures conceived on the same scale, so typical, so colossal ; looming upon us from a stage of mighty amplitude, with a grand Greek background of mountain and sky. They have the Greek freedom and the Greek limitations. Jean Valjean, just as surely as Prometheus, wears the mask, and is elevated on the cothurnus ; whence at once his extraordinary stature and his one fixed expression of changeless and monotonous pain.

Would one choose rather the mobile human face and the free motion of men on a small stage, he must enter

M

the Globe Theatre and hear the wonderful acting of the
English players; but with Victor Hugo, as with the
father of Athenian drama, we are limited to one mood
and wearied by one high-pitched chant. Even if this
were perfectly done, it would grow wearisome; but being
far from perfectly done, being at once wearisome and
chaotic, it depresses as often as it elevates, and makes us
long for a breezier music and a fresher, kindlier movement of face and limb. Nor can Victor Hugo's greatest
admirers deny the fact that he deliberately overclouds his
conceptions with verbiage, and blurs what was originally
a noble outline by subsequent attempts at elaboration.
Our first glimpse of his figures moves us most; our
further examination of them is fraught with pain; and
not till we have closed our eyes to contemplate the impression left upon the mind, do we again feel how greatly
the figures were originally conceived. This writer
triumphs invariably by sheer force of primary pictorial
vision; triumphs generally in defiance of his own in-
capacity to *paint* exquisitely. Reckless (as we have expressed it) of all literary consequences, he produces works
which are at once miracles of imagination and marvels of
bad taste. Directly we have got the outline of his
picture, all further study of it is unsatisfactory: we must
fill in the tints for ourselves. Compare the "Prometheus" of Æschylus with "Les Misérables" of Victor
Hugo and perceive the difference between power concentrated and power recklessly drivelled away. The
whole episode of Jean Valjean could have been com-

pressed into a tragedy, and, given in such quintessence, would have been an unmixed pleasure to all time. As it is, we doubt whether posterity will do justice to a production so shapeless, so interminable; and this is the more irritating, as it contains in dilution more colossal imagery than anything we have had in Europe since the " Divine Comedy."

Viewed simply for what he is, Hugo is very great; but viewed for what he might have been he is persistently disappointing. With every fresh year of his life he has grown two-fold—in power of conception and power of windiness; until we now recognise in him a god of the elements indeed, but one with more affinity to Boreas than to Apollo. It was doubtless in an unlucky moment that he first freed himself from rhythmic fetters. His was just the sort of genius that needed to be bound and drilled. Let loose on the mighty fields of prose, he knows no limit to his wanderings, and he follows his jerky fancies from one sentence to another, like a snipe-shooter floundering, popping, and perspiring in an Irish marsh. He will go epigram-hunting through a whole series of chapters, at the most critical point of his narrative. A single word (take " Waterloo " in a certain part of " Les Misérables ") is Will-o'-the-wisp enough to keep him rushing through the dark till the reader faints for very weariness. If Goethe was, as Novalis described him to be, the Evangelist of Economy, Victor Hugo is assuredly the Evangelist of Waste. A prodigy of less supreme energy would have collapsed long ago under such tremendous exertions ; but he, just when we expect to see him sink altogether, springs from the solid earth with fresh vigour. Genius, he has told us in "William Shakespeare," is not circumscribed.   Exaggeration, moreover, is the glory of genius.   "Cela c'est l'Inconnu !   Cela c'est l'Infini !   Si Corneille avait cela, il serait l'égal d'Eschyle.   Si Milton avait cela, il serait l'égal d'Homère.   Si Molière avait cela, il serait l'égal de Shakspeare."

We have here, in a nutshell, the Apotheosis of literary Waste ; but it would not be difficult to show that none of Hugo's typical sublimities—Homer, Job, Isaiah, Ezekiel, Juvenal, Percival, St. John, St. Paul, Tacitus, Dante, Rabelais, Cervantes, Shakespeare—exhausted their energies in the fashion peculiar to the author of "L'Homme. qui Rit."   The truth is, Hugo attempts to elevate into a system the recklessness which, in his own case, is sheer matter of temperament.   His mind is for ever pitched in too high a tone of excitement : febrile symptoms, with him, characterise the normal intellectual condition.   He is always high-strung, with or without provocation, evincing that excited French power of superficial passion, whether his themes be the wrongs of poor humanity or the loss of a hat-box at a railway station.   A cynical foreigner would accuse him of attitudinising.   He spouts and strides. Not content with being recognised as Æschylus, he at times affects the graces of La Fontaine.   His humour, nevertheless, is very grim.   Nor is his satire much better. His true mood is Ercles' mood—your true nineteenth century heroic.

PROSE AND VERSE:

A STRAY NOTE.

THE "music of the future is at last slowly approaching its apotheosis ; since "Lohengrin" has signally triumphed in Italy, and the South is opening its ears to the subtle secrets of the Teutonic Muse. The outcome of Wagner's consummate art is a war against mere melody and tintinabulation, such as have for many long years delighted the ears of both gods and groundlings. Is it too bold, then, to anticipate for future "Poetry" some such similar triumph ? Freed from the fetters of pedantry on the one hand, and escaping the contagion of mere jingle on the other, may not Poetry yet arise to an intellectual dignity parallel to the dignity of the highest music and philosophy ? It may seem at a first glance over sanguine to hope so much, at the very period when countless Peter Pipers of Verse have overrun literature so thoroughly, robbing poetry of all its cunning, and "picking their pecks of pepper" to the delight of a literary Music Hall; but, in good truth, when disease has come to a crisis so enormous, we have good reason to hope for amendment.

A surfeit of breakdowns and nigger melodies, or of Offenbach and Hervé, or of "Lays" and "Rondels," is certain to lead to a reaction all in good time. A vulgar taste, of course, will always cling to vulgarity, preferring in all honesty the melody of Gounod to the symphony of Beethoven, and the tricksy shallow verse of a piece like Poe's 'Bells' to the subtly interwoven harmony of a poem like Matthew Arnold's "Strayed Reveller." True art, however, must triumph in the end. Sooner or later, when the Wagner of poetry arises, he will find the world ready to understand him; and we shall witness some such effect as Coleridge predicted—a crowd, previously familiar with Verse only, vibrating in wonder and delight to the charm of *oratio soluta*, or loosened speech.

Already, in a few words, we have sketched out a subject for some future æsthetic philosopher or philosophic historian. A sketch of the past history of poetry, in England alone, would be sufficiently startling; and surely a most tremendous indictment might be drawn thence against Rhyme. Glance back over the works of British bards, from Chaucer downwards; study the *delitiæ Poetarum Anglicorum.* What delightful scraps of melody! what glorious bursts of song! Here is Chaucer, wearing indeed with perfect grace his metrical dress; for it sits well upon him, and becomes his hoar antiquity, and we would not for the world see him clad in the freedom of prose.   Here is Spenser; and Verse becomes *him* well, fitly modulating the faëry tale he has to tell. Here are Gower, Lydgate, Dunbar, Surrey, Gascoigne, Daniel, Drayton, and many others; each full of dainty devices; none strong enough to stand without a rhyme-prop on each side of him.   Of all sorts of poetry, except the very best, these gentlemen give us samples; and their works are delightful reading.   As mere metrists, cunning masters of the trick of verse, Gascoigne and Dunbar are acknowledged masters.   Take the following verses from the "Dance of the Seven Deadly Sins:"

> Then Ire came in with sturt and strife,
> His hand was aye upon his knife,
> > He brandeist like a beir;
> Boasters, braggarts, and bargainers,
> After him passit in pairs,
> > All boden in feir of weir . . .
> Next in the dance followed **Envy**,
> Fill'd full of feid and felony,
> > Hid malice and despite.
> For privy hatred that traitor trembled,
> Him follow'd many freik dissembled,
> > With fenyit wordis white;
> And flatterers unto men's faces,
> And back-biters in secret places,
> > To lie that had delight,
> With rowmaris of false leasings;
> Alas that courts of noble kings
> > Of them can ne'er be quite !

This, allowing for the lapse of years, still reads like "Peter Piper" at his best; easy, alliterative, pleasant, if neither deep nor cunning.   For this sort of thing, and for many higher sorts of things, Rhyme was admirably adapted, and is still admirably adapted. When, however, a larger music and a more loosened speech was wanted, Rhyme went overboard directly.

On the stage even, Rhyme did very well, as long as the matter was in the *Ralph Royster Doyster* vein; but a larger soul begot a larger form, and the blank verse of Gorboduc was an experiment in the direction of loosened speech. How free this speech became, how by turns loose and noble, how subtle and flexible it grew, in the hands of Shakespeare and the Elizabethans, all men know; and rare must have been the delight of listeners whose ears had been satiated so long with mere alliteration and jingle. The language of Shakespeare, indeed, must be accepted as the nearest existing approach to the highest and freest poetical language. Here and there rhymed dialogue was used, when the theme was rhythmic and not too profound; as in the pretty love scenes of *A Midsummer Night's Dream* and the bantering, punning chat of *Love's Labour's Lost.* True song sparkled up in its place like a fountain. But the level dialogue for the most part was loosened speech. Observe the following speech of Prospero, usually printed in lines each beginning with a capital :—

This King of Naples, being an enemy to me inveterate, hearkens my brother's suit; which was,—that he, in lieu of the premises, of homage and I know not how much tribute, should presently extirpate me and mine out of the dukedom, and confer fair Milan, with all the honours, on my brother. Whereon, a treacherous army levied, one midnight fated to the purpose did Antonio open the gates of Milan ; and, in the dead of darkness, the ministers for the purpose hurried thence *me* and thy crying self !

Tempest, act i., scene 2.

Any poet since Shakespeare would doubtless have modulated this speech more *exquisitely*, laying special stress on the five accented syllables of each line.   Shakespeare, however, was too true a musician.   He knew when to use careless dialogue like the above, and when to break in with subtle modulation; and he knew, moreover, how the loose prose of the one threw out the music of the other.   He knew well how to inflate his lines with the measured oratory of an offended king :

> The hope and expectation of thy time
> Is ruin'd ; and the soul of every man
> Prophetically doth forethink thy fall.
> Had *I* so lavish of my presence been,
> So common-hackney'd in the eyes of men,
> So stale and cheap to vulgar company ;
> Opinion, that did help me to the crown,
> Had still kept loyal to possession ;
> And left me in reputeless banishment,
> A fellow of no mark, nor likelihood.
> By being seldom seen, I could not stir,
> But, like a comet, I was wonder'd at ;
> That men would tell their children, *This is he !*
> Others would say, *Where? which is Bollingbroke?* &c.

Henry IV., Part I., act iii., scene 2.

In the hands of our great Master, indeed, blank verse becomes almost exhaustless in its powers of expression ; but nevertheless, prose is held in reserve, not merely as the fitting colloquial form of the "humorous" scenes, but as the appropriate loosened utterance of strong emotion. The very highest matter of all, indeed, is sometimes delivered in prose, as its most appropriate medium. Take the wonderful set of prose dialogues in the second act of "Hamlet," and notably that exquisitely musical speech of the Prince, beginning, "I have of late, but wherefore I know not, lost all my mirth." Turn, also, to Act V. of the same play, where the "mad matter" between Hamlet and the Gravediggers, so full of solemn significance and sound, is prose once more. The noble tragedy of "Lear," again, owes much of its weird power to the frequent use of broken speech. And is the following any the less powerful or passionate because it goes to its own music, instead of following any prescribed form?—

1 am a Jew. Hath not a Jew eyes? hath not a Jew hands, organs, dimensions, senses, affections, passions? fed with the same food, hurt with the same weapons, subject to the same diseases, healed by the same means, warmed and cooled by the same winter and summer, as a Christian is? If you prick us, do we not bleed? If you tickle us, do we not laugh? If you poison us, do we not die? and if you wrong us, shall we not revenge?

Merchant of Venice, act iii., scene 1.

It would be tedious to prolong illustrations from an author with whom everybody is supposed to be familiar. Enough to say that the careful student of Shakespeare will find his most common magic to lie in the frequent use, secret or open, of the *oratio soluta.* And what holds of him, holds in more or less measure of his contemporaries—of Jonson, Marston, Webster, Massinger, Beaumont and Fletcher, Greene, Peele, and the rest; just as it holds of the immediate predecessor of Shakespeare, whose "mighty line" led the way for the full Elizabethan choir of voices. Then, as now, society had been surfeited with tedious jingle; and only waited for genius to set it free. It is difficult to say in what respect the following scene differs from first-class prose; although we have occasionally an orthodox blank verse line, the bulk of the passage is free and unencumbered; yet its weird imaginative melody could scarcely be surpassed.

> *Duch.* Is he mad, too?
> *Servant.* Pray question him; I'll leave you.
> *Bos.* I am come to make thy tomb.
> *Duch.* Ha! my tomb?
> Thou speak'st as if I lay upon my death-bed
> Gasping for breath. Dost thou perceive me such?
> *Bos.* Yes.
> *Duch.* Who am I? am not I thy duchess?
> *Bos.* That makes thy sleep so broken:
> Glories, like glow-worms, afar off shine bright,
> But looked to near have neither heat nor light.
> *Duch.* Thou art very plain.
> *Bos.* My trade is to flatter the dead, not the living,
> I am a tomb-maker.
> *Duch.* And thou hast come to make my tomb?
> *Bos.* Yes!
> *Duch.* Let me be a little merry:
> Of what stuff wilt thou make it?
> *Bos.* Nay, resolve me first: of what fashion?
> *Duch.* Why do we grow phantastical on our death-bed?
> Do we affect fashion in the grave?
> *Bos.* Most ambitiously. Princes' images on the tombs
> Do not lie as they were wont, seeming to pray
> Up to heaven; but with their hands under their cheeks,
> As if they died of the toothache! They are not carved

> With their eyes fixed upon the stars ; but as
> Their minds were wholly bent upon the world,
> The self-same way they seem to turn their faces.
>   *Duch.* Let me know fully, therefore, the effect
> Of this thy dismal preparation !—
> This talk fit for a charnel.
>   *Bos.* Now I shall (*a coffin, cords, and a bell*).
> Here is a present from your princely brothers ;
> And may it arrive welcome, for it brings
> Last benefit, last sorrow.[1]

He who will carefully examine the works of our great dramatists, will find everywhere an equal freedom ; rhythm depending on the emotion of the situation and the quality of the speakers, rather than on any fixed laws of verse.

If we turn, on the other hand, to dramatists and poets of less genius—if we open the works of Waller, Cowley, Marvell, Dryden, and even of Milton, we shall find much exquisite music, but little perhaps of that wondrous cunning familiar to us in Shakespeare and the greatest of his contemporaries. Shallow matter, as in Waller ; ingenious learned matter, as in Cowley ; dainty matter, as in Andrew Marvell ; artificial matter, as in Dryden ; and puritan matter, as in Milton, were all admirably fitted for rhymed or some other formal sort of Verse. Rhyme, indeed, may be said, while hampering the strong, to

---

[1] "The Duchess of Malfy," act iv. sc. 2. The above extract is much condensed. The reader who would fully feel the force of our allusion, cannot do better than study Webster's great tragedy as a whole. It utterly discards all metrical rules, and abounds in wonderful music.

strengthen and fortify the weak. But, of the men we have just named, the only genius approaching the first class was Milton; and so no language can be too great to celebrate the praises of *his* singing.

Passage after passage, however, might be cited from his great work, where, like Molière's "Bourgeois Gentil-homme," he talks prose without knowing it; and, to our thinking, his sublimest feats of pure music are to be found in that drama[1] where he permits himself, in the ancient manner, the free use of loosened cadence. Milton, however, great as he is, is a great formalist, sitting "stately at the harpsichord." A genius of equal earnestness, and of almost equal strength—we mean Jeremy Taylor—wrote entirely in prose; and it has been well observed by a good critic that "in any one of his prose folios there is more fine fancy and original imagery —more brilliant conceptions and glowing expressions— more new figures and new applications of old figures— more, in short, of the body and soul of poetry, than in all the odes and epics that have since been produced in Europe." Nor should we have omitted to mention, in glancing at the Elizabethan drama, that the prose of Bacon is as poetical, as lofty, and in a certain sense as musical, as the more formal "poetry" of the best of his contemporaries.

Very true, exclaims the reader, but what *are* we driving at? Would we condemn verse altogether as a form of speech, and abolish rhyme from literature for ever?

[1] "Samson Agonistes."

Certainly not! We would merely suggest the *dangers* of Verse, and the *limitations* of Rhyme, and briefly show how the highest Poetry of all answers to no fixed scholastic rules, but embraces, or ought to embrace, all the resources both of Verse generally and of what is usually, for want of a better name, entitled Prose. On this, as on many points, tradition confuses us. The word "Poet" means something more than a singer of songs or weaver of rhymes. What are we to say to a literary classification which calls "Absalom and Achitophel" a poem, and denies the title to "The Pilgrim's Progress;" which includes "Cato" and the "Rape of the Lock" under the poetical head, and excludes Sidney's "Arcadia" and the "Vicar of Wakefield;" which extends to Cowper, Chatterton, Gray, Keats, and Campbell the laurel it indignantly denies to Swedenborg, Addison (who created Sir Roger de Coverley!), Burke, Dickens, and Richter; and which has for so long delayed the placing of Walter Scott's novels in their due niche just below the plays of Shakespeare?

Instead of being the *spontaneous* speech of inspired men in musical moods, Verse has become a "form of literature," binding so-called "poets" as strictly as bonds of brass and iron; and the effort of most of our strong men has been to free their limbs as much as possible, by working in the most flexible chain of all, that of *blank* verse. If the reader will take the trouble to compare the early verse of Tennyson with his later works, wherein he has found it necessary to shake his soul free of its overmodulated formalism, he will understand what we mean. If, just after a perusal of even "Guinevere" and "Lucretius," he will read Whitman's "Centenarian's Story" or Coleridge's "Wandering of Cain," his feeling of the "wonderfulness of prose" will be much strengthened. That feeling may thereupon be deepened to conviction by taking up and reading any modern poet immediately before a perusal of the authorised English version of the "Book of Job," "Ecclesiastes," or the wonderful "Psalms of David."

It is really strange that Wordsworth just hit the truth, in the masterly preface to his "Lyrical Ballads." "It may be safely affirmed," he says, "that there neither is, nor can be, any *essential* difference between the language of prose and metrical composition. . . . Much confusion has been introduced into criticism by this contradistinction of Poetry and Prose, instead of the more philosophical one of Poetry and Matter of Fact, or Science. The only strict antithesis to Prose is Metre ; nor is *this* in truth a strict antithesis, because lines and passages of metre so naturally occur in writing prose that it would be scarcely possible to avoid them, even were it desirable." Theoretically in the right, this great poet was often practically in the wrong ; using rhythmic speech habitually for non-rhythmic moods, and leaving us no example of glorious loosened speech, combining all the effects of pure diction and of metre. After generations of "Pope"-ridden poets, the Wordsworthian language was "loosened" indeed ; but it sounds now sufficiently formal and pedantic. His only contemporaries of equal greatness—we mean of course Scott and Byron—were sufficiently encumbered by verse. Scott soon threw off his fetters, and rose to the feet of Shakespeare. Byron never had the courage to abandon them altogether; but he played fine pranks with them in "Don Juan," and, had he lived, would have pitched them over entirely. On the other hand, the fine genius of Shelley and the wan genius of Keats worked with perfect freedom in the form of verse : first, because they neither of them possessed much humour or human unction ; second, because their subjects were vague, unsubstantial, and often (as in the "Cenci") grossly morbid ; and third, because they were both of them overshadowed by false models, involving a very retrograde criterion of poetic beauty. Writers of the third or perhaps of the fourth rank, they occupy their places, masters of metric beauty, often deep and subtle, never very light or strong. Once more, what shall we say to a literary classification which grants Shelley the name of "poet" and denies it to Jean Paul ; and which (since poetry is admittedly the highest literary form of all, and worthy of the highest honour) sets a falsetto singer like John Keats high over the head of a consummate artist like George Sand ?

We have had it retorted, by those who disagreed with Wordsworth's theory, that its *reductio ad absurdum* was to be found in Wordsworth's own "Excursion ;" that "poem" being full of the most veritable prose that was ever penned by man. Very good. Take a passage :—

Ah, gentle sir! slight, if you will, the *means*, but spare to slight the *end*, of those who did, by system, rank as the prime object of a wise man's aim—security from shock of accident, release from fear; and cherished peaceful days for their own sakes, as mutual life's chief good and only reasonable felicity. What motive drew, what impulse, I would ask through a long course of later ages, drove the hermit to his cell in forest wide; or what detained him, till his closing eyes took their last farewell of the sun and stars, fast an‐chored in the desert?—*Excursion,* Book III.

This is not only prose, but indifferent prose; poor, collo‐quial, ununctional; and no amount of modulation could make it poetry. Contrast with it another passage, of great and familiar beauty :—

I have seen a curious child, who dwelt upon a tract of inland ground, applying to his ear the convolutions of a smooth-lipped shell, to which, in silence hushed, his very soul listened intently. His countenance soon brightened with joy; for from within were heard murmurings, whereby the monitor expressed mysterious union with its native sea. Even such a shell the universe itself is to the ear of Faith. And there are times, I doubt not, when to you it doth impart authentic tidings of invisible things, of ebb and flow, and ever-during power, and central peace subsisting at the heart of endless agitation.—*Excursion,* Book IV.

Prose again, but how magnificent! poetical imagery worthy of Jeremy Taylor; but losing nothing by being printed naturally. The conclusion of the whole matter, so far as it affects the " Excursion," is that the work, while essentially fine in substance, suffers from an unnatural form. Read as it stands, it is rather prosy poetry. Written properly, it would have been admitted universally as a surpassing poem in prose; although it contains a great deal which, whither printed as prose or verse, would be unanimously accepted as commonplace and unpoetic.

Our store of acknowledged poetry is very precious; but it might be easily doubled, were we suffered to select from our prose writers—from Plato, from Boccaccio, from Pascal, from Rousseau, from Jean Paul, from Novalis, from George Sand, from Charles Dickens, from Nathaniel Hawthorne—the magnificent nuggets of pure poetic ore in which these writers abound. Read Boccaccio's story of Isabella and the Pot of Basil, or Dickens' description of a sea-storm in " David Copperfield," or Hawthorne's picture of Phœbe Pyncheon's bed-chamber, and confess that, if these things be not poetry, poetry was never written. If you still doubt that the rhythmic form is essential to the highest poetic matter, read that wondrous dream of the World without a Father at the end of Jean Paul's "Siebenkäs," and then peruse Heine's description of the fading away of the Hellenic gods before the thorn-crowned coming of Christ. What these prose frag-ments lose in neatness of form, they gain in mystery and glamour.

Illustrations so crowd upon us as we write, that they threaten to swell this little paper out of all moderate limits. We must conclude; and what shall be our con-clusion? This. A truly good Poet is not he who wearies us with eternally jingling numbers; is not Pope, is not Poe, is not even Keats. It is he who is master of all speech, and uses all speech fitly; able, like Shake-speare, to chop the prosiest of prose with Polonius and the Clowns, as well as to sing the sweetest of songs with Ariel and the outlaws "under the greenwood tree." It is not Hawthorne, because his exquisite speech never once *rose* to pure song; it is Dickens, because (as could be easily shown, had we space) he was a great master of melody as well as a great workaday humorist. It is not Thackeray, because he never reached that subtle modulation which comes of imaginative creation ; and it is not Shelley, because he was essentially a *singer*, and many of the profoundest and delightfullest things absolutely *refuse* to be sung. It is Shakespeare *par excellence*, and it is Goethe *par hasard*. Historically speaking, however, it may be observed that the greatest Poets have not been those men who have used Verse habitually and necessarily ; and if we glance over the names of living men of genius, we shall perhaps not count those most poetic who call their productions openly "poems." Meanwhile, we wait on for the Miracle-worker who never comes—*the* Poet. We fail as yet to catch the tones of his voice; but we have no hesitation in deciding that his first proof of ministry will be dissatisfaction with the limitations of Verse as at present written.

NATURE SKETCHES.

THE HIGHLAND SEASONS.

AS the year passes there is always something new to attract one who loves Nature. When the winds of March have blown themselves faint, and the April heaven has ceased weeping, there comes a rich sunny day, and all at once the cuckoo is heard telling his name to all the hills. Never was such a place for cuckoos in the world. The cry comes from every tuft of wood, from every hillside, from every projecting crag. The bird himself, so far from courting retirement, flutters across your path at every step, attended invariably by half a dozen excited small birds; alighting a few yards off, crouches down for a moment between his slate-coloured wings; and finally, rising again, crosses your path with his sovereign cry—

"O blithe new-comer, I have heard,
I hear thee, and rejoice!"

Then, as if at a given signal, the trout leaps a foot into

the air from the glassy loch, the buds of the water-lily float to the surface, the lambs bleat from the green and heathery slopes; the rooks caw from the distant rookery; the cock grouse screams from the distant hill-top; and the blackthorn begins to blossom over the nut-brown pools of the burn. Pleasant days follow, days of high white clouds and fresh winds whose wings are full of warm dew. Wherever you wander over the hills, you see the lambs leaping, and again and again it is your lot to rescue a poor little one from the deep pool, or steep ditch, which he has vainly sought to leap in following his mother. If you are a sportsman, you rejoice, for there is not a hawk to be seen anywhere, and the weasel and foumart have not yet begun to promenade the mountains. About this time more rain falls, preliminary to a burst of fine summer weather, and innumerable glow-worms light their lamps in the marshes. At last, the golden days come, and all things are busy with their young. Frequently, in the midsummer, there is drought for weeks together. Day after day the sky is cloudless and blue; the mountain lake sinks lower and lower, till it seems about to dry up entirely; the mountain brooks dwindle to mere silver threads for the water-ousel to fly by, and the young game often die for lack of water; while afar off, with every red vein distinct in the burning light, without a drop of vapour to moisten his scorching crags, stands Ben Cruachan. By this time the hills are assuming their glory:—the mysterious bracken has shot up all in a night, to cover them with a green carpet between the knolls of heather, the lichen is pencilling the crags with most delicate silver, purple, and gold, and in all the valleys there are stretches of light yellow corn and deep green patches of foliage. The corn-crake has come, and his cry fills the valleys. Walking on the edge of the corn-field, you put up the partridges—fourteen cheepers the size of a thrush, and the old pair to lead them. From the edge of the peat-bog the old cock grouse rises, and if you are sharp you may see the young following the old hen through the deep heather close by. The snipe drums in the marsh. The hawk, having brought out his young among the crags of Kerrera, is hovering still as stone over the edge of the hill. Then perchance, just at the end of July, there is a gale from the south, blowing for two days black as Erebus with cloud and rain; then going up into the north-west and blowing for one day with little or no rain ; and dying away at last with a cold puff from the north. All at once, as it were, the sharp sound of firing is echoed from hill to hill ; and on every mountain you see the sportsman climbing, with his dog ranging above and before him, the keeper following, and the gillie lagging far behind. It is the twelfth of August. Thenceforth, for two months at least, there are broiling days, interspersed with storms and showers, and the firing continues more or less from dawn to sunset.

Day after day, as the autumn advances, the tint of the hills is getting deeper and richer, and by October, when the beech leaf yellows and the oak leaf reddens, the dim purples and deep greens of the heather are perfect. Of all seasons in Lorne the late autumn is perhaps the most beautiful. The sea has a deeper hue, the sky a mellower light. There are long days of northerly wind, when every crag looks perfect, wrought in gray and gold and silvered with moss, when the high clouds turn luminous at the edges, when a thin film of hoar-frost gleams over the grass and heather, when the light burns rosy and faint over all the hills, from Morven to Cruachan, for hours before the sun goes down. Out of the ditch at the roadside flaps the mallard, as you pass in the gloaming, and, standing by the side of the small mountain loch, you see the flock of teal rise, wheel thrice, and settle. The hills are desolate, for the sheep are being smeared. There is a feeling of frost in the air, and Ben Cruachan has a crown of snow.

When dead of winter comes, how wondrous look the hills in their white robes! The round red ball of the sun looks through the frosty steam. The far-off firth gleams strange and ghostly, with a sense of mysterious distance. The mountain loch is a sheet of blue, on which you may disport in perfect solitude from morn to night, with the hills white on all sides, save where the broken snow shows the red-rusted leaves of the withered bracken. A deathly stillness and a death-like beauty reign everywhere, and few living things are discernible, save the hare plunging heavily out of her form in the snow, or the rabbit scuttling off in a snowy spray, or the small birds piping disconsolate on the trees and dykes. Then Peter, the tame rook, brings three or four of his wild relations to the back door of the White House, and they stand aloof with their heads cocked on one side, while he explains their position, and suggests that they, being hard-working rooks who never stooped to beg when a living could be got in the fields, well deserve to be assisted. Then comes the thaw. As the sun rises, the sunny sides of the hills are seen marked with great black stains and winding veins, and there is a sound in the air as of many waters. The mountain brook leaps, swollen, over the still clinging ice, the loch rises a foot above its still frozen crust, and a damp steam rises into the air. The wind goes round into the west, great vapours blow over from the Atlantic, and there are violent storms.

LAKES AND WOODS.

WHEREVER one wanders, on hill or in valley, there is something to fascinate and delight. Those moorland lochs, for example! Those deep pure pools of dew distilled from the very heart of the mountains—changing as the season changes—lying blue as steel in the bright clear light, or turning to rich mellow brown in the times of flood. On all of them the water-lily blows, creeping up magically from the under-world, and covering the whole surface with white, green, and gold—its broad and well-oiled leaves floating dry in delicious softness in the summer sun, and its milk-white cups opening wider and wider, while the dragon-fly settles and sucks honey from their golden hearts. How exquisitely the hills are mirrored, the images only a shade darker than the heights above ! Perhaps there is a faint breeze blowing, leaving here and there large flakes of glassy calm, which it refuses to touch for some mysterious reason, and the edges of which—

just where wind and gleam meet—calm the colour of golden fringe. Often in midsummer, however, the loch almost dries up in its bed ; and innumerable flies—veritable gad-flies with stings—make the brink of the water unpleasant, and chase one over the hills. In such weather, there is nothing for it but to make off to the fir-woods, and there to dream away the summer's day, with the bell-shaped flowers around you in one gleaming sheet—

"Blue as a little patch of fallen sky,"

and the primroses fringing the tree-roots with pallid beauty that whitens in the shadow. The wood is delicious ; not too dark and cold, but fresh and scented, with open spaces of green sward and level sunshine. The fir predominates, dark and enduring in its loveliness; but there are dwarf oaks, too, with twisted limbs and thick branches, and the mountain ash is there with its innumerable beads of crimson coral, and the fluttering aspen, and the birch, whose stem is pencilled with threads of frosty silver, and the thorns snowed over with delicate blossoms.

THE MOOR.

HE great glory of Lorne is the open Moor, where the heather blows from one end of the year to the other. There is something sea-like in the moor, with its long free stretch for miles and miles, its great rolling hills, its lovely solitude, broken only by the cry of sheep and the scream of birds. Lakes and water-lilies are to be found far south. There are richer woods in Kent than any in the Highlands. But the moors of the western coast of Scotland stand alone, and the moors of Lorne are finest of all. Nowhere in the world, perhaps, does nature present a scene of greater beauty than that you may behold, with the smell of thyme about your feet, and the mountain bee humming in your ears, from any of the sea-commanding heights of Lorne. Turn which way you will, the glorious moors stretch before you; wave after wave of purple heather, broken only by the white farm with its golden fields, and the mountain loch high up among the hills;

while the arms of the sea steal winding, now visible, now invisible, on every side, and the far-off Firth, with its gleaming sail, stretches from the white lighthouse of Lismore far south to Isla and its purple caves. Then the clouds! White and high, they drift overhead,

"Slow traversing the blue ethereal field,"

and you can watch their shadows moving on the moor for miles and miles, just as if it were the sea! Nor is the scene barren of such little touches as make English landscape sweet. There are bees humming everywhere, and skylarks singing, and the blackbird whistling wherever there is a bush, and the swift wren darting in and out of the stone dykes, like a swift-winged insect. There are flowers too—little unobtrusive things, flowers of the heath—primroses, tormentil, bog-asphodel, and many others. But nothing is purchased at the expense of freedom. All is fresh and free as the sea. After familiarity with the moor you turn from the macadamised road with disgust, and will not even visit the woods till the fear of a sun-stroke compels you. Did we compare the moor to the sea? Yes; but you yourself are like an inhabitant thereof; not a mere sailor on the surface, but a real haunter of the deep. What hours of indolence in the deep heather, so long as the golden weather lasts!

THE SHIELINGS.

WHEREVER you wander over the moors, you will see piteous little glimpses of former cultivation—the furrow marks which have existed for generations. Wherever there is a bit of likely ground on the hillside, be sure that it has been ploughed, or rather dug with the spade. Standing on any one of the great heights, you see on every side of you the green slopes marked with the old ridges; and you remember that Lorne in former days was a thickly populated district. We have heard it stated, and even by so high an authority as the Duke of Argyll, that these marks do not necessarily indicate a higher degree of prosperity than exists in the same district at present. We are not so sure of that. Nor may the husbandry have been so rude; since the spade must have gone deep to leave its traces so long; and busy hands can do much even to supply the want of irrigation. Attached to some of the existing crofts, which work entirely by hand labour and till the most unlikely ground, we have seen some of the best bits of crop in the district. Be that as it may, the fact remains that once upon a time these hills of heather swarmed with crofts, and were covered with little fields of grain.

Remote, too, among the hills, in the most lonely situations, distant by long stretches of bog and moorland from any habitation, you will find here and there, if you wander so far, a Ruin in the midst of green slopes and heathery bournes. This is the ruin of the old Shieling, which in former days so resounded with mirth and song.

> " O sad is the shieling,
> Gone are its joys ! "

as Robb Dunn sings in the Gaelic. Hither, ere sheep-farming was invented, came the household of the peasant in the summer time, with sheep and cattle ; and here, while the men returned to look after matters at home, the women and young people abode for weeks, tending the young lambs and kids, watching the milch cow, and making butter and cheese that were rich with the succulent juices of the surrounding herbage. Then the milk-pan foamed, the distaff went, the children leapt for joy with the lambs ; and in the evening the girls tried charms, and learned love-songs, and listened to the tales of their elders, with dreamy eyes. Better still, there was real love-making to be had ; for some of the men remained, generally unmarried ones, and others came and went ; and somehow in those long summer nights, it was pleasant to sit out in the flood of moonlight, and whisper, and perhaps kiss, while the lambs bleated from the pens, and the silent hills slept shadowy in the mystic light. No wonder that Gaelic literature abounds in "shieling songs," and that most of these are ditties of love! The shieling was rudely built, as a mere temporary residence, but it was snug enough when the peat bog was handy. In the wilds of the Long Island it is still used in the old manner, and the Wanderer has many a time crept into it for shelter when shooting wild-fowl. The Norwegian saeter is precisely the same as the Scottish shieling, and still, as every traveller knows, flourishes in all its glory.

We are no melancholy mourner of the past, rather a sanguine believer in progress and the future; but alas! whenever we look on the lonely ruins among the hills, we feel inclined to sing a Dirge. The "Big Bed in the Wilderness," as the Gaelic bard named the saeter and pasture, is empty now, empty and silent, and the children that shouted in it are buried in all quarters of the earth; ay—and many had reason to curse the cruelty of man ere they died, for they were driven forth across the waters from all that they loved. Some lived on, to see the change darker and darker, and then were carried on handyspokes, in the old Scottish fashion, to the grave. Many a long summer day could we spend in meditation over the places where they sleep.

DUNOLLIE CASTLE.

THE ruins of Dunollie Castle stand on the very point of the promontory to the north-west of Oban, and form one of the finest foregrounds possible for all the scenery of the Firth. There is no old castle in Scotland quite so beautifully situated. On days of glassy calm, every feature of it is mirrored in the sea, with browns and grays that ravish the artistic eye. There is not too much of it left : just a wall or two, lichen-covered and finely broken. Seen from a distance, it is always a perfect piece of colour, in fit keeping with the dim and doubtful sky; but in late autumn, when the woods of the promontory have all their glory—fir-trees of deep black green, intermixed with russet and golden birches—Dunollie is something to watch for hours and wonder at. The day is dark, but a strong silvern light is in the air, a light in which all the blue shadows deepen, while far off in the west, over green Kerrera, is one long streak of faint violet, above which gather strongly defined clouds in a brooding slate-coloured mass. On such a day—and such days are numberless in the Highland autumn—the silvern light strikes strong on Dunollie, bringing out every line and tint of the noble ruin, while the sea beneath, with the merest shadow of the cold faint wind upon it, shifts its tints like a sword-blade in the light, from soft steel-gray to deep slumbrous blue. It only wants Morven in the background, dimly purple with dark plum-coloured stains, and the swathes of white mist folded round the high peaks, to complete the perfect picture.

RAIN AND RAINBOWS.

THE visitor to the west coast of Scotland is doubtless often disappointed by the absence of bright colours and brilliant contrasts, such as he has been accustomed to in Italy and in Switerzland, and he goes away too often with a malediction on the mist and the rain, and an under-murmur of contempt for Scottish scenery, such as poor Montalembert sadly expressed in his life of the Saint of Iona. But what many chance visitors despise, becomes to the living resident a constant source of joy. Those infinitely varied grays—those melting, melodious, dimmest of browns—those silvery gleams through the fine neutral tint of cloud ! One gets to like strong sunlight least ; it dwarfs the mountains so, and destroys the beautiful distance. Dark, dreamy days, with the clouds clear and high and the wind hushed ; or wild days with the dark heavens blowing past like the rush of a sea, and the shadows driving like mad things over the long grass and the marshy pool ; or sad days of rain, with dim pathetic glimpses of the white and weeping orb; or nights of the round moon, when the air throbs with strange electric light, and the hill is mirrored dark as ebony in the glittering sheet of the loch; or nights of the Aurora and the lunar rainbow: on days and nights like those is the Land of Lorne beheld in its glory. Even, during those superb sunsets, for which its coasts are famed —sunsets of fire divine, with all the tints of the prism— only west and east kindle to great brightness; while the landscape between reflects the glorious light dimly and gently, interposing mists and vapours, with dreamy shadows of the hills. These bright moments are exceptional; yet is it quite fair to say so when, a dozen times during the rainy day, the heart of the grayness bursts open, and the Rainbow issues forth in complete semicircle, glittering in glorious evanescence, with its dim ghost fluttering faintly above it on the dark heaven :

> " My heart leaps up when I behold
> A Rainbow in the sky ! "

The Iris comes and goes, and is, indeed, like the sunlight, " a glorious birth " wherever it appears; but for rainbows of all degrees of beauty, from the superb arch of delicately defined hues that spans a complete landscape for minutes together, to the delicate dying thing that flutters for a moment on the skirt of the storm-cloud and dies to the sudden sob of the rain, I know no corner of the earth to equal Lorne and the adjacent Isles.

DROUGHT IN THE HIGHLANDS.

E have not had a drop of rain for a fortnight. The days have been bright and short, and the nights starry and bright, with frequent flashes of the Aurora. It is the gloaming of the year—

> " ——To russet brown
> The heather fadeth. On the treeless hill,
> O'er-rusted with the red decaying bracken,
> The sheep crawl slow."

This is the brooding hush that precedes the stormy wintry season, and all is inexpressibly beautiful. The wind blows chill and keen from the north, breaking the steel-gray waters of the Firth into crisp-white waves; and though it is late afternoon, the western sky hangs dark and chill over the mountains of Mull, while the east is softly bright, with clouds tinted to a faint crimson. There is no brightness on any of the hills save to the east, where, suffused with a roseate flush, stands Ben

Cruachan, surrounded by those lesser heights, beautifully christened the "Shepherds of Loch Etive," a space of daffodil sky just above him and them, and then, a mile higher, like a dome, one magnificent rose-coloured cloud. Thus much it is possible to describe, but not so the strange vividness of the green tints everywhere, and the overpowering sense of height and distance. Though every fissure and cranny of Cruachan seems distinct in the red light, the whole mountain seems great, dreamy, and glorified. Walking on one of the neighbouring hills the Wanderer seems lifted far up into the air, into a still world, where the heart beats wildly and the eyes grow dizzy looking downward on the mother-planet.

In autumn, and even in winter, stillness like this, dead brooding calm, sometimes steals over Lorne for weeks together, and all the colours deepen and brighten ; but at such times as at all others, the finest effects are those of the rain-cloud and the vapour, and no overpowering sense of sunlight comes to trouble the vision.

THE ASCENT OF CRUACHAN.

FOLLOWING the road along the Pass of Awe, you reach Tyanuilt, whence the ascent of Ben Cruachan is tolerably easy. Mountain climbing is always glorious, be the view obtained at the highest point ever so unsatisfactory; for do not pictures arise at every step, beautiful exceedingly, even if no more complex than a silver-lichened boulder half buried in purple heather and resting against the light blue mountain air; or a mountain pool fringed with golden mosses and green cresses, with blue sky in it and a small white cloud like a lamb; or a rowan tree with berries red as coral, sheltering the mossy bank where the robin sits in his nest? He who climbs Cruachan will see not only these small things, but he will behold a series of rag-pictures of unapproachable magnificence—corriess, red and rugged, in the dark fissures of which snow lingers even as late as June, pyramids and minarets of granite, glistering in the sunshine through the moisture of their own dew, stained by rain and light into darkly beautiful hues, and speckled by innumerable shadows from the passing clouds. There is a certain danger in roaming among the precipices near the summit, as the hill is subject to sudden mists, sometimes so dense that the pedestrian can scarcely see a foot before him; but in summer time, when the heights are clear as amber for days together, the peril is not worth calculating. On a fine clear day, the view from the summit—which is a veritable red ridge or cone, not a flat table-land like that of some mountains—is very peculiar. It can scarcely be called picturesque, for there is no power in the eye to fix on any one picture; and on the other hand, to liken it to a map of many colours would be conveying a false impression. The effect is more that of a map than of a picture, and more like the sea than either. The spectator loses the delicate æsthetic sense, and feels his whole vision swallowed up in immensity. The mighty waters of Awe brood sheer below him, under the dark abysses of the hill, with the islands like dark spots upon the surface. Away to the eastward rise peaks innumerable, mountain beyond mountain, from the moor of Rannoch to Ben Lomond, some dark as night with shadow, others dim as dawn from sheer distance, all floating limitless against a pink horizon and brooded over by a heaven of most delicate blue, fading away into miraculous tints, and filling the spirit with intensest awe; while in the west is visible the great ocean, stretching arms of shining sheen into the wildly broken coast, brightening around the isles that sleep upon its breast—Tiree, Coll, Rum, Canna, Skye,—and fading into the long vaporous line where the setting sun sinks into the underworld. Turn where it may, the eye is satisfied, overcharged. Such another panorama of lake, mountain, and ocean is not to be found in the Highlands. As for Lorne, you may now behold it indeed, gleaming with estuaries and lakes:—Loch Linnhe, the Bay of Oban, and the mighty Firth as far south as Jura, and, northward over the moors, a divine glimpse of the head of Loch Etive, blue and dreamy as a maiden's eyes. The head swims, the eyes dazzle. Are you a god, that you should survey these wonders in such supremacy? Look which way you will, you behold immensity, measureless ranges of mountains, measureless tracts of inland water, the measureless ocean, lighted here and there by humanity in the shape of some passing sail smaller to view than a sea-bird's wing. For some little time at least the spectator feels that spiritual exaltation which excludes perfect human perception; he yields to a wave of awful emotion, and bows before it as before God. He can be æsthetic again when he once more descends to the valleys.

A DAY AFLOAT.

IT was a good day, and a long one. The wind came and went, shifting between west and west-by-south, often failing altogether; and the rain fell, more or less, constantly. We made slow work of it, though we carried our gaff-topsail, and though now and then we got a squall which shook and buried the boat. By three in the afternoon we were only off the mouth of Loch Aline, fifteen miles from our starting-place, floating on the slack tide, and hardly making an inch of way. But, nevertheless, it was a day to be remembered. Never did the Wanderer feast his vision on finer effects of vapour and cloud; never did he see the hills possessed with such mystic power and meaning. The "grays" were everywhere, of all depths, from the dark slumberous gray of the unbroken cloud-mass on the hill-top to the silvery gray of the innumerable spears of the rain; and there were bits of brown, too, when the light broke out, which would have gladdened the inmost

soul of a painter.   One little picture, all in a sort of
neutral tint, abides in his memory as he writes.   It was
formed by the dark silhouette of Ardtornish Castle and
promontory, with the winter sky rent above it; and
a flood of white light behind it just reaching the stretch of
sea at the extremity of the point, and turning it to the
colour of glistening white-lead.   That was all; and the
words convey little or nothing of what I saw.   But the
effect was ethereal in the extreme, finer by far than that of
any moonlight.

CANNA AND SKYE.

CANNA never looked more beautiful than that day—her cliffs were wreathed into wondrous forms and tinctured with deep ocean-dyes, and the slopes above were rich and mellow in the light. Beyond her, was Rum, always the same, a dark beauty with a gentle heart. But what most fascinated the eye was the southern coast of Skye, lying on the starboard bow as we were beating northward. The Isle of Mist[1] was clear on that occasion, not a vapour lingering on the heights, and although it must be admitted that much of its strange and eerie beauty was lost, still we had a certain gentle loveliness to supply its place. Could that be Skye, the deep coast full of rich warm under-shadow, the softly-tinted hills, " nakedly visible without a cloud," sleeping against the " dim sweet harebell-colour " of the heavens ? Where was the thunder-cloud, the weeping

[1] This name is purely Scandinavian—*Sky* signifying " cloud ;" whence, too, our own word " sky," the under, or vapour, heaven.

shadows of the cirrus, the white flashes of cataracts through the black smoke of rain on the mountain-side? Were those the Cuchullins—the ashen-gray heights turning to solid amber at the peaks, with the dry seams of torrents softening in the sunlight to golden shades? Why, Blaven, with its hooked forehead, would have been bare as Primrose Hill, save for one slight white wreath of vapour, that, glittering with the hues of the prism, floated gently away to die in the delicate blue. Dark were the headlands, yet warmly dark, projecting into the sparkling sea and casting summer shades. Skye was indeed transformed, yet its beauty still remained spiritual, still it kept the faint feeling of the glamour. It looked like witch-beauty, wondrous and unreal. You felt that an instant might change it,— and so it might and did. Ere we had sailed many miles away, Skye was clouded over with a misty woe, her face was black and wild, she sobbed in the midst of the darkness with the voice of falling rain and moaning winds.

CELTIC SUPERSTITION:

A YARN AFLOAT.

BEGAN talking to the steersman about super-stition. It was a fine eerie situation for a talk on that subject, and the still summer night with the deep dreary murmur of the sea, powerfully stimulated the imagination.

"I say, Hamish," said the Wanderer, abruptly, "do you believe in ghosts?"

Hamish puffed his pipe leisurely for some time before replying.

"I'm of the opinion," he replied at last, beginning with the expression habitual to him—"I'm of the opin-ion that there's strange things in the world. I never saw a ghost, and I don't expect to see one. If the Scripture says true—I mean the Scripture, no' the ministers—there has been ghosts seen before my time, and there may be some seen now. The folk used to say there was a Ben-shee in Skipness Castle—a Ben-shee with white hair and a mutch like an old wife—and my father saw it with his own een before he died. They're curious people over in Barra, and they believe stranger things than that."

"In witchcraft, perhaps?"

"There's more than them believes in witchcraft. When I was a young man on board the *Petrel* (she's one of Middleton's fish-boats, and is over at Howth now) the winds were that wild, there seemed sma' chance of winning hame before the new year. Weel, the skipper was a Skye man, and had great faith in an auld wife who lived alone up on the hillside; and without speaking a word to any o' us, he went up to bid wi' her for a fair wind. He crossed her hand wi' siller, and she told him to bury a live cat wi' its head to the airt wanted, and then to steal a spoon from some house, and get awa'. He buried the cat, and he stole the spoon. It's curious, but sure as ye live, the wind changed that night into the northwest, and never shifted till the *Petrel* was in Tobermory."

"Once let me be the hero of an affair like that," cried the Wanderer, "and I'll believe in the devil for ever after. But it was a queer process."

"The ways o' God are droll," returned Shaw seriously. "Some say that in old times the witches made a causeway o' whales from Rhu Hunish to Dunvegan Head. There are auld wives o'er yonder yet who hae the name of going out wi' the Deil every night in the shape o' blue hares, and I kenned a man who thought he shot one wi' a siller button. I dinna believe all I hear, but I dinna just disbelieve, either. Ye've heard o' the Evil Eye?"

"Certainly."

"When we were in Canna, I noticed a fine cow and calf standing by a house near the kirkyard, and I said to the wife as I passed (she was syning her pails at the door), 'Yon's a bonnie bit calf ye hae with the auld cow.' 'Ay,' says she, 'but I hope ye didna look at them o'er keen'—meaning, ye ken, that maybe I had the Evil Eye. I laughed and told her that wàs a thing ne'er belong't to me nor mine. That minds me of an auld wife near Loch Boisdale, who had a terrible bad name for killing kye and doing mischief on corn. She was gleed,[1] and had black hair. One day, when the folk were in kirk, she reached o'er her hand to a bairn that was lying beside her, and touched its cheek wi' her finger. Weel, that moment the bairn (it was a lassie, and had red hair) began greeting and turning its head from side to side like folk in fever. It kept on sae for days. But at last anither woman, who saw what was wrang, recommended eight poultices o' kyedung (one every night) from the innermost kye i' the byre. They gied her the poultices, and the lassie got weel."

"That was as strange a remedy as the buried cat," observed the Wanderer; "but I did not know such people possessed the power of casting the trouble on human beings."

Hamish puffed his pipe, and looked quietly at the sky. It was some minutes before he spoke again.

"There was a witch family," he said at last, "in Loch

____
[1] She squinted.

Carron, where I was born and reared. They lived their lane[1] close to the sea. There were three o' them—the mither, a son, and a daughter. The mither had great lumps all o'er her arms, and sae had the daughter; but the son was a clean-hided lad, and he was the cleverest. Folk said he had the power o' healing the sick, but only in ae way, by transferring the disease to him that brought the message seeking help. Once, I mind, a man was sent till him on horseback, bidding him come and heal a fisher who was up on the hill and like to dee. The warlock mounted his pony, and said to the man, " Draw back a bit, and let me ride before ye." The man, kenning nae better, let him pass, and followed ahint. They had to pass through a glen, and in the middle o' the glen an auld wife was standing at her door. When she saw the messenger riding ahint the warlock, she screeched out to him as loud as she could cry—" Ride, ride, and reach the sick lad first, or ye're a dead man." At that the warlock looked black as thunder, and galloped his pony; but the messenger being better mounted, o'ertook him fast, and got first to the sick man's bedside. In the night the sick man died. Ye see, the warlock had nae power o' shifting the complaint but on him that brought the message, and no on him if the warlock didna reach the house before the messenger."

Here the Viking emerged wlth the whisky-bottle, and Hamish Shaw wet his lips. We were gliding gently along now, and the hills of Uist were still dimly visible.

[1] *Their lane*—alone.

The deep roll of the sea would have been disagreeable, perhaps, to the uninitiated, but we were hardened. While the Viking sat by, gazing gloomily into the darkness, the Wanderer pursued his chat with Shaw, or, rather, incited the latter to further soliloquies.

"Do you know, Hamish," he said, slyly, "it seems to me very queer that Providence should suffer such pranks to be played, and should entrust that marvellous power to such wretched hands. Come, now, do you actually fancy these things have happened?"

But Hamish Shaw was not the man to commit himself. He was a philosopher.

"I'm of the opinion," he replied, "that it would be wrong to be o'er positive. Providence does as queer things, whiles,[1] as either man or woman. There was a strange cry, like the whistle of a bird, heard every night close to the cottage before Wattie Macleod's smack was lost on St. John's Point, and Wattie and his son drowned; then it stoppit. Whiles it comes like a sheep crying, whiles like the sound o' pipes. I heard it mysel' when my brither Angus died. He had been awa' o'er the country, and his horse had fallen and kicket him on the navel. But before we heard a word about it, the wife and I were on the road to Angus' house, and were coming near the burn that parted his house from mine. It was night, and bright moonlight. The wife was heavy at the time, and suddenly she grippit me by the arm and whispered, "Wheesht! do you hear?" I listened, and at

---

[1] At times.

first heard nothing. "Wheesht, again!" says she; and then I heard it plain—like the low blowing o' the bagpipes, slowly and sadly, wi' nae tune. "O, Hamish," said the wife, "*wha* can it be?" I said naething, but I felt my back all cold, and a sharp thread running through my heart. It followed us along as far as Angus' door, and then it went awa'. Angus was sitting by the fire; they had just brought him hame, and he told us o' the fall and the kick. He was pale, but didna think much was wrang wi' him, and talked quite cheerful and loud. The wife was sick and frighted, and they gave her a dram; they thought it was her trouble, for her time was near, but she was thinking o' the sign. Though we knew fine that Angus wouldna live, we didna dare to speak o' what we had heard. Going hame that nicht, we heard it again, and in a week he was lying in his grave."

The darkness, the hushed breathing of the sea, the sough of the wind through the rigging, greatly deepened the effect of this tale; and the Viking listened intently, as if he expected every moment to hear a similar sound presaging his own doom. Hamish Shaw showed no emotion. He told his tale as mere matter-of-fact, with no elocutionary effects, and kept his eye to windward all the time, literally looking out for squalls.

"For God's sake," cried the Viking, "choose some other subject of conversation. We are in bad enough plight already, and don't want any more horrors."

"What! afraid of ghosts?"

"No, dash it!" returned the Viking; "but—but—as sure as I live, there's storm in yon sky!"

The look of the sky to windward was certainly not improving; it was becoming smoked over with thick mist. Though we were now only a few miles off the Uist coast, the loom of the land was scarcely visible; the vapours peculiar to such coasts seemed rising and gradually wrapping everything in their folds. Still, as far as we could make out from the stars, there was no carry in the sky.

"I'll no' say," observed Hamish, taking in everything at a glance—"I'll no' say but there may be wind ere morning; but it will be wind off the shore, and we hae the hills for shelter."

"But the squalls! the squalls!" cried the Viking.

"The land is no' so high that ye need to be scared. Leave you the vessel to me, and I'll take her through it snug. But we may as weel hae the third reef in the mainsail, and mak' things ready in case o' need."

This was soon done. The mainsail was reefed, and the small jib substituted for the large one; and after a glance at the compass, Hamish again sat quiet at the helm.

"Barra," he said, renewing our late subject of talk, "is a great place for superstition, and sae is Uist. The folk are like weans, simple and kindly. There is a Benshee weel-known at the head o' Loch Eynort, and anither haunts one o' the auld castles o' the great Macneil o' Barra. I hae heard, too, that whiles big snakes, wi' manes like horses, come up into the fresh-water lakes and lie in wait to devour the flesh o' man. In a fresh-water loch at the Harris, there was a big beast like a bull, that came up ae day and ate half the body o' a lad when he was bathing. They tried to drain the loch to get at the beast, but there was o'er muckle water. Then they baited a great hook wi' the half o' a sheep, but the beast was o'er wise to bite. Lord, it was a droll fishing! They're a curious people. But do ye no' think, if the sea and the lochs were drainit dry, there would be all manner o' strange animals that nae man kens the name o'? There's a kind o' water-world—nae man kens what it's like—for the drown'd canna see, and if they could see, they couldna speak. Ay!" he added, suddenly changing the current of his thoughts, "ay! the wind's rising, and we're no' far off the shore, for I can smell the land."

By what keenness of sense Hamish managed to "smell the land" we had no time just then to inquire, for all our wits were employed in looking after the safety of the *Tern*. She was bowling along under three-reefed mainsail and stormjib, and was getting just about as much as she could bear. With the rail under to the cockpit, the water lapping heavily against the cooming, and ever and anon splashing right over in the cockpit itself, she made her way fast through the rising sea. In vain we strained our eyes to discern the shore—

> "The blinding mist came down and hid the land
> As far as eye could see!"

All at once the foggy vapours peculiar to the country

had steeped everything in darkness ; we could guess from the helm where the land lay, but how near it was we were at a loss to tell. What with the whistling wind, the darkness, the surging sea, we felt quite bewildered and amazed.

The Wanderer looked at his watch, and it was past midnight. Even if the fog cleared off, it would not be safe to take Loch Boisdale without good light, and there was nothing for it but to beat about till sunrise. This was a prospect not at all comfortable, for we might even then be in the neighbourhood of dangerous rocks, and if the wind rose any higher, we should be compelled to run before the wind, God knew whither. Meantime, it was determined to stand off a little to the open, in dread of coming to over-close quarters with the shore.

HERRING FISHERS.

 BUSY sight indeed is Loch Boisdale or Stornoway in the herring season. Smacks, open boats, skiffs, wherries, make the narrow waters shady; not a creek, however small, but holds some boat in shelter. A fleet, indeed!—the Lochleven boat from the east coast, with its three masts and three huge lugsails; the Newhaven boat with its two lugsails; the Isle of Man "jigger;" the beautiful Guernsey runner, handsome as a racing yacht, and powerful as a revenue-cutter; besides all the numberless fry of less noticeable vessels, from the fat west-country smack with its comfortable fittings down to the miserable Arran wherry.[1] Swarms of seagulls float

[1] The Arran wherry, now nearly extinct, is a wretched-looking thing without a bowsprit, but with two strong masts. Across the foremast is a bulkhead, and there is a small locker for blankets and bread. In the open space between bulkhead and locker birch tops are thickly strewn for a bed, and for covering there is a huge woollen waterproof blanket ready to be stretched out on spars. Close to the

everywhere, and the loch is so oily with the fishy deposit that it requires a strong wind to ruffle its surface. Everywhere on the shore and hill-sides, and on the numberless islands, rises the smoke of camps. Busy swarms surround the curing-houses and the inn, while the beach is strewn with fishermen lying at length, and dreaming till work-time. In the afternoon, the fleet slowly begins to disappear, melting away out into the ocean, not to re-emerge till long after the grey of the next dawn.

Did you ever go out for a night with the herring fishers? If you can endure cold and wet, you would enjoy the thing hugely, especially if you have a boating mind. Imagine yourself on board a west-country smack, running from Boisdale Harbour with the rest of the fleet. It is afternoon, and there is a nice fresh breeze from the south-west. You crouch in the stern by the`side of the helmsman, and survey all around you with the interest of a novice. Six splendid fellows, in various picturesque attitudes, lounge about the great, broad, open hold, and another is down in the forecastle boiling coffee. If you were not there, half of these would be taking their sleep down below. It seems a lazy business, so far; but wait! By sunset the smack has run fifteen miles up the coast, and is going seven or eight miles east of Ru Hunish lighthouse; many of the fleet still keep her company,

mast lies a huge stone, and thereon a stove. The cable is of *heather rope*, the anchor *wooden*, and the stock a *stone*. Rude and ill-found as these boats are, they face weather before which any ordinary yachtsman would quail.

steering thick as shadows in the summer twilight. How the gulls gather yonder! That dull plash ahead of the boat was caused by the plunge of a solan goose. That the herrings are hereabout, and in no small numbers, you might be sure, even without that bright phosphorescent light which travels in patches on the water to leeward. Now is the time to see the lounging crew dart into sudden activity. The boat's head is brought up to the wind, and the sails are lowered in an instant.[1] One man grips the helm, another seizes the back rope of the net, a third the "skunk" or body, a fourth is placed to see the buoys clear and heave them out, the rest attend forward, keeping a sharp look-out for other nets, ready, in case the boat should run too fast, to steady her by dropping the anchor a few fathoms into the sea. When all the nets are out, the boat is brought bow on to the net, the "swing" (as they call the rope attached to the net) secured to the smack's "bits," and all hands then lower the mast as quickly as possible. The mast lowered, secured, and made all clear for hoisting at a moment's notice, and the candle lantern set up in the iron stand made for the purpose of holding it, the crew leave one look-out on deck, with instructions to call them up at a fixed hour, and turn in below for a nap in their clothes: unless it so happens that your brilliant conversation, seasoned with a few bottles of whisky, should tempt them to steal a

---

[1] There is fashion everywhere. An east-country boat always shoots *across* the wind, of course carrying some sail; while a west country boat shoots *before* the wind, with bare poles.

few more hours from the summer night. Day breaks, and every man is on deck. All hands are busy at work, taking the net in over the bow, two supporting the body, the rest hauling the back rope, save one who draws the net into the hold, and another who arranges it from side to side in the hold to keep the vessel even. Tweet! tweet! that thin cheeping sound, resembling the razor-like call of the bat, is made by the dying herrings at the bottom of the boat. The sea to leeward, the smack's hold, the hands and arms of the men, are gleaming like silver. As many of the fish as possible are shaken loose during the process of hauling in, but the rest are left in the net until the smack gets to shore. Three or four hours pass away in this wet and tiresome work. At last, however, the nets are all drawn in, the mast is hoisted, the sail set, and while the cook (there being always one man having this branch of work in his department) plunges below to prepare breakfast, the boat makes for Loch Boisdale. Everywhere on the water, see the fishing-boats making for the same bourne, blessing their luck or cursing their misfortune, just as the event of the night may have been. All sail is set if possible, and it is a wild race to the market. Even when the anchorage is reached, the work is not quite finished: for the fish has to be measured out in "cran" baskets,[1] and delivered at the curing station. By the time that the crew have got their morning dram, have arranged the nets snugly in the

---

[1] A cran holds rather more than a herring barrel, and the average value of a cran measure of herrings is about one pound sterling.

stern, and have had some herrings for dinner, it is time to be off again to the harvest field. Half the crew turn in for sleep, while the other half hoist sail and conduct the vessel out to sea.

Huge, indeed, are the swarms that inhabit Boisdale, afloat or ashore, during this harvest; but, partly because each man has business on hand, and partly because there is plenty of sea-room, there are few breaches of the peace. On Saturday night the public-house is crowded, and now and then the dull roar ceases for a moment as some obstreperous member is shut out summarily into the dark. Besides the regular fishermen and people employed at the curing stations, there are the herring-gutters —women of all ages, many of whom follow singly the fortunes of the fishers from place to place. Their business is to gut and salt the fish, which they do with wonderful dexterity and skill.

Hideous, indeed, looks a group of these women defiled from head to foot with herring garbage, and laughing and talking volubly, while gulls innumerable float above them and fill the air with their discordant screams. But look at them when their work is over, and they are changed indeed. Always cleanly, and generally smartly dressed, they parade the roads and wharf. Numbers of them are old and ill-favoured, but you will see among them many a blooming cheek and beautiful eye. Their occupation is a profitable one, especially if they be skilful; for they are paid according to the amount of work they do.

It is the custom of most of the east-country fishers to
bring over their own women—one to every boat, sleeping
among the men, and generally related to one or more of
the crew. We have met many of these girls, some of
them very pretty, and could vouch for their perfect purity.
Besides their value as cooks, they can gut herrings and
mend nets; but their chief recommendation in the eyes
of the canny fishermen is that they are kith and kin,
while the natives are strangers "no' be trusted." The
east-country fisherman, on his arrival, invariably encamps
on shore, and the girl or woman "keeps the house" for
the whole crew.

For the fisherman of the east coast likes to be comfortable. He is at once the most daring and the most
careful. He will face such dangers on the sea as would
appal most men, while at the same time he is as cautious
as a woman in providing against cold and ague. How
he manages to move in his clothes is matter for marvel,
for he is packed like a patient after the cold-water
process. Only try to clothe yourself in all the following
articles of attire:—pair of socks, pair of stockings over
them half up the leg, to be covered by the long fishing-
boots; on the trunk, a thick flannel, covered with an
oilskin vest; after that, a common jacket and vest; on
the top of these, an oilskin coat; next, a mighty muffler
to wind round the neck and bury the chin and mouth;
and last of all, the sou'-wester! This is the usual costume
of an east-country fisherman, and he not only breathes
and lives in it, but manages his boat on the whole better

than any of his rivals on the water. He drags himself along on land awkwardly enough ; and on board, instead of rising to walk, he rolls, as it were, from one part of the boat to the other. He is altogether a more calculating dog than the west-country man, more eager for gain, colder and more reticent in all his dealings with human kind.

THE OUTER HEBRIDES.

HIS must be a strange soul who, wandering over these hillocks and gazing westward and seaward in calm weather, is not greatly awed and moved. There is no pretence of effect, no tremendousness, no obtrusive sign of power. The sea is glassy smooth, the long swell does not break at all, until, reaching the smooth sand, it fades softly with deep monotonous moan. Here and there, sometimes close to land, sometimes far out seaward, a horrid reef slips its black back through the liquid blue, or a single rock emerges, toothlike, thinly edged with foam. Southward loom the desolate heights of Barra, with crags and rocks beneath, and although there is no wind, the ocean breaks there with one broad and frightful flash of white. The sea-sound in the air is faint and solemn ; it does not cease at all. But what deepens most the strangeness of the scene, and weighs most sadly on the mind, is the pale sick colour of the sands. Even on the green heights the wind and rain have washed out great hollows, wherein the powdered shells are drifted like snow. You are solemnised as if you were walking on the great bed of the ocean, with the serene depths darkening above you. You are ages back in time, alone with the great forces antecedent to man ; but humanity comes back upon you creepingly, as you think of wanderers out upon that endless waste, and search the dim sea-line in vain for a sail.

Calm like this is even more powerful than the storm. Under that stillness you are afraid of something—nature, death, immortality, God. But at the rising of the winds rises the savage within you : the blood flows, the heart throbs, the eyes are pinched close, the mouth shut tight. You can resist now as mortal things resist. Lifted up into the whirl of things, life is all; the stillness—nature, death, God—is nought.

Terrific, nevertheless, is the scene on these coasts when the storm wind rises,—

    " Blowing the trumpet of Euroclydon."

Westward above the dark sea-line, rise the purple-black clouds, driving with a tremendous scurry eastward, while fresh vapours rise swiftly to fill up the rainy gaps they leave behind them. As if at one word of command, the waters rise and roar, their white crests, towering heaven-ward, glimmering against the driving mist. Lightning, flashing out of the sky, shows the long line of breakers on the flat sand, the reefs beyond, the foamy tumult around the rocks southward. Thunder crashes afar, and the earth reverberates. So mighty is the wind at times that no man can stand erect before it; houses are thrown down, boats lifted up and driven about like faggots. The cormorants, ranged in rows along their solitary cliffs, eye the wild waters in silence, starving for lack of fish, and even the nimble seagull beats about screaming, unable to make way against the storm.

These are the winter gales,—the terror alike of husbandmen and fishers. The west wind begins to blow in October, and gradually increases in strength, till all the terrors of the tempest are achieved. Hailstorms, rainstorms, snowstorms alternate, with the terrific wind trumpeting between; though the salt sea-breath is so potent, even in severe seasons, that the lagoons seldom freeze, and the snow will not lie. The wild wandering birds—the hooper, the bean-goose, the gray-lag, all the tribes of ducks—gather together on the marshes, sure of food here, though the rest of the north be frozen. The great Arctic seal sits on Haskier and sails through the Sound of Harris. Above the wildest winds are heard the screams of birds.

Go in December to the Sound of Harris, and on some stormy day gaze on the wild scene around you; the whirling waters, sown everywhere with isles and rocks— here the tide foaming round and round in an eddy powerful enough to drag along the largest ship—there a huge patch of seaweed staining the waves and betraying the lurking reef below. In the distance loom the hills of Harris, blue-white with snow, and hidden ever and anon

in flying mist.   Watch the terrors of the great Sound--the
countless reefs and rocks, the eddies, the furious wind-
swept waters, and pray for the strange seamen whose fate
it may be to drive helpless thither.

HEBRIDEAN LAGOONS.

STANDING on Kenneth Hill, a rocky eleva-
tion on the north side of Loch Boisdale,
and looking westward on a summer day,
one has a fine glimpse of Boisdale and its
lagoons, stretching right over to the edge of the Western
Ocean, five miles distant. The inn and harbour, with
the fishing-boats therein, make a fine foreground, and
thence the numerous ocean fjords, branching this way
and that like the stems of seaweeds, stretch glistening
westward into the land. A little inland, a number of
huts cluster, like beavers' houses, on the site of a white
highway; and along the highway peasant men and
women, mounted or afoot, come wandering down to the
port. Far as the eye can see the land is quite flat and
low, scarcely a hillock breaking the dead level until the
rise of a row of low sandhills on the very edge of the
distant sea. The number of fjords and lagoons, large
and small, is almost inconceivable; there is water every-

where, still and stagnant to the eye, and so constant
is its presence that the mind can scarcely banish the
fancy that this land is some floating, half-substantial mass,
torn up in all places to show the sea below. The highway meanders through the marshes until it is quite lost
on the other side of the island, where all grows greener
and brighter, the signs of cultivation more noticeable, the
human habitations more numerous. Far away, on the
long black line of the marshes, peeps a spire, and the
white church gleams below, with school-house and hovels
clustering at its feet.

A prospect neither magnificent nor beautiful, yet surely
full of fascination; its loneliness, its piteous human
touches, its very dreariness, win without wooing the soul.
And if more be wanted, wait for the rain—some thin
cold "smurr" from the south, which will clothe the
scene with gray mist, shut out the distant sea, and brooding over the desolate lagoons, draw from them pale and
beautiful rainbows, which come and go, dissolve and
grow, swift as the colours in a kaleidoscope, touching
the dreariest snatches of water and waste with all the
wonders of the prism. Or if you be a fair-weather
voyager, afraid of wetting your skin, wait for the sunset.
It will not be such a sunset as you have been accustomed
to on English uplands or among high mountains, but
something sullener, stranger, and more sad. From a
long deep bar of cloud, on the far-off ocean horizon, the
sun will gleam round and red, hanging as if moveless,
scarcely tinting the deep watery shadow of the sea, but

turning every lagoon to blood.   There will be a stillness
as if Nature held her breath.   You will have no sense of
pleasure or wonder—only hushed expectation, as if something were going to happen ; but if you are a saga-reader,
you will remember the death of Balder, and mutter the
rune.   Such sunsets, alike yet ever different, we saw, and
they are not to be forgotten.   Then most deeply did the
soul feel itself in the true land of the glamour, shut out
wholly from the fantasies of mere fairyland or the
grandeurs of mere spectacle.   The clouds may shape
themselves into the lurid outlines of the old gods, crying,

> Suinken i Gruus er
> Midgards stad !

the mist on the margins of the pools may become the
gigantic witch-wife, spinning out lives on her bloody distaff, and croaking a prophecy; but gentler things may
not intrude, and the happy sense of healthy life dies
utterly away.

THE LOCHAN.

PLEASANT it is, after such an hour, to wander across the bogs and marshes, and come down on the margin of a little lake, while the homeward passing cattle low in the gloaming. You are now in fairyland. With young buds yellow, and flowers as white as snow, floating freely among the floating leaves, the water-lilies gather, and catch the dusky silver of the moon. The little dab-chick cries, and you see her sailing, a black speck, close to shore, and splashing the pool to silver where she dives. The sky clears and the still spaces between the lilies glisten with stars, whose broken rays shimmer like hoar-frost and touch with crystal the edges of leaves and flowers. You are a child at once, and think of Oberon.

EAGLES AND RAVENS.

FEW have ever killed an eagle in its full pride of strength and flight. It is the sickly, half-starved, feeble bird that inadvertently crosses the shepherd's gun, and yields a lean and unwholesome body to the stuffer's arts. Such an one we saw low down on the crags of Ben Eval, passing with a great heavy beat of the wing from rock to rock, now hovering for an instant over some object among the heather, then rising painfully and drifting along on the wind. We had no gun with us that day, or we think that, by cautiously stalking among the heights, we might have made the bird our own; and, indeed, our hearts were sad for the great bird, with that fierce hunger tearing at his heart, while, doubtless, the yellow eyes burnt terribly through the gathering films of death. Out of the hollow crags gathered six ravens, rushing with hoarse shrieks at the fallen king, and turning away with horrible yells whenever he turned towards them with sharp talon and opened beak ; attracted by the noise, flocked from all the surrounding pastures the hideous hooded crows, with their sick gray coats and sable heads, cawing like devils ; and these, too, rushed at the eagle, to be beaten back by one wave of the wrathful wings. It was a sad scene—power eclipsed on the very throne of its glory, taunted and abused by carrion.

" Sick in the world's regard, wretched and low,"

yet preserving the mournful shadow of its dignity and kingly glory. Every movement of the eagle was still kingly, nor did he deign to utter a sound ; while the crows and ravens were detestable in every gesture, mean, grovelling, and unwieldy, and their cruel cries made the echoes hideous. Round the shoulder of the hill floated the king, with the imps of darkness at his back. We fear his day of death, so nigh at hand, was to be very sad. Better that the passing shepherd should put a bullet through his heart and carry him away to deck some gentle-man's hall, than that he should fall spent yonder, insulted at his last gasp, torn at by the fiends, seeing the leering raven whet his beak for slaughter, and the corby perched close by, eager to pick out the golden and beautiful eyes.

> " By too severe a fate,
> Fallen, fallen, fallen, fallen,
> Fallen from his high estate,
>   And weltering in his blood ;
> On the bare earth exposed he lies,
> With not a friend to close his eyes."

We were not loath to see him go. It would have required a hard heart to take advantage of him, in the last forlorn moments of his reign.

Just as he passed away, there started out from the side of a rock a ghastly apparition, glaring at us with a face covered with blood, and looking as if it meant murder. It was only a sheep, and for the moment it amazed us, for it seemed like the ghost of a sheep, horrid and forbidding. Alas! though it glared in our direction, it could not see; its poor gentle eyes had just been destroyed, the red blood from them was coursing down its cheeks; and it was staggering, drunken with the pain. It was the victim of the hoody or the raven, ever on the watch for the unwary, ready in a moment to dart down on the sleeping lamb or the rolling sheep, and make a meal of its eyes; then, with devilish chuckle, to track the blind and tottering victim hither and thither, as it feels its feeble way among the heights, until, standing on the edge of some high rock, it can be startled, with a wild beat of wings and a hoarse shriek, right down the fatal precipice to the rocks beneath; and there the murderer, while a dozen others of his kind gather around him in carnival, croaks out a discordant grace, and plunges his reeking beak into the victim's heart.

HAWKS AND OWLS.

EXT in rank to the Golden Eagle stands the Erne,—a pluckier and altogether a fiercer bird, resembling in character one of those fierce Highland caterans, who were wont to flock in the neighbourhood of its haunts. In spite of the brutal butchery of keepers and collectors, this noble bird, unlike the other, still abounds, breeding in all the headlands, of Skye, on the breast of one of Macleod's Maidens in the wild Scuir, of Eigg, in Scalpa, North Uist, Shiant Isles, Benbecula, and in Lewis and Harris. He is an unclean feeder, seldom slaughtering his own food, but seeking everywhere for garbage—dead sheep, stranded fish, or a salmon out of the neck of which the otter has taken its own tasty bite. His eyrie is generally among the most inaccessible crags, but he has been known to rear the mighty fabric in a tree, in the midst of some lonely island. Macgillivray found a Sea Eagle's nest in an island in a Hebridean lake, in a mound of rock "not higher than could have been reached with a fishing-rod " He varies greatly in size, "some specimens measuring only six feet from tip to tip of the wings, while others are at least one half more." He is pugnacious as a Cock-robin, and as vulgar as a Vulture, but he can be tamed, and in his tame state becomes an interesting pet. The finest extant specimen is in the Stornoway collection of Sir James Matheson; it was killed in the island of Lewis, and is of gigantic size, and very light in colour.

Many other rapacious birds frequent the Hebrides from the Osprey down to the Kestrel, or Wind-hover; but the most interesting of all, perhaps, is the Peregrine Falcon, so lovely in form and plumage, and so elegant of flight. The Peregrine breeds in all the outer islands, on the outlying rocks of Haskair, and even in St. Kilda. He is a murderous fellow, killing far more than he can eat, for the sheer sake of killing, twisting off the head of a snipe or a ptarmigan as unconcernedly as a waiter draws a bottle of beer! When he resides near the sea, he makes sad havoc among the Puffins and Guillemots. Next to him, in point of beauty, is his swift little kinsman, the Merlin, pluckiest of all the hawks, and deftest in the hunt. Game to the bone is the Soog, as he is called by the Celts, and will tackle a quarry out of all proportion to his strength. Snipes and Golden Plovers are his favourite feeding, and he will beat the marshes and sea-sands as carefully as an old pointer beats the turnips in September.

While the Eagle and Hawks hunt by day, the Owls

prowl by night. These latter birds are not numerous in the Hebrides, the short-eared Owl being the most common, but we have here and there seen the tawny Owl hovering on the skirts of the plantations, oftentimes enough put up awkwardly by the dogs when beating cover, and likely to share a sudden fate at the hands of some bungler, unless protected by the sympathetic "It's only an Old Wife— poor thing !" of some friendly keeper. The last Owl we saw was last night, beating the margin of Loch Bee for mice, with that curious limp flap of its downy wing, and occasionally resting as still as stone on the overhanging cone of a damp boulder, in just the same attitude in which we had not long before seen one of his kinsmen resting on Robert Browning's shoulder, in the very heart of London. As to the White Owl, the *true* Cailleach, or Old Woman, she seems to have taken some deathly offence at our islands, for though there is a ruin on every headland, sorry a one of them all will she inhabit. Her ghastly presence would indeed become the gloaming hour, when the moon is shining on the ruined belfry of Icolmkill ; but not even *there*, where the Spirit of the sea-loving Saint still walks o' nights, is her weird cry heard, or her ghostly flight beheld.

> Not a whit of her tuwhoo !
> Her to woo to her tuwhit !

We have sought her in vain in Iona, in Dunstaffnage, in Rodel, and in many kindred places, chiefly desolate graveyards ; finding in her stead, among the tombs, only the little Clacharan,[1] in his white necktie, cluck-clucking as monotously as a death-watch, and conducting eternally, on his own account, a kind of lonely *spirit-rapping*, in the most appropriate place.   Among the same desolate homes of the dead, we have also found (as Dr. Gray seems to have found) the Sea-gulls coming to rest for the night, stealing through the twilight with a slow flight, which might be mistaken, at the first glance, for that of the Cailleach herself.

[1] Celtic name of the Stone-chat *(Saxicola Rubicola)*.

THE WATER-OUZEL.

WHAT the Stone-chat is to graveyards, the Dipper is to lonely burns. He has many names in the Isles,— *Lon uisge, Gobha dubh nan Allt*, &c.—but none so sweet as the name familiar to every Saxon ear, that of Water-Ouzel. Who has not encountered the little fellow, with his light eye and white breast, dipping backwards and forwards as he sits on a stone amid the tiny pools and freshets, and rising swiftly to follow with swift but exact flight the windings and twistings of the stream? and who that has ever so met him, has failed to see in his company his faithful and inseparable little mate? He likes the waterfall and the brawling linn, as well as the dark pools amid the green and mossy heath; and he is to be found building from head to foot of every mountain that can boast a burn, however tiny and unpretending. The young are born with the cry of water in their ears; often the nest where they lie and cheep is within a few feet of a torrent, the voice of which is a roaring thunder ; and close at hand, amid the spray, the little father-ouzels sit on a mossy stone, and sing aloud.

> What pleasures have great princes? &c.,

they seem to be crying, in the very words of the old song. To search for water-shells and eat the toothsome larvæ of the water-beetle, and to have the whole of a mountain brook for kingdom,—what royal lot can compare with this ?

> Whiles thro' a linn the burnie plays,
>   Whiles thro' a glen it wimples,
> Whiles bickering thro' the golden haze
>   With flickering dauncing dazzle,
> Whiles cookin' underneath the braes
>   Beneath the flowing hazel ! [1]

To the eye of the little feathered king and queen, the bubbling waters are a world miraculously tinted and sweet with summer sound.   The life of the twain is full of calm joy.   So at least thinks the angler, as he crouches under the bank from the shower, and sees the cool drops splashing like countless pearls round the Ouzel's mossy throne in the midst of the pool.   We hear for the first time, on the authority of Dr. Gray, that the Ouzel has been proscribed and decimated in many Highland parishes, because, forsooth, he is supposed to interfere with the rights of human fishermen !   In former times, whoever slew one

[1] The lover of Burns must forgive blunders, as I quote from memory.

of these lovely birds received as his reward the privilege
of fishing in the close season ; and a reward of sixpence a
head is this day given for the " Water Craw " in some
parts of Sutherlandshire.   To such a pass come mortal
ignorance and greed !—ignorance, here quite unaware that
the Ouzel never touches the spawn of fish at all ; and
greed, unwilling to grant to a bird so gentle and so beauti·
ful even a share of the prodigal gifts of nature.

THE KINGFISHER.

AR more persecuted than the Bird of the Burn is that other frequenter of inland waters, the Kingfisher: so lovely that every cruel hand is raised against his life; so rare, through such slaughter, that one may now search long and far without ever perceiving the azure gleam of its wing. Its head is not unlike that of a Heron, on a diminutive scale; and its attitude, as it sits motionless for hours together, on some bough overhanging the stream, is heron-like in its steadfastness and patience. Unsocial and solitary, it deposits its pink-white eggs and rears its young in a hole in the green bank. Flashing past, it seems like a winged emerald; in repose, its colour is ruddy brown. Seen in any light, it is a thing of perfect beauty, not to be spared from the precious things of the student of nature. To these Outer Hebrides, it never comes; but it has been found in the island of Skye. The dark, shrubless banks of these streams do not attract it ; and, moreover, for so sportsmanlike and indefatigable a bird, the fishing is bad.   It loves a stream shaded with alders and dwarf willows, and affects, too, spots well-warmed by the sun.   When the buds of the water-lilies blow, and the well-oiled leaves float around them, when the dragon-fly poises in the leaves and gleams brilliantly, when the sun shines golden overhead and, be-low in the pool, you see the shadows of the motionless trout on the bright stones—*then*, creeping near, warily, look for the Kingfisher.   There he sits, on a green branch near the mouth of his dwelling, arrayed as Solomon never was in all his glory, and shadowed by the willow tree,

> That grows aslant the brook,
> And shows his hoar leaves in the glassy stream.

The sun creeps behind a cloud for a moment; a tiny trout splashes, leaving a circle that widens and fades. What was that, the flash of an emerald or the gleam of some passing insect?   'Twas the King of Fishers darting down to seize his tiny prey; but so swiftly is he back again to his point of vantage, that he scarcely seems to have stirred at all.

HEBRIDEAN BIRDS.

WHAT picture next appears? In a lonely lochan, glossy black, and with never reed or flower to relieve its sadness, under a dark sky seamed with silvern streaks, there rises a rocky isle, and close to the isle swims the Learga, or Black-throated Diver, troubling the brooding silence with his weird cry—*Deoch! deoch! tha'n loch a traogbadh !*[1] Sunset on Loch Scavaig, the ocean glassy-still, and the Coolins rising lurid in the red light streaming over the western ocean, while the Solan drops like a bullet to his prey, and

> The cormorant flaps o'er a sleek ocean-floor
> Of tremulous mother-of-pearl,

Twilight on the slopes of the mountains of Mull, and the evening star glimmering over the dark edge of the fir-wood, while the ghost-moths begin to issue from their green hiding-places, and the Night gar, looming on the

[1] "Drink ! drink ! the lake is nearly dried up."

summit of a tree, utters his monotonous call. A spring morning, with broken clouds and a rainbow, gleaming on the isles of Loch Awe, and cuckoos multitudinous as leaves in Vallambrosa telling their name to all the hills. The prospects are endless, the cries confusing as the chorus of birds in Aristophanes:

> Toro, toro, toro, toro, toro, toro, toro, toro, toro,
> Kickabau, kickabau,
> Toro, toro, toro, toro, tobrix!

With these for guides, one may wander further and see stranger scenes than ever came under the eyes of the Nephelococcygians; but, indeed, modern culture scarcely knows even their names, and the spots where they dwell scarcely attract even the passing tourist. Wonderful indeed is modern ignorance, only to be paralleled by modern fatuity. Few men know the difference between the Birch and the Hornbeam, the Curlew and the Whimbrel. Modern authors, poets particularly, write as if they had been brought up in a dungeon or a hothouse, never breathing the fresh air or beholding plants and birds in a state of nature. "It is a fool's life, as they will find when they get to the end of it, if not before." The pursuit of false comforts, the desire of vain accomplishments, the sucking of social lollipops, these are modern vanities. We were speaking the other day with one of the best educated men in England, a party finished to the finger-tips, great in philosophy, and "in Pindar and poets unrivalled." He had never seen an eagle or a red deer; he could neither shoot, fish, nor swim; he

was sea-sick whenever he left dry land; he believed the
"sheets" of a boat to be her "sails;" he knew (as
Browning expresses it) the "Latin word for Parsley," but
he had never even heard of "white" heather. For this
being, his University had done all it could, and had
turned him out in the world about as ignorant as a parrot
and as helpless, for all manly intents and purposes, as a
new-born baby.

NIGHT IN THE SEA.

EARLY in the afternoon we passed Dunvegan, Head, and then Vaternish Point; but by this time the breeze had grown very faint indeed, and when we were in the middle of the great mouth of Loch Snizort, the wind ceased altogether. For hours we rolled about on a most uncomfortable sea, till the sun sank far away across the Minch, touching with red light the hazy outline of the Long Island. Then, all in a moment as it were, the eyes of heaven opened, very dim and feeble, and the night—if night it could be called—came down with a chilly sprinkle of invisible dew. All round the yacht the sea burnt, flashed, and murmured, lit up by innumerable lights. Wherever a wave broke, there was a phosphorescent gleam. The punt astern floated in a patch as bright as moonlight; and every time the counter of the yacht struck the water the latter emitted a flash like sheet-lightning. The whole sea was alive with millions of miraculous creatures, each with a tiny light to pilot him about the abysses. Here and there the Medusa moved luminous, devouring the minute creatures that swarmed around it, terrible in its way as the Poulp that Victor Hugo has caricatured so immortally;[1] and other creatures of volition, to us nameless, passed, mysteriously; while ever and anon a shoal of tiny sethe would dart to the surface and hover in millions around the yacht. Though there was no moon, the waters and the sky seemed full of moonlight. The silence was profound, only broken by a dull heavy sound at intervals—whales blowing off the headland of Dunvegan.

Midnight; and no breeze came. The sky to the north unfolded like a flower blossoming, and the northern lights flitted up from the horizon, flashing like quicksilver, and filling the sight with a peculiar thrill of mesmeric sensation. Lights gleaming on the ocean, the eyes of heaven glittering, the aurora flashing and fading—with all these the sense seemed overburthened. Now and then, as if the pageant were incomplete, a star shot from its sphere, gleamed, and disappeared.

[1] "Les Travailleurs de la Mer."

MORNING GLIMPSES: OFF SKYE.

WHEN day broke, red and sombre, we were off Hunish Point, and saw on every side of us the basaltic columns of the coast flaming in the morning light, and behind us, in a dark hollow of a bay, the ruins of Duntulm Castle, gray and forlorn. The coast views here were beyond expression magnificent. Tinted red with dawn, the fantastic cliffs formed themselves into shapes of the wildest beauty, rain-stained and purpled with shadow, and relieved at intervals by slopes of emerald, where the sheep crawled. The sea through which we ran was a vivid green, broken into thin lines of foam, and full of innumerable Medusæ drifting southward with the tide. Leaving the green sheep-covered island of Trody on our left, we slipt past Aird Point, and sped swift as a fish along the coast, until we reached the two small islands off the northern point of Loch Staffin—so named, like the island of Staffa, on account of its columnar ridges of coast. Here we beheld a sight which seemed the glorious fabric of a vision:—a range of small heights sloping from the deep green sea, every height crowned with a columnar cliff of basalt, and each rising over each, higher and higher, till they ended in a cluster of towering columns, minarets, and spires, over which hovered wreaths of delicate mist, suffused with the pink light from the east. We were looking on the spiral pillars of the Quirang. In a few minutes the vision had faded; for the yacht was flying faster and faster, assisted a little too much by a savage puff from off the Quirang's great cliffs ; but other forms of beauty arose before us as we went. The whole coast from Aird point to Portree forms a panorama of cliff-scenery quite unmatched in Scotland. Layers of limestone dip into the sea, which washes them into horizontal forms, resembling gigantic slabs of white and gray masonry, rising sometimes stair above stair, water-stained, and hung with many-coloured weed; and on these slabs stand the dark cliffs and spiral columns: towering into the air like the fretwork of some Gothic temple, roofless to the sky ; clustered sometimes together in black masses of eternal shadow ; torn open here and there to show glimpses of shining lawns sown in the heart of the stone, or flashes of torrents rushing in silver veins through the darkness ; crowned in some places by a green patch, on which the goat feed small as mice ; and twisting frequently into towers of most fantastical device, that lie dark and spectral against the gray background of the air. To our left we could now behold the island of

Rona, and the northern end of Raasay. All our faculties, however, were soon engaged in contemplating the Storr, the highest part of the northern ridge of Skye, terminating in a mighty insulated rock or monolith which points solitary to heaven, two thousand three hundred feet above the sea, while at its base rock and crag have been torn into the wildest forms by the teeth of earthquake, and a great torrent leaps foaming into the sound. As we shot past, a dense white vapour enveloped the lower part of the Storr, and towers, pyramids, turrets, monoliths were shooting out above it like a supernatural city in the clouds.

A SUNSET.

WHAT with the slight wind, and the weary beating down the Sound, we did not sight Sconser Lodge, which lies just at the mouth of Loch Sligachan, until the sunset. By this time the clouds had somewhat cleared away about Glamaig, and glorious shafts of luminous silver were working wondrous chemistry among the dark mists. We put about close to Raasay House, a fine dwelling in the midst of well cultivated land, and feasted our eyes with the fantastic forms and colours of the Skye cliffs to the westward, grouped together in the strange wild illumination of a cloudy sunset : domes, pinnacles, spires, rising with dark outlines against the west, and flitting from shade to light, from light to shade, as the mist cleared away or darkened against the sinking sun ; with vivid patches between of dark brown rocks and of green grass washed to glistening emerald by recent rain. It was a scene of strange beauty—Nature mimicking with unnatural perfection the mighty works of men, colouring all with the wildest hues of the imagination, and revealing beyond at intervals, glimpses of other domes, pinnacles, and spires, flaming duskly in the sunset, and crumbling down, like the ruins of a burning city, one by one. What came into the mind just then was not Wordsworth's sonnet on a similar cloudy pageant, but those wonderful stanzas of a wonderful poem by the same great poet on the eclipse of the sun in 1820 :—

> " Awe-stricken she beholds the array
> That guards the temple night and day ;
> Angels she sees, that might from heaven have flown,
> And virgin saints, who not in vain
> Have striven by purity to gain
> The beatific crown—
>
> " Sees long-drawn files, concentric rings,
> Each narrowing above each ; the wings,
> The uplifted palms, the silent marble lips,
> The starry zone of sovereign height—
> All steeped in the portentous light !
> All suffering dim eclipse ! "

It is difficult to tell why these lines should have arisen in our mind at that moment; for no stronger reason, perhaps, than that which caused the figures themselves to rise before Wordsworth by the side of Lugano. He had once seen the Cathedral at Milan, and when the eclipse came, he could not help following it thither in imagination. These faint associations are the strangest things in life, and the sweetest things in song. Portentous light ! dim eclipse ! These were the only words truly applicable to the scene we were gazing upon at that moment; and those few words were the chain of the association—the magical charm linking sense and soul— bringing Milan to Skye, filling the sunset picture with the wings, uplifted palms, and silent lips of angels and virgin saints—

> " All steeped in the portentous light ;
> All suffering dim eclipse !"

THE BIRTH OF THE CUCHULLINS:

A RETROSPECT.

E have no patience with those imaginative people who are so far fascinated by transcendental meteors as to class Geology in the prose sisterhood of Algebra and Mathematics. The typical geologist, indeed, whom we meet prowling, hammer in hand, in the darknesss of Glen Sannox, or rock-tapping on the sea-shore in the society of elderly virgins, or examining Agassiz' atlas through blue spectacles on board the Highland steamboat—this typical being, we repeat, is frequently duller company than the Free Church minister or the dominie ; but he is a mere fumbler about the footprints of the fair science, with never the courage to look straight into those beautiful blind eyes of hers and discover that she has a soul. By what name shall we call her, if not by the divine name of Mnemosyne —the sphinx-like spirit that broods and remembers : a soul, a divinity, brooding blind in the solitude, and feeling

with her fingers the raised letters of the stone book, which
she holds in her lap, and wherein God has written the
veritable " Legend of the World ? "   A prose science ?—
say rather a sublime Muse !   Why, her throne is made of
the mountains of the earth, and her speech is the earth-
slip and the volcano, and her taper is the lightning, and
her forehead touches a coronal of stars.   Only the fool
misapprehends her and blasphemes.   Whoso looks into
her face with reverend eyes is appalled by the light of God
there, and sinks to his knees, crying, " I would seek unto
God, and unto God would I commit my cause, who doeth
great things and unsearchable, marvellous things without
number."

In sober words, without fine writing or rapture, it must
be said that the Cuchullins cannot long be contemplated
apart from their geology.   Turn your eyes again for a
moment on Scuir-na-Gillean !   Note those sombre hues,
those terrific shadows, that jagged outline traced as with a
frenzied finger along the sky.   It is a gentle autumn morning, and the film of white cloud resting on yonder topmost peak, is moveless as the ghost of the moon in an
April heaven.   There is no sound save the melancholy
murmur of water.   A strange awe steals over you as you
gaze ; the soul broods in its own twilight.   Then, as the
first feeling of almost animal perception fails, the mind
awakens from its torpor, and with it comes a sudden
illumination.   Along these serrated peaks runs a fiery
tongue of flame, the abysses blacken, the air is filled with
a deep groan, and a thunder-cloud, driving past in a great

wind, clutches at the mountain, and clinging there, belches flame, and beats the darkness into fire with wings of iron. From a rent above, the drifting stars gaze, like affrighted; yes, dim as corpse-lights. In a moment, this wonder passes: the sudden tension of the mind fails, and with it the phantasm, and you are again in the torpid condition, gazing dreamily at the jagged outline of the Titan, dark and silent in the brightness of the autumn morning. Again Mnemosyne waves her hand, and again the mind flashes into picture.

You have now a glimpse of the ninth circle of the Inferno. Surrounded by the region of the Cold Clime, girt round on every side by unearthly forms of ice and rock, you see below you vales of frozen water, and un-fathomable deeps blue as the overhanging heaven. Where fire once raved snow now broods. Dome, pyramid, and pinnacle tower around with walls and crags of glittering ice. Winds contend silently, and heap the snow with rapid breath. Here and there gleams the vaporous light-ning, innocent as the aurora. The glaciers slip, and ever change. And down through the heart of all this desola-tion, past the very spot where you stand, filling the gigantic hollow of Glen Sligachan, welling onward with one deep murmur, carrying with it mighty rocks and blasted pine trees, rolls a majestic river, here burnished black as ebony in the rush of its own speed, there foamins over broken boulders and tottering crags, and everywhere gathering into its troubled bosom the drifting glacier and the melting snow.

The Wanderer at least saw all this plain enough as he passed along the weary glen in the rear of his party; and the fanciful retrospect, instead of dulling the scene, lends it a solemn consecration.   Poor indeed would be the songs of all the Muses, compared with the tale of Mnemosyne, if she could only be brought to utter half she knows.

HART-O'-CORRY.

PAUSE here, where your path is the dry bed of a torrent, and look yonder to the north-east. Between two hills opens the great gorge of Hart-o'-Corry, which is closed in again far away by a wall of livid stone. 'Tis broad day here, but gray twilight yonder. In the hollow of the corry broods a dense vapour, and above it, down the deep green fissures of the hypersthene, trickle streams like threads of hoary silver, frozen motionless by distance; while higher, far above the rayless abyss, the sky is serene and hyacinthine blue. That black speck over the topmost peak, that little mark scarce bigger than the dot of an *i* is an eagle; it hovers for many minutes motionless, and then melts imperceptibly away. From the side of Hart-o Corry, Scuir-na-Gillean shoots up its rugged columns; and close to the mouth of the corry, the sharply-defined sweep of the deep green hypersthene, overlying the pale yellow felspar, has an effect of rare beauty.   Turning now, and looking up the Glen towards Camasunary, you behold Ben Blaven closing in the view, and towering into the sky from precipice to precipice, its ashen gray flanks corroding everywhere into veins of mineral green, until it cuts the ether with a sharp hooked forehead of solid stone.

LOCH CORRUISK.

CORRUISK, or the Corry of the Water, is a wild gorge, oval in shape, about three miles long and a mile broad, in the centre of which a sheet of water stretches for about two miles, surrounded on every side by rocky precipices totally without vegetation, and towering in one sheer plane of livid rock, until they mingle with the wildly picturesque and jagged outlines of the topmost peak of the Cuchullins. Directly on entering its sombre darkness, the student is inevitably reminded of the awful region of Malebolge :

> "Luogo è in Inferno detto Malebolge
> Tutto di pietra e di color ferrigno,
> Come la cerchia, che d'intorno 'l volge."

The Mere is black as jet, its waters only broken and brightened by four small grassy islands, on the edges of the largest of which that summer day the black-backed gulls were sitting, with the feathery gleam of their sha·dows faintly breaking the glassy blackness below them.

These islands form the only bit of vegetable green in all
the lonely prospect.　Close to the shores of the loch, and
at the foot of the crags, there are dark-brown stretches of
heath ; but the heights above them are leafless as the
columns of a cathedral.

Coming abruptly on the shores of this loneliest of lakes,
the Wanderer had passed instantaneously from sunlight to
twilight, from brightness to mystery, from the gladsome stir
of the day to a silence unbroken by the movement of any
created thing.　Every feature of the scene was familiar to
him—he had seen it in all weathers, under all aspects—
yet his spirit was possessed as completely, as awe-stricken,
as solemnised, as when he came thither out of the world's
stir for the first time.　The brooding desolation is there
for ever.　There was no sign to show that it had ever been
broken by a human foot since his last visit.　He left it in
twilight, and in twilight he found it.　Since he had departed, scarce a sunbeam had broken the darkness of the
dead Mere ; so close do the mountain pinnacles tower on
all sides, that only when the sun is sheer above can the
twilight be broken ; and when it is borne in mind that the
Cuchullins are the chosen lairs of all the winds, that the
hollows are the dark breeding-places of all the monsters
of storm, that scarce a day passes over them without mist
and tears, one ceases to wonder at the unbroken darkness.
A great cathedral is solemn, solemner still is such an island
as Haskeir when it sleeps silent amid the rainy grief of
a dead still sea, but Corruisk is beyond all expression
solemnest of all.　Perpetual twilight, perfect silence,

terribly brooding desolation. Though there are a thousand voices on all sides—the voices of winds, of wild waters, of shifting crags—they die away here into a heartbeat. See! down the torn cheeks of all those precipices tear head-long torrents white in foam, and each is crying, though you cannot hear it. Only one low murmur, deeper than silence, fills the dead air. The black water laps silently on the dark claystone shingle of the shore. The cloud passes silently, far away over the melancholy peaks.

Streams innumerable come from all directions to pour themselves into the abyss ; and enormous fragments of stone lie everywhere, as if freshly fallen from the precipices, while many of these gigantic boulders, as MacCulloch observes, are " poised in such a manner on the very edges of the precipitous rocks on which they have fallen, as to render it difficult to imagine how they could have rested in such places, though the presence of *snow* at the time of their fall may perhaps explain this difficulty." These indeed, are the true *blocs perchés*, marking the course of the glacier which once invaded these wilds. " The interval between the borders of the lake and the side of Garsven is strewed with them ; the whole, of whatever size, lying on the surface in a state of uniform freshness and integrity, unattended by a single plant or atom of soil, as if they had all but recently fallen in a single shower." The mode in which they lie is no less remarkable. The bottom of the valley is covered with rocky eminences, of which the summits are not only bare, but often very narrow, while their declivities are always steep, and often perpendicular.

Upon these rocks the fragments lie just as on the more level ground. One, weighing about one hundred tons, has become a rocking-stone; another, of not less than fifty, stands on the narrow edge of a rock a hundred feet higher than that ground which must have first met it in the descent.

> " Mighty rocks,
> Which have from unimaginable years
> Sustained themselves with terror and with toil
> Over a gulf, and with the agony
> With which they cling seem slowly coming down ;
> Even as a wretched soul hour after hour
> Clings to the mass of life ; yet, clinging, lean ;
> And leaning, make more dark the dread abyss
> In which they fear to fall."[1]

Strangely beautiful as is the scene, it is a ruin. The vast fragments are the remains of a magnificent temple rising into pinnacles and minarets of ice, glittering with all the colours of the prism. Here the silent-footed glacier slipped, and the snow shifted under the footsteps of the wind, and there perhaps, where the lonely lake lies, glittered a cold sheet of hyacinthine blue; and no gray rain-cloud brooded on the temple's dome—only delicate spirits of the vapour, drinking soft radiance from the light of sun and star. Around this temple crawled the elk and bear, and swift-footed mountain deer. Summer after summer it abode in beauty, not stable like temples built by hands, but ever changing, full of the low murmur of its change, the melancholy sound of its

[1] Shelley's " Cenci."

own shifting walls and domes. Then more than once Fire swept out of the abyss, and clung like a snake about the temple, while Earthquake, like a chained monster, groaned below; wild elements came from all the winds to overthrow it; wall after wall fell, fragment after fragment was dashed down. The fairy fretwork of snow melted, the fair carvings of ice were obliterated, pinnacle and minaret dissolved in the sun, like the baseless fragment of a vision. Dark twilight settled on the ruin, and Melancholy marked it for her own. The walls of livid rock remain, gray from the volcano, and torn into rugged rents, casting perpetual darkness downward, where the water bubbling up from unseen abysses has spread itself into a mirror. All ruins are sad, but this is sad utterly. All ruins are beautiful, but this is beautiful beyond expression. The solemn Spirit of Death comes more or less to all ruins, whenever the meditative mind conjures and wishes; but here it abides, at once overshadowing whosoever approaches by the still sense of doom. "Thus saith the Lord God, Behold, O Mount Seir, I am against thee, and I will make thee most desolate. When the whole earth rejoiceth, I will make thee desolate." The fiat has also been spoken here. The place has been solemnised to desolation.

In deep unutterable awe does the human visitant explore with timid eye the mighty crags above him, the layers of volcanic stone, until he finds himself fascinated by the strange outlines of the peaks where they touch the sky, and detecting fancied resemblances to things that live. Yonder crouches, black and distinct against the light, a maned beast, like a lion, watching; its eyes invisible, but fixed doubtless on yours. Higher still is a dimmer outline, as of some huge bird, winged like the griffin. These two resemblances infect the whole scene instantaneously. There are shapes everywhere—in the peaks, in the gorges, by the torrents—living shapes, or phantoms, frozen still to listen, or to watch; and horrifying you with their deathly silence. Your heart leaps as if something were going to happen; and you feel if the stillness were suddenly broken, and these shapes were to spring into motion, you would shriek and faint.

How dark and fathomless look the abysses yonder, at the head of the loch! A wild scarf of mist is folding itself round the peaks (betokening surely that the clear still weather will not remain much longer unbroken), and faint gray light travels along the wildly indented wall beneath. It is not two miles to the base of the crags, yet the distance seems interminable; and shadows, shifting and deepening, weary the eye with mysterious and dimly-reflected vistas.

CANNA AND ITS PEOPLE.

ANNA is the child of the great waters, and such children, lonely and terrible as is their portion, seldom lack loveliness—often their only dower. From the edge of the lapping water to the peak of the highest crag, it is clothed with ocean gifts and signs of power. Its strange under-caves and rocks are coloured with rainbow hues, drawn from glorious-featured weeds ; overhead its cliffs of basalt rise shadowy, ledge after ledge darkened by innumerable little wings ; and high over all grow soft greenswards, knolls of thyme and heather, where sheep bleat and whence the herd boy crawls over to look into the raven's nest. On a still summer day, when the long Atlantic swell is crystal smooth, Canna looks supremely gentle on her image in the tide, and out of her hollow under-caves comes the low weird whisper of a voice ; the sunlight glimmers on peaks and sea, the beautiful shadow quivers below, broken here and there by drifting weeds, and the bleating sheep on the high swards soften the stillness. But when the winds come in over the deep, the beauty changes—it darkens, it flashes from softness into power. The huge waters boil at the foot of the crags, and the peaks are caught in mist; and the air, full of a great roar, gathers around Canna's troubled face. Climb the crags, and the horrid rocks to westward, jutting out here and there like shark's teeth, spit the lurid white foam back in the glistening eyes of the sea. Slip down to the water's edge, and amid the deafening roar the spray rises far above you in a hissing shower. The whole island seems quivering through and through. The waters gather on all sides, with only one long glassy gleam to leeward. No place in the world could seem fuller of supernatural voices, more powerful, or more utterly alone.

It is our fortune to see the island in all its moods; for we are in no haste to depart. Days of deep calm alternate with days of the wildest storm—there is constant change.

Everywhere in the interior of the island there are sweet pastoral glimpses. On a summer afternoon, while we are wandering in the road near the shore, we see the cattle beginning to flock from the pastures, headed by two gentle bulls, and gathering round the dairy house, where, in " short gowns," white as snow, the two head dairymaids sit on their stools. The kine low softly, as the milk is drawn from the swelling udder, and now and then a calf, desperate with thirst, makes a plunge at his mother and drinks eagerly with closed eyes till he is driven away. Men and children gather around, looking on idly. As we pass by, the dairy-maid offers us a royal drink of fresh warm milk, and with that taste in our lips we loiter away. Now we are among fields, and we might be in England—so sweet is the scent of hay. Yonder the calm sea glimmers, and one by one the stars are opening like forget-me-nots, with dewdrops of light for reflections in the water below. Can this be Canna? Can this be the solitary child of the ocean? Hark! That is the corn-crake crying in the corn—the sound we have heard so often in the southern fields !

When there is little or no sea, it is delightful to pull in the punt round the precipitous shores, and come upon the lonely haunts of the ocean birds. There is one great cliff, with a hugh rock rising out of the water before it, which is the favourite breeding haunt of the puffins, and while swarms of these little creatures, with their bright parrot-like bills and plump white breasts, flit thick as locusts in the air, legions darken the waters underneath, and rows on rows sit brooding over their young on the dizziest edges of the cliff itself. The noise of wings is ceaseless, there is constant coming and going, and so tame are the birds that one might almost seize them, either on the water or in the air, with the outstretched hand. Discharge a gun into the air, and, as the hollow echoes roar upward and inward to the very hearts of the caves, it will suddenly seem as if the tremendous crags were loosening to fall,— but the dull dangerous sound you hear is only the rush of wings. A rock farther northward is possessed entirely by gulls, chiefly the smaller species ; thousands sit still and fearless, whitening the summit like snow, but many hover with discordant scream over the passing boat, and seem trying with the wild beat of their wings to scare the intruders away.   Close in shore, at the mouth of a deep dark cave, cormorants are to be found, great black " scarts," their mates and the young, preening their glistening plumage leisurely, or stretching out their snake-like necks to peer with fishy eyes this way and that.   They are not very tame here, and should you present a gun, will soon flounder into the sea and disappear ; but at times, when they have gorged themselves with fish, so awkward are they with their wings, and so muddled are their wits, that one might run right abreast of them, and knock them over with an oar.

Everywhere below, above, on all sides, there is nothing but life—birds innumerable, brooding over their eggs or fishing for the young.   Here and there, a little fluff of down just launched out into the great world paddles about bewildered, and dives away from the boat's bow with a faint troubled cry.   On the outer rocks gulls and guillemots, puffins on the crags, and cormorants on the ledges of the caves.   The poor reflective human being brought into the sound of such a life, gets quite scared and dazed.   The air, the rocks, the waters are all astir. The face turns for relief upward, where the blue sky meets the summit of the crags.   Even yonder, on the very ledge, a black speck sits and croaks;   and still farther upward, dwarfed by distance to the size of a sparrow-hawk, hovers a black eagle, fronting the sun.

There is something awe-inspiring, on a dead calm day,

in the low hushed wash of the great swell that for ever
sets in from the ocean; slow, slow, it comes, with the
regular beat of a pulse, rising its height, without breaking, against the cliff it mirrors in its polished breast, and
then dying down beneath with a murmuring moan.
What power is there! what dreadful, fatal ebbing and
flowing! No finger can stop that under-swell, no breath
can come between that and its course; it has rolled
since time began, the same, neither more nor less,
whether the weather be still or wild, and it will keep
on when we are all dead. Bah! that is hypochondria.
But look! what is that floating yonder, on the glassy
water?

> " O is it fish, or weed, or floating hair,
>   O' drownëd maiden's hair ? "

No; but it tells us clear a tale. Those planks formed
lately the sides of a ship, and on that old mattress with
the straw washing out of the rents, some weary sailor
pillowed his head not many hours ago. Where is the
ship now? Where is the sailor? Oh, if a magician's
wand could strike these waters, and open them up to our
view, what a sight should we see!—the slimy hulls of
ships long submerged; the just sunken fish-boat, with
ghastly faces twisted among the nets; the skeleton suspended in the huge under-grass and monstrous weeds,
the black shapes, the fleshless faces looming green in the
dripping foam and watery dew! Yet how gently the
swell comes rolling, and how pleasant look the depths,

this summer day,—as if death were not, as if there could be neither storm nor wreck at sea.

More hypochondria, perhaps. Why the calm sea should invariably make us melancholy we cannot tell, but it does so, in spite of all our efforts to be gay. Walt Whitman used to sport in the great waters as happily as a porpoise or a seal, without any dread, with vigorous animal delight; and we, too, can enjoy a glorious swim in the sun, if there is just a little wind, and the sea sparkles and freshens full of life. But to swim in a dead calm is dreadful to a sensitive man. Something mesmeric grips and weakens him. If the water be deep, he feels dizzy, as if he were suspended far up in the air.

We are harping on delicate mental chords, and forgetting Canna; yet we have been musing in such a mood as Canna must inevitably awaken in all who feel the world. She is so lonely, so beautiful; and the seas around her are so full of sounds and sights that seize the soul. There is nothing mean, or squalid, or miserable about Canna; but she is melancholy and subdued,—she seems, like a Scandinavian Havfru, to sit her with hand to her ear earnestly listening to the sea.

That, too, is what first strikes one in the Canna people, —their melancholy look, not grief-worn, not sorrowful, not passionate, but simply melancholy and subdued. We cannot believe they are unhappy beyond the lot of other people who live by labour, and it is quite certain that, in worldly circumstances, they are much more comfortable than the Highland poor are generally. Nature, however, with her wondrous secret influences, has subdued their lives, toned their thoughts, to the spirit of the island where they dwell. This is more particularly the case with the women. Poor human souls, with that dark, searching look in the eyes, those feeble flutterings of the lips! They speak sad and low, as if somebody were sleeping close by. When they step forward and ask you to walk into the dwelling, you think (being new to their ways) that some one has just died. All at once, and inevitably, you hear the leaden wash of the sea, and you seem to be walking on a grave.

" A ghostly people !" exclaims the reader ; " keep me from Canna !" That is an error. The people do seem ghostly at first, their looks do sadden and depress ; but the feeling soon wears away, when you find how much quiet happiness, how much warmth of heart, may under·lie the melancholy air. When they know you a little, ever so little, they brighten, not into anything demonstrative, not into sunniness, but into a silvern kind of beauty, which we can only compare to moonlight. A veil is quietly lifted, and you see the soul's face ; and then you know that these folk are melancholy, not for sorrow's sake, but just as moonlight is melancholy, just as the wash of water is melancholy, because *that* is the natural expression of their lives. They are capable of a still, heart-suffering tenderness, very touching to behold.

We visit many of their houses, and hold many of their hands. Kindly, gentle, open-handed as melting charity, we find them all ; the poorest of them as hospitable as

T

the proudest chieftain of their race. There is a gift everywhere for the stranger, and a blessing to follow,—for they know that after all he is bound for the same bourne.

Theirs is a quiet life, a still passage from birth to the grave; still, untroubled, save for the never-silent voices of the waves. The women work very hard, both indoors and afield. Some of the men go away herring-fishing in the season, but the majority find employment either on the island or the circumjacent waters. We cannot credit the men with great energy of character; they do not seem industrious. An active man could not lounge as they lounge, with that total abandonment of every nerve and muscle. They will lie in little groups for hours looking at the sea, and biting stalks of grass—not seeming to talk, save when one makes a kind of grunting observation, and stretches out his limbs a little farther. Some one comes and says, " There are plenty of herring over in Loch Scavaig—a Skye boat got a great haul last night." Perhaps the loungers go off to try their luck, but very likely they say, " Wait till to-morrow—it may be all untrue ;" and in all probability, before they get over to the fishing ground, the herrings have disappeared.

Yet they can work, too, and with a will, when they are fairly set on to work. They can't speculate, they can't search for profit; the shrewd man outwits them at every turn. They keep poor—but keeping poor, they keep good. Their worst fault is their dreaminess ; but surely as there is light in heaven, if there be blame here, God is to blame here, who gave them dreamy souls! For our part, keep us from the man who could be born in Canna, live on and on with that ocean murmur around him, and elude dreaminess and a melancholy like theirs!

"Bah!" cries a good soul from a city; "they are lazy, like the Irish, like Jamaica niggers; they are behind the age; let them die!" You are quite right, my good soul; and if it will be any comfort to you to hear it, they, and such as they, are dying fast. They can't keep up with you; you are too clever, too great. You, we have no doubt, could live at Canna, and establish a manufactory there for getting the sea turned into salt for export. You wouldn't dream—not you! Ere long these poor High-landers will die out, and with them may die out gentle-ness, hospitality, charity, and a few other lazy habits of the race.

In a pensive mood, with a prayer on our lips for the future of a noble race destined to perish locally, we wander across the island till we come to the little grave-yard where the people of Canna go to sleep. It is a desolate spot, commanding a distant view of the Western Ocean. A rude stone wall, with a clumsy gate, surrounds a small square, so wild, so like the stone-covered hill-side all round, that we should not guess its use without being guided by the fine stone-mausoleum in the midst. That is the last home of the Lairds of Canna and their kin; it is quite modern and respectable. Around, covered knee-deep with grass, are the graves of the islanders, with no other memorial stones than simple pieces of rock, large and small, brought from the sea-shore and placed as foot-stones and headstones. Rugged as water tossing in the wind is the old kirk-yard, and the graves of the dead therein are as the waves of the sea.

In a place apart lies the wooden bier, with handspokes on which they carry the cold men and women hither; and by its side—a sight indeed to dim the eyes—is another smaller bier, smaller and lighter, used for little children. Well, there is not such a long way between parents and offspring ;—the old here are children too, silly in worldly matters, loving, sensitive, credulous of strange tales. They are coming hither, faster and faster ; bier after bier, shadow after shadow. It is the tradesman's day now, the day of progress, the day of civilisation, the day of shops ; but high as may be your respect for the commercial glory of the nation, stand for a moment in imagination among these graves, listen to one tale out of many that might be told of those who sleep below, and join me in a prayer for the poor islanders whom they are carrying, here and in a thousand other kirkyards, to the rest that is without knowledge and the sleep that is without dream.

EIRADH OF CANNA.

EIRADH OF CANNA.[1]

A TALE.

" She was a woman of a steadfast mind,
    Tender and deep in her excess of love ;
    Not speaking much, pleased rather with the joy
    Of her own thoughts.
                        WORDSWORTH'S " *Excursion.*"

THERE was a man named Ian Macraonail, who lived at Canna in the sea. In the days of his prosperity God sent him issue,—five lads and a lass. Now Ian had great joy in his five sons, for they grew up to be fine young men, straight-limbed, clean-skinned, clever with their hands ; and in the girl he had not joy, but pain, for she was a sickly child and walked lame through a trouble in the spine. Her name was Eiradh, and she was born to many thoughts.

When she was born she cried ; nor did she cease crying

---

[1] This tale, or poem in prose, is supposed to be told by a native of the Highlands in the Highland tongue.

after long days ; and folk seeing that she was so sickly a child, thought that she would die soon.   Yet Eiradh did not die, but cried on, so that the house was never quiet, and the neighbours, when they heard the sound in the night, said, "That is Ian Macraonail's bairn; the Lord has not yet taken her away."   When she was three years old she lay in the cradle still, and could not run upon her feet : and then foul sores came out upon her head—after they burst she had sound sleeps, and her trouble passed away.

The mother's heart was glad to see the little one grow stiller and brighter every day, and try to prattle like other children at the hearth ; and she nursed her with care, slowly teaching her to move upon her feet.   Afterwards they taught her how to use a little crutch of wood which Ian himself cut in the long winter nights when he was at home.

Ian Macraonail was a just man, and his house was a well-doing house, but Eiradh saw little of her father's face. In the summer season he was far away chasing the herring on the great sea, and even on the stormy winter days he was fishing cod and ling with a mate on the shores of Skye and Mull.   When he came home he was wet and sleepy, and all the children had to keep very still.   Then Eiradh would sit in a corner of the hearth and see his dark face in the peat smoke.   If he took her upon his knee she felt afraid and cried ; so that the father said, "The child is stupid, take her away." But when he took her young brother upon his knee, the boy laughed and played with his beard.

For all that the mother held Eiradh dear above all her

other children, because she was sickly, and had given ner so much care.

Ian had built the house with his own hands, and it looked right out upon the sea. All the day and night the water cried at the door. Sometimes it was low and still and glistening; and it was pleasant then to sit out on the sand and throw stones into the smooth and glassy tide. But oftenest it was wild and loud, shrieking out as if it were living, dashing in the seaweed and planks of ships, and seeming to say, "Come out here, come out here, that I may eat you up alive!" All the long night it cried on, while the wind tore at the roof of the house, and would have carried it far away if the straw ropes and heavy stones had not been there to hold it down.

Then Eiradh would hide her head under the blankets and think of her father upon the sea.

The water cried at the door. When Eiradh's eldest brother grew up into a strong youth, he went away with his father upon the sea. He stayed away so long that his face grew strange. When he came home he was sleepy and tired, like his father, and said little to his sister and brothers; but one day he brought Eiradh home a little round-eyed owl, like a little old woman in a tufted wig. Eiradh was proud that day. When the calliach opened its mouth and roared for food, she laughed and clapped her hands; and she made the bird a nest in an old basket, and fed it with her own hands. She loved her great brother very much after that, and was happy when he came home.

The water cried at the door. One day Eiradh's second brother joined his father and brother upon the sea, and ever after that was sleepy and tired like the others when he came home. The mother said to Eiradh, " That is always the way; boys must work for their bread." But Eiradh thought to herself, " It is the sea calling them away. I shall soon not have a brother left in the house."

The water cried at the door till all Eiradh's five brothers went away. Then it was very lonely in the dwelling, and the days and nights were long and dull. When the fishers came home, their faces were all strange to her, and they seemed great rough men, while she was only a little sickly child. But they were kind. They told her wild stories about the sea and the people they had seen, and laughed out loud and merry at the wonder in her great staring eyes. They told her of the great whales and the sea-snakes that have manes like a horse and teeth like a saw; and how the old witch of Barra smoked her pipe over her pot and sold the fishermen winds.

One night when Eiradh was twelve years of age, she sat with her mother over the fire, waiting for her father and brothers to come home in the skiff from Mull. It was a rainy night, late in the year. Now, the mother had been ailing for many days with a heaviness and pain about the heart, and she said to Eiradh: " I feel sick, and I will lie down upon the bed to rest a little." Eiradh kept very still that her mother might sleep, and the pot, with the supper in it, bubbled, the rain went splash-splash at the door, till Eiradh fell to sleep herself. She woke up with a loud cry, and looking round her saw her father and brothers in the room. The steam was coming thick like smoke from their clothes, their faces were white, and they were talking to one another. She called to them not to make a noise because mother was asleep; but her father said, in a sharp voice, "Take the girl away—she is better out of the house." Then a neighbour woman stepped forward, out of the shadow of the door, and said, " she shall go with me." When the woman took her by the hand and led her to the other house through the rain, she was so frightened she could not say a word. The woman led her in, and bade her seat herself beside the fire, where a man sat smoking his pipe and mending his nets. Then Eiradh heard her whisper in his ear, as she passed him, "This is lame Eiradh with the red hair—her mother has just died."

It seemed to Eiradh that the ground was suddenly drawn from under her feet, and she was walking high up in the air, and all around her were voices crying : " Eiradh ! Eiradh with the red hair ! your mother has just died." When that passed away, a sharp thread was drawn through her heart, and she could scarcely cry for pain ; but when the tears came they did her good, washing the pang away. But it was like a dream.

It was like a dream, too, the day when the woman took her by the hand and led her back to the house. The sea was loud that day—loud and dark—and it seemed to be saying, with its great voice: " Eiradh !

Eiradh! your mother has just died." The home was clean and still; father was sitting on a bench beside the fire in his best clothes, looking very white. When she went in he drew her to him and kissed her on the forehead, and she sobbed sore. The woman said, " Come, Eiradh;" and led her aside. Something was lying on the bed all white, and there was a smell like fresh-bleached linen in the air; then the woman lifted up a kerchief, and Eiradh saw her mother's face dressed in a clean cap, and the grey hair brushed down smooth and neat. Eiradh's tears stopped, and she was afraid— it looked so cold. The woman said: " Would you like to kiss her, Eiradh, before they take her away?" but Eiradh drew her breath tight, and cried to be taken out of the house.

That night she slept in the neighbour's house, and the next day her mother was taken to the graveyard on the hill. Eiradh did not see them take her away; but in the afternoon she went home and found the house empty. It was clean and bright. The peat fire was blazing on the floor, and there were bottles and glasses on the press in the corner. By-and-by her father and brothers came in, all dressed in their best clothes, and with red eyes; and many fishermen—neighbours—stood at the door to take the parting glass, and went away quite merry to their homes. But the priest came and sat down by the fire with her father and brothers, and patted Eiradh on the head, telling her not to cry any more, because her mother was happy with God. She went and sat on the ground in a corner, looking at them through her tears. Her father was lighting his pipe, and she heard him say, "She was a good wife to me;" and the priest answered, "She was a good wife and a good mother; she has gone to a better place." Eiradh wondered very much to see them so quiet and hard.

With that, the days of Eiradh's loneliness began. She had no mother now to talk to her in the long nights when her father and brothers were away upon the sea; but she used to go to the neighbour-woman's house and sleep among the children. Oftener than ever before, she loved to sit by the water and listen, playing alone; so that her playmates used to say, "Eiradh is a stupid girl, and likes to sit by herself." One day she went to the graveyard on the hill and searched about for the place where her mother was laid. The grass was long and green, and there were great weeds everywhere; but there was one place where the earth had been newly turned, and blades of young grass were beginning to creep through the clay. She felt sure that her mother must be sleeping there. So she sat down on the grave and began to knit. It was a clear bright day, the sheep were crying on the hills, and the sea far off was like a glass; and it was strange to think her mother was lying down there, so near to her, with her face up to the sky. Eiradh began wondering how deep she was lying and whether she was still dressed in white. Her thoughts made her afraid, and she looked all around her. Though it was daytime, she could not bear to stay any longer, for she had heard about ghosts. As she walked home on her crutch, she looked round her very often, fancying she heard some one at her back.

Though Eiradh Nicraonail was a sickly girl, she was clever and quick, and she soon began to take a pleasure in the house. The neighbour-woman helped about the place and taught Eiradh many things—how to cook, how to make cakes of oatmeal on the brander, and how to wash clothes. She was so quick and willing, and longed so much to please her father and brothers, that they said, "Eiradh is as good as a woman in a house, though she is so young." Then Eiradh brightened full of pride, and ever after that kept the home clean and pleasant, and forgot her griefs.

There was a man in Canna, a little old man with a club foot, who got his living in many ways, for he could make shoes and knew how to mend nets, and besides, he was a learned man, having been taught at a school in the south. Some of the children used to go to him in the evenings, and he taught them how to read; but he was so sharp and cross that sometimes he would have nothing to say to them though they came. Now and then, Eiradh went over to him, and he was gentler with her than with the rest, because she had a trouble of the body like himself. He learned her her letters, and afterwards, with a wooden trunk for a desk, made her try to write. Often, too, he came over to her in the house, and smoked his pipe while she knitted; but if her father or any of her brothers came in, he gave them sharp answers and soon went away, while they laughed and said, "It is a pity that his learning does not make him more free." He was a strange old man, and believed in ghosts and witches. Eiradh liked to sit and listen to his tales. He told her how the bagpipes played far off when any one was going to die. He told her of a young man in Skye, who could cause diseases by the power of the evil eye, and of a woman in Barra, who used to change into a hare every night and run up to the top of the mountains to meet a spirit in black by the side of a fire made out of the coffins of those who died in sin. He had seen every loophole in Skipness Castle full of cats' heads, with red eyes, and every head was the head of a witch. He believed in dreams, and thought that the dead rose every night and walked together by the side of the sea. Often in the dark evenings, when Eiradh was sitting at his knee, he would take his pipe out of his mouth and tell her to listen ; if she listened very hard in the pauses of the wind, she would hear something like a voice crying, and he told her that it was the spirit of the poor lady who died in the tower, walking up and down, moaning and wringing its hands.

As Eiradh grew older she had so much to do in the house that she thought of these things less than before. But when she sat by herself knitting, and the day's work was over, voices came about her that belonged to another land, and she grew so used to them that their presence seemed company to her, and she was not afraid. By the time that she was seventeen years of age God's strength had come upon her, and she could walk about without her crutch. She had red hair, her face was white and well-favoured, and her eyes were the colour of the green sea.

One night, when her father and brothers were sleeping with her in the house, Eiradh Nicraonail had a dream. She thought she was standing by the sea, and it was full of moonlight and the shadows of the stars. While she stood looking and listening there came up out of the sea a black beast like a seal, followed by five young ones, and they floated about in the light of the moon with their black heads up listening to a sound from far away like the music of a harp. All at once the wind rose and the sea grew rough and white, and the lift was quite dark. In a little time the distant music grew louder and the wind died away. Then Eiradh saw the beast floating about alone in the white moonlight and bleating like a sheep when robbed of its lamb; and at last it gave a great cry and stretched itself out stiff and dead, with its speckled belly shining uppermost and the herring-syle playing round it like flashes of silver light. With that she awoke, and it was dark night; the wind was crying softly outside, and she could hear her father and brothers breathing heavy in their sleep.

The next day, when her father and brothers sat mending their nets at the door she told them her dream. They only laughed, and said it was folly put into her head by the old man who taught her to read. But she saw that they looked at one another, and were not well pleased. All that day the dream troubled her at her work, and whenever she heard the sheep bleat from the hill-side she felt faint. The next night she said a long prayer for her father and brothers, and slept sound. The dream did not come again, and in a few days the trouble of it wore away. But when the news came that they were catching herring in Loch Scavaig, and the fisherman and his sons began preparing their boat to sail over and try their chance, all Eiradh's fears came back upon her twentyfold. It was changeful weather early in the year; there were strong winds and a great sea.

The day before the boat went away Ian had the rheumatic trouble so sore in his bones that he could not rise out of his bed; and he was still so sick next day that he told the young men to go away alone, for fear of missing the good fishing. They went off with a light heart—four strong men and a tall lad.

Ian Macraonail never saw his sons any more. Three days afterwards news was brought that the boat had laid over and filled in a squall, and that every one on board had been drowned in the sea.

Then Eiradh knew that her strange dream had partly come true, but that more was to come true yet. The water cried at the door. Ian sat like a frozen man in the house, and when Eiradh looked at him her tears ceased —she felt afraid. He scarcely said a word, and did not cry, but he paid no heed to his meat. He looked like the man on the hill-side when the voice of God came out of the burning bush.

U

Again and again Eiradh cried " Father ! " and looked into his face, but he held up his hand each time to warn her away. A thread ran through her heart at this, for she had always known he loved her brothers best, and now he did not seem to remember her at all. She went outside the home, and looked at the crying water, and hated it for all it had done. Her heart was sad for her five brothers who were dead, but it was saddest of all for her father who was alive.

The priest came, and prayed for the dead. Ian prayed too, with a cold heart. Afterwards the priest took him by the hand, looking into his eyes, and said, " Ian, you have suffered sore, but those the Lord loves are born to many troubles." Ian looked down, and answered in a low voice, "That is true ; I have nothing left now to live for." But the priest said, "You have Eiradh, your daughter; she is a good girl." Ian made no answer, but sat down and smoked his pipe. Eiradh went out of the house, and cried to herself.

Now, that day Ian Macraonail put on his best black gear and the black hat with the broad crape band. The black clothes made him look whiter. He took his staff, and went up over the hill on to the cliffs, over the place where the black eagle builds, and stood close to the edge, looking over at Loch Scavaig, where the lads were drowned. While he stood there a shepherd that knew him came by, and seeing him look so wild, fancied that he meant to take the short road to the kirkyard. So the man touched him on the shoulder, saying, " He sleeps ill that rocks himself to sleep—we are in God's hands, and must bide His time." Ian knew what the shepherd meant, and shook his head. "I have been a well-doing man," he said, "and mine has been a well-doing house. I have drunk a bitter cup, but the Lord forbid that I should do the sin you think of." So the shepherd made the sign of the blessed cross, and went away.

After that Ian wore his black gear every day, and every day he went up on the high cliffs to walk. He ate his meat quite hearty, and he was gentle with Eiradh in the house; but he stared all around him like a man at the helm in a thick mist, and listened as the man at the helm listens in the mist for the wind that is coming. It was plain that he took little heart in his dwelling, or in the good money he had saved. One day he said, "When I go again to the herring-fishing, I must pay wages to strangers I cannot trust, and things will not go well." The day after that, at the mouth of lateness they found him leaning against a stone, close over the place where the black eagle builds; and his heart was turned to lead, and his blood was water, and there were no pictures in his eyes.

Now Eiradh Nicraonail was alone in the whole world.

II.

When Ian was in the narrow house where the fire is cold and the grass grows at the door, Eiradh sold the boats and the nets, and all but the house she lived in;

and when she counted the good money, she found there was enough to keep her from hunger for a little time. In these days she had little heart to work in the house and in the fields, and every time she thought of those who were lying under the hill she felt a salt stone rise in her throat. In the long nights, when she was alone, voices came out of the sea, and eyes looked at her,—she heard the wind calling, and the ghost of the lady crying up in the tower,—and she thought of all the strange things the old man had told her when she was small. Often her heart was so troubled that she had to run away to the neighbours and sit among them for company. She often said, "I would rather be far away than here, for it is a dull place;" and she planned to take service on some farm across the water.

The women bade her wait and look out for a man, but Eiradh said, "The man is not born that would earn meat for me." She was dull and down-looking in these days, speaking little, but her bodily trouble was all gone, and she was clean-limbed and had a soft face. More than one lad looked her way, and would have come courting to her house at night, but she barred the door and would let no man in. One night, when a fisher lad got in, and came laughing to her bedside, he was sore afraid at the look of her face and the words of her mouth, though she only cried, "Go away this night, for the love of my father and mother. I am sick and heavy with sleep."

These were decent and well-doing lads, shepherds

earning good wages, but Eiradh had a face to frighten them away.

The winter after Ian Macraonail died, Calum Eachern, the tailor, came north to Canna. The folk had been waiting for him since long, and there was much work to be done—so that Calum was busy morning and night in one house or another; but though he had been busier, his tongue could never have kept still. Every night people gathered in the place where he worked, and those were merry times. He was like a full kist, never empty; his tales were never done. He had the story of the king of Lochlan's daughter, and how Fionn killed the great bird of the red beak, and many more beside. He loved best to tell about the men of peace, with their green houses under the hillside, and about the changeling bairns that play the fairy pipes in the time of sleep, and about the ladies with green gowns, that sit in the magic wells and tempt the herdboys with silver rings. He had that many riddles they were like the limpets on the seashore. He knew old songs, and he had the gift of making rhymes himself to his own tune. So the coming of Calum Eachern was like the playing of pipes at a wedding on a summer day.

Calum was little, narrow in the shoulders, and short in the legs. His face was like a china cup for neatness. He had a little turned-up nose, and white teeth, and he shaved his beard clean every day. He had little twinkling eyes like a fox's, and when he talked to you he cocked his head on one side, like a sparrow on a dyke.

One night, he was at work in a neighbour's house, and Eiradh went in with the rest. Calum sat on his board, and some were looking on and listening to his talk. When Eiradh went in, he put his head on one side and looked at her, and said in a rhyme—

> " What did the fox say?
> Huch ! huch ! huch ! cried the fox ;
> Cold are my bones this day—
> I have leant my skin to cover the head
> Of the girl with the red hair."

All the folk laughed, and Eiradh laughed too. Then she sat down on the floor by the fire, and hearkened with her cheek on her hand. Calum Eachern was like a bee in the time of honey. He stitched, and sang, and told tales about the men of peace, and the land where jewels grew as thick as chuckie-stones, and gold is as plenty as the sand of the sea. Whenever Eiradh looked up, he had his head on one side, and his eyes were laughing at her. By-and-by he nodded and said :

> " What did the sea-gull say?
> Kriki ! kriki ! cried the sea-gull ;
> Hard it is to hatch my eggs this day—
> I have lent my white breast
> To the girl with the red hair."

Then he nodded again and said :

> " What did the heron say?
> Kray ! kray ! said the heron ;
> Poor is my fishing in the loch to-day—
> I have lent my long straight leg
> To the girl with the red hair.

With that, he flung down his shears, and laughed till the tears were in his eyes. Eiradh felt angry and ashamed, and went away.

But for all that, she was not ill pleased. Listening to Calum Eachern had been like sitting out of doors on a bright sunny day. It made her heart light. All the night long she thought of his talk. She had never heard tales like those before—all about brightness and a pleasant place. When she went to sleep, she dreamed she was in an enchanted castle all made of silver mines and precious stones, and that Calum Eachern was showing her a fountain full of gold fish, and the fountain seemed to fall in rhyme. All at once, Calum laughed so loud that the castle was broken into a thousand pieces, and when she woke up it was bright day.

The day after that who should come into the house but Calum Eachern. "A blessing on this house!" said he, and sat down beside the fire. Eiradh was putting the potatoes in the big pot, and Calum pointed at the pot and said :

> " Totoman, totoman,
> Little black man,
> Three feet under
> And bonnet of wood ! "

Eiradh laughed at the riddle. Then Calum, seeing she was pleased, began to talk and sing, putting his head on one side and laughing. All at once he said, looking quite serious, " It's not much company you will be having here, Eiradh Nicraonail."

"That's true enough," said Eiradh.

"It's a dull house that is without the cry of bairns, I'm thinking."

"And that's true too," said Eiradh.

"Then why don't you take a man?" said he, looking at her very sharp.

Eiradh gave her head a toss, and lifted up the lid of the pot to look in.

"Your cheek is like a rose for redness," said Calum. "Are ye ashamed to answer?"

At that, Eiradh lifted up her head and looked him straight in the face.

"The man is not born that I heed a straw," said she.

Calum laughed out loud to hear her say that, and a little after he went away.

Eiradh did not know whether she was pleased or angry, and all that night she had little sleep. She did not like to be laughed at, and yet she could not be rightly angry with such a merry fellow as Calum. It seemed strange to her that he should come to the house at all.

It seemed stranger, the next night, when Calum came in again, and sat down by the fire.

"How does the Lord use you this night, Eiradh Nicraonail?"

"The Lord is good," answered Eiradh.

"Can you read print?" he said, smiling.

"Ay," answered Eiradh, "print and writing too."

"And that's a comfort," said Calum. "But I've

brought you somebody to sit with ye by the fire in the long nights."

"And what's he like?" asked Eiradh, thinking that Calum meant himself.

"He's not over fine to look at, but he's mighty learned. He's a little old man with a leather skin, and his name written on his face, and the marks o' thumbs all over his inside."

"And where is he this night?"

"This is him, and here he is, and many a merry thing he'll teach you, if you attend to his talking," said Calum; and he gave her a little book in the Gaelic, very old and covered with black print; and soon after that he went away.

When he was gone, Eiradh sat down by the fire and turned over the leaves of the book that he had given her, and it seemed like the voice of Calum talking in her ear. There were stories about the fairies and the men of peace, and shieling songs of the south country, and riddles for the fireside in the south country on Halloween. Eiradh read till she was tired, and some of the stories made her laugh afterwards as she sat by the fireside with her cheek on her hand. She could not help thinking that it would be fine to live in the south country, where there was corn growing everywhere, and gardens full of flowers, and no sea.

After that Calum Eachern came often to the house and Eiradh did not tell him to stay away. Some of the folk said, "Calum Eachern has a bad name," and bade

Eiradh beware, because he had a false tongue. Eiradh laughed and said, " I fear the tongue of no man." Every night she read the printed book, till she knew it from the first page to the last, and when she was alone she would sing bits of the songs to Calum Eachern's tunes. Sometimes she would stand on the sea-shore, and look out across the water, and wonder what like was the country on the other side of the Rhu. In those days she was sick of Canna, and thought to herself, " If I was living in the south country, I should not be afraid of them that are dead; " and she remembered Calum's words, " It's not much company you will be having here, Eiradh Nicraonail."

One night there was a boat from Tyree in the harbour, and when Calum came in late Eiradh knew that he had been drinking with the Tyree men. His face was red, and his breath smelt strong of the drink. He tried hard to get his will of her that night, but Eiradh was a well-doing girl and pushed him out of the house. She was angry and fit to cry, thinking of the words, " Calum Eachern has a bad name." That night she had a dream. She thought she has walking by the side of the sea on a light night, and she had a bairn in her arms, and she was giving it the breast. As she walked she could hear the ghost of the lady crying in the tower. Then she felt the babe she carried as heavy as lead, and it spoke with a man's voice, and had white teeth ; and when she looked at its face, it was Calum's face laughing, all cocked on one side. With that she woke.

When she saw Calum next, he hung down his head, and looked so strange and sad that she could not help laughing as she passed by. Then he ran after, and she turned on him full of anger. But Calum had a smooth tongue, and she soon forgot her anger listening to one of his tales. She liked him best of all that day, for he was quiet and serious, and never laughed once. Eiradh thought to herself, "The man is no worse than other men, and drink will change a wise man into a fool."

Calum never tried to wrong her again, but one night he spoke out plain and asked her to marry him, and go home with him in a Canna boat to the south. It was a long while ere Eiradh answered a word. She sat with her cheek on her hand looking at the fire, and thinking of the night her mother died, and of her father and brothers that were drowned, and of the voices that came to her out of the sea. It was a rough night, and the wind blew sharp from the east, and she could hear the water at the door. Then she looked at Calum, and he had a bright smile, and held out his hand. But she only said, "Go away this night," and he went away without a word. All night long she thought of his words, "It's a dull house without the cry of bairns," and she remembered the days when her mother used to nurse her, and her father cut her the crutch of wood with his own hands. Next morning the sea was still, and the light was the colour of gold on the land beyond the Rhu. That day the folk seemed sharp and cold, and more than one mocked her with the name of Calum; so that she said to herself, "They shall not mock me without a cause;" and when Calum came to her the next night, she said she would be his good wife.

Soon after that Calum Eachern and Eiradh Nicraonail were married by the priest from Skye; and the day they married they went on board a Canna smack that was sailing south. An old man from Tyree was at the helm, and she sat on her kist close to him. Calum sat up by the mast with the men, who were all Canna lads, and as they all talked together Calum whispered something and laughed, and all the lads looked at her and laughed too. Calum was full of drink. He had a bottle of whisky in the breast of his coat, and as the boat sailed out of the bay he waved it to the folk on shore, and laughed like a wild man.

Now Eiradh felt sadder and sadder as she saw Canna growing farther and farther away; for she thought of her father and mother, and of the graveyard on the hill. The more she thought, the more she felt the tears in her eyes and the stone in her throat. Going round the Rhu she had the sea-sickness, and thought she was going to die. Though she had dwelt beside the sea so many years, she had never sailed on the water in a boat.

III.

Where Calum Eachern lived, the folk had strange ways, and many of them had both the Gaelic and the English. Their houses were whitewashed and roofed with slate, and there was a long street with shops full of all things that man could wish, and there was a house for the sale of drink. The roads were broad and smooth as your hand, and on the sides of the hills were fields of corn and potatoes. The sea was twenty miles away, but there was a burn, on the banks of which the women used to tread their clothes. Eiradh thought to herself, "It is not as fine a country as Calum said."

Calum's house was the poorest house there. It had two rooms, and in the front room Calum worked; the back room was a kitchen with a bed in the wall. Eiradh had brought with her some of the furniture from her father's house, and plenty of woollen woof made by her mother's own hands; and she soon made the place pleasant and clean. They had not been home a day when the laird came in for the back rent that was due, and Eiradh paid the money out of her own store. She had the money in a stocking inside her kist, and some of it was in copper and silver, but there were pound notes quite ragged and old with being kept so many years.

It would take me a long winter's night to tell all that Eiradh thought in those days. She was like one in a dream. She felt it strange to see so many people coming and going in and out of the shops and houses, and the crowds on market days, and the great heap of sheep and cattle. The folk were civil and fair-spoken, but most of the men drank at the public house. There was a man next door who would get mad-drunk every night he had the money, and it was a sad sight to see his wife's face cut and bruised and the bairns at her side crying for lack of food. Many of the men were weavers, and walked lame as Eiradh used to do, and had pale sickly faces, black under the eyes. The Gaelic they had was a different Gaelic from that the folk had in Canna, and sometimes Eiradh could not understand it at all.

Now, it was not long ere Eiradh found that Calum had a bad name in the place for drinking; and besides he had beguiled a servant lass the year before under the promise of marriage. Eiradh thought of the night when he had come drunk to the house, but she said nothing to Calum. She would sit and watch him for hours, and wonder she had thought him so bright and free ; for she soon saw he was a double man, with a side for his home and another for strangers ; and the first side was as dull as the second was bright. He never raised his hand to her in those days, and was sober ; but he would sit with a silent tongue, and sometimes give her a strange look. Eiradh thought to herself " Calum is like the south country, and looks brightest to them that are farthest away."

A year after they had come to the south country, Calum turned his front room into a shop, and made Eiradh look after it while he was at work. The goods were bought with her own good money, and were tea, sugar, tobacco, and meal. The first month, Eiradh got all her money back. It was pleasant to sit there and sell, and know that she made a profit on each thing she sold ; and Calum was light and merry, when he saw that his idea had turned out well. Eiradh's health was not so good in those days, and she had no children.

After that came days of trouble, for Calum grew worse and worse. He would take the money that Eiradh had earned, and spend it in the public-house; and when he came home in drink, he raised his hand to her more than once. Then Eiradh thought to herself, "My father did not love me, but he never struck me a blow; there is not a man in Canna who would lift his hand to a woman." After that she took no pleasure in trade, but would sit with a sick face and a silent tongue, thinking of Canna in the sea. Calum liked her the less because she did not complain. One day he told her that he did not marry her for herself, but for the money she had saved; and this was a sore thing to say to her; but though the tears made her blind, she only looked at him, and did not answer a word. There was some of the money left in her kist, but she never cared to look at it after what Calum had said.

After the day he married Eiradh, Calum had never left his home to work through the country as he once did. But one night late in the year he said he must go south on business, and in the morning he went away. Eiradh never saw him again on this side the narrow house. He went straight to the big city of Glasgow, and there he met the lass he had beguiled the year he married Eiradh, and the two sailed over the seas to Canada. The news came quick to Eiradh by the mouth of one who saw them on the quay.

One would need the tongue of a witch to tell all

Eiradh's thoughts in those days.   The first news seemed like the roar of the sea the time her brothers died, and the words stopped in her ears like the crying of the water day and night.   She felt ashamed to show herself in the street, and she could not bear the comfort of the good wives; for they all said, "Calum had ever a bad name," and she remembered how the folk in Canna had used the same words.   She would sit with her apron over her face, and greet[1] for hours with no noise.   It seemed dreadful to be there in the south country, without friend or kindred, and the folk having a different Gaelic from her own.   She felt sick and stupid, just like herself when she would cry night and day from the cradle, without strength to run upon her feet.   She thought to herself, "I may cry till my heart breaks now, but no one heeds ;" and the thought brought up the picture of her mother lying in the bed all white, and made her cry the more.   Now in those days voices came about her that belonged to another land, and the faces of her father and mother went past her like the white breaking of a wave on the beach in the night.   She had dreams whenever she slept, and in every one of her dreams she heard the sough of the sea.

But Eiradh Eachern was a well-doing lass, and had been bred to face trouble when it came.   Her first thought was this : "I will go back to Canna in the sea, and work for my bread in the fields."   But when she looked in the kist, she found that Calum had been there and taken away all the good money out of the stocking,

[1] Weep.

and a picture besides of the Virgin Mary, set round with yellow gold and precious stones the colour of blood. Now, this grieved Eiradh most. She did not heed the money so much, but the picture had belonged to her mother, and she would not have parted with it for hundreds of pounds. She felt a sharp thread run through her heart and she was sick·for pain.

It is a wonder how much trouble a strong man or woman in good health can bear when it comes. Eiradh thought to herself at first, "I shall die," but she did not die. The Lord was not willing that she should be taken away then. He spared her, as he had spared her in her sickness when a bairn at the breast.

One day a neighbour came in and said, "Will you not keep open the shop the same as before? You have always paid for your goods, and those that sent them will not press for payment at first." Now, Eiradh had never thought of that, and her heart lightened. That same day she got the schoolmaster to write a letter, in the English, to the big city, asking goods. The next week the goods came.

Then Eiradh thought, "God has not forgotten me," and worked hard to put all in order as before. Many folk came and bought from her, out of kindness at first, but afterwards because they said she was a just woman, and gave full value for their money. All this gladdened her heart. She said, "God helps those that are fallen," and every penny that she earned seemed to have the blessing of God.

x

In those times she would lock up the house when the day was done, and walk by herself along the side of the burn; for the sound of the water seemed like old times; and when the moon came out on the green fields, they looked for all the world like smooth water. Voices from another land came to her, and spirits passed before her eyes; so that she often thought to herself, " I wonder how Canna looks this night, and whether it is storm or calm?"

I might talk till the summer came, and not tell you half of the many thoughts Eiradh had in the south country. She loved to sit by herself, as when she was a child; and the folk thought her a dull woman with a white face. The women said, " Calum Eachern's wife has the greed of money strong in her heart, but she is a just-dealing woman." It was true that Eiradh found pleasure in trade, and would not sell to those who did not come to buy money in hand. Every piece she saved she put in the stocking in the old kist, and every week she counted it out in her lap.

So the time passed, and sometimes Eiradh could hardly call up right the memory of Calum's face. It seemed like a dream. These were the days of her prosperity, and every week she saved something, and every second Sabbath she saw the priest. Now, the folk in those parts had a religion of their own, and did not believe in the Virgin Mary or the Pope of Rome. Some of them were worse than that, and did not believe in the Lord Jesus Christ. All the children had the English as well as the Gaelic; and the preachings were in the English, and the English was taught in the school. But all the time she lived in the south Eiradh could not speak a word of that tongue. It seemed to her like the chirping of birds, with little meaning and a heap of sound.

All the years Eiradh sat in the shop, the Lord drew silver threads in her hair, and made lines like pencil-marks over her face ; and when she was thirty-five years of age her sight failed her, and she had to wear glasses. She had little sickness, but she stooped in the shoulders, and had a dry cough. In those days she did not go out of the house at night, but sat over the fire reading the book Calum had given her long years before. The leaves of the book were all black and torn, and many of the pages were gone. Every time she looked at it she thought of old times. She had little pleasure in the tales and riddles of the south country—all about brightness and a pleasant place ; for she thought to herself, "The tales are all lies, and the south country looks brightest far off, and the folk do not believe in the Virgin Mary or the saints." For all that she liked to look at the old book ; and to let her thoughts go back of their own accord, like the flowing of water in a burn. Best of all, she loved to count the bright money into her lap, and think how the neighbours praised her as a just-dealing woman who throve well.

IV

The years went past Eiradh Eachern like the waves breaking on the shore, and the days were as like each other as the waves breaking, and she could not count

them at all.   She was like the young man that went to
sleep on the Island of Peace, and had a dream of watching
the fairy people, and when he woke he was old and frail
upon his feet.   Eiradh was fifty years of age when she
counted the money in her kist for the last time, and found
that she had put by a hundred and twenty pounds in good
money.   That night she sat with the heap of money in
her lap, and the salt tears running down her cheeks, and
her bottom-lip quivering like the withered leaf on the
bough of a tree.

Now all these years Eiradh had one thought, and it was
this : " Before I die I will go back to Canna in the sea."
Every day of her life she fancied she saw the picture of
the green cliffs covered with goats and sheep, and the
black scarts sitting on the weedy rocks in a row, and the
sea rising and falling like the soft breasts of a woman in
sound sleep.   Every night of her life she had a dream of
her father's house by the shore, and the water crying at
the door.   It seemed ever calm weather to her thoughts,
and the sea was kinder and sweeter than when she was a
child.   Eiradh often thought to herself, " The water took
away my five brothers, and close to the water my father
and mother closed their eyes ; " and the more she thought
of them sleeping the less she was afraid.

So when she had saved one hundred and twenty pounds
in good money, she felt that she could abide no longer in
the south country.   The more she tried to stay a little
longer, the more voices from another land came to her,
saying, " Eiradh, Eiradh ! go back to Canna in the sea."

At last she had a dream ; and she thought she was lying in her sowe[1] in a dark land, waiting to be laid in the earth. All at once she felt herself rocking up and down, and heard the sound of the sea crying, and when she put out her hand at the side it was dripping wet. Then Eiradh knew that she was drifting in a boat, and the boat was a coffin with the lid off, and though there was a strong wind she floated on the waves like a cork. All night long she floated and never saw land ; only a light shining far, far off, over the dark water. When she woke up, she was sore troubled, and said to herself, " It is my wraith that I saw, and unless I haste I may never see my home again."

After that she never rested till she had sold the trade of her shop in the south country, and all she kept to herself was the old kist full of her clothes and the money she had saved. But she made a pouch of leather with her own hands, and put the money in it, and fastened the pouch to her waist underneath her clothes, and the only thing in the pouch beside the money was the old book in the Gaelic Calum had given her when she was a young woman.

I have told you that the place was twenty miles from the sea. One day she put her kist in a cart that was going that way, and the day after she took the road. It was a fine morning, early in the year. When she got to the top of the hill, and saw the place below her where she had lived so long, all asleep and still, with the smoke going straight up out of the houses, and not a soul in the

Shroud.[1]

street, it seemed like a dream. As she went on, the
country was strange, but it looked finer and bonnier than
any country she had ever seen. Now, her heart was so
light that day that she could walk like a strong man.
The sun came out and the birds sang, and the land was
green, and wherever she went the sheep cried. Eiradh
thought to herself, " My dream was true after all, and the
south country is a pleasant place."

For all that she was wearying to see Canna in the sea,
and wondering if it was the same all those years. She
counted on her fingers the names of the folk she knew,
and wondered how many were dead. Every one of them
seemed like a friend. She was keen to hear her own
Gaelic again after so many years in a foreign land.

She walked twelve miles that day, and slept at a farm
by the road at night. The next day she saw the sea.

It was good weather, and the sea was covered with
fishing-boats and ships. She could hear the sough of the
water a long way off, and it seemed like old times. There
was a bit village on the shore, full of fisher folk, and the
houses minded her of those where she was born. There
were skiffs drawn up on the shore, and nets put out to
dry, and the air was full of the smell of fish.

She slept in the house of a fisher-woman that night, and
the next day a fishing-boat took her out to catch the big
steamboat to Tobermory. It was the first time that
Eiradh had seen a boat like that, and it seemed to her like a
great beast panting and groaning, and swimming through
the water with its fins and tail. It was full of the smell of

fish, and the decks were covered with herring-barrels, and where there were no herring-barrels there were cattle and sheep. In one part of the boat there was a long box like a coffin, covered over with a piece of tarpaulin to keep it dry ; and one of the sailors told Eiradh that it held the dead body of an old man from Skye, who had died on the Firth o' Clyde, and was being carried home to be with his kindred at home. Eiradh said, " It is a sad thing to be buried far away from kindred ; " and she thought to herself, " If I had died in the south country, there would have been no kin or friend to carry me to Canna in the sea."

Neither wind nor tide could keep the big steamboat back; so wonderful are the works of the hand of man, when God is willing. Late at night Eiradh landed at Tobermory in Mull, but the moon was bright, and she saw that the bay was full of fishing-boats at anchor. Eiradh wondered to herself if any of the boats were from Canna.

She got a lodging in the inn that night, and the next morning she went down to the shore. There were heaps of fishermen on the beach, and many of them passed her the sign of the day, but none of them seemed to have her own Gaelic. Then Eiradh said, " Is there a Canna boat in the bay ? " and they said " Ay," and pointed out a big smack with her sails up, and a great patch on the mainsail. The skipper of the smack was on shore, and his name was Alastair. He was a big black-whiskered man, with large silly eyes like a seal's. Eiradh minded him well, though he was a laddie when she left, and went up and called him by his name, but he stared at her and shook his head. Then Eiradh said, "Do you mind Eiradh Nicraonail, who dwelt in the small house by the sea?" and the man laughed, and asked after Calum Eachern, Eiradh told him her troubles, and got the promise of a passage to Canna that day.

In the afternoon it blew hard from the east, but Eiradh went on board the smack with her kist. They ran out of the Sound of Mull with the wind, and kept in close to the Rhu, for the sake of smooth water. Eiradh felt a heaviness and pain about her heart, and sat on the kist with her head leaning against the side of the boat. She had a touch of the sea-sickness, but that passed away.

Alastair steered the smack on the west side of Eig, and the squalls came so sharp off the Scaur that they had to take down the topsail. As they sailed in the smooth water on the leeside of Eig Eiradh asked about the Canna folk she had known, and most of them were dead and buried. Then she asked about the old man who had taught her to read and write, and he was dead too. Many of the young folk had gone away across the ocean, to work among strangers and wander in a foreign land.

The heart of Eiradh sank to hear the news; for she thought to herself, "Every face will be as strange as the faces in the south." Then Alastair, seeing she put her hand to her heart, said "What ails ye, wife? are you sick?" Eiradh nodded, and leant her head over the boat, looking at the sea.

A little after that the smack rounded the north end of

Rum, and Eiradh saw Canna in the sea, just as she had left it long ago. There was a shower all over the ocean, but the green side of Canna was shining with the light through a cloud. Eiradh looked and looked; for there was not an inch of the green land but she knew by heart.

The wind blew fresh and keen, and they had to lower the peak of the mainsail running for the harbour. Eiradh saw the tower, all gray and wet in the rain, and she thought she heard the lady's voice calling as in old times. Then she looked over to the mouth of Loch Scavaig, thinking to herself, " There is the place where my brothers were lost !" and that brought up the picture of her father, sitting dead on the cliffs, and looking out to sea. Eiradh's eyes were blind with tears, and she could not see Canna any more ; but as they ran round into the bay, her eyes cleared, and she saw her home close by the water-side, with the roof all gone, and the walls broken down, and a cow looking out of the door.

A little after that, when the anchor was down and the mainsail lowered, Alastair touched Eiradh on the arm, thinking she was asleep, for she was leaning back with her face in her cloak. Then he drew back the cloak, and saw her face with a strange smile on it, and the eyes wide open. Though he was a big man, he was scared, and called out to his mates, and an old man among them said, " Sure enough she is dead." So they carried her body ashore in their boat, and put it in one of the houses, and sent word to the laird.

Y

Eiradh Eachern had died of the same disease that killed her mother. She had o'er many thoughts to live long, and she knew the name of trouble. In her kist they found her grave-clothes all ready made and neatly worked with her own hands, and they buried her on the hill-side close to her father and mother. May the Lord God find her ready there to answer to her name at the Last Day!

THE END.

S. Cowan & Co., Strathmore Printing Works, Perth.

CHATTO & WINDUS'S
LIST OF BOOKS.

* * * * * * * * * * * * *

About.—The Fellah: An Egyptian Novel. By EDMOND ABOUT. Translated by Sir RANDAL ROBERTS. Post 8vo, illustrated boards, 2s. ; cloth limp, **2s. 6d.**

Adams (W. Davenport), Works by:

A Dictionary of the Drama. Being a comprehensive Guide to the Plays, Playwrights, Players. and Playhouses of the United Kingdom and America, from the Earliest to the Present Times. Crown 8vo, halfbound, **12s. 6d.** [*In preparation.*

Latter-Day Lyrics. Edited by W. DAVENPORT ADAMS. Post 8vo, cloth limp, **2s. 6d.**

Quips and Quiddities. Selected by W. DAVENPORT ADAMS. Post 8vo, cloth limp, **2s. 6d.**

Advertising, A History of, from the Earliest Times. Illustrated by Anecdotes. Curious Specimens, and Notices of Successful Advertisers. By HENRY SAMPSON. Crown 8vo, with Coloured Frontispiece and Illustrations, cloth gilt, **7s. 6d.**

Agony Column (The) of "The Times," from 1800 to 1870. Edited, with an Introduction, by ALICE CLAY. Post 8vo, cloth limp, **2s. 6d.**

Aïde (Hamilton), Works by:

Carr of Carrlyon. Post 8vo, illustrated boards, **2s.**

Confidences. Post 8vo, illustrated boards, **2s.**

Alexander (Mrs.).—Maid, Wife, or Widow? A Romance. By Mrs. ALEXANDER. Post 8vo, illustrated boards, 2s. ; cr. 8vo, cloth extra, **3s. 6d.**

Allen (Grant), Works by:

Colin Clout's Calendar. Crown 8vo, cloth extra, **6s.**

The Evolutionist at Large. Crown 8vo, cloth extra, **6s.**

Vignettes from Nature. Crown 8vo, cloth extra, **6s.**

Architectural Styles, A Handbook of. Translated from the German of A. ROSENGARTEN, by W. COLLETT-SANDARS. Crown 8vo, cloth extra, with 639 Illustrations, **7s. 6d.**

Art (The) of Amusing: A Collection of Graceful Arts, Games, Tricks, Puzzles, and Charades. By FRANK BELLEW. With 300 Illustrations. Cr. 8vo, cloth extra, **4s. 6d.**

Artemus Ward :

Artemus Ward's Works: The Works of CHARLES FARRER BROWNE, better known as ARTEMUS WARD. With Portrait and Facsimile. Crown 8vo, cloth extra, **7s. 6d.**

Artemus Ward's Lecture on the Mormons. With 32 Illustrations. Edited, with Preface, by EDWARD P. HINGSTON. Crown 8vo, **6d.**

The Genial Showman: Life and Adventures of Artemus Ward. By EDWARD P. HINGSTON. With a Frontispiece. Crown 8vo, cloth extra, **3s. 6d.**

Ashton (John), Works by :

A History of the Chap-Books of the Eighteenth Century. With nearly 400 Illustrations, engraved in fac-simile of the originals. Crown 8vo, cloth extra, 7s. 6d.

Social Life in the Reign of Queen Anne. Taken from Original Sources. With nearly One Hundred Illustrations. New and cheaper Edition, crown 8vo, cloth extra, 7s. 6d.

Humour, Wit, and Satire of the Seventeenth Century. With nearly 100 Illustrations. Crown 8vo, cloth extra, 7s. 6d. One Hundred large-paper copies (only seventy-five of them for sale) will be carefully printed on hand-made paper, crown 4to, parchment boards, price 42s. Early application must be made for these.   [*In preparation.*

Ballad History (The) of England

By W. C. BENNETT. Post 8vo, cloth limp, 2s.

Balzac's " Comedie Humaine "

and its Author. With Translations by H. H. WALKER. Post 8vo, cloth limp, 2s. 6d.

Bankers, A Handbook of London;

together with Lists of Bankers from 1677. By F. G. HILTON PRICE. Crown 8vo, cloth extra, 7s. 6d.

Bardsley (Rev. C.W.), Works by :

English Surnames: Their Sources and Significations. Crown 8vo, cloth extra, 7s. 6d.

Curiosities of Puritan Nomenclature. Crown 8vo, cloth extra, 7s. 6d.

Bartholomew Fair, Memoirs

of. By HENRY MORLEY. A New Edition, with One Hundred Illustrations. Crown 8vo, cloth extra, 7s. 6d.

Beauchamp. — Grantley

Grange: A Novel. By SHELSLEY BEAUCHAMP. Post 8vo, illustrated boards, 2s.

Beautiful Pictures by British

Artists: A Gathering of Favourites from our Picture Galleries. In Two Series. All engraved on Steel in the highest style of Art. Edited, with Notices of the Artists, by SYDNEY ARMYTAGE, M.A. Imperial 4to, cloth extra, gilt and gilt edges, 21s. per Vol.

Bechstein. — As Pretty as

Seven, and other German Stories. Collected by LUDWIG BECHSTEIN. With Additional Tales by the Brothers GRIMM, and 100 Illusts. by RICHTER. Small 4to, green and gold, 6s. 6d.; gilt edges, 7s. 6d.

Beerbohm. — Wanderings in

Patagonia; or, Life among the Ostrich Hunters. By JULIUS BEERBOHM. With Illusts. Crown 8vo, cloth extra, 3s. 6d.

Belgravia for 1883.

One Shilling Monthly, Illustrated.—" Maid of Athens," JUSTIN McCARTHY's New Serial Story, Illustrated by FRED. BARNARD, was begun in the JANUARY Number of BELGRAVIA, which Number contained also the First Portion of a Story in Three Parts, by OUIDA, entitled " Frescoes ; " the continuation of WILKIE COLLINS's Novel, " Heart and Science ; " a further instalment of Mrs. ALEXANDER's Novel, " The Admiral's Ward ; " and other Matters of Interest.

*** *Now ready, the Volume for* MARCH *to* JUNE, 1883, *cloth extra, gilt edges,* 7s. 6d.; *Cases for binding Vols.,* 2s. *each.*

Belgravia Holiday Number,

written by the well-known Authors who have been so long associated with the Magazine, is now ready, price 1s.

Besant (Walter) and James

Rice, Novels by. Each in post 8vo, illust. boards, 2s. ; cloth limp, 2s. 6d.; or crown 8vo, cloth extra, 3s. 6d.

Ready-Money Mortiboy.

With Harp and Crown.

This Son of Vulcan.

My Little Girl.

The Case of Mr. Lucraft.

The Golden Butterfly.

By Celia's Arbour.

The Monks of Thelema.

'Twas in Trafalgar's Bay.

The Seamy Side.

The Ten Years' Tenant.

The Chaplain of the Fleet.

Besant (Walter), Novels by :

All Sorts and Conditions of Men: An Impossible Story. With Illustrations by FRED. BARNARD. Crown 8vo, cloth extra, 3s. 6d.

The Captains' Room, &c. With Frontispiece by E. J. WHEELER. Crown 8vo, cloth extra, 3s. 6d.

All in a Garden Fair. Three Vols., crown 8vo, 31s. 6d.   [*Shortly.*

Birthday Book.—The Starry Heavens: A Poetical Birthday Book. Square 8vo, handsomely bound in cloth, 2s. 6d. *[Shortly.*

Birthday Flowers: Their Language and Legends. By W. J. GORDON. Beautifully Illustrated in Colours by VIOLA BOUGHTON. In illuminated cover, crown 4to, 6s. *[Shortly.*

Blackburn's (Henry) Art Handbooks. Demy 8vo, Illustrated, uniform in size for binding.

Academy Notes, separate years, from 1875 to 1882, each 1s.

Academy Notes, 1883. With Illustrations. 1s.

Academy Notes, 1875-79. Complete in One Volume, with nearly 600 Illustrations in Facsimile. Demy 8vo, cloth limp, 6s.

Grosvenor Notes, 1877. 6d.

Grosvenor Notes, separate years, from 1878 to 1882, each 1s.

Grosvenor Notes, 1883. With Illustrations. 1s.

Grosvenor Notes, 1877-82. With upwards of 300 Illustrations. Demy 8vo, cloth limp, 6s.

Pictures at South Kensington. With 70 Illustrations. 1s.

The English Pictures at the National Gallery. 114 Illustrations. 1s.

The Old Masters at the National Gallery. 128 Illustrations. 1s. 6d.

A Complete Illustrated Catalogue to the National Gallery. With Notes by H. BLACKBURN, and 242 Illusts. Demy 8vo, cloth limp, 3s.

The Paris Salon, 1883. With over 300 Illustrations. Edited by F. G. DUMAS. (English Edition.) Demy 8vo, 3s.

At the Paris Salon. Sixteen large Plates, printed in facsimile of the Artists' Drawings, in two tints. Edited by F. G. DUMAS. Large folio, 1s.

The Art Annual. Edited by F. G. DUMAS. With 250 full-page Illusts. Demy 8vo, 3s. 6d.

Blake (William): Etchings from his Works. By W. B. SCOTT. With descriptive Text. Folio, half-bound boards, India Proofs, 21s.

Boccaccio's Decameron; or, Ten Days' Entertainment. Translated into English, with an Introduction by THOMAS WRIGHT, F.S.A. With Portrait, and STOTHARD's beautiful Copperplates. Cr. 8vo, cloth extra, gilt, 7s. 6d.

Bowers'(G.) Hunting Sketches:

Canters in Crampshire. Oblong 4to, half-bound boards, 21s.

Leaves from a Hunting Journal. Coloured in facsimile of the originals. Oblong 4to, half-bound, 21s.

Boyle (Frederick), Works by:

Camp Notes: Stories of Sport and Adventure in Asia, Africa, and America. Crown 8vo, cloth extra, 3s. 6d.; post 8vo, illustrated bds., 2s.

Savage Life. Crown 8vo, cloth extra, 3s. 6d.; post 8vo, illustrated bds., 2s.

Brand's Observations on Popular Antiquities, chiefly Illustrating the Origin of our Vulgar Customs, Ceremonies, and Superstitions. With the Additions of Sir HENRY ELLIS. Crown 8vo, cloth extra, gilt, with numerous Illustrations, 7s. 6d.

Bret Harte, Works by:

Bret Harte's Collected Works. Arranged and Revised by the Author. Complete in Five Vols., crown 8vo, cloth extra, 6s. each.

Vol. I. COMPLETE POETICAL AND DRAMATIC WORKS. With Steel Plate Portrait, and an Introduction by the Author.

Vol. II. EARLIER PAPERS—LUCK OF ROARING CAMP, and other Sketches —BOHEMIAN PAPERS — SPANISH AND AMERICAN LEGENDS.

Vol. III. TALES OF THE ARGONAUTS —EASTERN SKETCHES.

Vol. IV. GABRIEL CONROY.

Vol. V. STORIES — CONDENSED NOVELS, &c.

The Select Works of Bret Harte, in Prose and Poetry. With Introductory Essay by J. M. BELLEW, Portrait of the Author, and 50 Illustrations. Crown 8vo, cloth extra, 7s. 6d.

Gabriel Conroy: A Novel. Post 8vo, illustrated boards, 2s.

An Heiress of Red Dog, and other Stories. Post 8vo, illustrated boards, 2s.; cloth limp, 2s. 6d.

The Twins of Table Mountain. Fcap 8vo, picture cover, 1s.; crown 8vo, cloth extra, 3s. 6d.

The Luck of Roaring Camp, and other Sketches. Post 8vo, illustrated boards, 2s.

Jeff Briggs's Love Story. Fcap 8vo, picture cover, 1s.; cloth extra, 2s. 6d.

Flip. Post 8vo, illustrated boards, 2s.; cloth limp, 2s. 6d.

Brewer (Rev. Dr.), Works by :

The Reader's Handbook of Allusions, References, Plots, and Stories. Third Edition, revised throughout, with a New Appendix, containing a COMPLETE ENGLISH BIBLIOGRAPHY. Crown 8vo, 1,400 pages, cloth extra, **7s. 6d.**

A Dictionary of Miracles: Imitative, Realistic, and Dogmatic. Crown 8vo, cloth extra, **7s. 6d.** [*In preparation.*

Buchanan's (Robert) Works :

Ballads of Life, Love, and Humour. With a Frontispiece by ARTHUR HUGHES. Crown 8vo, cloth extra, **6s.**

Selected Poems of Robert Buchanan. With Frontispiece by T. DALZIEL. Crown 8vo, cloth extra, **6s.**

Undertones. Crown 8vo, cloth extra, **6s.**

London Poems. Crown 8vo, cloth extra, **6s.**

The Book of Orm. Crown 8vo, cloth extra, **6s.**

White Rose and Red: A Love Story. Crown 8vo, cloth extra, **6s.**

Idylls and Legends of Inverburn. Crown 8vo, cloth extra. **6s.**

St. Abe and his Seven Wives: A Tale of Salt Lake City. With a Frontispiece by A. B. HOUGHTON. Crown 8vo, cloth extra, **5s.**

The Hebrid Isles: Wanderings in the Land of Lorne and the Outer Hebrides. With Frontispiece by W. SMALL. Crown 8vo, cloth extra, **6s.**

Selections from the Prose Writings of Robert Buchanan. Crown 8vo, cloth extra, **6s.** [*Shortly.*

Robert Buchanan's Complete Poetical Works. Crown 8vo, cloth extra, **7s. 6d.** [*In preparation.*

The Shadow of the Sword: A Romance. Crown 8vo, cloth extra, **3s. 6d.**; post 8vo, illust. boards, **2s.**

A Child of Nature: A Romance. With a Frontispiece. Crown 8vo, cloth extra, **3s. 6d.**; post 8vo, illustrated boards, **2s.**

God and the Man: A Romance. With Illustrations by FRED. BARNARD. Crown 8vo, cloth extra, **3s. 6d.**

The Martyrdom of Madeline: A Romance. With a Frontispiece by A. W. COOPER. Crown 8vo, cloth extra, **3s. 6d.**

Love Me for Ever. With a Frontispiece by P. MACNAB. Crown 8vo, cloth extra, **3s. 6d.**

Annan Water: A Romance. Three Vols., cr. 8vo, **31s. 6d.** [*Immediately.*

Brewster (Sir David), Works by:

More Worlds than One: The Creed of the Philosopher and the Hope of the Christian. With Plates. Post 8vo, cloth extra, **4s. 6d.**

The Martyrs of Science: Lives of GALILEO, TYCHO BRAHE, and KEPLER. With Portraits. Post 8vo, cloth extra, **4s. 6d.**

Letters on Natural Magic. A New Edition, with numerous Illustrations, and Chapters on the Being and Faculties of Man, and Additional Phenomena of Natural Magic, by J. A. SMITH. Post 8vo, cloth extra, **4s. 6d.**

Brillat-Savarin.—Gastronomy

as a Fine Art. By BRILLAT-SAVARIN. Translated by R. E. ANDERSON, M.A. Post 8vo, cloth limp, **2s. 6d.**

Browning.—The Pied Piper of

Hamelin. By ROBERT BROWNING. Illust. by GEORGE CARLINE. Large 4to. illum. cover. **1s.** [*In preparation.*

Burnett (Mrs.), Novels by :

Surly Tim, and other Stories. Post 8vo, illustrated boards, **2s.**

Kathleen Mavourneen. Fcap. 8vo, picture cover, **1s.**

Lindsay's Luck. Fcap. 8vo, picture cover, **1s.**

Pretty Polly Pemberton. Fcap. 8vo, picture cover, **1s.**

Burton (Robert):

The Anatomy of Melancholy. A New Edition, complete, corrected and enriched by Translations of the Classical Extracts. Demy 8vo, cloth extra, **7s. 6d.**

Melancholy Anatomised: Being an Abridgment, for popular use, of BURTON'S ANATOMY OF MELANCHOLY. Post 8vo, cloth limp, **2s. 6d.**

Burton (Captain), Works by :

To the Gold Coast for Gold: A Personal Narrative. By RICHARD F. BURTON and VERNEY LOVETT CAMERON. With Maps and Frontispiece. Two Vols., crown 8vo, cloth extra, **21s.**

The Book of the Sword: Being a History of the Sword and its Use in all Countries, from the Earliest Times. By RICHARD F. BURTON. With over 400 Illustrations. Square 8vo, cloth extra, **32s.** [*In preparation.*

Bunyan's Pilgrim's Progress.

Edited by Rev. T. SCOTT. With 17 Steel Plates by STOTHARD, engraved by GOODALL, and numerous Woodcuts. Crown 8vo, cloth extra, gilt, **7s. 6d.**

Byron (Lord):

Byron's Letters and Journals. With Notices of his Life. By THOMAS MOORE. A Reprint of the Original Edition, newly revised, with Twelve full-page Plates. Crown 8vo, cloth extra, gilt, 7s. 6d.

Byron's Don Juan. Complete in One Vol., post 8vo, cloth limp, 2s.

Cameron (Commander) and Captain Burton.—To the Gold Coast for Gold: A Personal Narrative. By RICHARD F. BURTON and VERNEY LOVETT CAMERON. With Frontispiece and Maps. Two Vols., crown 8vo, cloth extra, 21s.

Cameron (Mrs. H. Lovett), Novels by:

Juliet's Guardian. Post 8vo, illustrated boards, 2s.; crown 8vo, cloth extra, 3s. 6d.

Deceivers Ever. Post 8vo, illustrated boards, 2s.; crown 8vo, cloth extra, 3s. 6d.

Campbell.—White and Black: Travels in the United States. By Sir GEORGE CAMPBELL, M.P. Demy 8vo, cloth extra, 14s.

Carlyle (Thomas):

Thomas Carlyle: Letters and Recollections. By MONCURE D. CONWAY, M.A. Crown 8vo, cloth extra, with Illustrations, 6s.

On the Choice of Books. By THOMAS CARLYLE. With a Life of the Author by R. H. SHEPHERD. New and Revised Edition, post 8vo, cloth extra, Illustrated, 1s. 6d.

The Correspondence of Thomas Carlyle and Ralph Waldo Emerson, 1834 to 1872. Edited by CHARLES ELIOT NORTON. With Portraits. Two Vols., crown 8vo, cloth extra, 24s.

Century (A) of Dishonour: A Sketch of the United States Government's Dealings with some of the Indian Tribes. Crown 8vo, cloth extra, 7s. 6d.

Chapman's (George) Works:

Vol. I. contains the Plays complete, including the doubtful ones. Vol. II., the Poems and Minor Translations, with an Introductory Essay by ALGERNON CHARLES SWINBURNE. Vol. III., the Translations of the Iliad and Odyssey. Three Vols., crown 8vo, cloth extra, 18s.; or separately, 6s. each.

Chatto & Jackson.—A Treatise on Wood Engraving, Historical and Practical. By WM. ANDREW CHATTO and JOHN JACKSON. With an Additional Chapter by HENRY G. BOHN; and 450 fine Illustrations. A Reprint of the last Revised Edition, Large 4to, half-bound, 28s.

Chaucer:

Chaucer for Children: A Golden Key. By Mrs. H. R. HAWEIS. With Eight Coloured Pictures and numerous Woodcuts by the Author. New Ed., small 4to, cloth extra, 6s.

Chaucer for Schools. By Mrs. H. R. HAWEIS. Demy 8vo, cloth limp, 2s. 6d.

Cobban —The Cure of Souls: A Story. By J. MACLAREN COBBAN. Post 8vo, illustrated boards, 2s.

Collins (C. Allston).—The Bar Sinister: A Story. By C. ALLSTON COLLINS. Post 8vo, illustrated boards, 2s.

Collins (Mortimer & Frances), Novels by:

Sweet and Twenty. Post 8vo, illustrated boards, 2s.

Frances. Post 8vo, illust. bds., 2s.

Blacksmith and Scholar. Post 8vo, illustrated boards, 2s.; crown 8vo, cloth extra, 3s. 6d.

The Village Comedy. Post 8vo, illust. boards, 2s.; cr. 8vo, cloth extra, 3s. 6d.

You Play Me False. Post 8vo, illust. boards, 2s.; cr. 8vo, cloth extra, 3s. 6d.

Collins (Mortimer), Novels by:

Sweet Anne Page. Post 8vo, illustrated boards, 2s.; crown 8vo, cloth extra, 3s. 6d.

Transmigration. Post 8vo, illustrated boards, 2s.; crown 8vo, cloth extra, 3s. 6d.

From Midnight to Midnight. Post 8vo, illustrated boards, 2s.; crown 8vo, cloth extra, 3s. 6d.

A Fight with Fortune. Post 8vo, illustrated boards, 2s.

Colman's Humorous Works: "Broad Grins," "My Nightgown and Slippers," and other Humorous Works, Prose and Poetical, of GEORGE COLMAN. With Life by G B BUCKSTONE, and Frontispiece by HOGARTH. Crown 8vo, cloth extra, gilt, 7s. 6d.

Collins (Wilkie), Novels by.
Each post 8vo, illustrated boards, 2s; cloth limp, 2s. 6d.; or crown 8vo, cloth extra, Illustrated, 3s. 6d.

Antonina. Illust. by A. CONCANEN.

Basil. Illustrated by Sir JOHN GILBERT and J. MAHONEY.

Hide and Seek. Illustrated by Sir JOHN GILBERT and J. MAHONEY.

The Dead Secret. Illustrated by Sir JOHN GILBERT and A. CONCANEN.

Queen of Hearts. Illustrated by Sir JOHN GILBERT and A. CONCANEN.

My Miscellanies. With Illustrations by A. CONCANEN, and a Steel-plate Portrait of WILKIE COLLINS.

The Woman in White. With Illustrations by Sir JOHN GILBERT and F. A. FRASER.

The Moonstone. With Illustrations by G. DU MAURIER and F. A. FRASER.

Man and Wife. Illust. by W. SMALL.

Poor Miss Finch. Illustrated by G. DU MAURIER and EDWARD HUGHES.

Miss or Mrs.? With Illustrations by S. L. FILDES and HENRY WOODS.

The New Magdalen. Illustrated by G. DU MAURIER and C. S. RANDS.

The Frozen Deep. Illustrated by G. DU MAURIER and J. MAHONEY.

The Law and the Lady. Illustrated by S. L. FILDES and SYDNEY HALL.

The Two Destinies.

The Haunted Hotel. Illustrated by ARTHUR HOPKINS.

The Fallen Leaves.

Jezebel's Daughter.

The Black Robe.

Heart and Science: A Story of the Present Time. Three Vols., crown 8vo, 31s. 6d.

Convalescent Cookery: A Family Handbook. By CATHERINE RYAN. Post 8vo, cloth limp, 2s. 6d.

Conway (Moncure D.), Works by:

Demonology and Devil-Lore. Two Vols., royal 8vo, with 65 Illusts., 28s.

A Necklace of Stories. Illustrated by W. J. HENNESSY. Square 8vo, cloth extra, 6s.

The Wandering Jew. Crown 8vo, cloth extra, 6s.

Thomas Carlyle: Letters and Recollections. With Illustrations. Crown 8vo, cloth extra, 6s.

Cook (Dutton), Works by:

Hours with the Players. With a Steel Plate Frontispiece. New and Cheaper Edit., cr. 8vo, cloth extra, 6s.

Nights at the Play: A View of the English Stage. Two Vols., crown 8vo, cloth extra, 21s.

Leo: A Novel. Post 8vo, illustrated boards, 2s.

Paul Foster's Daughter. Post 8vo, illustrated boards, 2s.; crown 8vo, cloth extra, 3s. 6d.   [*Shortly.*

Copyright.—A Handbook of English and Foreign Copyright in Literary and Dramatic Works. By SIDNEY JERROLD, of the Middle Temple, Esq., Barrister-at-Law. Post 8vo, cloth limp, 2s. 6d.

Cornwall.—Popular Romances of the West of England; or, The Drolls, Traditions, and Superstitions of Old Cornwall. Collected and Edited by ROBERT HUNT, F.R.S. New and Revised Edition, with Additions, and Two Steel-plate Illustrations by GEORGE CRUIKSHANK. Crown 8vo, cloth extra, 7s. 6d.

Creasy.—Memoirs of Eminent Etonians: with Notices of the Early History of Eton College. By Sir EDWARD CREASY, Author of "The Fifteen Decisive Battles of the World." Crown 8vo, cloth extra, gilt, with 13 Portraits, 7s. 6d.

Cruikshank (George):

The Comic Almanack. Complete in TWO SERIES: The FIRST from 1835 to 1843; the SECOND from 1844 to 1853. A Gathering of the BEST HUMOUR of THACKERAY, HOOD, MAYHEW, ALBERT SMITH, A'BECKETT, ROBERT BROUGH, &c. With 2,000 Woodcuts and Steel Engravings by CRUIKSHANK, HINE, LANDELLS, &c. Crown 8vo, cloth gilt, two very thick volumes, 7s. 6d. each.

The Life of George Cruikshank. By BLANCHARD JERROLD, Author of "The Life of Napoleon III.," &c. With 84 Illustrations. New and Cheaper Edition, enlarged, with Additional Plates, and a very carefully compiled Bibliography. Crown 8vo, cloth extra, 7s. 6d.

Robinson Crusoe. A choicely-printed Edition, with 37 Woodcuts and Two Steel Plates, by GEORGE CRUIKSHANK. Crown 8vo, cloth extra, 7s. 6d. 100 Large Paper copies, carefully printed on hand-made paper, with India proofs of the Illustrations, price 36s.   [*In preparation.*

Crimes and Punishments. Including a New Translation of Beccaria's "De Delitti e delle Pene." By JAMES ANSON FARRER. Crown 8vo, cloth extra, 6s.

Cumming.—In the Hebrides. By C. F. GORDON CUMMING, Author of "At Home in Fiji." With Autotype Facsimile and Illustrations. Demy 8vo, cloth extra, 8s. 6d. [*Preparing.*

Cussans.—Handbook of Heraldry; with Instructions for Tracing Pedigrees and Deciphering Ancient MSS., &c. By JOHN E. CUSSANS. Entirely New and Revised Edition, illustrated with over 400 Woodcuts and Coloured Plates. Crown 8vo, cloth extra, 7s. 6d.

Cyples.—Hearts of Gold: A Novel. By WILLIAM CYPLES. Crown 8vo, cloth extra, 3s. 6d.

Daniel. — Merrie England in the Olden Time. By GEORGE DANIEL. With Illustrations by ROBT. CRUIKSHANK. Crown 8vo, cloth extra, 3s 6d.

Daudet.—Port Salvation; or, The Evangelist. By ALPHONSE DAUDET. Translated by C. HARRY MELTZER. Two Vols., post 8vo, 12s.

Davenant. — What shall my Son be? Hints for Parents on the Choice of a Profession or Trade for their Sons. By FRANCIS DAVENANT, M.A. Post 8vo, cloth limp, 2s. 6d.

Davies' (Sir John) Complete Poetical Works, including Psalms I. to L. in Verse, and other hitherto Unpublished MSS., for the first time Collected and Edited, with Memorial-Introduction and Notes, by the Rev. A. B. GROSART, D.D. Two Vols., crown 8vo, cloth boards, 12s.

De Maistre.—A Journey Round My Room. By XAVIER DE MAISTRE. Translated by HENRY ATTWELL. Post 8vo, cloth limp, 2s. 6d.

Derwent (Leith), Novels by:

Our Lady of Tears. Crown 8vo, cloth extra, 3s. 6d.; post 8vo, illustrated boards, 2s.

Circe's Lovers. Three Vols., crown 8vo, 31s. 6d.

Dickens (Charles), Novels by:
Post 8vo, illustrated boards, 2s. each.
Sketches by Boz.
The Pickwick Papers.
Oliver Twist.
Nicholas Nickleby.

The Speeches of Charles Dickens. Post 8vo, cloth limp, 2s. 6d.

Charles Dickens's Speeches, Chronologically Arranged: with a New Life of the Author, and a Bibliographical List of his Published Writings in Prose and Verse, from 1833 to 1883. Crown 8vo, cloth extra, 6s. [*In preparation.*

About England with Dickens. By ALFRED RIMMER. With 57 Illustrations by C. A. VANDERHOOF, ALFRED RIMMER, and others. Sq. 8vo, cloth extra, 10s. 6d.

Dictionaries:

A Dictionary of Miracles: Imitative, Realistic, and Dogmatic. By the Rev. E. C. BREWER, LL.D. Crown 8vo, cloth extra, 7s. 6d. [*Preparing.*

A Dictionary of the Drama: Being a comprehensive Guide to the Plays, Playwrights, Players, and Playhouses of the United Kingdom and America, from the Earliest to the Present Times. By W. DAVENPORT ADAMS. A thick volume, crown 8vo, half-bound, 12s. 6d. [*In preparation.*

Familiar Allusions: A Handbook of Miscellaneous Information; including the Names of Celebrated Statues, Paintings, Palaces, Country Seats, Ruins, Churches, Ships, Streets, Clubs, Natural Curiosities, and the like. By WM. A. WHEELER and CHARLES G. WHEELER. Demy 8vo, cloth extra, 7s. 6d.

The Reader's Handbook of Allusions, References, Plots, and Stories. By the Rev. E. C. BREWER, LL.D. Third Edition, revised throughout, with a New Appendix, containing a Complete English Bibliography. Crown 8vo, 1,400 pages, cloth extra, 7s. 6d.

Short Sayings of Great Men. With Historical and Explanatory Notes. By SAMUEL A. BENT, M.A. Demy 8vo, cloth extra, 7s. 6d.

The Slang Dictionary: Etymological, Historical, and Anecdotal. Crown 8vo, cloth extra, 6s. 6d.

DICTIONARIES, *continued—*

Words, Facts, and Phrases: A Dictionary of Curious, Quaint, and Out-of-the-Way Matters By ELIEZER EDWARDS. Crown 8vo, half-bound, 12s. 6d.

Dobson (W. T.), Works by:

Literary Frivolities, Fancies, Follies, and Frolics. Post 8vo, cloth limp, 2s. 6d.

Poetical Ingenuities and Eccentricities. Post 8vo, cloth limp, 2s. 6d.

Doran. — Memories of our

Great Towns; with Anecdotic Gleanings concerning their Worthies and their Oddities. By Dr. JOHN DORAN, F.S.A. With 38 Illustrations. New and Cheaper Edition, crown 8vo, cloth extra, 7s. 6d.

Drama, A Dictionary of the.

Being a comprehensive Guide to the Plays, Playwrights, Players, and Playhouses of the United Kingdom and America, from the Earliest to the Present Times. By W. DAVENPORT ADAMS. (Uniform with BREWER'S "Reader's Handbook") Crown 8vo, half-bound, 12s. 6d.   [*In preparation.*]

Dramatists, The Old. Crown

8vo, cloth extra, with Vignette Portraits, 6s. per Vol.

Ben Jonson's Works. With Notes Critical and Explanatory, and a Biographical Memoir by WM. GIFFORD. Edited by Colonel CUNNINGHAM. Three Vols.

Chapman's Works. Complete in Three Vols. Vol. I. contains the Plays complete, including the doubtful ones; Vol. II., the Poems and Minor Translations, with an Introductory Essay by ALGERNON CHAS. SWINBURNE; Vol. III., the Translations of the Iliad and Odyssey.

Marlowe's Works. Including his Translations. Edited, with Notes and Introduction, by Col. CUNNINGHAM. One Vol.

Massinger's Plays. From the Text of WILLIAM GIFFORD. Edited by Col. CUNNINGHAM. One Vol.

Dyer. — The Folk-Lore of

Plants. By T. F. THISELTON DYER, M.A. Crown 8vo, cloth extra, 6s.   [*In preparation.*]

Edwards, Betham-. — Felicia:

A Novel. By M. BETHAM-EDWARDS. Post 8vo, illustrated boards, 2s.; crown 8vo, cloth extra, 3s. 6d.

Early English Poets. Edited,

with Introductions and Annotations, by Rev. A. B. GROSART, D.D. Crown 8vo, cloth boards, 6s. per Volume.

Fletcher's (Giles, B.D.) Complete Poems. One Vol.

Davies' (Sir John) Complete Poetical Works. Two Vols.

Herrick's (Robert) Complete Collected Poems. Three Vols.

Sidney's (Sir Philip) Complete Poetical Works. Three Vols.

Herbert (Lord) of Cherbury's Poems. Edited, with Introduction, by J. CHURTON COLLINS. Crown 8vo, parchment, 8s.

Edwardes (Mrs. A.), Novels by:

A Point of Honour. Post 8vo, illustrated boards, 2s.

Archie Lovell. Post 8vo, illust. bds., 2s.; crown 8vo, cloth extra, 3s. 6d.

Eggleston.—Roxy: A Novel. By

EDWARD EGGLESTON. Post 8vo, illust. boards, 2s.; cr. 8vo, cloth extra, 3s. 6d.

Emanuel.—On Diamonds and

Precious Stones: their History, Value, and Properties; with Simple Tests for ascertaining their Reality. By HARRY EMANUEL, F.R.G.S. With numerous Illustrations, tinted and plain. Crown 8vo, cloth extra, gilt, 6s.

Englishman's House, The: A

Practical Guide to all interested in Selecting or Building a House, with full Estimates of Cost, Quantities, &c. By C. J. RICHARDSON. Third Edition. With nearly 600 Illustrations. Crown 8vo, cloth extra, 7s. 6d.

Ewald (Alex. Charles, F.S.A.),

Works by:

Stories from the State Papers. With an Autotype Facsimile. Crown 8vo, cloth extra, 6s.

The Life and Times of Prince Charles Stuart, Count of Albany, commonly called the Young Pretender. From the State Papers and other Sources. New and Cheaper Edition, with a Portrait, crown 8vo, cloth extra, 7s. 6d.

Fairholt.—Tobacco: Its History and Associations; with an Account of the Plant and its Manufacture, and its Modes of Use in all Ages and Countries. By F. W. FAIRHOLT, F.S.A. With Coloured Frontispiece and upwards of 100 Illustrations by the Author. Crown 8vo, cloth extra, 6s.

Familiar Allusions: A Handbook of Miscellaneous Information; including the Names of Celebrated Statues, Paintings, Palaces, Country Seats, Ruins, Churches, Ships, Streets, Clubs, Natural Curiosities, and the like. By WILLIAM A. WHEELER, Author of "Noted Names of Fiction;" and CHARLES G. WHEELER. Demy 8vo, cloth extra, 7s. 6d.

Faraday (Michael), Works by:

The Chemical History of a Candle: Lectures delivered before a Juvenile Audience at the Royal Institution. Edited by WILLIAM CROOKES, F.C.S. Post 8vo, cloth extra, with numerous Illustrations, 4s 6d.

On the Various Forces of Nature, and their Relations to each other: Lectures delivered before a Juvenile Audience at the Royal Institution. Edited by WILLIAM CROOKES, F.C.S. Post 8vo, cloth extra, with numerous Illustrations, 4s. 6d.

Fin-Bec.— The Cupboard Papers: Observations on the Art of Living and Dining. By FIN-BEC. Post 8vo, cloth limp, 2s. 6d.

Fitzgerald (Percy), Works by:

The Recreations of a Literary Man; or, Does Writing Pay? With Recollections of some Literary Men, and a View of a Literary Man's Working Life. Crown 8vo, cloth extra, 6s.

The World Behind the Scenes. Crown 8vo, cloth extra, 3s. 6d.

Post 8vo, illustrated boards, 2s. each.
Bella Donna.
Never Forgotten.
The Second Mrs. Tillotson.
Polly.
Seventy-five Brooke Street.

Fletcher's (Giles, B.D.) Complete Poems: Christ's Victorie in Heaven, Christ's Victorie on Earth, Christ's Triumph over Death, and Minor Poems. With Memorial-Introduction and Notes, by the Rev. A. B. GROSART, D.D. Crown 8vo, cloth boards, 6s.

Fonblanque.—Filthy Lucre: A Novel. By ALBANY DE FONBLANQUE. Post 8vo, illustrated boards, 2s.

Francillon (R. E.), Novels by:
Crown 8vo, cloth extra, 3s. 6d. each; post 8vo, illust. boards, 2s. each.
Olympia.
Queen Cophetua.
One by One.

Esther's Glove. Fcap. 8vo, picture cover. 1s.

French Literature, History of. By HENRY VAN LAUN. Complete in 3 Vols., demy 8vo, cl. bds., 7s. 6d. each.

Frost (Thomas), Works by:
Crown 8vo, cloth extra, 3s. 6d. each.
Circus Life and Circus Celebrities.
The Lives of the Conjurers.
The Old Showmen and the Old London Fairs.

Fry.—Royal Guide to the London Charities, 1883-4. By HERBERT FRY. Showing, in alphabetical order, their Name, Date of Foundation, Address, Objects, Annual Income, Chief Officials, &c. Published Annually. Crown 8vo, cloth, 1s 6d.

Gardening Books:

A Year's Work in Garden and Greenhouse: Practical Advice to Amateur Gardeners as to the Management of the Flower, Fruit, and Frame Garden. By GEORGE GLENNY. Post 8vo, cloth limp, 2s. 6d.

Our Kitchen Garden: The Plants we Grow, and How we Cook Them. By TOM JERROLD, Author of "The Garden that Paid the Rent," &c. Post 8vo, cloth limp, 2s. 6d.

Household Horticulture: A Gossip about Flowers. By TOM and JANE JERROLD. Illustrated. Post 8vo, cloth limp, 2s. 6d.

The Garden that Paid the Rent. By TOM JERROLD. Fcap. 8vo, illustrated cover, 1s.; cloth limp, 1s. 6d.

My Garden Wild, and What I Grew there. By FRANCIS GEORGE HEATH. Crown 8vo, cloth extra, 5s.; gilt edges, 6s.

Gentleman's Magazine (The) for 1883. One Shilling Monthly. "The New Abelard," ROBERT BUCHANAN'S New Serial Story, was begun in the JANUARY Number of THE GENTLEMAN'S MAGAZINE. This Number contained many other interesting Articles, the continuation of JULIAN HAWTHORNE'S Story, "Dust," and a further instalment of "Science Notes," by W. MATTIEU WILLIAMS, F.R.A.S.

*** *Now ready, the Volume for* JANUARY *to* JUNE, 1883, *cloth extra, price* 8s. 6d.; *Cases for binding,* 2s. *each.*

Garrett.—The Capel Girls: A Novel. By EDWARD GARRETT. Post 8vo, illustrated boards, 2s.; crown 8vo, cloth extra, 3s. 6d.

German Popular Stories. Collected by the Brothers GRIMM, and Translated by EDGAR TAYLOR. Edited, with an Introduction, by JOHN RUSKIN. With 22 Illustrations on Steel by GEORGE CRUIKSHANK. Square 8vo, cloth extra, 6s. 6d.; gilt edges, 7s. 6d.

Gibbon (Charles), Novels by:

Each in crown 8vo, cloth extra, 3s. 6d.; or post 8vo, illustrated boards, 2s.
  Robin Gray.
  For Lack of Gold.
  What will the World Say?
  In Honour Bound.
  In Love and War.
  For the King.
  Queen of the Meadow.
  In Pastures Green.

Post 8vo, illustrated boards, 2s.
The Dead Heart.

Crown 8vo, cloth extra, 3s. 6d. each.
  The Braes of Yarrow.
  The Flower of the Forest.
  A Heart's Problem.
  The Golden Shaft.

Three Vols., crown 8vo, 31s. 6d. each.
Of High Degree.
Fancy-Free.   *[In the press.*

Gilbert (William), Novels by:
Post 8vo, illustrated boards, 2s. each.
  Dr. Austin's Guests.
  The Wizard of the Mountain.
  James Duke, Costermonger.

Gilbert (W. S.), Original Plays by: In Two Series, each complete in itself, price 2s. 6d. each. FIRST SERIES contains The Wicked World—Pygmalion and Galatea — Charity — The Princess—The Palace of Truth—Trial by Jury. The SECOND SERIES contains Broken Hearts — Engaged — Sweethearts—Gretchen—Dan'l Druce —Tom Cobb—H.M.S. Pinafore—The Sorcerer—The Pirates of Penzance.

Glenny.—A Year's Work in Garden and Greenhouse: Practical Advice to Amateur Gardeners as to the Management of the Flower, Fruit, and Frame Garden. By GEORGE GLENNY. Post 8vo, cloth limp, 2s. 6d.

Godwin.—Lives of the Necromancers. By WILLIAM GODWIN. Post 8vo, cloth limp, 2s.

Golden Library, The:
Square 16mo (Tauchnitz size), cloth limp, 2s. per volume.
Ballad History of England. By W. C. BENNETT.
Bayard Taylor's Diversions of the Echo Club.
Byron's Don Juan.
Godwin's (William) Lives of the Necromancers.
Holmes's Autocrat of the Breakfast Table. With an Introduction by G. A. SALA.
Holmes's Professor at the Breakfast Table.
Hood's Whims and Oddities. Complete. All the original Illustrations.
Irving's (Washington) Tales of a Traveller.
Irving's (Washington) Tales of the Alhambra.
Jesse's (Edward) Scenes and Occupations of a Country Life.
Lamb's Essays of Elia. Both Series Complete in One Vol.
Leigh Hunt's Essays: A Tale for a Chimney Corner, and other Pieces. With Portrait, and Introduction by EDMUND OLLIER.
Mallory's (Sir Thomas) Mort d'Arthur: The Stories of King Arthur and of the Knights of the Round Table. Edited by B. MONTGOMERIE RANKING.
Pascal's Provincial Letters. A New Translation, with Historical Introduction and Notes, by T. M'CRIE, D.D.
Pope's Poetical Works. Complete.
Rochefoucauld's Maxims and Moral Reflections. With Notes, and Introductory Essay by SAINTE-BEUVE.
St. Pierre's Paul and Virginia, and The Indian Cottage. Edited, with Life, by the Rev. E. CLARKE.
Shelley's Early Poems, and Queen Mab. With Essay by LEIGH HUNT.
Shelley's Later Poems: Laon and Cythna, &c.
Shelley's Posthumous Poems, the Shelley Papers, &c.
Shelley's Prose Works, including A Refutation of Deism, Zastrozzi, St. Irvyne, &c.
White's Natural History of Selborne. Edited, with Additions, by THOMAS BROWN, F.L.S.

Golden Treasury of Thought, The: An ENCYCLOPÆDIA OF QUOTATIONS from Writers of all Times and Countries. Selected and Edited by THEODORE TAYLOR. Crown 8vo, cloth gilt and gilt edges, 7s. 6d.

Gordon Cumming. — In the Hebrides. By C. F. GORDON CUMMING, Author of "At Home in Fiji." With Autotype Facsimile and numerous full-page Illustrations. Demy 8vo, cloth extra, 8s. 6d. [*In preparation.*

Graham. — The Professor's Wife: A Story. By LEONARD GRAHAM. Fcap. 8vo, picture cover, 1s.; cloth extra, 2s. 6d.

Greeks and Romans, The Life of the, Described from Antique Monuments. By ERNST GUHL and W. KONER. Translated from the Third German Edition, and Edited by Dr. F. HUEFFER. With 545 Illustrations. New and Cheaper Edition, demy 8vo, cloth extra, 7s. 6d.

Greenwood (James), Works by:

The Wilds of London. Crown 8vo, cloth extra, 3s. 6d.

Low-Life Deeps: An Account of the Strange Fish to be Found There. Crown 8vo, cloth extra, 3s. 6d.

Dick Temple: A Novel. Post 8vo, illustrated boards, 2s.

Guyot.—The Earth and Man; or, Physical Geography in its relation to the History of Mankind. By ARNOLD GUYOT. With Additions by Professors AGASSIZ, PIERCE, and GRAY; 12 Maps and Engravings on Steel, some Coloured, and copious Index. Crown 8vo, cloth extra, gilt, 4s. 6d.

Hair (The): Its Treatment in Health, Weakness, and Disease. Translated from the German of Dr. J. PINCUS. Crown 8vo, 1s.; cloth, 1s. 6d.

Hake (Dr. Thomas Gordon), Poems by:

Maiden Ecstasy. Small 4to, cloth extra, 8s.

New Symbols. Crown 8vo, cloth extra, 6s.

Legends of the Morrow. Crown 8vo, cloth extra, 6s.

The Serpent Play. Crown 8vo, cloth extra, 6s.

Half-Hours with Foreign Novelists. With Notices of their Lives and Writings. By HELEN and ALICE ZIMMERN. A New Edition. Two Vols., crown 8vo, cloth extra, 12s.

Hall.—Sketches of Irish Character. By Mrs. S. C. HALL. With numerous Illustrations on Steel and Wood by MACLISE, GILBERT, HARVEY, and G. CRUIKSHANK. Medium 8vo, cloth extra, gilt, 7s. 6d.

Halliday.—Every-day Papers. By ANDREW HALLIDAY. Post 8vo, illustrated boards, 2s.

Handwriting, The Philosophy of. With over 100 Facsimiles and Explanatory Text. By DON FELIX DE SALAMANCA. Post 8vo, cloth limp, 2s. 6d.

Hanky-Panky: A Collection of Very Easy Tricks, Very Difficult Tricks, White Magic, Sleight of Hand, &c. Edited by W. H. CREMER. With 200 Illustrations. Crown 8vo, cloth extra, 4s. 6d.

Hardy (Lady Duffus). — Paul Wynter's Sacrifice: A Story. By Lady DUFFUS HARDY. Post 8vo, illust. boards, 2s.

Hardy (Thomas).—Under the Greenwood Tree. By THOMAS HARDY, Author of "Far from the Madding Crowd." Crown 8vo, cloth extra, 3s. 6d.; post 8vo, illustrated boards, 2s.

Haweis (Mrs. H. R.), Works by:

The Art of Dress. With numerous Illustrations. Small 8vo, illustrated cover, 1s.; cloth limp, 1s. 6d.

The Art of Beauty. Square 8vo, cloth extra, gilt edges, with Coloured Frontispiece and nearly 100 Illustrations, 10s. 6d.

The Art of Decoration. Square 8vo, handsomely bound and profusely Illustrated, 10s. 6d.

Chaucer for Children: A Golden Key. With Eight Coloured Pictures and numerous Woodcuts. New Edition, small 4to, cloth extra, 6s.

Chaucer for Schools. Demy 8vo, cloth limp, 2s. 6d.

Haweis (Rev. H. R.).—American Humorists. Including WASHINGTON IRVING, OLIVER WENDELL HOLMES, JAMES RUSSELL LOWELL, ARTEMUS WARD, MARK TWAIN, and BRET HARTE. By the Rev. H. R. HAWEIS, M.A. Crown 8vo, cloth extra, 6s.

Hawthorne (Julian), Novels by.
Crown 8vo, cloth extra, 3s. 6d. each;
post 8vo, illustrated boards, 2s. each.

> Garth.
>
> Ellice Quentin.
>
> Sebastian Strome.

Mrs. Gainsborough's Diamonds. Fcap. 8vo, illustrated cover, 1s.; cloth extra, 2s. 6d.

Prince Saroni's Wife. Crown 8vo, cloth extra, 3s. 6d.

Dust: A Novel. Crown 8vo, cloth extra, 3s. 6d.

Fortune's Fool. Three Vols., crown 8vo, 31s. 6d. *[Shortly.*

Heath (F. G.). — My Garden
Wild, and What I Grew There. By
FRANCIS GEORGE HEATH, Author of
" The Fern World," &c. Crown 8vo,
cloth extra, 5s.; cloth gilt, and gilt
edges, 6s.

Helps (Sir Arthur), Works by :

Animals and their Masters. Post 8vo, cloth limp, 2s. 6d.

Social Pressure. Post 8vo, cloth limp, 2s. 6d.

Ivan de Biron: A Novel. Crown 8vo, cloth extra, 3s. 6d.; post 8vo, illustrated boards, 2s.

Heptalogia (The); or, The
Seven against Sense. A Cap with
Seven Bells. Cr. 8vo, cloth extra, 6s.

Herbert.—The Poems of Lord
Herbert of Cherbury. Edited, with
an Introduction, by J. CHURTON
COLLINS. Crown 8vo, bound in parchment, 8s.

Herrick's (Robert) Hesperides,
Noble Numbers, and Complete Collected Poems. With Memorial-Introduction and Notes by the Rev. A. B.
GROSART, D.D., Steel Portrait, Index
of First Lines, and Glossarial Index,
&c. Three Vols., crown 8vo, cloth
boards, 18s.

Hesse - Wartegg (Chevalier
Ernst von), Works by :

Tunis: The Land and the People.
With 22 Illustrations. Crown 8vo,
cloth extra, 3s. 6d.

The New South-West: Travelling
Sketches from Kansas, New Mexico,
Arizona, and Northern Mexico.
With 100 fine Illustrations and 3
Maps. Demy 8vo, cloth extra,
14s. *[In preparation.*

Hindley (Charles), Works by :
Crown 8vo, cloth extra, 3s. 6d. each.

Tavern Anecdotes and Sayings: Including the Origin of Signs, and
Reminiscences connected with
Taverns, Coffee Houses, Clubs, &c.
With Illustrations.

The Life and Adventures of a Cheap
Jack. By One of the Fraternity.
Edited by CHARLES HINDLEY.

Holmes(Oliver Wendell),Works
by :

The Autocrat of the Breakfast-
Table Illustrated by J. GORDON
THOMSON. Post 8vo, cloth limp,
2s. 6d.; another Edition in smaller
type, with an Introduction by G. A.
SALA. Post 8vo, cloth limp, 2s.

The Professor at the Breakfast-
Table; with the Story of Iris. Post
8vo, cloth limp, 2s.

Holmes. — The Science of
Voice Production and Voice Preservation: A Popular Manual for the
Use of Speakers and Singers. By
GORDON HOLMES, M.D. Crown 8vo,
cloth limp, with Illustrations, 2s. 6d.

Hood (Thomas):

Hood's Choice Works, in Prose and
Verse. Including the Cream of the
Comic Annuals. With Life of the
Author, Portrait, and 200 Illustrations. Crown 8vo, cloth extra, 7s. 6d.

Hood's Whims and Oddities. Complete. With all the original Illustrations. Post 8vo, cloth limp, 2s.

Hood (Tom), Works by :

From Nowhere to the North Pole:
A Noah's Arkæological Narrative.
With 25 Illustrations by W. BRUNTON and E. C. BARNES. Square
crown 8vo, cloth extra, gilt edges, 6s.

A Golden Heart. A Novel. Post 8vo,
illustrated boards, 2s.

Hook's (Theodore) Choice Humorous Works, including his Ludicrous Adventures, Bons Mots, Puns and
Hoaxes. With a New Life of the
Author, Portraits, Facsimiles, and
Illustrations. Crown 8vo, cloth extra,
gilt, 7s. 6d.

Horne.—Orion : An Epic Poem,
in Three Books. By RICHARD HENGIST HORNE. With Photographic
Portrait from a Medallion by SUMMERS. Tenth Edition, crown 8vo,
cloth extra, 7s.

Howell.—Conflicts of Capital and Labour, Historically and Economically considered: Being a History and Review of the Trade Unions of Great Britain, showing their Origin, Progress, Constitution, and Objects, in their Political, Social, Economical, and Industrial Aspects. By GEORGE HOWELL. Crown 8vo, cloth extra, 7s. 6d

Hugo. — The Hunchback of Notre Dame. By VICTOR HUGO. Post 8vo, illustrated boards, 2s.

Hunt.—Essays by Leigh Hunt. A Tale for a Chimney Corner, and other Pieces. With Portrait and Introduction by EDMUND OLLIER. Post 8vo, cloth limp, 2s.

Hunt (Mrs. Alfred), Novels by:
Thornicroft's Model. Crown 8vo, cloth extra, 3s. 6d.; post 8vo, illustrated boards, 2s.

The Leaden Casket. Crown 8vo, cloth extra, 3s. 6d.; post 8vo, illustrated boards, 2s.

Self-Condemned. Three Vols., crown 8vo. 31s. 6d.

Ingelow.—Fated to be Free : A Novel. By JEAN INGELOW. Crown 8vo, cloth extra, 3s. 6d.; post 8vo, illustrated boards, 2s.

Irving (Henry).—The Paradox of Acting. Translated, with Annotations, from Diderot's "Le Paradoxe sur le Comédien," by WALTER HERRIES POLLOCK. With a Preface by HENRY IRVING. Crown 8vo, in parchment, 4s 6d.

Irving (Washington), Works by:
Post 8vo, cloth limp, 2s. each.
Tales of a Traveller.
Tales of the Alhambra.

James.—Confidence : A Novel. By HENRY JAMES, Jun. Crown 8vo, cloth extra, 3s. 6d.; post 8vo, illustrated boards, 2s.

Janvier.—Practical Keramics for Students. By CATHERINE A. JANVIER. Crown 8vo, cloth extra, 6s.

Jay (Harriett), Novels by. Each crown 8vo, cloth extra, 3s. 6d.; or post 8vo, illustrated boards, 2s.
The Dark Colleen.
The Queen of Connaught.

Jefferies.—Nature near London. By RICHARD JEFFERIES, Author of "The Gamekeeper at Home." Crown 8vo, cloth extra, 6s.

Jennings (H. J.).—Curiosities of Criticism. By HENRY J. JENNINGS. Post 8vo, cloth limp, 2s. 6d.

Jennings (Hargrave). — The Rosicrucians: Their Rites and Mysteries. With Chapters on the Ancient Fire and Serpent Worshippers. By HARGRAVE JENNINGS. With Five full-page Plates and upwards of 300 Illustrations. A New Edition, crown 8vo, cloth extra, 7s. 6d.

Jerrold (Tom), Works by :
The Garden that Paid the Rent. By TOM JERROLD. Fcap. 8vo, illustrated cover, 1s. ; cloth limp, 1s. 6d.

Household Horticulture: A Gossip about Flowers. By TOM and JANE JERROLD. Illustrated. Post 8vo, cloth limp, 2s. 6d.

Our Kitchen Garden: The Plants we Grow, and How we Cook Them. By TOM JERROLD. Post 8vo, cloth limp, 2s. 6d.

Jesse.—Scenes and Occupations of a Country Life. By EDWARD JESSE. Post 8vo cloth limp, 2s.

Jones (William, F.S.A.), Works by :
Finger-Ring Lore: Historical, Legendary, and Anecdotal. With over 200 Illustrations. Crown 8vo, cloth extra, 7s. 6d.

Credulities, Past and Present; including the Sea and Seamen, Miners, Talismans, Word and Letter Divination, Exorcising and Blessing of Animals, Birds, Eggs, Luck, &c. With an Etched Frontispiece. Crown 8vo, cloth extra, 7s. 6d.

Crowns and Coronations: A History of Regalia in all Times and Countries. With about 150 Illustrations. Crown 8vo, cloth extra, 7s. 6d.
[In preparation.

Jonson's (Ben) Works. With Notes Critical and Explanatory, and a Biographical Memoir by WILLIAM GIFFORD. Edited by Colonel CUNNINGHAM. Three Vols., crown 8vo, cloth extra, 18s. ; or separately, 6s. per Volume.

Josephus, The Complete Works of. Translated by WHISTON. Containing both "The Antiquities of the Jews" and "The Wars of the Jews." Two Vols., 8vo, with 52 Illustrations and Maps, cloth extra, gilt, 14s.

Kavanagh.—The Pearl Fountain, and other Fairy Stories. By BRIDGET and JULIA KAVANAGH. With Thirty Illustrations by J. MOYR SMITH. Small 8vo, cloth gilt, 6s.

Kempt.—Pencil and Palette: Chapters on Art and Artists. By ROBERT KEMPT. Post 8vo, cloth limp, 2s. 6d.

Kingsley (Henry), Novels by: Each crown 8vo, cloth extra, 3s. 6d.; or post 8vo, illustrated boards, 2s.

    Oakshott Castle.
    Number Seventeen.

Lace (Old Point), and How to Copy and Imitate it. By DAISY WATERHOUSE HAWKINS. With 17 Illustrations by the Author. Crown 8vo, illustrated boards, 2s. 6d.

Lamb (Charles):
    Mary and Charles Lamb: Their Poems, Letters, and Remains. With Reminiscences and Notes by W. CAREW HAZLITT. With HANCOCK'S Portrait of the Essayist, Facsimiles of the Title-pages of the rare First Editions of Lamb's and Coleridge's Works, and numerous Illustrations. Crown 8vo, cloth extra, 10s. 6d.

    Lamb's Complete Works, in Prose and Verse, reprinted from the Original Editions, with many Pieces hitherto unpublished. Edited, with Notes and Introduction, by R. H. SHEPHERD. With Two Portraits and Facsimile of a Page of the "Essay on Roast Pig." Crown 8vo, cloth extra, 7s. 6d.

    The Essays of Elia. Complete Edition. Post 8vo, cloth extra, 2s.

    Poetry for Children, and Prince Dorus. By CHARLES LAMB. Carefully Reprinted from unique copies. Small 8vo, cloth extra, 5s.

Lane's Arabian Nights, &c.:
    The Thousand and One Nights: commonly called, in England, "THE ARABIAN NIGHTS' ENTERTAINMENTS." A New Translation from the Arabic, with copious Notes, by EDWARD WILLIAM LANE. Illustrated by many hundred Engravings on Wood, from Original Designs by WM. HARVEY. A New Edition, from a Copy annotated by the Translator, edited by his Nephew, EDWARD STANLEY POOLE. With a Preface by STANLEY LANE-POOLE. Three Vols., demy 8vo, cloth extra, 7s. 6d. each.

Lane's Arabian Nights, &c.:
    Arabian Society in the Middle Ages: Studies from "The Thousand and One Nights." By EDWARD WM. LANE, Author of "The Modern Egyptians," &c. Edited by STANLEY LANE-POOLE. Cr. 8vo, cloth extra, 6s.

Lares and Penates; or, The Background of Life. By FLORENCE CADDY. Crown 8vo, cloth extra, 6s.

Larwood (Jacob), Works by:
    The Story of the London Parks. With Illustrations. Crown 8vo, cloth extra, 3s. 6d.

    Clerical Anecdotes. Post 8vo, cloth limp, 2s. 6d.

    Forensic Anecdotes. Post 8vo, cloth limp, 2s. 6d.

    Theatrical Anecdotes. Post 8vo, cloth limp, 2s. 6d.

Leigh (Henry S.), Works by:
    Carols of Cockayne. With numerous Illusts. Post 8vo, cloth limp, 2s. 6d.

    A Town Garland. Crown 8vo, cloth extra, 6s.

    Jeux d'Esprit. Collected and Edited by HENRY S. LEIGH. Post 8vo, cloth limp, 2s. 6d.

Life in London; or, The History of Jerry Hawthorn and Corinthian Tom. With the whole of CRUIKSHANK'S Illustrations, in Colours, after the Originals. Crown 8vo, cloth extra, 7s. 6d.

Linton (E. Lynn), Works by:
    Witch Stories. Post 8vo, cloth limp, 2s. 6d.

    The True Story of Joshua Davidson. Post 8vo, cloth limp, 2s. 6d.

Crown 8vo, cloth extra, 3s. 6d. each; post 8vo, illustrated boards, 2s.

    Patricia Kemball.
    The Atonement of Leam Dundas.
    The World Well Lost.
    Under which Lord?
    With a Silken Thread.
    The Rebel of the Family.
    "My Love!"

    Ione Steuart. 3 vols., crown 8vo. *[Shortly.*

Locks and Keys.—On the Development and Distribution of Primitive Locks and Keys. By Lieut.-Gen. PITT-RIVERS, F.R.S. With numerous Illustrations. Demy 4to, half Roxburghe, 16s.

Longfellow:

Longfellow's Complete Prose Works. Including "Outre Mer," "Hyperion," "Kavanagh," "The Poets and Poetry of Europe," and "Driftwood." With Portrait and Illustrations by VALENTINE BROMLEY. Crown 8vo, cloth extra, 7s. 6d.

Longfellow's Poetical Works. Carefully Reprinted from the Original Editions. With numerous fine Illustrations on Steel and Wood. Crown 8vo, cloth extra, 7s. 6d.

Lucy.—Gideon Fleyce: A Novel. By HENRY W. LUCY. Crown 8vo, cloth extra, 3s. 6d.

Lunatic Asylum, My Experiences in a. By A SANE PATIENT. Crown 8vo, cloth extra, 5s.

Lusiad (The) of Camoens. Translated into English Spenserian Verse by ROBERT FFRENCH DUFF. Demy 8vo, with Fourteen full-page Plates, cloth boards, 18s.

McCarthy (Justin, M.P.), Works by:

A History of Our Own Times, from the Accession of Queen Victoria to the General Election of 1880. Four Vols. demy 8vo, cloth extra, 12s. each.—Also a POPULAR EDITION, in Four Vols. crown 8vo, cloth extra, 6s. each.

A Short History of Our Own Times. One Volume, crown 8vo, cloth extra, 6s. [*Shortly.*

History of the Four Georges. Four Vols. demy 8vo, cloth extra, 12s. each. [*In preparation.*

Crown 8vo, cloth extra, 3s. 6d. each post 8vo, illustrated boards, 2s. each.

Dear Lady Disdain.
The Waterdale Neighbours.
My Enemy's Daughter.
A Fair Saxon.
Linley Rochford
Miss Misanthrope.
Donna Quixote.

The Comet of a Season. Crown 8vo, cloth extra, 3s. 6d.

Maid of Athens. With 12 Illustrations by F. BARNARD. 3 vols., crown 8vo, 31s. 6d. [*Shortly.*

McCarthy (Justin H.), Works by:

Serapion, and other Poems. Crown 8vo, cloth extra, 6s.

An Outline of the History of Ireland. from the Earliest Times to the Present Day. Cr. 8vo, 1s. ; cloth, 1s. 6d.

MacDonald (George, LL.D.), Works by:

The Princess and Curdie. With 11 Illustrations by JAMES ALLEN. Small crown 8vo, cloth extra, 5s.

Gutta-Percha Willie, the Working Genius. With 9 Illustrations by ARTHUR HUGHES. Square 8vo, cloth extra, 3s. 6d.

Paul Faber, Surgeon. With a Frontispiece by J. E. MILLAIS. Crown 8vo, cloth extra, 3s. 6d. ; post 8vo, illustrated boards, 2s.

Thomas Wingfold, Curate. With a Frontispiece by C. J. STANILAND. Crown 8vo, cloth extra, 3s. 6d. ; post 8vo, illustrated boards, 2s.

Macdonell.—Quaker Cousins: A Novel. By AGNES MACDONELL. Crown 8vo, cloth extra, 3s. 6d. ; post 8vo, illustrated boards, 2s.

Macgregor. — Pastimes and Players. Notes on Popular Games. By ROBERT MACGREGOR. Post 8vo, cloth limp, 2s. 6d.

Maclise Portrait-Gallery (The) of Illustrious Literary Characters; with Memoirs—Biographical, Critical, Bibliographical, and Anecdotal—illustrative of the Literature of the former half of the Present Century. By WILLIAM BATES, B.A. With 85 Portraits printed on an India Tint. Crown 8vo, cloth extra, 7s. 6d.

Macquoid (Mrs.), Works by:

In the Ardennes. With 50 fine Illustrations by THOMAS R. MACQUOID. Square 8vo, cloth extra, 10s. 6d.

Pictures and Legends from Normandy and Brittany. With numerous Illustrations by THOMAS R. MACQUOID. Square 8vo, cloth gilt, 10s. 6d.

Through Normandy. With 90 Illustrations by T. R. MACQUOID. Square 8vo, cloth extra, 7s. 6d.

Through Brittany. With numerous Illustrations by T. R. MACQUOID. Square 8vo, cloth extra, 7s. 6d.

About Yorkshire. With 67 Illustrations by T. R. MACQUOID, Engraved by SWAIN. Square 8vo, cloth extra, 10s. 6d.

The Evil Eye, and other Stories. Crown 8vo, cloth extra, 3s. 6d. ; post 8vo, illustrated boards, 2s.

Lost Rose, and other Stories. Crown 8vo, cloth extra, 3s. 6d. ; post 8vo, illustrated boards, 2s.

Mackay.—Interludes and Undertones: Poems of the End of Life. By CHARLES MACKAY, LL.D. Crown 8vo, cloth extra, 6s. *[In the press.*

Magician's Own Book (The): Performances with Cups and Balls, Eggs, Hats, Handkerchiefs, &c. All from actual Experience. Edited by W. H. CREMER. With 200 Illustrations. Crown 8vo, cloth extra, 4s. 6d.

Magic No Mystery: Tricks with Cards, Dice, Balls. &c., with fully descriptive Directions; the Art of Secret Writing; Training of Performing Animals, &c. With Coloured Frontispiece and many Illustrations. Crown 8vo, cloth extra, 4s. 6d.

Magna Charta. An exact Facsimile of the Original in the British Museum, printed on fine plate paper, 3 feet by 2 feet, with Arms and Seals emblazoned in Gold and Colours. Price 5s.

Mallock (W. H.), Works by:

The New Republic; or, Culture, Faith and Philosophy in an English Country House. Post 8vo, cloth limp, 2s. 6d.; Cheap Edition, illustrated boards, 2s.

The New Paul and Virginia; or, Positivism on an Island. Post 8vo, cloth limp, 2s. 6d.

Poems. Small 4to, bound in parchment, 8s.

Is Life worth Living? Crown 8vo, cloth extra, 6s.

Mallory's (Sir Thomas) Mort d'Arthur: The Stories of King Arthur and of the Knights of the Round Table. Edited by B. MONTGOMERIE RANKING. Post 8vo, cloth limp, 2s.

Marlowe's Works. Including his Translations. Edited. with Notes and Introduction, by Col. CUNNINGHAM. Crown 8vo, cloth extra, 6s.

Marryat (Florence), Novels by:

Crown 8vo, cloth extra, 3s. 6d. each; or, post 8vo, illustrated boards, 2s.

Open! Sesame!
Written in Fire.

Post 8vo, illustrated boards, 2s. each.
A Harvest of Wild Oats.
A Little Stepson.
Fighting the Air.

Mark Twain, Works by:

The Choice Works of Mark Twain. Revised and Corrected throughout by the Author. With Life, Portrait, and numerous Illustrations. Crown 8vo, cloth extra, 7s. 6d.

The Adventures of Tom Sawyer. With 100 Illustrations. Small 8vo, cloth extra, 7s. 6d. CHEAP EDITION, illustrated boards, 2s.

An Idle Excursion, and other Sketches. Post 8vo, illustrated boards, 2s.

The Prince and the Pauper. With nearly 200 Illustrations. Crown 8vo, cloth extra, 7s. 6d.

The Innocents Abroad; or, The New Pilgrim's Progress: Being some Account of the Steamship " Quaker City's " Pleasure Excursion to Europe and the Holy Land. With 234 Illustrations. Crown 8vo, cloth extra, 7s. 6d. CHEAP EDITION (under the title of " MARK TWAIN'S PLEASURE TRIP "), post 8vo, illust. boards, 2s.

A Tramp Abroad. With 314 Illustrations. Crown 8vo, cloth extra, 7s. 6d.

The Stolen White Elephant, &c. Crown 8vo, cloth extra, 6s.

Life on the Mississippi. With about 300 Original Illustrations. Crown 8vo, cloth extra, 7s. 6d.

Massinger's Plays. From the Text of WILLIAM GIFFORD. Edited by Col. CUNNINGHAM. Crown 8vo, cloth extra, 6s.

Mayhew.—London Characters and the Humorous Side of London Life. By HENRY MAYHEW. With numerous Illustrations. Crown 8vo, cloth extra, 3s. 6d.

Mayfair Library, The:

Post 8vo, cloth limp, 2s. 6d. per Volume.

A Journey Round My Room. By XAVIER DE MAISTRE. Translated by HENRY ATTWELL.

Latter-Day Lyrics. Edited by W. DAVENPORT ADAMS.

Quips and Quiddities. Selected by W. DAVENPORT ADAMS.

The Agony Column of "The Times," from 1800 to 1870. Edited, with an Introduction, by ALICE CLAY.

Balzac's "Comedie Humaine" and its Author. With Translations by H. H. WALKER.

Melancholy Anatomised: A Popular Abridgment of " Burton's Anatomy of Melancholy."

Gastronomy as a Fine Art. By BRILLAT-SAVARIN.

MAYFAIR LIBRARY, *continued—*

The Speeches of Charles Dickens.

Literary Frivolities, Fancies, Follies, and Frolics. By W. T. DOBSON.

Poetical Ingenuities and Eccentricities. Selected and Edited by W. T. DOBSON.

The Cupboard Papers. By FIN-BEC.

Original Plays by W. S. GILBERT. FIRST SERIES. Containing: The Wicked World — Pygmalion and Galatea—Charity — The Princess—The Palace of Truth—Trial by Jury.

Original Plays by W. S. GILBERT. SECOND SERIES. Containing: Broken Hearts — Engaged — Sweethearts — Gretchen—Dan'l Druce—Tom Cobb —H.M.S. Pinafore — The Sorcerer —The Pirates of Penzance.

Animals and their Masters. By Sir ARTHUR HELPS.

Social Pressure. By Sir ARTHUR HELPS.

Curiosities of Criticism. By HENRY J. JENNINGS.

The Autocrat of the Breakfast Table. By OLIVER WENDELL HOLMES. Illustrated by J. GORDON THOMSON.

Pencil and Palette. By ROBERT KEMPT.

Clerical Anecdotes. By JACOB LARWOOD.

Forensic Anecdotes; or, Humour and Curiosities of the Law and Men of Law. By JACOB LARWOOD.

Theatrical Anecdotes. By JACOB LARWOOD.

Carols of Cockayne. By HENRY S. LEIGH.

Jeux d'Esprit. Edited by HENRY S. LEIGH.

True History of Joshua Davidson. By E. LYNN LINTON.

Witch Stories. By E. LYNN LINTON.

Pastimes and Players. By ROBERT MACGREGOR.

The New Paul and Virginia. By W. H. MALLOCK.

The New Republic. By W. H. MALLOCK.

Muses of Mayfair. Edited by H. CHOLMONDELEY-PENNELL.

Thoreau: His Life and Aims. By H. A. PAGE.

Puck on Pegasus. By H. CHOLMONDELEY-PENNELL.

Puniana. By the Hon. HUGH ROWLEY.

More Puniana. By the Hon. HUGH ROWLEY.

The Philosophy of Handwriting. By DON FELIX DE SALAMANCA.

MAYFAIR LIBRARY, *continued—*

By Stream and Sea. By WILLIAM SENIOR.

Old Stories Re-told. By WALTER THORNBURY.

Leaves from a Naturalist's Note-Book. By Dr. ANDREW WILSON.

Medicine, Family.—One Thousand Medical Maxims and Surgical Hints, for Infancy, Adult Life, Middle Age, and Old Age. By N. E. DAVIES, Licentiate of the Royal College of Physicians of London. Crown 8vo, 1s. ; cloth, 1s. 6d. [*In the press.*

Merry Circle (The): A Book of New Intellectual Games and Amusements. By CLARA BELLEW. With numerous Illustrations. Crown 8vo, cloth extra, 4s. 6d.

Middlemass (Jean), Novels by:

Touch and Go. Crown 8vo, cloth extra, 3s. 6d. ; post 8vo, illustrated boards, 2s.

Mr. Dorillion. Post 8vo, illustrated boards, 2s.

Miller. — Physiology for the Young; or, The House of Life: Human Physiology, with its application to the Preservation of Health. For use in Classes and Popular Reading. With numerous Illustrations By Mrs. F. FENWICK MILLER. Small 8vo, cloth limp, 2s. 6d.

Milton (J. L.), Works by:

The Hygiene of the Skin. A Concise Set of Rules for the Management of the Skin; with Directions for Diet, Wines, Soaps, Baths, &c. Small 8vo, 1s. ; cloth extra, 1s. 6d.

The Bath In Diseases of the Skin. Small 8vo, 1s. ; cloth extra, 1s. 6d.

The Laws of Life, and their Relation to Diseases of the Skin. Small 8vo, 1s. ; cloth extra. 1s. 6d.

Moncrieff. — The Abdication; or, Time Tries All. An Historical Drama. By W. D. SCOTT-MONCRIEFF. With Seven Etchings by JOHN PETTIE, R.A., W. Q. ORCHARDSON, R.A., J. MACWHIRTER, A R.A , COLIN HUNTER, R. MACBETH, and TOM GRAHAM. Large 4to, bound in buckram, 21s

Murray (D. Christie), Novels by:

A Life's Atonement. Crown 8vo, cloth extra. 3s. 6d. ; post 8vo, illustrated boards, 2s.

Joseph's Coat. With Illustrations by F. BARNARD. Crown 8vo, cloth extra, 3s 6d.

D. C. MURRAY'S NOVELS, *continued—*

Coals of Fire. With Illustrations by ARTHUR HOPKINS and others. Crown 8vo, cloth extra, 3s. 6d.

A Model Father, and other Stories. Crown 8vo, cloth extra, 3s. 6d.; post 8vo, illustrated boards, 2s.

Val Strange: A Story of the Primrose Way. Crown 8vo, cloth extra, 3s. 6d.

Hearts. Three Vols., cr. 8vo, 31s. 6d.

By the Gate of the Sea. Two Vols., post 8vo, 12s.

The Way of the World. Three Vols., crown 8vo, 31s. 6d. [*Shortly.*

North Italian Folk. By Mrs. COMYNS CARR. Illustrated by RANDOLPH CALDECOTT. Square 8vo, cloth extra, 7s. 6d.

Number Nip (Stories about), the Spirit of the Giant Mountains. Retold for Children by WALTER GRAHAME. With Illustrations by J. MOYR SMITH. Post 8vo, cloth extra, 5s.

Oliphant. — Whiteladies: A Novel. With Illustrations by ARTHUR HOPKINS and HENRY WOODS. Crown 8vo, cloth extra, 3s. 6d.; post 8vo, illustrated boards, 2s.

O'Reilly.—Phœbe's Fortunes: A Novel. With Illustrations by HENRY TUCK. Post 8vo, illustrated boards, 2s.

O'Shaughnessy (Arth.), Works by:

Songs of a Worker. Fcap. 8vo, cloth extra, 7s. 6d.

Music and Moonlight. Fcap. 8vo, cloth extra, 7s. 6d.

Lays of France. Crown 8vo, cloth extra, 10s. 6d.

Ouida, Novels by. Crown 8vo, cloth extra, 5s. each; post 8vo, illustrated boards, 2s. each.

Held in Bondage.
Strathmore.
Chandos.
Under Two Flags.
Idalia.
Cecil Castlemaine's Gage.
Tricotrin.
Puck.
Folle Farine.
A Dog of Flanders.
Pascarel.
Two Little Wooden Shoes.

OUIDA'S NOVELS, *continued—*

Signa.
In a Winter City.
Ariadne.
Friendship.
Moths.
Pipistrello.
A Village Commune.

In Maremma. Crown 8vo, cloth extra, 5s.

Bimbi: Stories for Children. Square 8vo, cloth gilt, cinnamon edges, 7s.6d.

Wanda: A Novel. Three Vols., crown 8vo, 31s. 6d.

The Wisdom, Wit, and Pathos of Ouida. Selected from her Works, by F. SYDNEY MORRIS. Small cr. 8vo, cloth extra, 5s. [*In the press.*

Page (H. A.), Works by:

Thoreau: His Life and Aims: A Study. With a Portrait. Post 8vo, cloth limp, 2s. 6d.

Lights on the Way: Some Tales within a Tale. By the late J. H. ALEXANDER, B.A. Edited by H. A. PAGE. Crown 8vo, cloth extra, 6s.

Pascal's Provincial Letters. A New Translation, with Historical Introduction and Notes, by T. M'CRIE, D.D. Post 8vo, cloth limp, 2s.

Paul Ferroll:

Post 8vo, illustrated boards, 2s. each.

Paul Ferroll: A Novel.

Why Paul Ferroll Killed His Wife.

Payn (James), Novels by:

Each crown 8vo, cloth extra, 3s. 6d.; or post 8vo, illustrated boards, 2s.

Lost Sir Massingberd.
The Best of Husbands.
Walter's Word.
Halves.
Fallen Fortunes.
What He Cost Her.
Less Black than We're Painted
By Proxy.
Under One Roof.
High Spirits.
Carlyon's Year.
A Confidential Agent
Some Private Views.
From Exile.

JAMES PAYN'S NOVELS, *continued—*

Post 8vo, illustrated boards, 2s. each.

A Perfect Treasure.
Bentinck's Tutor.
Murphy's Master.
A County Family.
At Her Mercy.
A Woman's Vengeance
Cecil's Tryst.
The Clyffards of Clyffe.
The Family Scapegrace.
The Foster Brothers.
Found Dead.
Gwendoline's Harvest.
Humorous Stories.
Like Father, Like Son.
A Marine Residence.
Married Beneath Him.
Mirk Abbey.
Not Wooed, but Won.
Two Hundred Pounds Reward.

Crown 8vo, cloth extra, 3s. 6d. each.

A Grape from a Thorn. With Illustrations by W. SMALL.
For Cash Only.
Kit: A Memory.

Pennell (H. Cholmondeley), Works by: Post 8vo, cloth limp, 2s. 6d. each.

Puck on Pegasus. With Illustrations.

The Muses of Mayfair. Vers de Société, Selected and Edited by H. C. PENNELL.

Pirkis.—Trooping with Crows: A Story. By CATHERINE PIRKIS. Fcap. 8vo, picture cover, 1s.

Planche (J. R.), Works by:

The Cyclopædia of Costume; or, A Dictionary of Dress—Regal, Ecclesiastical, Civil, and Military—from the Earliest Period in England to the Reign of George the Third. Including Notices of Contemporaneous Fashions on the Continent, and a General History of the Costumes of the Principal Countries of Europe. Two Vols., demy 4to, half morocco, profusely Illustrated with Coloured and Plain Plates and Woodcuts, £7 7s. The Volumes may also be had *separately* (each complete in itself) at £3 13s. 6d. each: Vol. I. THE DICTIONARY. Vol. II. A GENERAL HISTORY OF COSTUME IN EUROPE.

PLANCHE'S WORKS, *continued—*

The Pursuivant of Arms; or, Heraldry Founded upon Facts. With Coloured Frontispiece and 200 Illustrations. Crown 8vo, cloth extra, 7s. 6d.

Songs and Poems, from 1819 to 1879. Edited, with an Introduction, by his Daughter, Mrs. MACKARNESS. Crown 8vo, cloth extra, 6s.

Play-time: Sayings and Doings of Babyland. By EDWARD STANFORD. Large 4to, handsomely printed in Colours, 5s. [*Shortly.*

Plutarch's Lives of Illustrious Men. Translated from the Greek, with Notes Critical and Historical, and a Life of Plutarch, by JOHN and WILLIAM LANGHORNE. Two Vols., 8vo, cloth extra, with Portraits, 10s. 6d.

Poe (Edgar Allan):—

The Choice Works, in Prose and Poetry, of EDGAR ALLAN POE. With an Introductory Essay by CHARLES BAUDELAIRE, Portrait and Facsimiles. Crown 8vo, cloth extra, 7s. 6d.

The Mystery of Marie Roget, and other Stories. Post 8vo, illustrated boards, 2s.

Pope's Poetical Works. Complete in One Volume. Post 8vo, cloth limp, 2s.

Price (E. C.), Novels by:

Valentina: A Sketch. With a Frontispiece by HAL LUDLOW. Crown 8vo, cloth extra, 3s. 6d.; post 8vo, illustrated boards, 2s.

The Foreigners. Three Vols., crown 8vo, 31s. 6d. [*Shortly.*

Proctor (Richd. A.), Works by:

Flowers of the Sky. With 55 Illustrations. Small crown 8vo, cloth extra, 4s. 6d.

Easy Star Lessons. With Star Maps for Every Night in the Year, Drawings of the Constellations, &c. Crown 8vo, cloth extra, 6s.

Familiar Science Studies. Crown 8vo, cloth extra, 7s. 6d.

Myths and Marvels of Astronomy. Crown 8vo, cloth extra, 6s.

Pleasant Ways in Science. Crown 8vo, cloth extra, 6s.

Rough Ways made Smooth: A Series of Familiar Essays on Scientific Subjects. Crown 8vo, cloth extra, 6s.

R. A. Proctor's Works, *continued—*

Our Place among Infinities: A Series of Essays contrasting our Little Abode in Space and Time with the Infinities Around us. Crown 8vo, cloth extra, 6s.

The Expanse of Heaven: A Series of Essays on the Wonders of the Firmament. Cr. 8vo, cloth extra, 6s.

Saturn and its System. New and Revised Edition, with 13 Steel Plates. Demy 8vo, cloth extra, 10s. 6d.

The Great Pyramid: Observatory, Tomb, and Temple. With Illustrations. Crown 8vo, cloth extra, 6s.

Mysteries of Time and Space. With Illustrations. Crown 8vo, cloth extra, 7s. 6d.

Wages and Wants of Science Workers. Crown 8vo, 1s. 6d.

Pyrotechnist's Treasury (The); or, Complete Art of Making Fireworks. By Thomas Kentish. With numerous Illustrations. Crown 8vo, cloth extra, 4s. 6d.

Rabelais' Works. Faithfully Translated from the French, with variorum Notes, and numerous characteristic Illustrations by Gustave Dore. Crown 8vo, cloth extra, 7s. 6d.

Rambosson.—Popular Astronomy. By J. Rambosson, Laureate of the Institute of France. Translated by C. B. Pitman. Crown 8vo, cloth gilt, with numerous Illustrations, and a beautifully executed Chart of Spectra, 7s. 6d.

Reader's Handbook (The) of Allusions, References, Plots, and Stories. By the Rev. Dr. Brewer. Third Edition, revised throughout, with a New Appendix, containing a Complete English Bibliography. Crown 8vo, 1,400 pages, cloth extra, 7s. 6d.

Reade (Charles, D.C.L.), Novels by. Each post 8vo, illustrated boards, 2s.; or crown 8vo, cloth extra, Illustrated, 3s. 6d.

Peg Woffington. Illustrated by S. L. Fildes, A.R.A.

Christie Johnstone. Illustrated by William Small.

It is Never Too Late to Mend. Illustrated by G. J. Pinwell.

The Course of True Love Never did run Smooth. Illustrated by Helen Paterson.

Charles Reade's Novels, *continued—*

The Autobiography of a Thief; Jack of all Trades; and James Lambert. Illustrated by Matt Stretch.

Love me Little, Love me Long. Illustrated by M. Ellen Edwards.

The Double Marriage. Illustrated by Sir John Gilbert, R.A., and Charles Keene.

The Cloister and the Hearth. Illustrated by Charles Keene.

Hard Cash. Illustrated by F. W. Lawson.

Griffith Gaunt. Illustrated by S. L. Fildes, A.R.A., and Wm. Small.

Foul Play. Illustrated by George Du Maurier.

Put Yourself in His Place. Illustrated by Robert Barnes.

A Terrible Temptation. Illustrated by Edward Hughes and A. W. Cooper.

The Wandering Heir. Illustrated by Helen Paterson, S. L. Fildes, A.R.A., Charles Green, and Henry Woods, A.R.A.

A Simpleton. Illustrated by Kate Crauford.

A Woman-Hater. Illustrated by Thos. Couldery.

Readiana. With a Steel Plate Portrait of Charles Reade.

A New Collection of Stories. In Three Vols., crown 8vo. [*Preparing.*

Richardson. — A Ministry of Health, and other Papers. By Benjamin Ward Richardson, M.D., &c. Crown 8vo, cloth extra, 6s.

Riddell (Mrs. J. H.), Novels by:

Her Mother's Darling. Crown 8vo, cloth extra, 3s. 6d.; post 8vo, illustrated boards, 2s.

The Prince of Wales's Garden Party, and other Stories. With a Frontispiece by M. Ellen Edwards. Crown 8vo cloth extra, 3s. 6d.

Rimmer (Alfred), Works by:

Our Old Country Towns. By Alfred Rimmer. With over 50 Illustrations by the Author. Square 8vo, cloth extra, gilt, 10s. 6d.

Rambles Round Eton and Harrow. By Alfred Rimmer. With 50 Illustrations by the Author. Square 8vo, cloth gilt, 10s. 6d.

About England with Dickens. With 58 Illustrations by Alfred Rimmer and C. A. Vanderhoof. Square 8vo, cloth gilt, 10s. 6d.

Robinson (F. W.), Novels by:
Women are Strange. Crown 8vo, cloth extra, 3s. 6d.
The Hands of Justice. Three Vols., crown 8vo, 31s. 6d.

Robinson.—The Poets' Birds. By PHIL ROBINSON, Author of "Noah's Ark," &c. Cr. 8vo, cloth extra, 7s. 6d.

Robinson Crusoe : A beautiful reproduction of Major's Edition, with 37 Woodcuts and Two Steel Plates by GEORGE CRUIKSHANK, choicely printed. Crown 8vo, cloth extra, 7s. 6d. 100 Large-Paper copies, printed on hand-made paper, with India proofs of the Illustrations, price 36s. [*In preparation.*

Rochefoucauld's Maxims and Moral Reflections. With Notes, and an Introductory Essay by SAINTE-BEUVE. Post 8vo, cloth limp, 2s.

Roll of Battle Abbey, The; or, A List of the Principal Warriors who came over from Normandy with William the Conqueror, and Settled in this Country, A.D. 1066-7. With the principal Arms emblazoned in Gold and Colours. Handsomely printed, price 5s.

Ross.—Behind a Brass Knocker: Some Grim Realities in Picture and Prose. By FRED. BARNARD and C. H. Ross. Demy 8vo, cloth extra, with 30 full-page Drawings, 10s. 6d.

Rowley (Hon. Hugh), Works by:
Post 8vo, cloth limp, 2s. 6d. each.
Puniana: Riddles and Jokes. With numerous Illustrations.
More Puniana. Profusely Illustrated.

Sala.—Gaslight and Daylight. By GEORGE AUGUSTUS SALA. Post 8vo, illustrated boards, 2s.

Sanson.—Seven Generations of Executioners: Memoirs of the Sanson Family (1688 to 1847). Edited by HENRY SANSON. Crown 8vo, cloth extra, 3s 6d.

Saunders (John), Novels by:
Crown 8vo, cloth extra, 3s. 6d each ; or post 8vo, illustrated boards, 2s. each.
Bound to the Wheel.
One Against the World.
Guy Waterman.
The Lion in the Path.
The Two Dreamers.

Science Gossip : An Illustrated Medium of Interchange and Gossip for Students and Lovers of Nature. Edited by J. E. TAYLOR, Ph.D., F.L.S., F.G.S. Monthly, price 4d ; Annual Subscription 5s. (including Postage). Vols. I. to XIV. may be had at 7s. 6d. each; and Vols. XV. to XVIII (1882), at 5s. each. Among the subjects included in its pages will be found : Aquaria, Bees, Beetles, Birds, Butterflies, Ferns, Fish, Flies, Fossils, Fungi, Geology, Lichens, Microscopes, Mosses, Moths, Reptiles, Seaweeds, Spiders, Telescopes, Wild Flowers, Worms, &c.

Scott (Sir Walter).—The Lady of the Lake. With 120 fine Illustrations. Small 4to, pine-wood binding, 16s.

" Secret Out " Series, The :
Crown 8vo, cloth extra, profusely Illustrated, 4s. 6d. each.
The Secret Out: One Thousand Tricks with Cards, and other Recreations; with Entertaining Experiments in Drawing-room or "White Magic." By W. H. CREMER. 300 Engravings.
The Pyrotechnist's Treasury; or, Complete Art of Making Fireworks By THOMAS KENTISH. With numerous Illustrations.
The Art of Amusing: A Collection of Graceful Arts, Games, Tricks, Puzzles, and Charades. By FRANK BELLEW. With 300 Illustrations.
Hanky-Panky: Very Easy Tricks, Very Difficult Tricks, White Magic, Sleight of Hand. Edited by W. H. CREMER. With 200 Illustrations.
The Merry Circle: A Book of New Intellectual Games and Amusements. By CLARA BELLEW. Many Illusts.
Magician's Own Book: Performances with Cups and Balls, Eggs, Hats, Handkerchiefs, &c. All from actual Experience. Edited by W. H. CREMER. 200 Illustrations.
Magic No Mystery: Tricks with Cards, Dice, Balls, &c., with fully descriptive Directions; the Art of Secret Writing; Training of Performing Animals, &c. Coloured Frontispiece and many Illustrations.

Senior (William), Works by :
Travel and Trout in the Antipodes. Crown 8vo, cloth extra, 6s.
By Stream and Sea. Post 8vo, cloth limp, 2s. 6d.

Shakespeare :

The First Follo Shakespeare.—MR. WILLIAM SHAKESPEARE'S Comedies, Histories, and Tragedies. Published according to the true Originall Copies. London, Printed by ISAAC IAGGARD and ED. BLOUNT. 1623.—A Reproduction of the extremely rare original, in reduced facsimile, by a photographic process—ensuring the strictest accuracy in every detail. Small 8vo, half-Roxburghe, 7s. 6d.

The Lansdowne Shakespeare. Beautifully printed in red and black, in small but very clear type. With engraved facsimile of DROESHOUT'S Portrait. Post 8vo, cloth extra, 7s. 6d.

Shakespeare for Children: Tales from Shakespeare. By CHARLES and MARY LAMB. With numerous Illustrations, coloured and plain, by J. MOYR SMITH. Crown 4to, cloth gilt, 6s.

The Handbook of Shakespeare Music. Being an Account of 350 Pieces of Music, set to Words taken from the Plays and Poems of Shakespeare, the compositions ranging from the Elizabethan Age to the Present Time. By ALFRED ROFFE. 4to, half-Roxburghe, 7s.

A Study of Shakespeare. By ALGERNON CHARLES SWINBURNE. Crown 8vo, cloth extra, 8s.

Shelley's Complete Works, in Four Vols., post 8vo, cloth limp, 8s. ; or separately, 2s. each. Vol. I. contains his Early Poems, Queen Mab, &c., with an Introduction by LEIGH HUNT ; Vol. II., his Later Poems, Laon and Cythna, &c. ; Vol. III., Posthumous Poems, the Shelley Papers, &c. ; Vol. IV., his Prose Works, including A Refutation of Deism, Zastrozzi, St. Irvyne, &c.

Sheridan's Complete Works, with Life and Anecdotes. Including his Dramatic Writings, printed from the Original Editions, his Works in Prose and Poetry, Translations, Speeches, Jokes, Puns, &c. With a Collection of Sheridaniana. Crown 8vo, cloth extra, gilt, with 10 full-page Tinted Illustrations, 7s. 6d.

Short Sayings of Great Men. With Historical and Explanatory Notes by SAMUEL A. BENT, M.A. Demy 8vo, cloth extra, 7s. 6d.

Sidney's (Sir Philip) Complete Poetical Works, including all those in "Arcadia." With Portrait, Memorial-Introduction, Essay on the Poetry of Sidney, and Notes, by the Rev. A. B. GROSART, D.D. Three Vols., crown 8vo, cloth boards, 18s.

Signboards : Their History. With Anecdotes of Famous Taverns and Remarkable Characters. By JACOB LARWOOD and JOHN CAMDEN HOTTEN. Crown 8vo, cloth extra, with 100 Illustrations, 7s. 6d.

Sketchley.—A Match in the Dark. By ARTHUR SKETCHLEY. Post 8vo, illustrated boards, 2s.

Slang Dictionary, The : Etymological, Historical, and Anecdotal. Crown 8vo, cloth extra, gilt, 6s. 6d.

Smith (J. Moyr), Works by :

The Prince of Argolis : A Story of the Old Greek Fairy Time. By J. MOYR SMITH. Small 8vo, cloth extra, with 130 Illustrations, 3s. 6d.

Tales of Old Thule. Collected and Illustrated by J. MOYR SMITH. Crown 8vo, cloth gilt, profusely Illustrated, 6s.

The Wooing of the Water Witch : A Northern Oddity. By EVAN DALDORNE. Illustrated by J. MOYR SMITH. Small 8vo, cloth extra, 6s.

outh-West, The New : Travelling Sketches from Kansas, New Mexico, Arizona, and Northern Mexico. By ERNST VON HESSE-WARTEGG. With 100 fine Illustrations and 3 Maps. 8vo, cloth extra, 14s. [*In preparation.*

Spalding.-Elizabethan Demonology : An Essay in Illustration of the Belief in the Existence of Devils, and the Powers possessed by Them. By T. ALFRED SPALDING, LL.B. Crown 8vo, cloth extra, 5s.

Speight. — The Mysteries of Heron Dyke. By T. W. SPEIGHT. With a Frontispiece by M. ELLEN EDWARDS. Crown 8vo, cloth extra, 3s. 6d. ; post 8vo, illustrated boards, 2s.

Spenser for Children. By M. H. TOWRY. With Illustrations by WALTER J. MORGAN. Crown 4to, with Coloured Illustrations, cloth gilt, 6s.

Staunton.—Laws and Practice of Chess; Together with an Analysis of the Openings, and a Treatise on End Games. By HOWARD STAUNTON. Edited by ROBERT B. WORMALD. A New Edition, small crown 8vo, cloth extra, 5s.

Stedman. — Victorian Poets: Critical Essays. By EDMUND CLARENCE STEDMAN. Crown 8vo, cloth extra, 9s.

Sterndale.—The Afghan Knife: A Novel. By ROBERT ARMITAGE STERNDALE, F.R.G.S. Crown 8vo, cloth extra, 3s. 6d.; post 8vo, illustrated boards, 2s.

Stevenson (R.Louis),Works by:

Familiar Studies of Men and Books. Crown 8vo, cloth extra, 6s.

New Arabian Nights. New and Cheaper Edition. Crown 8vo, cloth extra, 6s.

St. John.—A Levantine Fami'y. By BAYLE ST. JOHN. Post 8vo, illustrated boards, 2s.

Stoddard.—Summer Cruising in the South Seas. By CHARLES WARREN STODDARD. Illustrated by WALLIS MACKAY. Crown 8vo, cloth extra, 3s. 6d.

St. Pierre.—Paul and Virginia, and The Indian Cottage. By BERNARDIN DE ST. PIERRE. Edited, with Life, by the Rev. E. CLARKE. Post 8vo, cloth limp, 2s.

Strahan.—Twenty Years of a Publisher's Life. By ALEXANDER STRAHAN. Two Vols., crown 8vo, with numerous Portraits and Illustrations, 24s. [*In preparation.*

Strutt's Sports and Pastimes of the People of England; including the Rural and Domestic Recreations, May Games, Mummeries, Shows, Processions, Pageants, and Pompous Spectacles, from the Earliest Period to the Present Time. With 140 Illustrations. Edited by WILLIAM HONE. Crown 8vo, cloth extra, 7s. 6d.

Suburban Homes (The) of London: A Residential Guide to Favourite London Localities, their Society, Celebrities, and Associations. With Notes on their Rental, Rates, and House Accommodation. With a Map of Suburban London. Crown 8vo, cloth extra, 7s. 6d.

Swift's Choice Works, in Prose and Verse. With Memoir, Portrait, and Facsimiles of the Maps in the Original Edition of "Gulliver's Travels." Cr. 8vo, cloth extra, 7s. 6d.

Swinburne (Algernon C.), Works by:

The Queen Mother and Rosamond. Fcap. 8vo, 5s.

Atalanta in Calydon. Crown 8vo, 6s.

Chastelard. A Tragedy. Crown 8vo, 7s.

Poems and Ballads. FIRST SERIES. Fcap. 8vo, 9s. Also in crown 8vo, at same price.

Poems and Ballads. SECOND SERIES. Fcap. 8vo, 9s. Also in crown 8vo, at same price.

Notes on Poems and Reviews. 8vo, 1s.

William Blake: A Critical Essay. With Facsimile Paintings. Demy 8vo, 16s.

Songs before Sunrise. Crown 8vo, 10s. 6d.

Bothwell: A Tragedy. Crown 8vo, 12s. 6d.

George Chapman: An Essay. Crown 8vo, 7s.

Songs of Two Nations. Crown 8vo, 6s.

Essays and Studies. Crown 8vo, 12s.

Erechtheus: A Tragedy. Crown 8vo, 6s.

Note of an English Republican on the Muscovite Crusade. 8vo, 1s.

A Note on Charlotte Bronte. Crown 8vo, 6s.

A Study of Shakespeare. Crown 8vo, 8s.

Songs of the Springtides. Crown 8vo, 6s.

Studies in Song. Crown 8vo, 7s.

Mary Stuart: A Tragedy. Crown 8vo, 8s.

Tristram of Lyonesse, and other Poems. Crown 8vo, 9s.

A Century of Roundels. Small 4to, cloth extra, 8s.

Syntax's (Dr.) Three Tours: In Search of the Picturesque, in Search of Consolation, and in Search of a Wife. With the whole of ROWLANDSON's droll page Illustrations in Colours and a Life of the Author by J. C. HOTTEN. Medium 8vo, cloth extra, 7s. 6d.

Taine's History of English Literature. Translated by HENRY VAN LAUN. Four Vols., small 8vo, cloth boards, 30s — POPULAR EDITION, in Two Vols., crown 8vo, cloth extra, 15s.

Taylor's (Bayard) Diversions of the Echo Club: Burlesques of Modern Writers. Post 8vo, cloth limp, 2s.

Taylor's (Tom) Historical Dramas: "Clancarty," "Jeanne Darc," "'Twixt Axe and Crown," "The Fool's Revenge," "Arkwright's Wife," "Anne Boleyn," "Plot and Passion." One Vol., crown 8vo, cloth extra, 7s. 6d.

₊ The Plays may also be had separately, at 1s. each.

Thackerayana: Notes and Anecdotes. Illustrated by Hundreds of Sketches by WILLIAM MAKEPEACE THACKERAY, depicting Humorous Incidents in his School-life, and Favourite Characters in the books of his every-day reading. With Coloured Frontispiece. Crown 8vo, cloth extra, 7s. 6d.

Thomas (Bertha), Novels by:

Each crown 8vo, cloth extra, 3s. 6d. ; or post 8vo, illustrated boards, 2s.

    Cressida.

    Proud Maisie.

    The Violin-Player.

Thomson's Seasons and Castle of Indolence. With a Biographical and Critical Introduction by ALLAN CUNNINGHAM, and over 50 fine Illustrations on Steel and Wood. Crown 8vo, cloth extra, gilt edges, 7s. 6d.

Thornbury (Walter), Works by:

Haunted London. Edited by EDWARD WALFORD, M.A. With Illustrations by F. W. FAIRHOLT, F.S.A. Crown 8vo, cloth extra, 7s. 6d.

The Life and Correspondence of J. M. W. Turner. Founded upon Letters and Papers furnished by his Friends and fellow Academicians. With numerous Illustrations in Colours, facsimiled from Turner's Original Drawings. Crown 8vo, cloth extra, 7s. 6d.

Old Stories Re-told. Post 8vo, cloth limp, 2s 6d.

Tales for the Marines. Post 8vo, illustrated boards, 2s.

Timbs (John), Works by:

The History of Clubs and Club Life in London. With Anecdotes of its Famous Coffee-houses, Hostelries, and Taverns. With numerous Illustrations. Crown 8vo, cloth extra, 7s. 6d.

English Eccentrics and Eccentricities: Stories of Wealth and Fashion, Delusions, Impostures, and Fanatic Missions, Strange Sights and Sporting Scenes, Eccentric Artists, Theatrical Folks, Men of Letters, &c. With nearly 50 Illusts. Crown 8vo, cloth extra, 7s. 6d.

Torrens. — The Marquess Wellesley, Architect of Empire. An Historic Portrait. By W. M. TORRENS, M.P. Demy 8vo, cloth extra, 14s.

Trollope (Anthony), Novels by:

The Way We Live Now. With Illustrations. Crown 8vo, cloth extra, 3s. 6d. ; post 8vo, illust. boards, 2s.

The American Senator. Crown 8vo, cloth extra, 3s. 6d ; post 8vo, illustrated boards, 2s.

Kept in the Dark. With a Frontispiece by J. E. MILLAIS, R.A. Crown 8vo, cloth extra, 3s. 6d.

Frau Frohmann, &c. With Frontispiece. Crown 8vo, cloth extra, 3s 6d.

Marion Fay. Cr. 8vo, cl. extra, 3s. 6d.

Mr. Scarborough's Family. Three Vols., crown 8vo, 31s 6d.

The Land Leaguers. Three Vols., crown 8vo, 31s. 6d.   [*Shortly*.

Trollope (T. A.). — Diamond Cut Diamond, and other Stories. By THOMAS ADOLPHUS TROLLOPE. Crown 8vo, cloth extra 3s. 6d.; post 8vo, illustrated boards. 2s.

Tytler (Sarah), Novels by:

What She Came Through. Crown 8vo, cloth extra. 3s. 6d.; post 8vo, illustrated boards, 2s.

The Bride's Pass. With a Frontispiece by P. MACNAB. Crown 8vo, cloth extra, 3s. 6d.

Van Laun. — History of French Literature. By HENRY VAN LAUN. Complete in Three Vols., demy 8vo, cloth boards, 7s. 6d. each.

Villari. — A Double Bond: A Story. By LINDA VILLARI. Fcap. 8vo, picture cover, 1s.

Walcott.— Church Work and Life in English Minsters; and the English Student's Monasticon. By the Rev. MACKENZIE E. C. WALCOTT, B.D. Two Vols., crown 8vo, cloth extra, with Map and Ground-Plans, **14s.**

Walford (Edw., M.A.), Works by:

The County Families of the United Kingdom. Containing Notices of the Descent, Birth, Marriage, Education, &c., of more than 12,000 distinguished Heads of Families, their Heirs Apparent or Presumptive, the Offices they hold or have held, their Town and Country Addresses, Clubs, &c. The Twenty-third Annual Edition, for 1883, cloth, full gilt, **50s.**

The Shilling Peerage (1883). Containing an Alphabetical List of the House of Lords, Dates of Creation, Lists of Scotch and Irish Peers, Addresses, &c. 32mo, cloth, **1s.** Published annually.

The Shilling Baronetage (1883). Containing an Alphabetical List of the Baronets of the United Kingdom, Short Biographical Notices, Dates of Creation, Addresses, &c. 32mo, cloth, **1s.** Published annually.

The Shilling Knightage (1883). Containing an Alphabetical List of the Knights of the United Kingdom, short Biographical Notices, Dates of Creation, Addresses, &c. 32mo, cloth, **1s.** Published annually.

The Shilling House of Commons (1883). Containing a List of all the Members of the British Parliament, their Town and Country Addresses, &c. 32mo, cloth, **1s.** Published annually.

The Complete Peerage, Baronetage, Knightage, and House of Commons (1883). In One Volume, royal 32mo, cloth extra, gilt edges, **5s.** Published annually.

Haunted London. By WALTER THORNBURY. Edited by EDWARD WALFORD, M.A. With Illustrations by F. W. FAIRHOLT, F.S.A. Crown 8vo, cloth extra, **7s. 6d.**

Walton and Cotton's Complete Angler; or, The Contemplative Man's Recreation; being a Discourse of Rivers, Fishponds, Fish and Fishing, written by IZAAK WALTON; and Instructions how to Angle for a Trout or Grayling in a clear Stream, by CHARLES COTTON. With Original Memoirs and Notes by Sir HARRIS NICOLAS, and 61 Copperplate Illustrations. Large crown 8vo, cloth antique, **7s. 6d.**

Wanderer's Library, The:

Crown 8vo, cloth extra, 3s. 6d. each.

Wanderings In Patagonia; or, Life among the Ostrich Hunters. By JULIUS BEERBOHM. Illustrated.

Camp Notes: Stories of Sport and Adventure in Asia, Africa, and America. By FREDERICK BOYLE.

Savage Life. By FREDERICK BOYLE.

Merrie England In the Olden Time. By GEORGE DANIEL. With Illustrations by ROBT. CRUIKSHANK.

Circus Life and Circus Celebrities. By THOMAS FROST.

The Lives of the Conjurers. By THOMAS FROST.

The Old Showmen and the Old London Fairs. By THOMAS FROST.

Low-Life Deeps. An Account of the Strange Fish to be found there. By JAMES GREENWOOD.

The Wilds of London. By JAMES GREENWOOD.

Tunis: The Land and the People. By the Chevalier de HESSE-WARTEGG. With 22 Illustrations

The Life and Adventures of a Cheap Jack. By One of the Fraternity. Edited by CHARLES HINDLEY.

The World Behind the Scenes. By PERCY FITZGERALD.

Tavern Anecdotes and Sayings Including the Origin of Signs, and Reminiscences connected with Taverns, Coffee Houses, Clubs, &c. By CHARLES HINDLEY. With Illustrations.

The Genial Showman: Life and Adventures of Artemus Ward. By E. P. HINGSTON. With a Frontispiece.

The Story of the London Parks. By JACOB LARWOOD. With Illusts.

London Characters. By HENRY MAYHEW. Illustrated.

Seven Generations of Executioners: Memoirs of the Sanson Family (1688 to 1847). Edited by HENRY SANSON.

Summer Cruising In the South Seas. By CHARLES WARREN STODDARD. Illust. by WALLIS MACKAY.

Warrants, &c. :—

Warrant to Execute Charles I. An exact Facsimile, with the Fifty-nine Signatures, and corresponding Seals. Carefully printed on paper to imitate the Original, 22 in. by 14 in. Price **2s.**

WARRANTS, &c., *continued—*

Warrant to Execute Mary Queen of Scots. An exact Facsimile, including the Signature of Queen Elizabeth, and a Facsimile of the Great Seal. Beautifully printed on paper to imitate the Original MS. Price 2s.

Magna Charta. An Exact Facsimile of the Original Document in the British Museum, printed on fine plate paper, nearly 3 feet long by 2 feet wide, with the Arms and Seals emblazoned in Gold and Colours. Price 5s.

The Roll of Battle Abbey; or, A List of the Principal Warriors who came over from Normandy with William the Conqueror, and Settled in this Country, A.D. 1066-7. With the principal Arms emblazoned in Gold and Colours. Price 5s.

Westropp.—Handbook of Pottery and Porcelain; or, History of those Arts from the Earliest Period. By HODDER M. WESTROPP. With numerous Illustrations, and a List of Marks. Crown 8vo, cloth limp, 4s. 6d.

Whistler v. Ruskin: Art and Art Critics. By J. A. MACNEILL WHISTLER. Seventh Edition, square 8vo, 1s.

White's Natural History of Selborne. Edited, with Additions, by THOMAS BROWN, F.L.S. Post 8vo, cloth limp, 2s.

Wilson (Dr. Andrew, F.R.S.E.), Works by:

Chapters on Evolution: A Popular History of the Darwinian and Allied Theories of Development. Second Edition. Crown 8vo, cloth extra, with 259 Illustrations, 7s. 6d.

Leaves from a Naturalist's Notebook. Post 8vo, cloth limp, 2s. 6d.

Leisure-Time Studies, chiefly Biological. Second Ed tion. Crown 8vo, cloth extra, with Illustrations, 6s.

Williams (W. Mattieu, F.R.A.S.), Works by:

Science in Short Chapters. Crown 8vo, cloth extra, 7s. 6d.

A Simple Treatise on Heat. Crown 8vo, cloth limp, with Illustrations, 2s. 6d.

Wilson (C. E.).—Persian Wit and Humour: Being the Sixth Book of the Baharistan of Jami, Translated for the first time from the Original Persian into English Prose and Verse. With Notes by C. E. WILSON, M.R.A.S., Assistant Librarian Royal Academy of Arts. Crown 8vo, parchment binding, 4s.

Winter (J. S.), Stories by:

Cavalry Life. Crown 8vo, cloth extra, 3s. 6d.

Regimental Legends. Crown 8vo, cloth extra, 3s. 6d.

Wood.—Sabina: A Novel. By Lady WOOD. Post 8vo, illustrated boards, 2s.

Words, Facts, and Phrases: A Dictionary of Curious, Quaint, and Out-of-the-Way Matters. By ELIEZER EDWARDS. Crown 8vo, half-bound, 12s. 6d.

Wright (Thomas), Works by:

Caricature History of the Georges. (The House of Hanover.) With 400 Pictures, Caricatures, Squibs, Broadsides, Window Pictures, &c. Crown 8vo, cloth extra, 7s. 6d.

History of Caricature and of the Grotesque in Art, Literature, Sculpture, and Painting. Profusely Illustrated by F. W. FAIRHOLT, F.S.A. Large post 8vo, cloth extra, 7s. 6d.

Yates (Edmund), Novels by:

Post 8vo, illustrated boards, 2s. each.
Castaway.
The Forlorn Hope.
Land at Last.

NOVELS BY THE BEST AUTHORS.

NEW NOVELS at every Library.

All in a Garden Fair. By WALTER BESANT. Three Vols. [*Shortly.*

Annan Water. By ROBERT BUCHANAN. Three Vols. [*Shortly.*

Heart and Science: A Story of the Present Day. By WILKIE COLLINS. Three Vols.

Port Salvation; or, The Evangelist. By ALPHONSE DAUDET. Translated by C. HARRY MELTZER. Two Vols., post 8vo, 12s.

Circe's Lovers. By J. LEITH DERWENT. Three Vols.

Of High Degree. By CHARLES GIBBON, Author of "Robin Gray," "The Golden Shaft," &c. Three Vols.

Fancy-Free, &c. By CHARLES GIBBON. Three Vols. [*Shortly.*

Fortune's Fool. By JULIAN HAWTHORNE. Three Vols. [*Shortly.*

Self-Condemned. By Mrs. ALFRED HUNT. Three Vols.

Ione Steuart. By E. LYNN LINTON. Three Vols. [*Shortly.*

The Way of the World. By D. CHRISTIE MURRAY. Three Vols. [*Shortly.*

Maid of Athens. By JUSTIN McCARTHY, M.P. With 12 Illustrations by F. BARNARD. Three Vols. [*Shortly.*

Hearts. By DAVID CHRISTIE MURRAY. Three Vols.

By the Gate of the Sea. By DAVID CHRISTIE MURRAY. Two Vols., post 8vo, 12s.

Wanda. By OUIDA. Three Vols., crown 8vo.

The Foreigners. By E. C. PRICE. Three Vols. [*Shortly.*

A New Collection of Stories by CHARLES READE is now in preparation, in Three Vols.

The Hands of Justice. By F. W. ROBINSON. Three Vols.

Behind a Brass Knocker: Some Grim Realities in Picture and Prose. By FRED BARNARD and C. H. ROSS. Demy 8vo, cloth extra, with 30 full-page Drawings, 10s. 6d.

Mr. Scarborough's Family. By ANTHONY TROLLOPE. Three Vols.

The Land Leaguers. By ANTHONY TROLLOPE. Three Vols. [*Shortly.*

THE PICCADILLY NOVELS.

Popular Stories by the Best Authors. LIBRARY EDITIONS, many Illustrated, crown 8vo, cloth extra, 3s. 6d. each.

BY MRS. ALEXANDER.
Maid, Wife, or Widow?

BY W. BESANT & JAMES RICE.
Ready-Money Mortiboy.
My Little Girl.
The Case of Mr. Lucraft.
This Son of Vulcan.
With Harp and Crown.
The Golden Butterfly.
By Celia's Arbour.
The Monks of Thelema.
'Twas in Trafalgar's Bay.
The Seamy Side.
The Ten Years' Tenant.
The Chaplain of the Fleet.

BY WALTER BESANT.
All Sorts and Conditions of Men.
The Captains' Room.

BY ROBERT BUCHANAN.
A Child of Nature.
God and the Man.
The Shadow of the Sword.
The Martyrdom of Madeline.
Love Me for Ever.

BY MRS. H. LOVETT CAMERON.
Deceivers Ever.
Juliet's Guardian.

BY MORTIMER COLLINS.
Sweet Anne Page.
Transmigration.
From Midnight to Midnight.

MORTIMER & FRANCES COLLINS.
Blacksmith and Scholar.
The Village Comedy.
You Play me False.

PICCADILLY NOVELS, *continued—*
BY WILKIE COLLINS.

Antonina.	Miss or Mrs ?
Basil.	New Magdalen.
Hide and Seek.	The Frozen Deep.
The Dead Secret.	The Law and the Lady.
Queen of Hearts.	
My Miscellanies.	The Two Destinies
Woman in White.	Haunted Hotel.
The Moonstone.	The Fallen Leaves
Man and Wife.	Jezebel's Daughter
Poor Miss Finch.	The Black Robe.

BY DUTTON COOK.
Paul Foster's Daughter.

BY WILLIAM CYPLES.
Hearts of Gold,

BY J. LEITH DERWENT.
Our Lady of Tears.

BY M. BETHAM-EDWARDS.
Felicia.

BY MRS. ANNIE EDWARDES.
Archie Lovell.

BY R. E. FRANCILLON.
Olympia. | Queen Cophetua.
One by One.

BY EDWARD GARRETT.
The Capel Girls.

BY CHARLES GIBBON.
Robin Gray.
For Lack of Gold.
In Love and War.
What will the World Say ?
For the King.
In Honour Bound.
Queen of the Meadow.
In Pastures Green.
The Flower of the Forest.
A Heart's Problem.
The Braes of Yarrow.
The Golden Shaft.

BY THOMAS HARDY.
Under the Greenwood Tree.

BY JULIAN HAWTHORNE.
Garth.
Ellice Quentin.
Sebastian Strome.
Prince Saroni's Wife.
Dust.

BY SIR A. HELPS.
Ivan de Biron.

PICCADILLY NOVELS, *continued—*
BY MRS. ALFRED HUNT.
Thornicroft's Model.
The Leaden Casket.

BY JEAN INGELOW.
Fated to be Free.

BY HENRY JAMES, Jun.
Confidence.

BY HARRIETT JAY.
The Queen of Connaught.
The Dark Colleen.

BY HENRY KINGSLEY.
Number Seventeen.
Oakshott Castle.

BY E. LYNN LINTON.
Patricia Kemball.
Atonement of Leam Dundas.
The World Well Lost.
Under which Lord ?
With a Silken Thread.
The Rebel of the Family.
"My Love!"

BY HENRY W. LUCY.
Gideon Fleyce.

BY JUSTIN McCARTHY, M.P.
The Waterdale Neighbours.
My Enemy's Daughter.
Linley Rochford. | A Fair Saxon.
Dear Lady Disdain.
Miss Misanthrope.
Donna Quixote.
The Comet of a Season.

BY GEORGE MACDONALD, LL.D.
Paul Faber, Surgeon.
Thomas Wingfold, Curate.

BY MRS. MACDONELL.
Quaker Cousins.

BY KATHARINE S. MACQUOID.
Lost Rose. | The Evil Eye.

BY FLORENCE MARRYAT.
Open! Sesame! | Written in Fire

BY JEAN MIDDLEMASS.
Touch and Go.

BY D. CHRISTIE MURRAY.
A Life's Atonement.
Joseph's Coat. | Coals of Fire.
A Model Father.

BY MRS. OLIPHANT.
Whiteladies.

PICCADILLY NOVELS, *continued—*
BY JAMES PAYN.
Lost Sir Massingberd.
Best of Husbands
Fallen Fortunes.
Halves.
Walter's Word.
What He Cost Her
Less Black than We're Painted.
By Proxy.
High Spirits.
Under One Roof.
Carlyon's Year.
A Confidential Agent.
From Exile.
A Grape from a Thorn.
For Cash Only.
Kit: A Memory.

BY E. C. PRICE.
Valentina.

BY CHARLES READE, D.C.L.
It is Never Too Late to Mend.
Hard Cash. | Peg Woffington.
Christie Johnstone.
Griffith Gaunt.
The Double Marriage.
Love Me Little, Love Me Long.
Foul Play.
The Cloister and the Hearth.
The Course of True Love.
The Autobiography of a Thief.
Put Yourself in His Place.
A Terrible Temptation.
The Wandering Heir. | A Simpleton.
A Woman-Hater. | Readiana.

BY MRS. J. H. RIDDELL.
Her Mother's Darling.
Prince of Wales's Garden-Party.

PICCADILLY NOVELS, *continued—*
BY F. W. ROBINSON.
Women are Strange.

BY JOHN SAUNDERS.
Bound to the Wheel.
Guy Waterman.
One Against the World.
The Lion in the Path.
The Two Dreamers.

BY T. W. SPEIGHT.
The Mysteries of Heron Dyke.

BY R. A. STERNDALE.
The Afghan Knife.

BY BERTHA THOMAS.
Proud Maisie. | Cressida.
The Violin-Player.

BY ANTHONY TROLLOPE.
The Way we Live Now.
The American Senator.
Frau Frohmann.
Marion Fay.
Kept in the Dark.

BY T. A. TROLLOPE.
Diamond Cut Diamond.

BY SARAH TYTLER.
What She Came Through.
The Bride's Pass.

BY J. S. WINTER.
Cavalry Life.
Regimental Legends.

CHEAP EDITIONS OF POPULAR NOVELS.
Post 8vo, illustrated boards, 2s. each.

[WILKIE COLLINS'S NOVELS and BESANT and RICE'S NOVELS may also be had in cloth limp at 2s. 6d. ' *See, too, the* PICCADILLY NOVELS, *for Library Editions.*]

BY EDMOND ABOUT.
The Fellah.

BY HAMILTON AÏDÉ.
Carr of Carrlyon. | Confidences.

BY MRS. ALEXANDER.
Maid, Wife, or Widow?

BY SHELSLEY BEAUCHAMP.
Grantley Grange.

BY W. BESANT & JAMES RICE.
Ready-Money Mortiboy.
With Harp and Crown.
This Son of Vulcan.
My Little Girl.
The Case of Mr. Lucraft.

BY BESANT AND RICE—*continued.*
The Golden Butterfly.
By Celia's Arbour.
The Monks of Thelema.
'Twas in Trafalgar's Bay.
The Seamy Side.
The Ten Years' Tenant.
The Chaplain of the Fleet.

BY FREDERICK BOYLE.
Camp Notes. | Savage Life.

BY BRET HARTE.
An Heiress of Red Dog.
Gabriel Conroy.
The Luck of Roaring Camp.
Flip.

CHEAP POPULAR NOVELS, *continued—*

BY ROBERT BUCHANAN.
The Shadow of the Sword.
A Child of Nature.

BY MRS. BURNETT.
Surly Tim.

BY MRS. LOVETT CAMERON.
Deceivers Ever.
Juliet's Guardian.

BY MACLAREN COBBAN.
The Cure of Souls.

BY C. ALLSTON COLLINS.
The Bar Sinister.

BY WILKIE COLLINS.
Antonina.
Basil.
Hide and Seek.
The Dead Secret.
Queen of Hearts.
My Miscellanies.
The Woman in White.
The Moonstone.
Man and Wife.
Poor Miss Finch.
Miss or Mrs. ?
The New Magdalen.
The Frozen Deep.
The Law and the Lady.
The Two Destinies.
The Haunted Hotel.
The Fallen Leaves.
Jezebel's Daughter.
The Black Robe.

BY MORTIMER COLLINS.
Sweet Anne Page.
Transmigration.
From Midnight to Midnight.
A Fight with Fortune.

MORTIMER & FRANCES COLLINS.
Sweet and Twenty.
Frances.
Blacksmith and Scholar.
The Village Comedy.
You Play me False.

BY DUTTON COOK.
Leo.
Paul Foster's Daughter.

BY J. LEITH DERWENT.
Our Lady of Tears.

CHEAP POPULAR NOVELS, *continued—*

BY CHARLES DICKENS.
Sketches by Boz. .
The Pickwick Papers.
Oliver Twist.
Nicholas Nickleby.

BY MRS. ANNIE EDWARDES.
A Point of Honour.
Archie Lovell.

BY M. BETHAM-EDWARDS.
Felicia.

BY EDWARD EGGLESTON.
Roxy.

BY PERCY FITZGERALD.
Bella Donna.
Never Forgotten.
The Second Mrs. Tillotson.
Polly.
Seventy-five Brooke Street.

BY ALBANY DE FONBLANQUE.
Filthy Lucre.

BY R. E. FRANCILLON.
Olympia.
Queen Cophetua.
One by One.

BY EDWARD GARRETT.
The Capel Girls.

BY CHARLES GIBBON.
Robin Gray.
For Lack of Gold.
What will the World Say ? ·
In Honour Bound.
The Dead Heart.
In Love and War.
For the King.
Queen of the Meadow.
In Pastures Green.

BY WILLIAM GILBERT.
Dr. Austin's Guests.
The Wizard of the Mountain.
James Duke.

BY JAMES GREENWOOD.
Dick Temple.

BY ANDREW HALLIDAY.
Every-Day Papers.

BY LADY DUFFUS HARDY.
Paul Wynter's Sacrifice.

BY THOMAS HARDY.
Under the Greenwood Tree.

HEAP POPULAR NOVELS, *continued—*

BY JULIAN HAWTHORNE.
Garth.
Ellice Quentin.
Sebastian Strome.

BY SIR ARTHUR HELPS.
Ivan de Biron.

BY TOM HOOD.
A Golden Heart.

BY VICTOR HUGO.
The Hunchback of Notre Dame.

BY MRS. ALFRED HUNT.
Thornicroft's Model.
The Leaden Casket.

BY JEAN INGELOW.
Fated to be Free.

BY HENRY JAMES, Jun.
Confidence.

BY HARRIETT JAY.
The Dark Colleen.
The Queen of Connaught.

BY HENRY KINGSLEY.
Oakshott Castle.
Number Seventeen.

BY E. LYNN LINTON.
Patricia Kemball.
The Atonement of Leam Dundas.
The World Well Lost.
Under which Lord?
With a Silken Thread.
The Rebel of the Family.
"My Love!"

BY JUSTIN McCARTHY, M.P.
Dear Lady Disdain.
The Waterdale Neighbours.
My Enemy's Daughter.
A Fair Saxon.
Linley Rochford.
Miss Misanthrope.
Donna Quixote.

BY GEORGE MACDONALD.
Paul Faber, Surgeon.
Thomas Wingfold, Curate.

BY MRS. MACDONELL.
Quaker Cousins.

BY KATHARINE S. MACQUOID.
The Evil Eye. | Lost Rose.

BY W. H. MALLOCK.
The New Republic.

CHEAP POPULAR NOVELS, *continued—*

BY FLORENCE MARRYAT.
Open! Sesame!
A Harvest of Wild Oats.
A Little Stepson.
Fighting the Air.
Written in Fire.

BY JEAN MIDDLEMASS.
Touch and Go. | Mr. Dorillion.

BY D. CHRISTIE MURRAY.
A Life's Atonement.
A Model Father.

BY MRS. OLIPHANT.
Whiteladies.

BY MRS. ROBERT O'REILLY.
Phœbe's Fortunes.

BY OUIDA.
LIBRARY EDITIONS of OUIDA's NOVELS may be had in crown 8vo, cloth extra, at 5s. each.

Held in Bondage.	Pascarel.
Strathmore.	Two Little Wooden Shoes.
Chandos.	
Under Two Flags.	Signa.
Idalia.	In a Winter City.
Cecil Castlemaine.	Ariadne.
Tricotrin.	Friendship.
Puck.	Moths.
Folle Farine.	Pipistrello.
A Dog of Flanders.	A Village Commune.

BY JAMES PAYN.

Lost Sir Massingberd.	Gwendoline's Harvest.
A Perfect Treasure.	Like Father, Like Son.
Bentinck's Tutor.	A Marine Residence.
Murphy's Master.	
A County Family.	Married Beneath Him.
At Her Mercy.	Mirk Abbey.
A Woman's Vengeance.	Not Wooed, but Won.
Cecil's Tryst.	£200 Reward.
Clyffards of Clyffe	Less Black than We're Painted.
The Family Scapegrace.	By Proxy.
Foster Brothers.	Under One Roof.
Found Dead.	High Spirits.
Best of Husbands	Carlyon's Year.
Walter's Word.	A Confidential Agent.
Halves.	
Fallen Fortunes.	Some Private Views.
What He Cost Her	
Humorous Stories	From Exile.

CHEAP POPULAR NOVELS, *continued—*

BY EDGAR A. POE.
The Mystery of Marie Roget.

BY E. C. PRICE.
Valentina.

BY CHARLES READE.
It is Never Too Late to Mend.
Hard Cash.
Peg Woffington.
Christie Johnstone.
Griffith Gaunt.
Put Yourself in His Place.
The Double Marriage.
Love Me Little, Love Me Long.
Foul Play.
The Cloister and the Hearth
The Course of True Love.
Autobiography of a Thief.
A Terrible Temptation.
The Wandering Heir.
A Simpleton.
A Woman-Hater.
Readiana.

BY MRS. RIDDELL.
Her Mother's Darling.

BY BAYLE ST. JOHN.
A Levantine Family.

BY GEORGE AUGUSTUS SALA.
Gaslight and Daylight.

BY JOHN SAUNDERS.
Bound to the Wheel.
One Against the World.
Guy Waterman.
The Lion in the Path.
The Two Dreamers.

BY ARTHUR SKETCHLEY.
A Match in the Dark.

BY T. W. SPEIGHT.
The Mysteries of Heron Dyke.

BY R. A. STERNDALE.
The Afghan Knife.

BY BERTHA THOMAS.
Cressida. | Proud Maisie
The Violin-Player.

CHEAP POPULAR NOVELS, *continued—*

BY WALTER THORNBURY.
Tales for the Marines.

BY T. ADOLPHUS TROLLOPE.
Diamond Cut Diamond.

BY ANTHONY TROLLOPE.
The Way We Live Now.
The American Senator.

BY MARK TWAIN.
Tom Sawyer.
An Idle Excursion.
A Pleasure Trip on the Continent
of Europe.

BY SARAH TYTLER.
What She Came Through.

BY LADY WOOD.
Sabina.

BY EDMUND YATES.
Castaway.
The Forlorn Hope.
Land at Last.

ANONYMOUS
Paul Ferroll.
Why Paul Ferroll Killed his Wife.

Fcap. 8vo, picture covers, 1s. each.
Jeff Briggs's Love Story. By BRET HARTE.
The Twins of Table Mountain. By BRET HARTE.
Mrs. Gainsborough's Diamonds. By JULIAN HAWTHORNE.
Kathleen Mavourneen. By Author of " That Lass o' Lowrie's."
Lindsay's Luck. By the Author of " That Lass o' Lowrie's."
Pretty Polly Pemberton. By the Author of " That Lass o' Lowrie's."
Trooping with Crows. By Mrs. PIRKIS.
The Professor's Wife. By LEONARD GRAHAM.
A Double Bond. By LINDA VILLARI.
Esther's Glove. By R. E. FRANCILLON.
The Garden that Paid the Rent. By TOM JERROLD.

J. OGDEN AND CO., PRINTERS, 172, ST. JOHN STREET, E.C.